She Lies Hidden

By

C M Stephenson

To Doreen, Jacky and Mel.

Prologue

January 1973

It's one o'clock Monday morning. Alice tosses and turns, the flock mattress a mess of lumps that seem to rub the very skin off her back. Threadbare sheets and worn woollen blankets fail to stop the cold creeping into her bones; she feels older than her sixty years.

A harsh January wind pierces the rotting window frame; the curtains flutter open and shut like a moth on a light. Heavy rain slashes against the window.

She cannot sleep; her granddaughter is still out. The alarm clock taunts her with every tick.

Veronica, barely eighteen, out on the town again, five miles away. The last bus long since been and gone. No idea of how she'll get back. The fear makes her feel sick to her stomach. Her fingers tug at the sheets and knot into a fist.

What's keeping her—I've had enough of her staying out all night. I'll give her what for when she turns up.

On top of the blankets, the cat stretches itself the length of her legs. Alice slides out her arm, scratches the nape of its neck.

Tomorrow, I'm putting a stop to this. It's not fair – I'm not her mother.

She turns onto her side, dozes in and out of consciousness. The cat shifts to the end of the bed.

Downstairs the grandfather clock chimes three times.

A feeling of despondency settles upon her chest; her tears soak into the pillow.

Where is she? By two o'clock in the afternoon on Sunday—that's what she promised me, that's when she said she'd be back. I had dinner all ready.

She ate it herself in the end, unwilling to let good food go to waste. No fridge to keep it in.

I should have made her go back home, let her mother deal with her.

'Please Gran, I promise,' she'd said. 'Just let me stay. A few months, that's all.' Veronica took hold of her hand, 'You know you miss me, anyway.'

And she had.

This was last April, it was lovely at first, just the two of them together. Then things had soured, someone had turned her head. Someone from college. From then on, bad habits had wrapped themselves around Veronica. She was either wide-awake or half dead.

Alice watches the shadows flicker across the wall. Her eyelids droop then close again.

The wind picks up, freezes, hailstones pelt against the window. Alice stirs, peers myopically at the alarm clock. The luminous hands glow in the dark, it's half-past four.

I've had enough now.

She gets out of bed, slips on her glasses, makes her way across the room. Takes her rosary off the hook beside the door. Its wooden beads and plastic cross give her comfort. In the shadows, Pope Paul VI looks down on her from a wooden frame on the wall. She kneels by the bed, clings onto the frame with one hand, runs the beads through her fingers with the other. Whispers the words, over and over again.

'Please Lord, bring Veronica back home, please let her be safe.'

The cat reaches out, claws at her fingers. Alice stays on her knees and waits, ears cocked, as though expecting an immediate miracle. After a while she gets to her feet, gazes out of the window. Dark shadows flood across the street; opposite, a tall leafless beech shudders and sighs.

The cat, unsettled yet again, bites at her toes as she pushes them beneath the blankets. Alice returns her glasses to their place on bedside table. Eyes closed, she on the edge of sleep, her body shifting restlessly, the discomfort of the mattress unending.

Light seeps through the curtain, it's gone eight o'clock. The cover on Veronica's bed lies untouched. The cat, now sitting on her chest, pats her face with its paw.

'You want to some food, do you, Blacky?'

It waits for a tickle behind its ears, just as it does every morning. Alice lets it snuggle into her hand before setting it down on the floor.

She reaches for her glasses, throws back the bedcovers, sniffs – a dank musty smell fills her nostrils. Her eyes trace the ceiling above Veronica's bed. They settle on a large patch of grey plaster.

Oh, God. The rain must have found its way in again.

There's no money to fix it.

The cat scurries past her as she takes the stairs. The house is silent. The living room stone cold. Veronica's coat isn't hung behind the door. Her shoes aren't abandoned in front of the fireplace.

At nine o'clock Alice goes to the shop, her eyes scan up and down the street for Veronica. A police car speeds by, then another a few minutes later.

Arlene, the shopkeeper, hands Alice a quarter of ham. Eyebrow arched, she leans forward.

'A girl has gone missing, a teenager,' she rubs her earlobe, then points through the window, 'a farm family, up on the tops. The Albrights—the mother comes in here.'

Slipping the ham into her bag, Alice's mouth goes dry. 'Missing?'

'Yes, when they got up this morning, she'd gone.'

Alice says nothing about Veronica, scurries back to her small two-bedroom cottage. Perhaps she's gone straight to college, she thinks to herself. Then waits another seven hours for her to come home.

The ham and pickle barm cake that Alice makes Veronica for tea, dries out.

As always, there's a queue outside the telephone box. Change clinking in her pocket, she stamps her feet, tries to get warm. Next in line, the door bangs shut, she jumps. Hands shaking, she dials 999.

The next day, a detective turns up on the doorstep, dishevelled, tired, disinterested. He looks around the room, at the hand-me down furniture, at the bare flagstones in the kitchen, at the wallpaper peeling from the ceiling. He was turning his nose up at her, and not even bothering to hide it.

Fifteen minutes later, he tells her that Veronica is likely a runaway, and nothing Alice says moves him from that theory. He pushes back in his seat, rubs his hands on the elbows of the chair, tells her he'll call in on the parents. His eyes narrow as he looks into her face.

'They go from staying out at the weekend to staying away for weeks. She'll probably turn up sooner or later.'

Two weeks later the headline of the Bolton Evening News shouts out.

'Missing girls not yet found.'

Six months later, the same newspaper runs another headline.

'Missing girls presumed dead.'

Chapter 1

Sunday, 10 January 2010

There are days when she doesn't think about the stuff. She no longer dwells on it. She has tools and techniques that help her block it out, learnt years ago on a course for therapists. That's what she does now, she's a therapist.

She tells me these things, I'm her best friend. Her only friend. She's not one for closeness. She's only close to me, and we are very close indeed.

I can read her like a book, like on the rare occasions she gets angry. Her pale cheeks, the pink flush on her chest that turns red as it works its way up her chin. The way she flexes her fingers, stretches them out then makes a fist. The pacing about. The grinding of her teeth as she drops off to sleep. And then, much later, the whimpering, the flickering of her eyelids. She can't keep the nightmares out, no matter how much she tries.

She doesn't use her full range of emotions, she has no self-compassion. *I can't believe I've just said that. Where the hell did that come from? Those books I bet, those self-help ones she reads, she's got hundreds of them. Some of it must be sinking into me.*

She blocks bad thoughts out by busyness. That's my word for it, I made it up and it fits perfectly. She's Miss Busyness. She rushes here, rushes there. Finds jobs to do, re-does jobs. Cleans things, cleans clean things. Scrubs and rescrubs. Anything to keep the dark stuff out. Even though it hurts her hands. He broke three of her fingers that night, too.

Talking of cleaning, I think it's time I came clean. She didn't tell me any of those things, I'm just surmising. We aren't best friends – our relationship is different. Special. Two minds intertwined. Destined to be together forever.

She feels old today. I can tell. It's the way she woke up. She pushed off the bedding, sat still for a moment, gathered her thoughts, stretched out the bones in her spine, one by one. Even her jaw hurt.

Her knees were sore, too. All that running on concrete pavements, rarely going off-road. Like she says though, it's always handy to be able to run as fast as you can.

I wish I'd done that, when I was younger, learnt to run fast.

It started when she signed up for the self-defence programme back in 2002. She got super-fit. Four weeks of unarmed combat run by a young thing from Warrington. Ex-Forces, slim, lightning fast and an expert in Wing Chun and Aikido.

Miss Therapist says that running is a way to create something positive out of something negative. Says it's good for your mental health. She says she started running years ago and hasn't looked back.

That's not true—she's telling a lie. She's always looking over her shoulder.

'You can run away from your problems and run towards a better future.'

That's what she tells her clients. Which is ironic – it truly is.

You see, you can run as fast as you like but one day your past will catch up with you.

Yesterday, ours did. A dirty great big black stain spread through our lives. Hers and mine.

Guilt.

And no amount of scrubbing will get rid of it.

Chapter 2

Friday, 8 January 2010

Thomasine Albright sprints up three flights of stairs, two at a time, her lanyard and ID card flapping around her neck, lungs bursting, her right arm straining on the bannister as she pulls herself up.

I'm too old for this.

She hurries down the corridor as fast as she can, the heels of her sodden boots scratch and slip on the hardwood floor. A thin trail of sweat makes its way down her spine.

Through plate-glass windows, her eyes snatch glimpses of the outside world. Heavy clouds filled with snow sweep across the sky, decanting their load as they go.

The text message had been short and to the point: Team Briefing @ 7.30 a.m. – Room C154, 3rd Floor, GMP HQ.

Yesterday morning the remains of a body had been found in woodland at the base of Anglezarke Moor. She expects to be Family Liaison Officer if forensics can identify the victim.

C152, C153, C154!

She cocks her head against the door, her senses tune into the muffled sounds emanating from the other side. The sharpness of a female officer's voice rises above the chatter, calling them to order, with an 'Oi, let's get on with it.'

Thomasine nudges the door open, attempts to render herself invisible, slips in behind a six-foot-five copper with a shaved head and swirling tattoos down his arms.

The room is crowded, every seat taken, a mix of black T-shirts, dark suits and white cotton blouses. The light in the room brightens, murmurs turn to silence, the overhead projector hums in the background then cuts out. Whatever presented on the wall now hidden from view.

She waits for the first utterance of contempt; someone must have noticed her sneaking in. Where are the comments about her being part-time, how lucky they were to be graced with her company? All barked out and laden with sarcasm. The usual.

Nothing. No one takes the piss; they always take the piss. It is as though the sound has been sucked out of the room. A bright red flush blotches her neck and chest. The DCI conducting the briefing acknowledges her presence with a narrowing of her eyes and a nod of her head.

'Chief Super wants to see you, Thom,' someone whispers from behind. 'Now.'

It's Jon Fisk. She'd know that thick citrus smell anywhere – the super-strength gel that keeps his hair bolt upright.

'What about?' she says under her breath.

Her question goes unanswered, his voice gives nothing away, 'Tenth floor, he's been waiting a while.'

'A while? Great,' she hisses out, 'bloody great! I wish someone had told me.'

As she rushes towards the stairs, a feeling of discomfort swirls in her stomach. Why did he want to see her? If he has anything to say he feeds it down the chain, why hasn't he? Her Detective Chief Superintendent wouldn't have called her in unless it was personal, and even then…

It can't be to do with our Karen – I would have known. She pushes the notion out her mind.

His office is seven floors up; her legs weaken at the thought of using the glass box that is the lift. She takes the stairs again, feels the energy sap from her thighs.

The elevator slides up and down seamlessly, taunting her, the large glass panels a witness to her dishevelled state. As she reaches the tenth floor, she pauses for breath, the corridor stretches out before her, abstract works of art line the walls.

So, this is how the top half live.

Room numbers are replaced by names and job titles. DCS Timothy Hardacre's office is the fourth on the right.

His secretary tells her to wait; he is on the phone, won't be long. Then carries on as before, her vermillion painted lips pursed in concentration, her fingers striking the keyboard at speed.

Thomasine sits in silence, the minutes ticking loudly inside her head. Her mind wanders back to the Incident Room, the vacuum of sound. She'd been in there less than a minute. It felt like a lifetime.

The shrill of the phone jars her back to the present, three solitary rings; the secretary nods her head, gestures for her to go inside. As her fingers reach for the handle, it twists, the door is wrenched open. Hardacre's tall frame looms over her, his thin, pale face wearing a cheerless look, a pair of slate grey eyes steady on her. He's not angry, she relaxes a little.

God, they're going to offer me early retirement.

'Sorry to have called you away from the briefing.' His voice has a sad note to it.

The tightness in her stomach returns. He never apologises for anything.

She takes in her surroundings. The room is large and sparsely furnished. She notices a row of trophies behind his desk – cross country running. They glisten in the luminescent glare of an anglepoise lamp. A brown envelope sits in the middle of his desk, three framed photographs face inwards towards his chair.

He offers his hand; there is a clamminess in his touch. 'Take a seat.' He inclines his head towards a table and chairs.

Her knees quake, the far wall is a single pane of glass, it's like walking towards the edge of a cliff.

'Thomasine, can I get you coffee or a tea?'

'A coffee would be great…' the words falter in her mouth, 'Sir.'

'I'll go get us a couple from the machine. It's quicker.'

The racing in her heart slows, he'd called her Thomasine; it would be Albright otherwise. And the tea, there would be no offer of tea if the shit was about to hit the fan. There was no beaming smile, but neither was there a frostiness that normally precedes a bollocking. She looks down at her hands, flexes her fingers, admires the manicure and polish she'd invested in the previous day – smoky plum.

Moments later he's back, each hand nursing a cheap, white, polystyrene cup. He kicks the door shut with the heel of his shoe, she takes a cup from him.

He seats himself down opposite her, places his cup on the table. 'There's been a development in the Anglezarke case. We've identified the remains.' His eyes fleetingly glance at the A3 buff envelope. 'I'm sorry, Thomasine, they're Karen's. The report came through about half an hour ago.'

She stares at him; his words juggling in her head.

Karen's remains?

'Are you sure?' Her chest tightens.

He nods. 'I'm truly sorry. I insisted that I be the one to tell you, I didn't want—'

Found?

'How did she die?' Her mouth goes dry; she sucks in her emotions, can't – won't let them out.

He folds his hands in his lap. 'We don't know that yet, there was an injury to the back of the skull.' He averts his gaze, looks out of the window; her eyes follow his – outside the world is covered in a thick carpet of snow. 'DCI Mel Phillips has been put in charge of the case, you'll be seconded to another team in the interim.'

'Pardon?'

'The case has been reopened. DCI Phillips has been put in charge; she's taking the briefing now. She'll be here in a minute.' His speech quickens, 'We can't have you working on the investigation. I know an officer with your experience will understand that.'

Understand?

Thomasine's face remains impassive; she shakes her head. It doesn't make any sense. 'It can't be Karen—it must be a mistake.'

'There is no mistake.' The frown on his forehead deepens, 'It's an accurate match on the dental records.'

'How did she get there? It's miles from the farm.' Her mouth feels as though it's full of cotton wool. 'She couldn't have walked it.'

She watches him scratch the inside of his wrist, it's a trick to check the time, the face of his watch lies above his pulse point. She uses it herself. He must be waiting for the DCI to turn up. He covers his mouth with a clenched fist, coughs.

'She must have been taken there. We don't yet know whether that was where she was killed.' He leans back in the chair, his arms loosely folded across his chest. 'That's as much as I can tell you.' His voice softens. 'Take some compassionate leave – you need to be with your family, just your mother now, isn't it?'

He has no idea what that will be like – not a clue, no one has.

At once she knows the envelope's contents: a summary of Karen's case file. Missing since the seventh of January 1973, sometime around nine o'clock on the Saturday evening and seven o'clock on the Sunday morning, when Thomasine herself had woken up, looked across the room and found her sister's bed empty. Thomasine had been eight-years-old; Karen had turned fifteen a few days earlier.

There's a knock at the door. Thomasine turns to look, a woman in her late thirties walks in. She's tall, like herself, similar in looks. Brown curly hair cut in at the jawline. A stress-filled body that no amount of food fattens up; her posture is as rigid as a brush handle. Dressed in a good-quality black trouser-suit, Thomasine has two like it hanging up in the wardrobe at home.

'DCI Mel Phillips,' she offers out her hand. The smile fades from her mouth. 'Sorry we couldn't meet under better circumstances.' The sharp edge gone from the voice she'd heard earlier. 'The team knows you won't be on the job, everyone understands.'

'Don't shut me out right now.' Thomasine's words are cold and flat.

Lips set in concentration, the DCI's eyes focus in on her.

'Look, I know how I would feel if I were you. I'd want to be in there, catching whoever did it. We can't allow that to happen though, you know that.' The plate glass window flexes as a gust of wind and snow slaps against it. 'Given the impact on you and your family, it will be impossible for you to be unbiased and non-judgemental. Copper or not. It would be the same for anybody in your position.' She takes in a deep breath. 'The whole team is on it. I realise that this is a difficult time, but we'll need to talk with you and your mother, go through your original statements.' She takes a business card out of her jacket pocket, slips it into Thomasine's hand. 'You can contact me on this number. We'll come out to you. Would tomorrow at about two o'clock be okay?'

'I want—' Thomasine's voice rises a pitch; her anger leaks out. 'I want to be involved.'

Hardacre interjects, raises his hand. 'Thomasine,' his face is impassive, 'we—'

'Of course.' Dry-eyed, she pushes back her anger. That battle can be fought later. 'We'll do whatever you want.' She stands up, makes for the door. 'I need to go, to get to Mam before the press do.'

The door slams behind her on her way out. Startled, the secretary jumps to her feet, her mouth opens, sounds come out, something about Family Liaison wanting to see her. Thomasine doesn't stop to listen; she hurries out into the corridor. Faces blur through glass walls, voices whisper, phones cry out. Her feet in flight mode take her down the stairs, out of the front door and onto the carpark. The freezing cold air cloaks her body; her heart thumps against her ribs. She wasn't going to cry in there, not in front of them. Not in front of anyone. She never cries. That stopped years ago. She slumps back against the wall, hands trembling.

Memories flood back in technicolour, she stands transfixed, a terrified eight-year-old child again. The front room, on the settee, the policemen kneeling in front of her, her mother standing by his side. She, powerless, shy, dressed in a matching navy-blue jumper and kilt, her sister's hand-me-downs, her hands tucked beneath her thighs, tears glistening in her eyes. Her father up on the moor searching for Karen.

There'd been a barrage of questions. She and Karen had shared a room. Was she sure she didn't wake up? She mustn't worry about telling the truth, she wouldn't get in trouble. Karen must have made a noise—did she hear it? It was dark, the lamp, Karen must have switched the lamp on, did it wake her up too? Did Karen say anything to her before she left? What was she wearing? If she made her promise to keep it secret, it's okay to tell them now. Did anyone come for her? The questions seemed endless. She had no answer for any of them. She didn't utter a word, total fear obliterating any memory she might have had. Her nose ran, tears streamed down her cheeks, dripped off her chin, soaked her jumper.

As the weeks went by she lost weight, everyone was too busy to eat. It would be wrong to eat. Why would they waste time cooking when they could be out looking for Karen? That would be a sin. She was already a sinner; she had allowed her sister to disappear. Her mother told her that day after day, if not in words, in silence.

Where the hell are they?

She hunts in her handbag for her car keys, tips the bag's contents onto the ground. Her keys lie like a broken body amongst a clump of tissues. Karen's face stares up at her from a photo keyring. Her dark brown eyes suddenly accusing her. She would have been fifty-one-years old last week.

Frantically, she gathers up her belongings, gets to her feet, throws her bag over her shoulder. She slips her keys and phone into her pocket, looks up, everything is a glaring white. Which car is hers? Where did she park? Her mind blanks—a band of anxiety binds her chest. In the distance a blue van approaches, its wheels skid and slide. Fingers grasping the ignition key, she presses down on the button. Muted red-lights flash in the distance. Seconds later she wrenches open the door, throws herself into the driver's seat.

Your fault! Your fault! Her mother's voice taunts her.

Blood thunders through her ears. What is inside of her screams its way out—the grief, the pain. A lifetime of it consumes her. Fists hammering relentlessly on the steering wheel, hot tears soak into the neck of her blouse.

The wind pummels the car; a thick layer of snow buries the windscreen. She thrusts her hands under her armpits, rocks in her seat, and with each breath the rage recedes—back into its cage just as it had as a child.

She pulls the mobile from her pocket, her fingers hover over the keypad. Anxiety kicks in. Why hadn't she got the detail from Hardacre? She'd had to get out of his office before she said something she'd regret. Her stomach flips.

Mam will want to know more; she'll want to know everything.

Had they rung her mother? If they had, *surely* they would have told her. Her neck stiffens. She can't ring her mother to check, if she did, and they hadn't, she'd have to tell her over the phone and that would be wrong, utterly wrong. She'd promised her mother that she would never do that.

This will kill her...

Thomasine had been the bringer of bad news to others, hundreds of times. Legs give way, bodies sink against the frame of the front door, some collapse, some shaken so badly they cannot get up without help. Occasionally they look at her blankly, unable to speak, unsure what to say.

'I'll make us a drink, shall I? A pot of tea? Let's go in.' Her own voice often barely above a whisper, the door to the world closing behind them. The next hour the delicate process of describing how their loved one was found. Getting it across in a kind way, sensitive to their months or years of waiting. Empathy and professionalism in equal measure. Knowing only too well the burden they have carried year after year.

Why can't I do this for myself?

She turns on the ignition, switches on the wipers; an arc of snow disappears from the windscreen. A thought occurs to her; she could ask someone else to tell her, a colleague, another FLO.

'No—I can't,' the words rush out of her; she doesn't want anyone else involved.

Of course, that's why they'd blanked the screen. So I wouldn't see the visual of the murder board and go off on my own, half-cocked, like a bull in a china shop. It didn't matter. She knew exactly what would be there. Maps of the farm, of the moorland. Photographs of Karen as a kid. Not the others, the age-progressed ones, thirty-five and forty-five, all worthless now. Photographs of new evidence will litter the board. Scene of Crime Officers will have done their work. All marked by a numbered card and photographed in situ. Hair, bones, teeth, clothing if it hasn't decomposed.

Every part of her wants to go up to the crime scene, but there's no point, she wouldn't even get past the tape. Her name won't be on the list of those allowed on site. She would be the same if she was in charge. Her best hope will be the Coroner's Report. Perhaps she can call in a favour. They've known her long enough.

She'll be sidelined after that.

Early morning briefings would pass down the orders from the Detective Superintendent. Hundreds of interview notes would be unpacked, reviewed and those involved re-interviewed – if they're still alive. Boxes of evidence, their seals broken, would be retested for DNA and particulates. Technology has moved on since the girls went missing. Soil samples would be taken; Karen's remains would be analysed for cause of death. The HOLMES database, the brain of the investigation, would be updated by the input clerk, all the evidence entered. Details on anyone connected with the investigation, their names, dates of birth, addresses, anything specific to them, would go on, too.

Perhaps Veronica's name will be up on the board as well, her pictures stuck on with tiny pieces of blue tack. She'd disappeared that night too, from town, not the moor, or so they believed at the time. The DI in charge had called her a runaway, there'd been no money for an abduction, no reason to believe anything else. Had they found her body, too? She hadn't asked. They would have said, *surely,* they would? Why hadn't she asked? There was never any evidence that Veronica and Karen knew each other. Her stomach sinks, Rosie – Veronica's sister. Her own best friend, she'll have to ring her.

If Rosie knew she would have rung me already, I've got to concentrate on Mam right now. She must be my priority.

The initial investigation broke her family. Everything, including the farm, fell apart. Her father's death had been the tipping point. People helped at first but, as the weeks went by, had to go back to their own farms, their own jobs. The final nail in the coffin came months later – the foot and mouth outbreak. Every single sheep had to be slaughtered.

Yet despite all of it, her love for the moorland never paled, not for the place that shaped her. Her fingernails dig into the leather cover of the steering wheel. The realisation of it cleaves her chest like an iron brace, Karen couldn't come home—it wasn't a choice that she made. All these years of waiting, all that hurt, the silent accusations, the disappointments. The anger. All wasted.

The windscreen wipers let out a high-pitched squeal. Thomasine closes her eyes and allows the tears to stream down her face.

She did everything she could to find her sister. She will sacrifice everything to find her killer.

And when she does—he's going to pay.

Chapter 3

Until yesterday, Saturday, *she* would say, life was better than it had ever been. I disagree. But then I would.

Her name is Lily, by the way. Lily Probisher – that's what she calls herself.

She lives in a great big Victorian villa in Lymm, double-fronted. Wrought iron railings painted a glossy black. Trees either side of the front door. Beautifully topiaried. You'd never guess they weren't real. Wooden shutters on the windows that cost a fortune. And a posh security system to keep it all safe. There's a camera over the front door and one out the back. She could access them online. *Could* is the operative word. Doesn't know how to switch them on. She's not read the manual yet. She's a bit of a Luddite.

She longs for a converted barn up on the moors with high ceilings, oak beams and a two-acre garden. The sort you see in *Homes & Gardens*, that in spring is pricked by snowdrops and daffodils. Where in winter the birds feast on the withered fruits of summer, blackberries, winberries, sloes. She'd never be happy there. She's not one for sinking her fingers into the soil. Thank God for Marigolds, that's what I say, she buys them in bulk. The rubber gloves, not the plant.

Lily's a therapist, like I said, she helps people to help themselves. She likes big words, like empowerment, is an expert on *paired comparisons* and *to-do* lists. Her current one is attached to the fridge door by a magnet that says *One Life – Live It*. She's booked herself onto a triathlon in three months' time. She can't even swim.

Anyway, like I said, yesterday happened. I'm sure somewhere in those self-help books, those that line the shelves of her study, there will be a paragraph that reads *things happen for a reason*. I'm

13

sure in the future we'll see the good that came out of yesterday. We'll look back and think, thank God that's all over.

Today, however, she's a right mess.

Yesterday started off as a good day. She got up early. Cleaned clean things. Rewashed washed stuff. Scrubbed the kitchen until her fingers bled. The house was clean as a pin when she left.

She went out for a run. It was one of those chilly days when it's so cold the tips of your ears feel like they're turning to ice. Where the end of your nose turns pink and the skin on your lips goes tight. One of those wonderful, crisp, winter days that make you want to be outside. The sun was a huge lemon disc in a bright blue sky. Beyond the moors, far away, snow-filled clouds drifted towards us like giant pulls of candy floss.

She was outside the local park, at the gates, jogging on the spot. Kitted out in a long-sleeved, black merino wool, running top, capri tights and a bright pink buff around her neck. She had a large water bottle in a carrier around her waist. It made a swishing noise as she ran.

There's an expensive running watch wrapped around her wrist. A Garmin. Its tiny screen feeds her statistics; how fast she's running, how many miles she's done. It's waterproof too, so she can wear it swimming. When she learns to swim, that is. It was a Christmas present to herself. Just like all her other gifts.

Yesterday was day one of the sixteen-week triathlon training programme. The one stuck on the door of the fridge, underneath her goals for the year. The one she typed up after she read that book, *Breaking the Mould – a Life Unlimited*.

As I mentioned, she was jogging on the spot. She looked down at her Garmin, it said she'd run one mile, three hundred and fifty yards. She wasn't very happy. She likes things going to plan. They weren't.

The gates were cordoned off by a row of bright, tangerine-coloured safety barriers. A white Ford Van was parked at the front. The rear doors were wide open, black rubber buckets, long-handled shovels, loads of cardboard food wrappers, empty tins of coca cola – it was full of crap. I could almost feel the tightness in her throat.

A couple of blokes in hard hats, hands wrestling with pneumatic drills, were breaking up the pavement. The jab and rattle of metal on concrete hurt her eardrums.

'Use the south entrance,' shouted one of them, gesturing down the road. She didn't hear him. She wasn't happy. Her fingernails raked the inside of her palms. A prickly flush crept up her neck.

'They're digging up the road,' said a voice loudly in her ear.

'What the—' Then she saw who it was. She recognised him. Patrick, he's a runner like herself. A local legend. Big, grey, bushy beard – a skinny Father Christmas in lycra tights. He'd had a heart attack, two weeks after his fifty-fifth birthday. It took him six months to learn to walk again. When she first met him, he said God gave him another chance at life. He's making the most of it now – six stones lighter, running seven-minute miles and winning his age category at 10k races.

She's on her second chance too—but only I know that. I know lots of her secrets.

'That short-cut… the one next to *Weatherspoon's*… it's grim though!' He panted the words out as he jogged backwards down the street.

So, it shouldn't have been much of a problem really, not for a runner like herself. A small detour. She was disappointed nevertheless. I could tell. It's the way she lifted her chin; that clenched jaw, the tiny pout on her lips. Stuff that she's completely unaware of.

Lily is my specialist subject – I know all her visual tics.

The High Street was two hundred yards away and an obstacle course – screeching children being dragged along by the scruff of their coats, pensioners wheeling their trollies. Teenage girls sauntering along as though auditioning for *Britain's Next Top Model*. Clamped on each other's arms, that's if they're not texting. Heads straining forward like monkeys. Fingers tapping and clicking, completely oblivious to anything around them. Stop-start all the way.

'Pillocks,' she whispered under her breath.

Her swear word of the day. She allows herself just the one. That was part of her transformation, her moving on. Her grand progression up *Maslow's Hierarchy of Needs*. It's a model. A diagram shaped like a pyramid. At the bottom, there's basic needs, for safety and sex. That's one thing that's rarely been ticked off the list—sex. At the top, self-actualisation. You are the best you can be. Confident, happy. Total control, that's what she really wanted. And, for that reason, I had to disappear from her life – completely.

So, she's jogging down the High Street at a snail's pace. Eight-minute miles drop to twelve, then sixteen; she was the salmon swimming upstream. Everyone headed for the New Year sales. She hates crowds—can't cope with all those bodies pressed against hers. Can't see who's coming her way. Can't get a feel for who's behind her. Her pulse races like an underground train.

'I'll pick up the pace later,' she probably told herself that through gritted teeth, frustration simmering towards anger, as she squeezed her way through the ten-deep queue outside *Glanville's Tea House*. The air nebuliser under the front entrance pumped out its little tease of freshly baked pork pies. The smell wove its way into her senses. I knew the image of a thick buttery crust and sweet onion gravy would be growling in her head. It certainly was in mine. She's a veggie now though, so those are off the menu.

Her training as a counsellor taught her to control her impulses. Like I said, she has this range of tools and techniques to keep her on the right track. Still, it must exhaust her, keeping all that anger in. She was going zero-minute miles right then. It said so on her Garmin. She swerved to the right.

'*Wetherspoons – shortcut – it's a bit grim.*'

It was.

Miss Therapist doesn't like alleyways. Places of shit and shadows she calls them. That commonness sometimes leaks out. Never in front of her clients, though. She's Miss Prim and Proper with them, no trace of that northern accent either. The one that held her back for years. She is the product of the full weight of her investment in elocution from that online subscription company on YouTube.

I've never seen her go down an alley. But like I said, she's trying to make progress. Facing her fears and all that. When she gets home she'll write it on her to-do list, then tick it off. She believes in retrospective recognition. Tick off what you've done; make it count.

I remember thinking, I hope she's careful running over those cobbles. Covered in frost, slippery as hell. It wouldn't have been the first time she'd fallen.

The stink hit her first. The alley was littered with cigarette butts, half-eaten bags of chips, plastic bottles, a used condom stuck against the brick wall. Her face reddened as she held her breath. In the shadows there's a man, she hasn't noticed him yet. His head protrudes from behind a large green waste bin. His back to her, his shoulders hunched against the wall. It was the noise that startled her—a spluttering stream of piss hitting the cobbles. The smell got a whole lot worst. Ammonia, flat beer, stale sweat. His boots stamped on the concrete. As he turned away from the wall, his eyes fixed on her.

He was barely out of his twenties. 'Hello,' he said, tucking his shirt into his trousers with a damp hand. 'Hello,' he repeated, leaning forward, his mouth widened into a supercilious grin.

Her whole body pulled back in disgust. It must have hurt him, that water bottle. Her fingers curled around the handle, striking him full in the face. Then with her right foot, she lashed out. Hit him right in the balls. He squealed like a pig, dropped to the ground, slid in his own piss. His left knee hit the cobbles with a crack.

That expensive self-defence programme finally paid off.

'Hello,' she said, without missing a beat.

Part of me was proud. Another part of me thought—shit where did that come from?

She leant over him. Whispered something under her breath, I didn't catch it. He shrank back against the wall.

A look of bewilderment crossed his face, 'Get… get away from me, you…'

I was shocked, completely shocked. She'd turned into a weirdo. Top of Maslow's Hierarchy of Needs – not taking any shit and all that. Someone I didn't recognise, and I've known her all her life.

'Okay,' her voice devoid of concern.

She looked over her shoulder. She must have decided the way back was better than the way forward. Moments later she was back on the main street, her teeth gritted, weaving her way through the crowd.

This story doesn't end yet, though. The weirdness continued.

Her eyes latched onto something. There was a massive flat screen TV in the centre of a shop window. She was drawn towards it like a magnet. The news silently played to all that looked.

The large plate glass window reflected a ghost of her image. The oval shape of her face, blonde hair, shaved short into her neck, her lean frame. Around her a stream of self-admirers. Their eyes flickering across the glass. Catching their likeness.

Her own eyes were captivated by the images of Scots Pine trees ripped from the ground. Their pale roots bursting through the soil like the arms of drowning men. The trees faded as they cut to another image – a girl. Hazel eyes with long black lashes stared out. Miss Therapist read the banner of text on the screen.

"Human remains found at Winter Hill construction site have been identified as those of Karen Albright – fifteen-years-old at the time of her disappearance on the seventh of January 1973. Police continue to excavate the site for the body of eighteen-year-old Veronica Lightfoot who went missing the same night."

I bet the hairs on the back of her neck stood on end.

White snowflakes clung to the reporter's slight frame. The camera scanned the crowd behind her, behind the yellow police tape. The camera zoomed out, then in, the scene changed. An old face with bright blue eyes and hooded lids came into view. Her hair glistened with tiny beads of hairspray. She blinked as the camera flashes bounced off her.

A sliver of recollection ran through Miss Therapist's head. I felt a tightness form across my chest.

The mother, that's what it said on the screen. The interviewer thrust a microphone out, the mother stepped forward, loosened her scarf – a pale white scar ran across the goitre on her neck.

The words travelled across the screen. She placed her forehead against the glass. Tried to hear what was being said. A look of confusion strewn across her face.

'Veronica, if you're watching this, please come back, we can start over. We love you. Rosie and I love you. We just want you home.'

Miss Therapist's mouth gaped open, she took a step back, her fingers let go of the water bottle – it clattered to the ground. The image faded, the news moved on. She stood in silence, tears stung her eyes. She rubbed them away. Strands of memories pulled themselves out and flexed.

Then she let out a low groan. Her legs crumbled beneath her. Someone, a young girl, grabbed her arm to steady her.

'Your… water bottle,' said the young girl who'd helped her up.

Lily, I think I'll call her Lily now, well, she bolted like a horse. Shoved her way through the crowds, didn't say sorry or I beg your pardon. Ran through the traffic. Almost got hit by a minibus. She kept going at full speed over the bridge. Out of town. Off road. Her eyes blind to everything around her. She scrambled over rubble and scree, her legs dragging her up onto the moors without her consent. Salty sweat ran down her forehead. Stinging her eyes. Blurring her vision. The snow blustered around her, pushing her back, then tugging her forwards. The sharp blade of the cotton-grass cut at her legs.

She ran on. Possessed by the face on the screen. By the bright blue eyes peering through hooded lids.

As though slapped back by the wind, she stopped dead. Her chest heaved. She couldn't breathe out, she couldn't breathe in. Her fingers fumbled for her water bottle. Gone. Lying by the plate glass window on the High Street. She had no idea where she was. Trembling uncontrollably, she stumbled to the ground. Perfect white snow crystals melted on the heat of her burning skin.

She covered her eyes with the palms of her hands. That life she mislaid, the one between hypnotherapy and Pentobarbital and things far worse. It flickered, like a light bulb about to blow. Splinters of memory cut through her like a knife through butter. The dance floor, the music, the Pakistani boy. Other memories. Her fingers in the soil, the foot, sticking out at an angle, refusing to be buried. Her hands, piling clumps of wet peat over bare toes. The pungent smell of newly turned earth, suddenly evoked within her.

Faces came out of the shadows, watching, judging. People, places. Forgotten on purpose, years ago. They butted against each other for her attention. The past flooded in, ruined the present, poisoned it. Her tools and techniques useless against the onslaught.

She retched as the snow settled upon her – its cold embrace slowing her heart.

Her last image my face. I couldn't save her.

Chapter 4

A freezing fog obliterates everything. Drivers, unable to see beyond the vehicle in front of them, slow the M62 to a snail's pace. Images of the meeting with Hardacre and DCI Phillips replay in Thomasine's head. The words she should have said mock her relentlessly.

The wind brings tide after tide of thick snowflakes that turn everything in their wake a glaring white. As she turns into the moor road, the tyres on her bright red Mini Cooper lose traction, the car unceremoniously sliding off to the left into a shallow ditch, she cannot stop it.

'Shit!' Her heart slams against her chest, her whole being shakes, she looks in the rear window.

Thank God there was no one behind me.

She tries to manoeuvre the car out, the wheels turn, fail to get purchase, the engine stalls. She turns on the hazard lights, pushes open the driver's door, clambers out. Still trembling, checks the car for damage; everything seems to be okay. An olive-green parka lies across the back seat, she tugs it on, zips it up. Her fingers fumbled with the latch on the boot, it springs open with a click; perching on the rim she struggles to get her feet into the thick red socks and black wellingtons she keeps in the boot for work.

The access to the farm is further down the road, the farmhouse is a couple of miles up the track – it's going to be a long trek. First, she must clamber over the lower gate, the lock is frozen shut.

Her progress through the thick fog of snow is painfully slow, feet soaked, her clothing her only defence against the freezing wind. Chilled to the bone, she cannot turn back for fear of getting lost; all evidence of her footsteps gone in minutes. As she presses on, a flock of horned sheep shiver behind a dilapidated drystone wall; their jet-black eyes fix on her, silver droplets of ice cling to their coarse woollen coats, their noses root in the snow for food.

Beneath its glimmering white sheet, the world before her has lain almost untouched for hundreds of years. Winter and summer alike, covered in purple moor grass and blanket bog. On the tops, shale and slate poke up through the shrub and heather. She tugs her hood down over her face, recovers against the wind for a moment. She loves this place. It was her escape. Her playground.

Outcrops of trees, like old men with twisted spines, cower amongst lumps of gritstone torn from the earth thousands of years ago. Too heavy for a man to carry, too many to make it worthwhile clearing. Her father's family has lived here since the early 1800s – she was forged in this landscape.

She hears a sharp crack, a gunshot going off.

Am I at the farm?

It's the barn door—still some way off. The wind is snatching it, slamming it to and fro. She follows the sound. Every few minutes she hears the dogs howl. She takes her mobile out of her pocket, squints at the screen. No signal; she cannot ring her mother for help.

Somewhere ahead, hidden by the weather, is the farmhouse. Two stories high with a steep roof, surrounded by a broken-down wall, a ramshackle of moss-covered stones. It is as though the wall itself thrust them out. They lie in piles of ten or twelve waiting to be put back in their rightful place. In clear weather, it can be seen from miles away. The lichen-covered slate roof, tall chimney and grey stone walls – a shadow on the moor, a darkness.

I can't understand why she still lives here. She can't cope with the place. She's on her own. Her foot sinks into another pothole, her father's voice rings in her ears.

'She'll never leave until Karen comes home.'

The day of Karen's disappearance, he'd hurt his back moving hay bales in the barn; that night he'd downed four painkillers with a pint of bitter, he'd barely been able to make it up the stairs to bed. He was out flat until the morning.

He said he'd never make that mistake again. He didn't – his side of her parents' marital bed lay empty from that night onwards. Each morning Thomasine would wake to find him slumped in the armchair, dozing, blocking the door to her bedroom from the inside. A blanket tucked under his chin, his eyes closed. Terrified that she, too, would be taken.

The rest of the time he'd be out on the moors, minding the sheep—looking for Karen even when everyone else had stopped.

A stroke followed by a massive heart attack. Forty-years-old. Dead within minutes. That's what the family doctor had said. Everyone else said it was a broken heart. That the guilt had taken him. They found him in the barn – he'd been working on the tractor, trying to change a wheel.

Oh God, I hope she doesn't ask me to stay the night.

With her father gone, the house became a time capsule. Karen was with them, yet not. Her mother had insisted their bedroom must stay as it was. Karen's made-up bed ready to be slept upon; her dressing table covered in her essentials. Small tubes of lipstick, matching bottles of nail varnish, creamy nudes, pale pinks, deep purples; their white plastic tops yellowed, their insides solidified. Long strands of dark brown hair lying in a small china pot, carefully eased from a plastic comb that her mother found behind the dressing table after the police had done their work. Her childhood dolls still rest on the shelf, their pale blue eyes open in constant surprise. Waiting.

Thomasine lifts her face to the wind and snow.

Their bedroom became a mausoleum, never to be left untidy. An irony, Karen's side of the room had always been a constant tip, clothes cast on the floor, half-read teen magazines thrown carelessly beneath the frame of her bed, makeup streaks on the white melamine top of the dressing table. Spots of pale pink nail varnish on the rug.

'See how nice Thomasine keeps her side.' Her mother would respond. 'Why can't you be like that?'

Karen would tilt her head to the side, put her hand on her hip. Say nothing. But it didn't end there, not for Thomasine, she'd pay one way or another for her tidiness. Usually, a Chinese burn on her wrist or a sharp pinch on the inside of her arm when she was least expecting it.

Now, Thomasine's side of the room is clear of clutter; her dressing table, her wardrobe never used.

The anniversary of Karen's disappearance—she always had be home for that. This year was the exception, she'd been working on a case, didn't feel she could ask for the time off.

Maybe we can clear all that stuff away, make it a decent place to stay.

To walk from one side of the bedroom to the other is to cross a time zone. Two countries, past and present. The window looks out across the valley, to Anglezarke, to Belmont. Where she lay hidden all those years. Thomasine knows that she will never be able to look out of that window again, neither will her mother. She'll want it sealed up.

The slamming of the barn door gets louder, the dogs howl. The stench of the slurry pit behind the farm catches in her throat. Even the snow couldn't snuff it out. She's nearly there.

The dreams started after her father had died, so vibrant, so real.

'They've found her,' her father would say, 'in Australia. She's very happy there. She's not coming back.' There was always relief in his voice.

In the dream, they'd sink down onto the settee beside her, her father's fingers linked through her own, her mother's arm around her shoulder. There was to be a new beginning. One where they could celebrate Christmas and she could have a birthday party every year, like the other kids in the village. The fire in the grate would be stoked high, yellow flames would lick up the chimney. Her mother would clean and cook; she'd make bread again.

Thomasine would be their number one daughter. They'd walk the moors, the dogs scampering behind them.

Then she'd wake with a start, her pillow soaked with tears. That mausoleum of a bedroom, freezing cold, her fingers still warm from her father's hand. Her mother across the room, in her sister's bed, knocked out each night by sleeping pills and vodka.

Eventually, Thomasine dragged her bedding down the stairs, slept on the settee in the kitchen. The dreams couldn't find her there.

The padlock to the farm gate refuses to open, like the one at the bottom of the track, it is frozen solid. The metal frame shakes as she clambers over it; her rubber boots slip on the cobblestones as she lands. For a moment, she struggles to stay upright.

Up close to the house, you can see the neglect; the decay. The dogs are tied up by the barn door, two of them, farm dogs, teeth bared, their black and white coats matted with mud. They lunge full pelt out of their kennel, chains straining their necks. They'd scare anyone else to death – not her. That's what her mother wants, to keep people out, especially the press. Thomasine knows it will soon start up again, the media circus will pry into every crevice of their lives. In the absence of the truth, digging up dirt, making up lies when it suits them; it sickens her.

'Down!' Her voice roars out over the yard. 'Sit.'

It is immediate, growls turn to whimpers, they drop down onto their hackles, tongues hanging out. She rubs their heads, runs her hand along their backs; they're underweight. She picks up the metal bowls by their feet, makes her way over to the barn, where their feed is kept. The wind catches the barn door again, slams it with such violence that it hurts her ears. The dogs whine, huddle together. The last three weeks have been full of storms; rain, freezing cold sleet then snow. The worst weather in thirty years. The damp will have swollen the wood, it always does, it will be impossible to shut the door properly until the summer sun dries it out. Either that or get it repaired and her mother flatly refuses to do that. Thomasine goes inside, picks up a bag of dried dog food, fills their bowls to the brim, places them down in front of the dogs. Within seconds the bowls are empty, so she fills them again.

Starving – they mustn't have been fed for days.

The constant banging of the door sets her on edge, she nudges a concrete block against it with her foot. The wind tugs at it angrily; the door holds fast. Silenced at long last.

She looks around the barn, it's deterioration shocks even her. The northern corner of the roof collapsed two winters ago. Wooden roof supports stick out like broken limbs, shattered tiles litter the ground beneath it. There is a strong tang of bird shit; droppings from pigeons and bats that nest in eaves. Years of it, layer upon layer. Occasionally, in the spring, her mother will take a knife to it, scrape it off, dig it into the small vegetable garden she keeps around the back of the house. Farm implements are scattered everywhere; a large, ancient Howard's Champion Plough lies covered in the muck that covers everything else.

She crosses the yard, heads for the farmhouse. Outside the front door is her mother's Range Rover, twenty years old and still going. The wheel arches covered in mud and dung.

She looks back the way she has just come, squints into the distance. Already all signs of her are obliterated.

Her attention returns to the house: either side of the front door two large windows, hung with long, green, velvet curtains, let in the cold daylight. On the left window sill, an oval-shaped cut glass vase is crammed with plastic snowdrops. On the right, a brown and white porcelain sheep dog stands guard.

Nothing changes.

Thomasine's frozen fingers linger above the door knocker. She gave back her key when she moved long ago. It must be over twenty years now, she thinks, as the matter ticks over in her mind. She can't quite remember why she left. Her mother thought it was the fear of being burdened with the farm, she'd said so at the time. But it wasn't that—it was more about distance, about giving herself a life that wasn't choked by her sister's absence. The key is lost now, or so her mother says. Thomasine thinks it's down the back of a settee or under piles of receipts at the back of a drawer. Her mother says she is too busy to search for it. A subtle hurt.

A thought drifts through her mind.

Perhaps now we can all start moving forward.

She imagines her mother living in a cottage next door to her sister, Aunt Elizabeth. She sees her mother and herself shopping together in town – laughing. Sharing an afternoon tea at the Crown. Then the images get sucked into the vast pool of hopelessness that fills her.

She wraps her fingers around the hoop on the black cast iron sheep's head knocker. It's like a pagan god, its horns curve towards the door, its eyes bulge out. It had been a gift from the local blacksmith, he said it was Duttur – the goddess and protector of flocks. A wedding gift to her mother and father. A shudder of cold passes through Thomasine's shoulders. She knocks on the door; the loud knock rattles back down her fingers.

Within moments, she sees her mother's face in the window, her long plait of grey hair swings down over her shoulder. Her eyes wide in surprise; she smiles then she disappears.

The press hasn't got to her yet. The wave of fear recedes.

It takes her mother some effort to open the front door. Like the others, the wood is swollen with damp. Thomasine pushes at it. It gives way with a ripping sound. The narrow hallway opens up, a bare light bulb swings from twisted flex from the ceiling. Her mother is cast in the shadows. Short wisps of hair curl over the tips of her ears; reading glasses hang from a chain around her neck. She is oblivious to the nightmare about to unfold around her. The lines in her forehead deepen.

'God, look at the state of you.' She grabs her by the hand. 'You're freezing cold—soaked to the skin! You shouldn't come out in this, Thomasine, you shouldn't.'

Thomasine draws her mother into an embrace. They have learnt to rub alongside each other, each with their own view of the world. The occasional spat turning to harsh words that must be forgotten and moved on from.

Perhaps it will be easier than I imagine? She could have reconciled herself to this moment years ago.

'Sorry I couldn't come home last week. It was work… we had a big investigation. I couldn't get time away.' It was a lie – she could have pushed for it. She holds her mother at arm's length. 'Mam, have you lost weight?' Her mother feels like skin and bones, like the owl she held in her hands when she was four-years-old. 'There is hardly anything of you—'

Her mother shrugs her off. 'Get on with you,' she forces a laugh, 'you've not seen us for a while, that's all.'

Thomasine knows better than to go over it again. Theirs is a fragile relationship, love based on acquiescence. Always the good daughter, saying and doing the right thing. She follows her mother down the hallway to the kitchen, the words about her sister still unsaid, the ticking time bomb in her head carries her forwards.

'Mam, I'll make us a pot of tea, I'm dying of thirst.'

As they walk into the kitchen, the warm aroma of drying clothes wafts in her face. Almost obscuring the fireplace, her mother's plain white cotton bras and knickers hang over the clothes maiden. On the mantle above is a row of photographs. Karen's five-year-old face looks out at her, her two front teeth barely visible beneath her lips. Thomasine feels a queasiness in her stomach—a dryness in her mouth.

'Let's get these off you.' Her mother tugs at her coat sleeve – it's soaked through, pulls it off Thomasine's back, hangs it on the end of the maiden. 'It'll dry quick enough here.'

As she fills the kettle, her mother chatters on about the weather, the damp in her bedroom, the price of dog vaccinations. Thomasine seats herself at the large oak kitchen table. Her mind wanders, her mother's voice melds into the background.

Karen is opposite her, eleven-years-old, a broad smile across her face. Auburn hair tied in a ponytail; coffee coloured freckles cover her nose and cheeks.

A loaf of freshly baked bread straight from the oven is on the table before them; the crust a crisp golden brown. Their mother cuts each a slice; she and her sister toast the bread on the open fire, layer it thick with butter and homemade wimberry jam. The memory envelops her. She remembers the crunch of the crust, the sharp sweetness of the jam. The longing to relive that memory time and time again.

These are the memories she ran away from, the ones that manifest themselves whenever she visits the farm. The hauntings – the true reason she moved out just after her twenty-first birthday.

The shrill tone of the phone startles them both. Thomasine's stomach lurches, she stands up, her mother already moving towards the hallway. She throws her arm out.

'Don't answer that, Mam!' Her voice rings out.

'But—'

'Don't answer it!' Thomasine's voice is sharp. 'Let them ring back.'

'It could be—' her mother's voice rises a pitch.

'Look, I'm sorry. I didn't mean to be… I need to tell you—it's really important.'

The whistle of the kettle rises above her voice, the ringing continues.

The hurt fades from her mother's face. 'Alright, but it had better be important.' She picks up a large white china teapot from the dresser. The ritual of making tea never varied; the swirling of water, leaf tea – a teaspoon per person and one for the pot. The topping up of water, the tea cosy, leaving it five minutes to brew.

Thomasine gets to her feet, goes out into the hall, takes the phone off the hook.

'Sit down, love.' Her mother pulls out a chair for her, puts the teapot down on the table, runs the back of her hand lightly across her cheek. 'I've missed you, why didn't you call?' Her voice softens. 'I'd have made us lunch.'

Thomasine feels a choke rising through her chest; she pushes it back.

'It's the job, it's hard to make plans, I…' her voice trails off, she picks up a spoon, stirs the teapot. Her heart beats against her ribs.

Now – tell her now.

She opens her mouth; no words come out. Beads of sweat form on her forehead.

Her mother places two white china pint pots on the table. Takes a jug of milk out of the table top fridge, puts a splash in each pint pot, fills them up with tea. Smiling, she sits down opposite her.

Not yet, she thinks, *I can't tell her yet.* Thomasine's cheeks burn hot.

'Still no sugar? Or are you still on that daft diet?'

Thomasine responds with a shake of her head, she picks up her tea, takes a sip, its strong and hot. *Now, now—do it now.* The words sit angrily on her tongue, she sucks in a breath.

'I've got something to tell you. It's—' She is standing on the edge of a cliff, her foot raised, ready to step out. She coughs, tries again. 'It's… Karen… she's been found.'

Her mother's eyes widen in surprise, her mouth gapes open, she rushes to her feet.

'Been found, what do you mean? Been found—where?' Voice raised, her face flushes with excitement. 'Is she alright? Why didn't you tell me as soon as you came in. Why didn't you ring me?'

Anxiety claws at Thomasine's chest. She'd said it wrong—said it all wrong. Tears sting her eyes; she grabs hold of her mother's hand. 'No… no… I'm sorry, I'm sorry. They've found her remains.'

The colour drains from her mother's face, her lips part, she covers her mouth with the palms of her hands. A loud wail pours out of her. Thomasine wraps her arms around her mother, stopping her before she falls to the flagstone floor.

'I'm so sorry,' the words tumble out of her mouth over and over. She takes her mother by the elbow, leads her over to the settee, sits down beside her, puts her arm around her shoulder.

They stay like that for a few moments, then her mother elbows her away. A sneer transforms her face, words shoot out of her like bullets.

'She can't be! I would have known if—'

'Forensics say she's been buried...' Thomasine's voice now barely audible, 'a long time. Probably since the time she disappeared.'

The lines on her mother's face carve deep, she wraps her arms around her chest, turns away from her. 'I don't believe you. I'm her mother—I would have known.'

Thomasine has heard these words many times. The telepathic link exists only in the minds of those left bereft. A balm used to hold back reality. Denial.

'Forensics don't make mistakes, they matched Karen's dental records.' She reaches out for her mother's hand, tries to cover it with her own. 'She was buried in the woods, at the base of the moor, over at Anglezarke. I'll get someone to come out, to tell you the full details.'

'She was,' her mother looks out into the distance, through the walls, across the fields and the valley. Tears redden her eyes, 'across the moor, the whole time?'

Thomasine nods. They have never truly talked, not openly and honestly, about what could have happened to Karen. In her mother's mind, Karen would always return home. She had constantly refused to accept that her daughter might be dead.

Her eyes harden. 'How did she die?'

'I don't know yet... the Coroner's report may take time.' Thomasine knows they'll need a forensic anthropologist to put together Karen's remains. She leaves those words unsaid, sure that they would tip her mother over the edge.

Her mother sinks down into the settee, her eyes close, thick tears run down the crevices in her cheeks.

'They thought I did it—did I tell you that?' A dark red rash slowly creeps its way up her neck.

'You?' Thomasine tries to warm her voice, knowing full well what happened. 'I'm sure they didn't. Sadly, it's routine to question the family.' She doesn't bother quoting the statistics.

'It wasn't *routine*!' her mother's eyes flash. 'Don't you remember? They picked me up in a police car, drove through the village.' Her hands shake. 'You could see them on the road, watching.'

Thomasine doesn't remember. She's packed all that up—locked the door on it.

'They had me in four times,' she spits the words out, 'four times! And your dad, too. And they never let us be together. I had to face them alone, so did he.'

And now it is going to start up all over again.

Thomasine tries to quell her mother's fears. 'I can put them off—'

'No! I want it over and done—' She sinks back into her chair.

Thomasine leans forward, reaches out for her mother's hand, covers it with hers.

'Mam, I promise you, whatever it takes, I'll find who did it,' gently, she squeezes her mother's fingers. 'And I promise you that they'll pay for all of pain they've caused us.'

Her mother's eyes dull, then fire into life.

'Just you make sure you do.'

Outside the wind roars up from the valley, tears around the house. Howls down the chimney, pulls at the tiles on the roof. The dogs cry out as though they too are grieving.

Chapter 5

He feels content. Tucked up in bed, Lottie folded into his back – the warmth of her breath on his neck. He imagines the winter sun rising over the fens, warming the landscape. Cormorants and swallows nesting in the rushes.

Today the light will be good. I'll go into the garden, watch the mist rise above the snow as the temperature rises. The frost will cling to the teasels in the field behind the house. Thousands of them. I'll have a coffee first, then I'll paint.

The shift of her cotton nightie touches his bare back. Carefully, he rolls over to face her; traces the curve of her cheeks with the tips of his fingers. Tenderly, he kisses her on the tip of her nose. She moves, lets out a sigh, rolls away from him to the edge of the mattress. Her body facing down; her chin juts out to the right. He leans over her; kisses her again.

'Sleepyhead,' he whispers in her ear.

She doesn't wake.

He eases himself out of the bed, dips to pick up the clothes he'd carelessly flung to the floor the previous night. He remembers the first time he saw her, twenty-five years ago; the shy but knowing smile, the denim cut-offs frayed at the edge, her sun blushed skin. The sunlight shimmering off the water at the swimming pool. Closing the door behind him, he creeps out of the bedroom.

'What—' Arm thrust out, he steadies himself with the wall. Horace, their aged chocolate Labrador, struggles to his feet. It isn't the first time he has tripped over the dog's prostrate body. It hates to be parted from Lottie and follows her around constantly.

He crosses the landing to the bathroom, drops his clothes on top of the washing basket. Urinates whilst looking at his face in the mirror. A dark shadow covers his chin and cheeks – he needs a shave. He grimaces, revealing two rows of gleaming white teeth. He'd not wanted them. His agent, Carlo had been pushy about it, said no one had coffee-stained teeth anymore. No one who was anyone, anyway. That had always been his weakness, giving in to other peoples' opinions. Now he had the smile of a twenty-year-old and forever conscious of it. The white teeth made his olive skin look even darker. He splashes cold water into his face, vigorously rubs his skin with a small hand towel. Still appraising himself, he squirts deodorant under his arms and down his underpants. A contingency—the sinus infection that's been plaguing him for months has obliterated his sense of smell.

He shrugs on last night's clothes. 'Mate, you look knackered!' he says *sotto voce* to the mirror on his way out of the bathroom. He goes downstairs; the dog clambers behind him, his long claws scratch the wooden boards.

At the bottom, he looks left, catches sight of the kitchen. It's a mess. Last night's meal a fragrant Thai green prawn curry served on coconut rice; he'd been the cook for the night. Next door neighbours, Ray and Kerry, their friends of ten years, had made up the four. Paul had arrived with two bottles of red, both demolished before the first course. The meal had gone down well, they'd had fun. Even the huge chocolate cheesecake he'd bought from the French Patisserie in town earlier that day had been finished.

'Shall I raid the cellar?' Lottie had asked, before launching herself towards the cellar door with what he thought was a little too much enthusiasm. A few minutes later she had staggered up the stairs with four bottles of 2006 Château Corton Grancey Grand Cru under her arms. A gift from Carlo last Christmas.

'Time to crack these babies open,' Lottie said, a wicked grin upon her lips, her deep blue silk top streaked with dust.

It had been a celebration, a good luck meal, a toast to his new art exhibition. *Genius Loci. The Protective Spirit.* Twenty-five paintings. At a gallery in Bow owned by one of Carlo's other clients, a restaurateur.

He gives out a sigh of pleasure. He's been asked many times why he became a painter. At first, he'd been unable to articulate it. Later, when he'd been planning his PhD thesis, he considered focusing on the work of Francis Bacon, *The Head VI*, the scream howling out of the gaping mouth. He'd spent hours staring at the painting. It was as though something slid out from under his skin during that time. The need for truth, for release. The need to pull the nightmares out of him and onto the canvas. His pallet knife dripping with raw sienna, cadmium red and phthalo green.

He picks up the Fairy Liquid. Gives one quick squirt of liquid into the bowl of hot water. It reminded him of the beginning. That hedonistic release of energy and creativity. A week of sleepless nights. He had emptied himself. Five huge canvases. A collection of paintings never to be exhibited. He'd even given them a name. *Unum Intra*. A loose interpretation of Only One Can Enter. His most significant work. The centrepiece of the collection, LD 1.

All hidden away. As a child, his grandfather told him that every man should have his own space. A secret place he can retreat to, to be himself. The lockup is his and only he knows about it. His mind returns to Carlo. He'd been insistent.

'Right now, is the best time for your work – the starkness, barren landscapes, woodlands ravaged by climate change and housing developers.'

He'd raised an eyebrow. The word *no* hovered on the tip of his tongue. Then he'd averted his gaze, looked out of the kitchen window, across the fens.

'Don't give me that look. I know that look. That, I'm not interested in the money shit look. You still have bills to pay just like every other bugger.' Carlo pulled himself up, his barrelled chest swelled like a peacock's. 'If you're not exhibiting, neither of us is earning. Lottie tells me you've been locked up there in your bloody garret for months. You must be doing something up there.'

True, he had been painting, playing around with the colour palette, experimental pieces that would probably get smothered in ivory white before the month was out.

'Okay, I'll get them out.' he capitulated. 'But not now.'

Weeks later he'd shown Carlo the new work, thirty-five paintings. Some good, a few really special – he'd known that himself. The rest had been wall fillers he'd hashed together in a hurry.

He holds up the palms of his hands, stained by red burnt sienna, yellow ochre and alizarin. He turns them over, his cuticles rimmed with ivory black acrylic paint.

An artist's hands.

He takes a tea towel out of the bottom drawer of an oversized armoire. A large, shabby chic monstrosity that Lottie had insisted he buy; it takes up half the back wall of the kitchen.

Footsteps sound above his head, the power shower roars into action. She's awoken. He knows she'll be down in a few minutes. *I'll wash up before Lottie comes downstairs. Maybe rustle up breakfast.*

For a second, he pictures himself, the perfect husband, the model of domesticity. Pulling croissants out of the Aga. Not putting the butter knife in the jam. Bringing the washing in. Hoovering…

He throws the tea towel on the kitchen table, laughs at himself.

No, I'm not that man and never will be. Cook up a meal now and then… perhaps.

He moves around the room, mindlessly picking up glasses. There's an image hovering at the front of his consciousness, it has been there for days, becoming more insistent. He closes his eyes, blanks out all the distractions. A broad forehead, full lips – drooped eyelids, half-open, corneas frosted white, skin tinged blue.

Lottie walks into the kitchen, a towel wrapped around her head, her dark brown dressing gown trailing on the floor.

'And how are you this morning, sleepyhead?' his words are gentle. He dips his knees, brings his face to hers. 'I didn't want to wake you.' It dawns on him – they talk to each other like children. Alternating – she as the parent, then he.

He feels a pang of discomfort at the intensity of her gaze. She slips her arms through his, lays her head upon his chest. He breathes in the faint odour of lavender, her shampoo.

'I forgot to tell you, I've got to go to the gallery today,' he blurts out brightly. 'You know, just to do the final check. Make sure everything is hung correctly, that the light is right. Things like that.' That would be the right thing to do, to drop in, to make sure everything is as it should be. A final check – ten minutes at the most, if he's lucky – he makes no mention of that point. He wants to paint, must paint. That woman, that image, has lodged itself in his head. The lock-up is only minutes away from the gallery.

Lottie withdraws her arms from around him. A shadow of doubt crosses her eyes; she's never been able to hide her feelings from him.

'Not again, today's a Sunday. You promised you'd not work Sundays.' Her voice has a sulky tone to it. 'You never mentioned it yesterday.'

'I forgot, I'm sorry. What with Ray and Kerry... well it completely slipped my mind. I'll only be three hours. Four at the most. Back by two o'clock. Promise.'

She turns her back, then casts a look at him over her shoulder.

'Don't leave me to deal with all *this,* then,' she gestures around the room with her arm. The petulance continues, 'and bring me something nice back from one of those market stalls on the embankment. Not food. A beautiful candle. One from Neale's Yard. For the bedroom.'

'I will, I promise.' He caresses her cheek with his fingers, slips his other hand inside her bathrobe, he dips his thigh between her legs.

She moves his hand, steps back. 'Not now.'

Untroubled, he smiles. 'Feeling a little rough, are you?' He touches her hair. 'Hangover is it?'

Lottie shakes her head, makes for the stairs, the belt of her bathrobe drags behind her.

He rinses the glasses before putting them in the dishwasher. Wipes down the worktops. Sweeps the floor. A shadow passes over his eyes. He should be painting. Before the memory fades. Before he loses it.

Sod it, I did everything last night; she can deal with this.

'I'm off now, Lottie!' he shouts up the stairs. The bedroom door opens, he sees her hand waving at him. He pulls on the black gabardine coat he wears day in, day out; buttoning it up to the neck. Taps the pockets with the palms of his hands – his wallet and keys are there.

'See you soon. Promise I won't be later than two!' He pulls the door shut behind him.

Four teenage girls walk down the London street, side by side on the pavement. A uniform of long straight brown hair, heavy mascara and duffle coats. It is as though he's back in the 1970s; he tightens his spine, pulls back his shoulders, drops off the kerb to let them pass. On the opposite side of the street, a man in orange overalls has his head dipped down under the bonnet of a car. Above him, a plane roars up into the clouds. The lock-up is fifty yards ahead. He's feeling positive, upbeat, invigorated. Eager to put paint to canvas. The girl from the gallery has inspired him.

Her name is Felicia – the girl organising the exhibition – he likes that name. He likes her a lot. She's a little flirt, underneath all the make-up was the face of a child. She'd excused herself to go to the toilet; came back with glossy lips and a waft of Calvin Klein. As he left, she took a card out of her purse, a mobile number written on the back in small red letters.

'Just in case you need to talk about anything,' that's what she'd said, her venetian blue eyes fixed on his. He'd felt a frisson of excitement in the base of his stomach. As he took it from her hand, he noticed her long, slender fingers, the small oval cuticles, the skin on the back of her hand, all flawless. Not a hint of a vein. Without looking, he'd turned the card over in his fingers, smiled and slipped it into his wallet. He thanked her for her help – he could have sworn he saw her irises dilate.

He pulls out the keys. One for the side door and one for the main entrance. He knows it will be freezing inside – the acrylics rock solid. As he unlocks the side door, twelve heavy-duty halogen bulbs spurt into life. From pitch black to bright light in less than a second. Thirteen hundred feet of space. His space. No natural light. No windows. No distractions. The place stinks of turpentine and stale air. The concrete floors are covered with paint-splattered Moroccan rugs. The walls filled with paintings, some hung, others propped against one another. Nudes, landscapes, abstracts.

His work.

In one corner of the room is a large architect's chest. Opposite are four metal shelves littered with tins of paint, an array of brushes, half-used bottles of white spirit. On the bottom shelf, a Nikon digital camera and two telephoto lenses, a macro for close-ups, beside them a small Canon automatic. In the middle of the room a single bed, unkempt. The duvet, half on, half off.

After closing the door behind him, he switches on the heaters. Their click, click, clicking noise bursts into a rattling hum. He takes off his coat, grabs a jumper off a peg on the wall. The navy Guernsey is stiff with acrylics. Blotches of vermillion, turquoise and viridian cover the arms and torso. *An abstract work of art in its own right*, he thinks to himself, as he tugs it down over his stomach.

This is where he is real, where he can peel back the skin of the life he lives; underneath is the man before Goldsmiths, before Lottie. The part of him that is in the middle of who he was and who he is. That one.

He'd not had anything to leave behind, no parents, no siblings, no one to pull him back; no embarrassments. His mother died four weeks before his tenth birthday in childbirth; a sister – the child had not survived. It was as though his mother had been ripped from him. He had been inconsolable. He lived with his paternal grandfather after that; his father disappeared for weeks on end. It was as though without the mother there was no son. He was a jigsaw piece that didn't fit in his father's new beginning. The memory of that last meeting was as vivid as ever.

'I need a clean slate.' His father's shirt and trousers had been cleanly pressed, the herringbone jacket that hung over his shoulder, new. He'd slapped an envelope on the table, his grandfather snatched it up, slipped it into the kitchen drawer as though in fear he would change his mind. A cheque – writing off all liability and responsibility. That was the last time he saw him.

He was at university when his grandfather died, leaving him with a blank canvas on which to paint a brand-new life for himself. Like father, like son, apparently. He was a phoenix rising from the flames, born again, brand new at age twenty, fuelled by the sale of his grandfather's back-to-back terraced house on the outskirts of a dreary, northern town. He'd assumed that there was no money; he was wrong.

He pulls himself up; a northern boy done good but with no one to brag to. A small downside, all things considered. He lets out a sigh of satisfaction, he's a man who likes to keep under the radar.

Lottie knows none of this, his artistic temperament included a reticence to talk about his youth. He left holes in his life, deep pools that she came to know in other ways. Unlike some of his contemporaries, he wasn't so famous that anyone had a need to peer into his past.

His reverie is pierced by the loud ring of his mobile.

He checks his watch. It's three o'clock. He's late. He has no idea where the time has gone. A flicker of irritation crosses his face. He takes out the phone from his trouser pocket, his home number flashes up on screen. He calls her back.

'Where the hell are you!' Her voice rings in his ears.

'I'm on my way home.' The words flow out easily.

She hangs up. The petulant teenager in her rearing its ugly head.

Lottie's eyes narrow in on him, she checks the small black plastic watch around her wrist.

'How long did you say you'd be?'

He shrugs his shoulders. 'Can't remember – *about four p.m*? His voice lilts as he smiles.

'Wrong—by two o'clock by the latest. You *promised*.'

He takes in the mess. The table still covered in dirty dishes; she's not moved a finger since he'd walked out of the door six hours ago. He clenches his fists. *Everything,* he thinks to himself, I did *every* damn thing last night, even laid the bloody table whilst she was upstairs preening herself. Surely, she could have stacked the dishwasher and turned it on? She's like a child that has never grown up, is that his fault? The thought niggles at his mind.

The TV blares in the background, Grand Designs; a repeat. He picks up the remote and switches it over to the news channel.

'Oi, I was watching that!'

'So, I can see.' He pulls off his coat, throws it on the bench in the corner.

She reaches for the remote – he snatches it away from her, moves towards the TV screen. Arms folded across his chest, he stands in front of it to make a point. He can feel her eyes bore into his back.

Dissatisfaction – he'd seen it often enough with his friends as their relationships slipped towards the rocks. He was growing older—she was barely middle-aged. She wanted to feel young again – he wanted her to be young again, the girl he'd met back in the eighties. Carefree, loquacious and up for anything. She wanted a designer home, open plan, large glass windows – he'd be happy with a new coat of paint on the walls and the house tidied by someone other than himself.

The glow from the previous evening leaches out of him. He empties the dishwasher, refills it; the clink of porcelain against porcelain fills the kitchen. He lets out a long sigh; wonders how long this sulk will last. His gaze returns to the TV.

'Well, if you're not wat—'

A face stares out of the screen at him. Large hazel eyes, the snub nose covered in freckles. Something grabs at his stomach—wrenches his innards. A stream of text crosses the bottom of the screen, the words blur before his eyes. Today's major story. He turns the volume up.

'You—'

'Quiet!'

'Oi!' he hears Lottie's voice in the background, whining. 'Don't talk to me like one of your students! You're doing this to—'

His eyes are fixed on the screen.

'Anyway, what are you interested in *that* for?'

He doesn't respond. He's no longer with her; he's someplace else.

'I'm going to take the dog for a walk, do you want to come?'

All his senses focus on the screen. He needs to take in every word; to remember exactly what is being said. Moments later the front door slams shut. He's relieved, the strength has gone out of him, he needs to sit down. *Now.* Before his legs give way.

He presses the playback button. Looking for more? Looking for who? The palms of his hands sweat. Frantically, he rubs them on his trousers, it is as though they're covered in blood.

The words run like a ticker tape in his head.

Human remains discovered.

A wave of nausea overtakes him. His world tilts, turns, crashes beneath his feet. He sinks back into his seat, drops his head into his hands. His heartbeat thunders in his ears. He closes his eyes – the faces of Karen Albright and Veronica Lightfoot rise to meet him.

How on earth can I explain this to Lottie?

Without finishing the train of thought, he knows he can never tell her. He moves over to the sink, opens the window. A blast of cold air hits his face.

She would never understand. Never. He takes in a breath, steadies himself.

Nobody came forward back in 1973—nobody. Why would they now? *Surely* not? Not after all this time. He wouldn't be the only one with something to lose.

He picks up a glass and fills it with water, gulps it down.

He can't stop the torrent. He feels it fly up his oesophagus, a bitter foul taste. He throws his upper body over the sink. His stomach wrenches out the dregs of the cup of coffee he'd drunk hours ago. The back of his throat burns with acid.

The lock on the front door clicks back noisily. Lottie. He wipes the spittle off his mouth just as she walks through to the kitchen, the dog leaping up at her thighs. He looks up at the clock, she's been gone for over an hour. He can't believe she's been out that long.

'Are you alright? You're white as a sheet.' She nears him, sniffs. 'What's that smell?'

'Just been sick. A migraine... I'm going to bed. I need to lie down'

The dog wanders by him, rubs up against his calf.

'I'd give you a hug, but...' She wriggles her nose then takes in the room. 'I suppose I'd best get this cleaned up, then.'

'That would be nice, Lottie. If you would.'

The ice between them melts.

Chapter 6

Margaret leans forward, takes hold of one drape, then the other. With one swift action she jerks the curtains shut. The cuffs of her cardigan catch tiny droplets of condensation off the glass. Every morning for the last thirty-seven years she has gazed out of this window, across the valley, across the fields, over the houses towards Anglezarke Moor. Every single morning without fail she has said the same prayer.

'Please Lord let her come home today safe and well.'

Did she say the prayer this morning? She can't remember. The day before? She can't remember that either.

It's my fault. It must be my fault.

The words jumble around in her head. The room spins. She stretches out her arm and steadies herself on the window frame, her arthritic hands knotted and bent, her nails bitten to the quick. The mirror on the wardrobe door captures her reflection. Her curved back; the thinness. The way her clothes hang off her like a scarecrow. Elasticated, pale blue denim jeans turned up at the heel, a long-sleeved, sky-blue blouse hides a woollen vest. Her cardigan, two sizes too big, needs the cuffs rolled over and over to fit. The seasons have carved their way into her skin, her forehead, her cheeks, down the side of her nose. Not a trace of make-up, not even a dab of Vaseline to heal her chafed lips.

A tiny metal dart of reality lodges in her heart. A grief-stricken look crosses her face. Karen won't recognise her, won't recognise the mother who loves her more than anything. The one who has waited all these years. She tries to summon up her thirty-year-old self. All she sees is an ancient woman with long grey hair and wrinkles; she feels as old and decrepit as the house itself.

She rubs her temples with her finger-tips. 'Maybe I need something to eat.' The urge fades as quickly as it came.

She feels a presence behind her – a movement, a smear of paint across a canvas. It's at the top of the stairs, barring her way. In the shadows. A fracture between dark and light. Standing still. The sallow skin, hazel eyes turned milky white, lips pinched in disapproval. Clumps of dried blood matt its hair. It, whatever *it* is, gazes directly into her eyes—judging. Margaret taps her forehead with the knuckles of her left hand. Tries to knock the malevolent changeling out of her head.

A cramp, an ache – makes its way down from her shoulder to her elbow.

It's still there. She takes a few paces towards it, then shrinks back. There's a smell, an off-ness, like rancid fat.

Her body jolts as the telephone reverberates up through the floor. She waits for the clanging noise to stop. It goes on and on. She covers her ears. Thomasine warned her—a reporter, that's who it'll be. The newspapers or some nosey parker from the village. Thomasine told her not to speak to anyone until she returned. She was vehement about it.

That's it. She's gone to get something out of her car, what is it? How long has she been gone?

Thomasine's words gnaw inside her, weave between the muscles of her ribs, 'human remains'. That's what she'd said. *Whatever it is, isn't my Karen.*

The pulse in her forehead flutters. *What was I going to do? The noise, that's it. I was going to stop the noise.* She pictures the phone sitting on the top of the hallway table. A long piece of plastic-covered wire connects the phone to a small cream junction box, just above the skirting boards beneath it. *I'll cut it, that's what I'll do, I'll do it right now.*

It takes her longer to climb down the narrow, wooden stairs than it did to get up. Eyes glazed in determination, she clings to the handrail. With every downward step, a flush of heat spreads across her chest, rises up her neck. At the bottom of the stairs, she tugs at the buttons on her cardigan; her fingers work them undone. Sweat glistens on her forehead, the woollen vest itches against her skin. The loud clanging noise hurts her head. With a flourish, Margaret jerks the plastic cable from the wall, knocks the telephone to the floor. Silence at last.

I'm too hot. She eases her arms out of the cardigan; it slips from her grasp to the floor. *Where's Thomasine, where's she gone?* Her feet drag as she makes her way through the kitchen. Her breathing labours; she sinks into the wooden back of the chair.

Margaret tilts her head to the side and remembers. Karen, her birth so quick – over in minutes, the softness of her skin as the midwife placed her in her arms. The mop of spiky black hair that none of them had expected. The way her teeny fingers grasped around her own. The smell of her wrapped in a towel, fresh from the womb. Born at home, here at the farm, upstairs in their bed. The winter sun peeking between the curtains that she'd insisted on being left open.

She can't be dead. I would have known. That fierce love she has carried in her heart all these years, since the moment of Karen's birth, *that* would have told her.

Margaret shuffles out into the hallway, goes to switch on the light, something grabs at her foot, pulls her back. Caught off guard, her arms flail out before her, the bones in her wrists snap as they collide with the freezing cold flagstones.

Chapter 7

Thomasine hurries out into the field, arms raised, her feet unsteady in the deep snow. The bright yellow air ambulance hovers mid-air. The blades let out a loud whine as they stir up a thick white mist that almost envelops them. As it lands, two medics leap out; they wade towards her.

Her mother, Margaret, lies motionless on the landing at the top of the stairs. Covered in a thick woollen blanket, left eye wide open; her right drooping as though tugged down by a hidden stitch in her cheek.

The next five minutes are a blur of activity; questions, medical checks, phone calls. A paramedic takes Thomasine aside.

'You're right—it's probably a stroke.' The woman's grey eyes peer from behind thick horn-rimmed glasses. 'More than likely a haemorrhagic stroke. Bleeding in the brain. We won't truly know until a scan is done. We'll take her to the Royal Blackburn. I've called it in.'

The colour seeps from Thomasine's face, her hands are trembling. 'I'd not been gone long, no more than thirty minutes, I'd gone to get my handbag.' She pushes her fingers through her hair. 'It was on the back seat of my car. I'd gone into a ditch, down on the road, couldn't get the car out.' The words stutter out. 'God, I can't… believe this… I shouldn't have left her. I found her at the top of the stairs, on the landing. The phone was pulled off the table, she must have tried to get up to…' She gazes down at her hands, takes in a breath. 'We'd just had some really bad news. Mam hadn't taken it well. She was sat in the kitchen when I left her.'

I'm blabbering, I'm blabbering.

The paramedic frowns, 'Was there anything special up here.'

Thomasine nods her head. 'My sister's bedroom.'

'We're ready.' The other medic interrupts as he checks the straps on the stretcher.

Exactly eight minutes later, the helicopter rises upwards, swoops over the barn, banks off to the right, towards Blackburn.

As the helicopter lands, its roaring engine shutting down, the clatter of the rotor blade stuttering to a stop, the hecticness truly begins. Her mother goes into cardiac arrest. The paramedics go into overdrive, words shoot between them that Thomasine doesn't recognise, Asystole… epinephrine… flatline. Flatline, the word ricochets around in her skull, she knows what that means. Her stomach plummets. They rush through to Resuscitation. She hurries after them.

'Sorry, you can't come inside,' a man in navy-blue scrubs blocks her way. 'I'll come and get you.' There's a firmness in his tone that is not unkind.

She takes a seat in the corridor, covers her face with her hands, lets her body fall forward.

Sometime later, she has no idea how long, there's a light touch on her shoulder.

'Are you Margaret's daughter?' It's the male nurse who spoke to her earlier.

She nods her head, gets to her feet.

'Sorry about that,' he gestures along the corridor, 'I'll take you along to the Family Room, you can wait there, it's a bit more comfortable.'

She follows him through A & E, then along a corridor to a room off to the left. He opens the door, offers her a drink.

'Thanks, tea, please. Milk, no sugar.'

Her eyes take in the room, an oblong window at shoulder height looks out into the corridor. Plain, wooden chairs with padded seats line one wall, a side table houses a small pile of magazines. In the corner is a box filled with red and yellow Lego bricks; cast aside on the floor are plastic cars, a wooden train, a doll with long black hair and bright blue eyes. The magnolia walls are covered in posters warning of the dangers of obesity, drug addiction, smoking.

A few minutes later, the nurse returns, tea in hand. 'From the machine, I'm afraid.'

'Thanks, that's okay,' she says, nestling the plastic cup in the palm of her hand. It's warm to the touch. She tries to smile but her lips seem locked in a frown.

He nods, hastens back towards A & E.

Muffled sounds filter through the glass window, the incessant ring of mobile phones, the chatter of voices, footsteps echoing up and down the corridor. Someone whistling, a cleaner, she watches his shoulders swing up and down, the mop in his hands moving from side to side. In the nape of his neck, a tattoo – one word in ornate block letters, DAD. The turquoise ink bleeds at the edges.

As she sips the tea, her mind wanders, memories of her father surface. His broad smile, the way his trousers always bagged at the knee. The thin line of soil that lay packed beneath his fingernails no matter how hard he tried to keep them clean. She, two-years-old, chubby-faced and curly-haired, sitting on his lap as he drove the tractor up and down the fields. One hand on the wheel, the other around her waist.

Good memories to hold back the chaos of the last hour; her mother's body on the landing, the spittle on the edge of her mouth. The panic in her eyes as her heart went into cardiac arrest.

Thomasine sips the final dregs of the tea now gone cold, deposits the plastic cup in the bin.

She checks her watch, it's over an hour since they admitted her mother into Resus.

Not long after, the door swings open, someone in a white coat strides in. A doctor, dark-skinned, dark-eyed, thick black hair swept back off his forehead. The door closes quietly behind him.

'Miss Albright, Thomasine is it?' The long drawn out vowels of his Northern Irish accent fill the room.

She nods her head, winces as she stretches out her back.

'Phillip O'Connell, I work in Resus.' He drags over a chair from against the wall. She notices that one of his nostrils is smaller than the other. Narrower.

'I'm sorry. Your mother—' his voice softens, 'there was a second stroke. We couldn't revive her—I'm sorry.' The dark shadows under his eyes give them a bruised look. 'It was quick. I don't think she felt any pain.'

There is a long silence between them. She senses he is expecting an outpouring of grief. That door is bolted shut and she cannot open it at will. Not even now.

The muffled sound of a woman's voice comes over the PA system.

'Adult Male Trauma, ETA fifteen minutes.'

His pager vibrates in his pocket. 'I'm sorry,' he says, glancing out of the window. 'I've got to go.' He fidgets in his seat, brushes the hair away from his eyes 'Would you like to spend some time with your mother before she's…?'

Her eyes widen in confusion.

'To say goodbye.'

There will be an autopsy, she knows that, Thomasine nods her head.

Better to say goodbye now before they…

He steps outside the room for a moment. There's a murmur of voices. A nurse appears in the doorway alongside him, her eyes soften in a smile.

'Jennifer here will take you to your mother.' His pager vibrates again. 'Sorry—' His hand rummages in his coat pocket, the vibrating stops. 'I've got to go back to Resus.'

Getting to her feet, Thomasine nods in acceptance. The nurse leads the way. They walk past a row of cubicles. Thin lengths of green plastic cloth flap open as people in scrubs go in and out, their shoes slap on the floor. She follows her down the corridor, they turn left, then right, down another corridor. People flow by them, technicians, bringers of life, their eyes focused on something in the distance, something behind her, through her. The noise drifts away the further they go.

Her mother is laid out in a private room, as though asleep, her body shrouded up to her chin in a navy-blue cotton sheet. Her head rests on a matching pillow. Her plaited hair curves around her head like a crown. Thomasine leans over, goes to kiss her forehead. She freezes – takes in a sharp breath. She has encountered hundreds of dead bodies during her career, yet nothing prepares her for this. Close up, everything changes. All the hurt and bitterness of her mother's life now written across her face. It is as though her skin has turned to plasticine. As if someone has dragged their fingers down the right side of her face – caught the edge of her eye. Her lips, already a bluish tinge, are twisted into a grimace. There is a strong smell of surgical spirit. Trembling, Thomasine steps back, covers her mouth and nose with the palm of her hand.

The nurse draws up a chair, tells her to sit down.

'Are you, okay. Can I get you anything?'

Thomasine slowly shakes her head, 'No, thank you.' She didn't say she was fine; the words wouldn't come out, not even in politeness.

Over time, Karen's disappearance had turned her mother harder than the gritstone boulders that littered the fields. Yet Thomasine had always sought her love. Her mind goes to earlier on that morning.

It could have been a good day.

Her mother smiled at her through the window, welcomed her in, tugged at her wet clothes to get them off, just like she had when she was a child. She'd made tea for them both, chattering away, happily. It would have been a good day if Thomasine hadn't ruined it. If Karen hadn't been found.

'Just let me know when you're ready.' Jennifer slips out into the corridor.

Thomasine gets to her feet. *If I'd not gone back for my bloody bag she might still be alive.* She takes in a deep breath, holds back the tears that threaten her eyes.

This is all my fault. And there's nothing I can do to change it.

Later that day she goes back to the farm; the snow had abated.

The dogs howled late into the night, as though they too were mourning her mother's death. It had been too much to take in, the broken wrists, the burn mark around her ankle.

Probably the telephone cord. She must have fallen; how did she get up the stairs? Why did she want to go up there? Nothing made sense. Yet in some way it did. Karen's bedroom, their bedroom, the one place her mother cared about above everything else.

When all this is done, I will grieve, she promises herself that. *I'll get some counselling, sort myself out.*

She refills her glass, until then it will have to be self-medication.

Chapter 8

Mel leans over her desk, arches her back, lifts her arms in a stretch. She's been sitting, hunched over the Albright evidence file for the last hour, fountain pen in hand, her thumb and forefinger now stained with red ink. The rank smell of stale cigarettes rises from every page. She gives herself a quick spray of Jo Malone to take the edge off it. Back in the 1970s, the squad room would have been a thick fog of smoke, a fag hanging off everyone's lips. Lung cancer two words rarely exchanged between them.

The notepad to her right is covered in small, neat handwriting. Comments and questions, a long list of them waiting to be answered. She could have got one of the team to do this, but there's something about this case that's piqued her interest.

The Albright case files are now in the murder room. All evidence from previous investigations is to be reviewed in light of new findings.

Mel had resumed the team briefing as soon as she returned from Hardacre's office. Her final words were specific and direct.

'And lastly, I know she's one of us, and to many of you a mate, but Thomasine Albright cannot be involved in this case. Any questions she has must be directed to me. Am I clear on that?' Her eyes scanned the room, looked for evidence of dissent. There were none. 'Right, let's crack on then, shall we?'

She looks through the plate glass window; the office is a hive of activity. Heads are down, phones busy, the murder board filling up.

Back aching, she slumps back into her seat, rubs her eyes. She recalls the look on Thomasine's face, the way the colour paled on her cheeks. How her hands bunched into fists—her knuckles white with anger. The slamming of the door. God knows how she would have behaved in the same circumstances. She would have told them to piss off, told them that they'd have to suspend her first. But then Thomasine Albright wasn't her.

'She's done well,' Hardacre said, 'she's got a talent for finding people and years of experience. There's always a lot of turnover in that job, she's stuck at it. She's a DI now, in charge of the whole team. The families like her, trust her. Her success rate is good. I don't want to lose her.'

Mel breathed out a sigh through her nose.

It must have been a heavy burden, knowing the one person you couldn't find was your own sister. Never knowing where she is, always wondering if she's alive or dead.

She has no doubt that transferring Thomasine to another team will have only a limited impact; she probably copied the case file years ago, she'd call in favours. That's what she herself would do.

She picks up her pen, at least now Thomasine and her mother know exactly where Karen is. But now a new kind of waiting has begun. The ugly question of *who killed her* had raised its head. A murder enquiry – that's a whole different ballgame.

And the first person she needs to interview is Margaret Albright, Thomasine's mother, but that will have to come a little later. She stands up, goes over to the window, the car park is half empty, non-operational staff will have gone home. Everything in sight is covered in a white layer of snow. She shakes her head.

When will this weather let up?

Mel knows she can't put it off, not now, she must visit the crime scene. On her own without anyone littering her mind with their own theories. She tugs a thick black parka off the back of the door, zips it up, takes the woollen hat out of the pocket and pulls it on.

It's going to be bloody cold out.

Chapter 9

Pick, pick, pick at the scab. Front door, back door, French doors, windows – all fourteen – *check, check, check*. Ten minutes later, Lily is doing it again.

Hyper-vigilance to go with hyper-cleaning? I'd say she's in the manic phase. She's a whole heap of things. Too long a list to go into here.

It was a while before those hikers found her up on the moors, middle-aged men having a day out. Their warm hands rubbed her face and fingers, they wrapped her in a coat. It was that bright pink buff around her neck they spotted.

'We'll call an ambulance,' one said. She didn't let them.

They gave her Kendal Mint Cake. Took her home to her perfect house with the trees either side of the door. They waited to be invited into the warmth, to be offered hot tea and biscuits. She stumbled up the front step, closed the door without a second look.

Clothes soaked, she opened the bathroom cabinet. Took out a small brown plastic bottle; knocked two tablets into her hand. Washed them down with a scoop of water from the tap. Turned on the shower, undressed, let the hot water rush over her, warm her.

Twelve hours later she woke. Covered in sweat. Trembling. Her dreams have turned to nightmares. I can tell. He'd been in her head again. He waits for her, taunts her.

She left the lamp on after that.

I think she can hear me sometimes. Lily, that is. To be exact, I'm not speaking out loud. I stopped that a long time ago. We had a going of our separate ways of sorts. She had to move on. I had to accept it.

The watch on her wrist vibrates, the alarm. It's six o'clock, where's the time gone? She scrambles out of bed – time to get ready for work.

Normally, she'd be cleaning the clean stuff. It's the first thing Lily does. But today she seems totally over that OCD thing. Doesn't even clean her teeth or wash her bits. She's charging at a great rate in the opposite direction. Transforming from Clean Queen to Filthy Cow. An *Oppositional Deviant*. Well, that's what *she'd* call it.

It's dark outside, she gets on the computer – Googling. Veronica Lightfoot. Karen Albright. Those are the names she's typed. Loads of stuff comes up, thousands of web pages. 377,451 pages to be exact. And that was just for Veronica Lightfoot. Fame at last.

It's seven o'clock. She digs out the manual for that fancy intruder alarm. The one she had installed when she bought the place. The one you can access through your phone. You can see and hear everything. She spends thirty minutes reading the manual, then another fifteen re-programming the alarm – setting up new codes, checking that the cameras work.

Now it's seven forty-five – she sprints upstairs, pulls open the wardrobe door. Stares at herself in the full-length mirror, gets right up close.

'Who… are… you?' The words come out in tiny faltering steps. Her head inclines to the side, her face right up to the mirror. Her breath blurs the glass. Her whole body quivers.

Something is going on inside that head of hers. She closes the wardrobe door, moves across the room, slumps onto the bed, lies back on the pillows.

Who are you?

I've realised what she'd just said.

Who are you?

She must believe there's another person in her head. We've read that. Post-Traumatic Stress can develop into MPD, Multiple Personality Disorder.

Lily closes her eyes, her body completely motionless. Like a toy whose batteries have run out.

Chapter 10

Mel focuses all her attention on the car; the tension on the accelerator, the traction of the tyres. The lightness of the steering wheel; she holds it steady with her right hand as she works down through the gears with her left. It's stupid to go out in this weather, but she wants to see the crime scene before the blustering snow and freezing cold temperatures obliterate everything.

Thirty minutes later, muted blue lights glint in the fog. She slows the car down, lets out a sigh of relief. The site looks deserted, yet as she nears, shadows appear out of the mist. TV crews cluster around the road closure sign. A long line of mobile media units, Sky, BBC, ITN, are parked up. Speculation, rumours, lies, a smidgeon of truth, she knows what to expect from the media at times like these. They'll be pissed off, frozen and hungry and with execs on their backs baying like wild dogs.

Occasionally there is someone decent, someone, who wants to know the truth, who won't sensationalise it. A journalist, a local one with a conscience, who helps rather than hinders. She's worked with one or two of them. At the other end, the nationals, pushing, demanding interviews. Preening themselves in front of the camera, wheedling their way into the investigation. Making promises to family and friends that they never keep. Writing whatever will make the best copy or get them a spot on the news.

The police tape is torn at by the wind, four marked vehicles are parked behind it and a large mobile CSI Unit behind them. The crime scene manager will have stopped the clock on the crime. They'll keep the press out. She runs the names of CSMs through her head and wishes she'd checked before she left.

Mel eases the car behind an ancient Peugeot, caked in mud, the windows misted up. There will be nothing of Karen left here now, she thinks to herself. Yet it is important she sees the place, gets a feel for it, fuels her imagination – gets inside the head of whoever did it. Her hands root around under the passenger seat, catch hold of a plastic bag. Mindful of her fingers, she takes hold of the rubber and steel crampons for weather like this. Stretches one then the other over the sole of her boots. At least she'll be able to stay on her feet, she thinks to herself.

The banter of the press pack enfolds her as she pushes her way through the barrier.

'Who is it?' calls a voice from the back.

'Do you know her?' It's a woman, accentless. Probably a TV reporter.

'A copper,' she recognises that voice, although the name of the owner eludes her. She looks to check. A rapid burst of camera flash blinds her momentarily. She squints, tries to cover her face with the back of her hand. A police community support officer ambles towards her, arm outstretched – he gestures for her to stop. Dark-skinned with a snubbed nose, water drips from the peak of his cap onto his chest – despondency writ large across his face.

He asks her name, she shows him her ID. He checks the list of authorised personnel in his hand, smiles, pulls up the tape and lets her pass, already aware that she'd be attending.

'Who's the CSM?'

'Dave Tanner,' he glances up towards the large mobile CSI unit further up the hill. 'He should be in there.

She'd heard of him; he plays five-a-side football with Badger on a Saturday. Her eyes strain to pick out the landscape, she totters towards the mobile unit, the ground beneath her feet now compacted with snow.

Nothing prepared her for the reality of the devastation. Shrouded by the mist, giant root formations taller than herself, ripped out of the earth by excavators. They lie on their sides like hundreds of victims, arms reaching out, begging for help; the property developers unaware of what lay hidden. Behind the carnage lay mile upon mile of unforgiving woodland, the trees intensively planted, barely a space between them.

A flurry of snow hits her in the face. Without missing a beat, she wipes the wetness away with the end of her sleeve. 'God knows what the crime scene will be like?'

Although she cannot see it, she knows in the distance will be a sealed off area, far away from prying eyes. The inner area is where the action is, at the point where the crime scene is screened off over head height, running straight through to the scene of the crime, metal tiles denoting the common approach path that all authorised personnel must take. Everyone must be suitably attired; no contamination, no transfer.

Ten minutes later she is kitted up and inside the evidence tent. The sides vibrate like a rattle, freezing cold air blasts its way through every nook and cranny. A good foot taller than herself, Dave Tanner looks nothing like she imagined, clearly five-a-side football was more combative then she thought. Two cauliflower ears and a broken nose give him the look of a boxer. He's gesturing to one of the tables. Photographs replace the original finds – human remains, scraps of clothing, a single hooped earring – all in situ, exactly where they were found. Beyond that another table, laden with physical evidence: curled up tissues, desiccated condoms, glass bottles, tin cans and fast food wrappers. All bagged and tagged.

'Any DNA?'

'None on the earring we found among the remains. However, there's lots of DNA around here,' He winks at her. 'Unlikely to be of help though.'

'You never know, he could have been back.' She resists the urge to over-speculate.

He nods his head in agreement. 'If it's a he? Who knows at this point? Maybe. It's all being processed anyway.' He takes off his latex gloves, pinches the bridge of his nose and closes his eyes momentarily. 'You've got a long list of people to interview, mainly men, I would think.'

And none of them are likely to be cooperative, she thinks to herself. Her eyes widen suddenly, 'Now that's interesting.' She points to the polyester gun bag.

'Not unexpected, though. We've found eight so far. The rest are back at the lab. All replica handguns – German. Been re-bored so they can fire live rounds.' He picks up the bag. 'Quite a trade in it – they go for about seven hundred pounds a time. No serial numbers, obviously.' He places it back on the table. 'The gangs stash them up here. Clearly whoever they belong to didn't get up here in time to retrieve them. Good to get them off the streets, though.'

'Any more remains?'

'Not yet, but we are extending the search area, I'll let you know what we find.'

She follows him out of the tent and into the falling snow.

'Thanks, I just wanted to get the feel of the place.'

He gives her his card. 'Just in case you need me direct.'

As Mel makes her way back to the car, she squints down at the card. Tanner – then it slips seamlessly into her memory. Of course, she'd read it in case notes. Frank Tanner was the name of the original investigating officer.

Was Dave his son?

A little unease settles into her, she'll have to be mindful of that.

Chapter 11

Jimmy Fairfax pulls out his earpiece, weaves his way around the tables in the restaurant, out of the front entrance and into the night. He lifts the lapels on his jacket to block the chill on the back of his neck, his suit not much protection from the icy temperature that greets him. He stamps his feet to keep warm, tiny balls of ice crunch beneath the soles of his shoes. Five minutes ago, hailstones as big as pearls drilled down onto the pavement like a power shower on full.

Headlights slowly stream by him, late night shoppers on their way back from Spinningfields; car boots crammed with the last remnants of the January sales. He sees a gap in the traffic, hurries across the road towards his car, parked four hours ago, and now covered in a thick layer of snow and ice. A metallic black Mercedes C300 with tinted windows; a personal indulgence that masquerades as a legitimate business expense. Hired out occasionally for special events – along with Sid, his driver and friend since he was sixteen years old. He eases himself into the driver's seat, turns on the ignition. Within seconds the heated seat gives warmth to his tired bones.

I'm getting too old for this.

He looks out of the window, back across the street. New York loft meets warehouse, his daughter had said; industrial lighting, steel girders, silver duct pipe, metres of it. The refurbishment had cost him plenty, but it had worked. Right now, the restaurant is half empty, a temporary lull, the tipping point between after-work diners and nightclub goers with something to celebrate. Within an hour every table will be occupied, the kitchen a frenzy of activity. Round two. Then through the night until six in the morning. He's always been a night-bird.

In the private room on the second floor, a group of women unwind with liqueurs and petit fours. Businesswomen at the top of their game, confident, articulate; wealthy. Feet shod in Jimmy Choo and Christian Louboutin, bodies clothed in Missoni and Vivienne Westwood. Their waistlines untroubled by fad diets and protein shakes. They revel in each other's company. It is one night per month where all pretence is discarded at the door.

He likes them – they like him.

A newspaper rests on the dashboard. He picks it up, turns the pages, skims the headlines. A photograph on page four is obscured by a yellow Post-It-Note. Sid's childlike handwriting scribbled across it.

'I think you should read this.'

He removes the note, reads what is beneath it, lets out a slow breath. He winds down the car window, rests the newspaper on the steering wheel. The blast of cold air sobers his mood.

'What—' He almost jumps out of his skin as two sharp fingernails prod him in the shoulder.

'Come on Dad. You're such a slack arse.' His daughter giggles at his unease, 'Get back in there and work.'

Thirty minutes later his mobile buzzes, drowned out by an impromptu karaoke session in the private room. The women conga around the table to an enthusiastic rendition of *I am What I am.* He claps in tune, a broad smile on his face, all thoughts of the newspaper article pushed to the rear of his brain. His daughter, the complete centre of his universe, dancing on the table, microphone in hand.

Chapter 12

'Don't...' The palm of her sister's hand covers her mouth. 'Don't you dare tell Mam and Dad I've gone out.'

She climbs out of the window, drops to the ground, the dogs snap at her heels. Her sister runs into the dark, into the fields. Thomasine hangs out of the window, cries out to her, begs her to come back, not to leave her. A gun goes off, again and again.

Bathed in sweat, Thomasine jolts herself out of her nightmare. She sits bolt upright, heart racing, barely able to breathe, tears streaming down her face.

The room is pitch black and freezing.

What was it? A memory, something repressed, a nightmare? Did she try to stop her, try to pull her back?

Why can't I remember?

She raises her head, eases her foot out from beneath her. Slowly her eyes adjust to the gloom. Out of the darkness, shapes form. A fringed shade. The turn and twist of oak. The standard lamp – she'd fallen asleep by the fire in the kitchen.

The muscles in the base of her spine cramp as she levers herself out of the chair. A dark-blue sky leaks in through the edges of crocheted curtains. The curtains had been Mam's distraction, her work. Night after night, the hooked needle looping around her finger and thumb, one tiny daisy linked to another, a look of concentration in her eyes. Something to engage her thoughts and hands, something to keep prying eyes out.

As Thomasine rises to her feet, her bare foot discovers something smooth – a wineglass on a side-plate. She rakes over the memories of the previous night. She'd come back to feed the dogs. Had gone into the pantry for a bag of dried food.

It was such a bloody shock in there. The shelves had been lined with tins of food. Her mother's cornucopia. She'd picked them up one by one. The use-by dates years since passed. Five half-eaten jars of fish paste, the jellied meat covered in a thick white mould.

Thank God, I didn't eat any of that.

On the top shelf, pushed to the back, was her dad's old hunting gun. He'd threatened journos with it time and time again. Beside it, a box of rat poison and four ancient traps, caked black with blood. Everything was covered in a thick layer of dust.

Beneath them, row upon row of Kilner jars lined the shelves. Each filled with homemade concoctions – lavender and applesauce; blackberry, onion and apple chutney. Wimberries glistening in a thick, sugary syrup. Her mother would give them as Christmas gifts. They were delicious, everyone loved them. Thomasine had felt an overwhelming sadness. Who would want them now?

On the floor, unopened bottles of dandelion and burdock pop and still lemonade, memories of summer picnics in the fields. Blue and white checked tablecloths, her mother and father drinking pale ale in pint glasses, holding hands, laughing. The valley, a brilliant mess of vibrant greens dotted with buttercups, dandelions and daisies. Blonde fields of hay lay ready to be shorn for animal feed. For a moment, she lets herself feel the warmth of that memory.

Too exhausted to cook, Thomasine cobbled together a chutney and cheese sandwich, washed it down with a glass of red wine. She only planned to have one glass, just to help her sleep. Yet, the empty bottle is evidence of the true story. One glass led to another, she had lit the fire, watched the logs burn, bathed in the glowing embers as they warmed the room. Now, there's a horrible bitter aftertaste of tannin on her tongue that even toothpaste will find hard to eradicate.

I must have nodded off.

There's a faint tang of stale sweat mixed with something sweet. Yesterday's clothes crushed by sleep; her mother's homemade cardigan scrunched up her back. The creamy Arran wool still bore her mother's scent. She shivers, pulls it tight around her, switches on the light; the forty-watt bulb casts the colour of weak tea.

There's wood and coal in the scuttle by the fire; newspaper on the stool by the door. She tears the paper into quarters, crunches them up into small paper balls, just as her father had taught her. Then takes up the poker, rakes over the ashes, the handle worn thin by her mother's fingers. Her cold hands layer the paper balls, kindling and coal in the grate. The box of matches on the mantelpiece is half-filled with used matches. A moment later, smoke rises from the paper. On her knees, she fans the flames with a piece of cardboard. Her mother had said the fire was like a hungry dog that's never satisfied.

She swivels around on her knees, takes in the room, takes a real look at it. Every piece of furniture, worn and shabby, stained and tattered. So-called antiques, ancient pieces bequeathed from her father's parents and their parents before them. Ladders of cobweb covered in dust drift noiselessly from the ceiling. Nature is taking over – a slender trail of ivy has worked its way through the rotting windowsill above the sink.

Her mother's underwear is neatly stacked on the seat of a chair, tucked beneath the table. The clothes maiden now folded up and hidden behind the back of the settee. Did she do that? Her mind goes blank. A tall pile of newspapers teeters on top of a small wooden stool. The dresser is laden with mismatched crockery, mixing bowls, plastic containers, spent envelopes filled with recipes and phone numbers written on torn up pieces of birthday card. A row of photographs sits behind the glass on the top shelf, faded by the sunlight, faces slowly disappearing.

That's me, I'm slowly disappearing. The real me, the person I could have been, never had a chance growing up here.

She rakes her fingers through her hair, rubs her eyes. She must keep going, keep busy. 'I'd better get on with it. Front room first,' she says to the walls.

As she opens the door, a stink of damp and moulding cheese cloys in her throat. The room must have been shut for months. A fine layer of dust clings to the dark-green velvet curtains. Around the window the red damask wallpaper is blown, peeling off; beneath, a thick black mould spreads like chicken pox.

Threadbare bed sheets cover the furniture; with a yank of her hand, the tall mahogany roll-top secretaire bookcase reveals itself. She runs her fingers over the narrow wooden slats. The dark wood feels cool to touch. This is a place of secrets. The one piece of furniture that has always been out of bounds. Inside it, all manner of things that she has never seen. As a child, she had longed to look inside.

The key is in the lock.

Thomasine hesitates, it is as though her mother is out in the fields with the dogs. As she turns the key, the roll-top slides back noiselessly. Her mouth falls open in dismay. Each cubicle is jam-packed with newspaper cuttings, old letters, more till receipts, handwritten notes and yet more photograph. There's no system to it as far as she can see.

It's going to take me ages to sort this lot out – most of it will probably need shredding or throwing out.

One by one she opens the drawers. Each the same, every single one filled to capacity. Balls of string, paper clips, spent pens, Sellotape, rolls of film in black plastic tubs – she picks one up, turns it over in her hand. Makes a mental note to get them developed.

I wonder how old they are, what memories are on them?

The next two hours are spent at the kitchen table, sorting through the contents of the secretaire. To her left, a plastic bucket filled with items for shredding. In front, three yellow envelope files, unread. While on the right, a wicker basket is piled high with miscellanea that she has no idea what to do with. The pot of tea by her hand goes cold.

She gets to her feet, places a log in the fire-grate. At long last the house is warming up; the room filled with the sweet smell of burning wood. An old familiar fragrance that brings with it memories. Winter evenings, jigsaw puzzles, baking cakes with her mother and sister. Her father, head back, mouth open, asleep in the chair. Laughter.

Tears prick her eyes. She brushes them away with the back of her hand, unwilling to open the gate: afraid of what might flood out.

Only the bad stuff drives her forward.

The fire has gone out. Thomasine unplugs the fridge, the rattle of the energy unit driving her mad. Stops the blast of cold air that rushes beneath the back door by stuffing a tea towel in the gap.

Silence at last.

The bottle of wine, a Pinot Noir, calls to her from the pantry. She'd brought it up at Christmas, they'd not drunk it. She takes three crystal glasses out of the dresser, washes them under the hot water, dries them with a cloth.

A copy of her mother's will lies open on the table, unread. Thomasine gathers it up and returns it to its hiding place – the left-hand drawer of the vestibule. She already knew that in the absence of her sister, everything would be left temporarily in her care. When she returned, everything would be shared, fifty-fifty. Desolation takes her.

Who'd want fifty-fifty of this, never mind a hundred per cent?

She takes the silver photo-frame off the mantelpiece, places it in the centre of the table. Karen – a mass of summer freckles, a wide grin upon her face, ensconced in their mother's arms. Their skin blushed by the sun. Peaceful, happy and content. She remembers that day well. The door to their Hillman Hunter Estate hung open. Dad listening to Rod Stewart playing on the car radio. The three of them together, she'd wandered off somewhere. Where? She can't remember. It had been perfect – a rare break from the work of the farm – a picnic. Yes, *perfect.* The pale-yellow dress, the one that fitted her mother so well, trimmed with daisies. Never worn again.

She wraps her fingers around the body of the bottle of wine, pulls the cork. The ruby red liquid flows easily into one glass, then another until all are filled. A wry smile crosses her lips.

'To you both, together at last, may you find happiness.' She lifts her eyes up to the ceiling, chinks one glass after another with her own. 'Rest in peace.'

They both smiled back at her, she sips her wine, they talk. Her mother tells her to refresh her glass. Thomasine pours herself another drink, allows herself to wallow in this temporary hallucination. They babble on. Karen never stops talking. Even on matters she knows, knew, little or nothing about. Her mother is much the same. They talk of summers gone by, of village fêtes, of her uncle Oliver and cousin Paul. Of her father, herding the sheep.

Despite Karen's apparent disdain for her younger sister, there had been times when they had been happy together. Thomasine's brow furrows, she can't quite remember the point when Karen went from being her sometimes-adorable sister to that other person. To the one who kept secrets. The one who manipulated. Perhaps it was the hormones, puberty? She doesn't know and probably never will.

After a while, the chatter quietens. She sits there, in comfortable silence, back pressed into the hard wooden seat, eyes gazing out of the window into the dark. Not even the birds are singing. Large flakes of white snow float by. She shrugs the blanket over her shoulders, returns her attention to the photograph. To Karen.

'So, give me a clue. Tell me who did it? Who hurt you?'

Silence.

Thomasine's eyes flicker then droop, Karen's face blurs. She downs the last drops of red wine from her glass. Heaves herself out of the chair, makes a bed for herself on the settee.

Outside, a fox snuffles at the front door. Tail held high and poker straight, it urinates on the step. The hot yellow liquid melts the snow. The dogs' strain at their metal chains, howl out a response; Thomasine's senses so attuned to it now she no longer hears their calls.

A yawn escapes from her mouth. She'll go home tomorrow, she's drunk too much to drive tonight. Exhaustion envelops her.

She's tired. So very tired.

Chapter 13

Perhaps she's a manic seasonal depressive. Lily that is. With aggressive tendencies linked to a traumatic incident in her past. *Where the hell did that come from?* Sometimes things come out of me before I've realised what I've said. I'm never sure if it's things I know or things I've picked up from those books she's read. The *Idiots' Guide to Psychotherapy*, I wonder if that book exists? If it doesn't, I could definitely write it.

As a kid, I was always up on the tops with my invisible friends. I found real ones quite hard to get. Huge grey skies and mile upon mile of moor grass, wide open spaces to play in, the wind tangling my hair. I knew those moors like the back of my hand. Massive granite rocks laced with silver to scramble over. The druid circle to fill my imagination. I spent hours up there. Alone, with no one to judge me. No one to look down on me.

Poverty is a slippery pit, hard to climb out of. University was never on my horizon. No matter how hard Mum tried—and she did. The more she pushed, the harder he pulled. My father the drunk, Mr Stir-It-Up. I don't like to call him Dad, that implies some sort of relationship. There wasn't one. He drank away my future.

As a kid, you dream all the time. I dreamt of the tens of lives I could live. Sometimes I was an actress, or an air hostess, or a nurse, or a nun. I was unstoppable.

Life wasn't like that. It was a glass box. I was always on the inside looking out. A lonely child, desperate for friendship. After puberty, it took hold of me like a virus. It compromised my ability to think. rationally that is. I made some stupid choices. But they were mine and I accept them. I learnt a valuable lesson, and this is it.

The people you hang around with determine who you become. Of all the things I tell you, please remember that.

I became part of the in-crowd. I thought it would be wonderful. It wasn't. You never truly know what you have to do to fit in.

Until it is too late.

And in the end, there was no turning back.

Chapter 14

'... drifts of up to four metres along the Pennines. Records show it has been the worst spell of weather in thirty—'

Thomasine's fingers reach out and press the snooze button on the radio alarm.

It's six forty-five. The central heating boiler bursts into life. Hot water rushes through the pipes, pockets of air trapped inside them. They wail and moan like ships gone aground. She's used to those sounds. They comfort her.

Her eyes peer into the darkness, no memory of dreaming. Any nightmares that may have tormented her are lost in the haze of a deep sleep. Warm for the first time in days, the king-size cotton duvet tucked up underneath her chin and over her feet.

Outside, she knows life will look much the same as the day before. The sky will be an inky black, street lights will blink on as instructed by their computer chips. Blankets of snow will cover the parkland across the road and everything else in its wake. In winter, this is a quiet street. In summer it's a riotous cacophony; picnic blankets, portable stereos, children screech and shout.

Her home is her place of safety – an Edwardian semi the other side of Manchester. Huge windows fill the house with light. French doors open onto a Japanese garden – it had taken her six months of back-breaking work. In summer it was her own personal haven. The sway of the bamboo, the music of flowing water, the shale path, the shimmering gold azaleas. Two large sandstone rocks hewn out of the soil behind the farm. Their bodies lined with feldspar and mica.

Unprompted, a memory pops into her head. Her mother, ambling across the yard, her long grey hair plaited, swishing across her back. She stops, rests her elbows on the farm gate, watches the sheep in the field. Oblivious to the fact that Thomasine is looking down on her from their bedroom window – a look of sadness on her face. An aeroplane leaves a white trail as it soars up into the clouds.

She stirs herself, clambers out of bed, looks in the bathroom mirror. There's a puffiness that wasn't there before, her eyes have sunk further into their sockets. Her lower lip swollen, the cold sore now hardening in the middle of her lip.

She steps into the shower, turns up the thermostat, lets her head fall back, lets the heat wash over her. It has always been there. The hurt, the paper cut that no sticking plaster can heal.

I need to get a grip; I can't be like this.

Mindlessly, she dries herself, pulls on some clothes. She must be ready. Ready for what? she asks herself.

She'd always thought she'd cope when the day came. It would be hard, but it would be easier – after all, she was used to death, in all its different forms. It came with the territory. She was hardened to it; had convinced herself of that. There were hundreds of them, the dead and missing, locked into her psyche. All filed away in her memory banks. What difference would two more make? She was wrong. Her mind steadfastly refuses to accept the reality of it. Her mother dead within twenty-four hours of being told that Karen's body had been discovered.

That thought wraps itself around her again. The naivety of it. Of course, her mother would be devastated. She should have been kinder, more observant, conscious of the impact the murder enquiry would have on her. Have on them both. She should have remembered what happened before. What it had done to her father. Why hadn't she? Another death on her conscience.

Thomasine puts the kettle on, makes herself a cup of strong black coffee. Random thoughts break through the fog in her head. *The funeral… the eulogy… what will I say?* Her hands start to shake. *Oh God, they'll be staring at me, pitying me. The farmhouse, I'll have to get it ready.*

A frown deepens across her forehead, her mother's voice sounds in her ears.

'I don't want a fuss. No fancy speeches. No flowers either.'

Did Mam actually say that? How much has she forgotten? Or repressed? Her ability to recall pieces of information is central to her work. She's known for it. Why has it deserted her now when she needs it the most?

The room smells stale, unused. She unlocks the French doors, steps outside into the morning light. The pale-yellow winter sun peeks through the clouds. The ice-cold air chills her breath; she shivers. A scattering of bright red berries peek through a latticework of white on the back fence.

Fat tears seep over the rims of her eyelids, she rubs them away with the heel of her hand, wants to curl up, shut out the world.

No tears, no tears! Come on, you can deal with this, you've dealt with worse!

That's a lie. She's never dealt with worse. She is an orphan now, living life on automatic.

The air is still, a bird trills in the distance, there's a flash of blue and red.

A chaffinch? This time of year? Her father's voice.

It's like the whole bloody family has moved in with me.

The bird swoops down beneath the feeding post, pecks at the seeds on the ground, then takes flight.

I wish I could do that. Just leave everything behind me. Take off.

The sharp ring of her mobile brings her back. It's the mortuary at the hospital, wanting to know the name of her mother's funeral directors. She has no idea.

'I'll ring you back.'

Thomasine gathers up, off the carpet, the hand-knitted throw her mother gave her years ago. Arranges it precisely on the back of the settee. Tugs at the ends to straighten it. Made from blonde wool shorn from the blackface sheep that roam their land; it's still beautiful.

Her mobile bursts into life again. One message after another flashes up.

'Would you be willing to talk?' Katie Morris, Northern Evening News.

'I know you'd like to get your story out there – we have an offer for you.' Jake Prentice, News North West.

There were seven more of that ilk.

How the bloody hell did they get my number? One of the families, they will have contacted one of the families.

She jabs at her phone. Each one gets the same response.

'Don't text me again. Am I clear?'

Mid punch, a message flashes up from Rosie.

'Tried calling you, I'm here for you, love you xxx.'

Tears prick her eyes again. She should have called Rosie yesterday, she had meant too. Thomasine texts her back.

'Sorry, it's hell here, will call you later.'

She switches off her mobile, unplugs the landline, shuts the curtains. Then it starts – constant rings on the doorbell, shouts through the letterbox, taps on the front window. It doesn't let up.

'I can't put up with this,' her anger bubbles up, she strides along the hallway, only just stops herself from ripping the door open. Instead, she turns on her heels, runs upstairs, throws some clothes and toiletries into a bag. She makes her getaway through her neighbour's garden. Takes the back streets to where she'd parked the four-by-four the night before.

Hands trembling, she utters a sigh of relief when it starts first time. She has no doubt where she'll be the safest.

I'll stay at the farm – scare the bastards off with the dogs!

Chapter 15

Whenever he closes his eyes, her face spreads across the back of his eyelids, her lips on his cheek, the downiness of her skin, the smell of bubble gum on her breath. Her hands pushing against his chest. Karen had been his first true infatuation. They'd met by chance. He'd not long had the car – the Capri. He was taking it out for a spin; up through town, onto the moors. It had been a cloudless sky, a summer's day, the sun high, the heat rising in waves off the tarmacked road.

He saw her before she saw him. She'd been walking through the fields. He'd got the windows down to let out the heat. His sleeveless T-shirt and shorts stuck to his skin. He thought he was the bee's knees. He'd brought the camera, planned to take a few snaps of the car, with himself on the bonnet. The camera had a timer on it.

The bee's knees – does anyone ever use that term anymore?

She wore a sugar pink ruched top. Her hair was tied back in a ponytail that swung from side to side; her jeans cut off at the knees. There was a languidness about her; fingertips trailing through the tips of the long grass. Singing to herself, he could hear her, even above the noise of the engine. He had to talk to her, pressed the horn, it startled her. Unafraid, she ran down to the gate, swung her legs over it and sat on the top bar, the sun glinting on her hair. It was the colour of chestnuts fresh out of their prickly skin.

He'd pulled over. Pretended to be lost.

'Do you know where Amplewood is?' A name he made up on the spot.

She smiled directly at him, her eyes laced by long dark lashes.

'Just keep on going down this road.' She knew he was lying.

'How old are you?' he asked, unable to stop himself.

A naughty grin spread across her lips, it set something off in him, he didn't know what it was back then. Then swung her legs back over the gate, dropped down onto the dirt track, started to jog back to wherever she'd come from.

'Wait!'

She turns to look, her eyes narrow. 'You hurt me.'

The air goes from his lungs. He springs to his feet. He's in the kitchen, in the here and now. Alone, except for the dog, who'd followed him downstairs hoping for food.

'I didn't, I didn't.' Words of denial rush out of his mouth, he's shouting out loud. 'It wasn't my fault. You should have...' He paces around the room, sits down, gets up, tries to think of something else; Lottie, the exhibition, anything. A self-induced hallucination brought on by what? Guilt? Fear? The look of her face as it stared out at him through the TV screen?

Grabbing the MacBook from the kitchen table, he silently takes the stairs, consumed by a sense of helplessness that won't lift. He winds his way up to the attic, opens the door to his office and switches on the light. His eyes blink and water in the glare of bright white walls and electric bulbs. Before he'd made money, this had been his 'painting place', Lottie's words, not his. She says it smells of methylated spirit and oils; he no longer notices. He puts the cup and laptop down on his desk, returns to the door and locks it, the way he always does. Not that Lottie would care, she never comes up.

He flips the lid up on the laptop, waits for the software to load. The room is comforting. The charcoal drawings, the waste paper bin overflowing with sweet wrappers, empty tubes of paint, discarded horse hair brushes stiff as oak. The wooden floors are a cacophony of paint; splashes of greenish yellows, oranges and deep maroons smear across the boards.

He types her name into the search engine: Karen Albright. There are thousands of listings, hundreds of Karen Albrights –

paid ads, LinkedIn, Facebook, Myspace. He clicks on images; a horde of photographs fills the screen. Hundreds of eyes stared back out at him. Hair of every possible colour and style, skin of every hue, some smiling, others not. His stomach lurches as his eye catches a photograph of her. She's standing by a Christmas tree in a pair of Levi's and a bright red woolly jumper. Her hair is loose. He slams the MacBook shut, tries to block her out. The muscles of his chest are so tight he thinks he's cracked a rib.

It's a good five minutes before he can go back to his task. This time he alters the search data.

Karen Albright body found.

There are newspaper articles, TV reports, pages and pages of them. He starts with the most recent. They'd sensationalised what few facts they'd had. She was no longer missing. Police were looking for her murderer; no mention of any persons of interest that they were seeking. Momentarily the tension in his chest subsides.

I'm right not to panic, he thinks to himself. He shuts the lid on the laptop. A wave of anxiety washes over him.

'Have you brought me a present?' Her voice echoes in his head again. She loved small things: a bar of chocolate, hair grips, a record. It became a tantalising game that they played, he'd hide them about his person, she'd search for them.

A physical memory jolts him. She loved gifts, he'd taken advantage of that. His gifts more expensive as time progressed – clothes, makeup – Mary Quant. She'd hide them in a barn, that's what she'd said. Or was it an attic? *What happened to those gifts?*

He lifts the lid of the laptop yet again, types in the words.

'How long do fingerprints last?'

Six million hits popped up. Each one contradicting the next. Both their fingerprints would be on every one of those gifts. His stomach drops. What if, even after all these years, they're still there. Waiting to be found.

Chapter 16

Lily's woken up, afraid – afraid that he's out there. The man from her nightmares. He's the roar of fear that stalks her. He was in her bedroom on Saturday night. He slid through the window, across the carpet, onto her bed. His hands itching to get around her neck. To put his fingers on her hyoid bone; to hear it snap. Just like he tried before.

It was a shadow that's all, a trick of the dark. She's unravelling, catastrophising. We've been here before. Not for a long time, but we have.

I know who he is. I knew him. He's a narcissist and a psychopath. Very charming. Can't bear criticism. Takes no responsibility when things go wrong. Loves the power he has over people. That's my opinion.

I want her to see him before he sees her. I want her to remember him. To be prepared. She's a therapist, for God's sake. She meditates, does Pilates, runs half-marathons. That might come in handy, I suppose. The ability to run a long way. She'd want to negotiate with him. Go win-win – he only likes win-lose.

She's unravelling, like I said, muttering on about being prepared. She puts on some Marigolds and climbs in the loft. What does she want, going up there? She's rooting around. It's full of crap. The loft is where the past lies, in boxes and suitcases never opened, gathering dust. It's the only place in the house where dust can survive.

What has she got in her hand? It's that old rucksack, that navy blue one. Thick with spider shit and mould. I'm surprised she even picked it up, even with the gloves on.

She's gone into the kitchen, shut herself in the utility. The scrubbing brush has come out. She's preparing her own special super-cleaning concoction. Two scoops of Vanish, one of bleach, one of disinfectant. All blasted together in the Nutribullet and – along with the rucksack – thrown into the washing machine. Sixty minutes at ninety degrees. She loves a power-clean. It's a disease really. Followed by twenty minutes in the tumble dryer. It will look brand new.

Now she's on phase two. The goodies, or the baddies depending on how you look at it. The ones in the box under the sink. Handy devices for the security minded. All bought on eBay, they're getting a clean, too. She always has a toothbrush and a bottle of Dettol at the ready. I'd say she's level two hypervigilant now. Although, she's always been a little afraid, always been careful.

Time to get ready for the weather – she nips upstairs and changes her clothes, then it's coat on, thick woollen socks and trail shoes on, grippers on, rucksack on her back. Her fingers grab the keys off the hook in the kitchen. As the door opens, she hesitates, looks down the pathway for footprints. There's a circle of tiny arrows around the doorstep. Bird tracks. That's all it is. Magpies. She hates them – thinks they're bad luck. Her shoes sink into freezing cold snow. Then she's through the gate and out onto the street. Her grippers gripping the ice.

She wants to run. I know she does. I can feel it. That's how she gets to work, always arriving healthy and flushed in the face. She likes the feeling of speed, not that she goes that fast to be honest. Her face might look forty, but her body is still fifty-five. I know she wins her *Good for Age* at races, but that doesn't mean everything is hunky-dory.

Oh my, these side roads are like sheets of ice. She's overtaking the cars – that'll go right to her head. Purposeful, that's how I would describe her right now. You'd never guess she was a fake waiting to be found out. Well, perhaps not waiting. It's like she's ready for it. What with all that secret weaponry. Miss Ninja Warrior. A name for her every occasion. Miss Clean, Miss Therapist, *Miss Take!* Not that she'd remember my name. The past is the other side of a glass window smeared with Vaseline.

Lily seems too comfortable. Far too confident. Weaving through the traffic like she's on a skateboard. There's something coming towards us, something silver. I think it's silver. She's not seen it. I can't understand that. I can see it. It's going to…

The snow-covered car glides towards Lily like a ship; just a patch of windscreen cleared for the driver to see out of.

Time slows down, tyres crunch on compacted ice. I hear the sound of windscreen wipers beating like the wings of an albatross soaring up to the sky. Lily stops. The stupid bitch stops. Halfway across the left-hand lane. A blast of ice-cold air burns her nose and cheeks. She holds out her hand. Tries to stop it, stop time. Stop the car. It is almost upon her, upon us. It will stop, she knows it will stop. She waves her arms about. Tries to see inside the car. She sees a face, a woman's face. Her own face reflected in the windscreen.

It doesn't stop. The car doesn't stop. The driver doesn't stop it.

'Run, get out of the way, run!' A boy's voice, unbroken, screams the words out. Lily turns to look at him, his face contorts as the words fly out again. 'Run, run!' He steps off the pavement, a horn blares, hands grab at his shoulders, they pull him back. A car goes by in the opposite direction, the driver blares his horn again.

'Watch out, watch out!' he shouts through the window.

Another voice roars.

'Move, for God's sake, MOVE!'

She doesn't.

Chapter 17

He rests his hand on the small of Felicia's back. 'The place looks great!' She looks great – her blonde, blunt-cut hair and loose black trousers give her the look of a young Jodie Foster.

'You've done a really good job.' Eyes scanning the wall before him, a broad smile spreads across on his face. 'They really look good, don't they?'

'Yes.'

He pulls her to him, momentarily feels the warmth of her breath on his neck. Her face upturned, flirting with him. Lottie is away powdering her nose in the unisex toilets.

'We try our best. So, are you ready for the party?' She checks her watch, bites her upper lip. 'Doors open in fifteen minutes. Shall I get you a drink?'

Ten bottles of Veuve Clicquot lie in wait on a table by the door, a row of champagne flutes in front of each.

'That would be nice.' He smiles benevolently at her, watches her saunter off in the direction of the drinks table. There's a sudden thump in his chest, his pulse races. He could if he wanted to. He should have left Lottie at home.

A crystal chandelier hangs from the ceiling. Hundreds of crystals linked together to form two silver discs twirling in opposite directions. The room ripples with light.

Pushing all thoughts of the girl away, he looks around for Carlo's squat frame and head of thick, steel-grey curly hair. *Where is he? How many invites did they send out?* His facial muscles tighten as he clenches his teeth. *What if people don't turn up? Oh, shit, what if no one else turns up?*

Lottie appears out of nowhere. He is constantly surprised by her capability to sneak up unheard.

'Well, *sweetheart,* isn't this nice. I need to be the *good* wife tonight, don't I?'

He slips his arm around her shoulders, nestles her into him. Doesn't know whether to risk a kiss. They'd exchanged less than four words in as many days. He isn't too sure what he's done wrong. Surely it isn't the argument over the TV.

Her hair is piled up on her head like a Greek goddess. A filigree of silver roses circles her neck; the long black dress hangs loosely on her. Barefoot, her toenails are painted a shimmering iridescent green.

She looks beautiful.

It sends a shiver down his back. He can still see the beauty in her even though she has aged.

Felicia returns with an open bottle of champagne sheltering in the curve of her elbow and an empty glass in each hand.

'Here—'

'Thanks,' says Lottie, sliding between them, deftly taking the bottle from Felicia's arms in one swift movement.

His eyes take in the scene, wary of what Lottie might do next. 'Felicia this is Lottie, my partner. Lottie, this is Felicia… she organised the show.'

Lottie's smile does not reach her heavily made-up eyes.

'*How nice,'* her voice is saccharine. 'Expecting many, are we?'

'Oh, about a hundred people.' Felicia, unruffled, looks towards the door. 'I'm sure they'll all turn up. They usually do, free drinks are always a pull.'

He feels a twinge of irritation, of feeling foolish.

'*My word*, you look *lovely* tonight, Lottie.' Carlo's voice booms as he takes her hand and kisses it. 'I'm worried all eyes will be on you rather than these fabulous canvases.'

Lottie giggles. Grins like a child given an ice cream. '*You* are *such* a flirt.' She heads off towards the rear of the gallery, closely followed by Carlo.

He feels the air change, it chills. Ben, Felicia's assistant, has unlocked the front door. Half a dozen people wrapped up against the cold walk in.

'Don't want them to be waiting outside in this weather,' says Felicia, sliding up beside him. She whispers in his ear, 'People don't spend money when they have to wait out in the cold.'

The slow beats of *I Heard it through the Grapevine* fill the room. Out of the corner of his eye he sees Carlo take Lottie in his arms, they dance. Their bodies fit together perfectly, too perfectly. He has to look away. He feels like a spare part.

Four large trays of canapés miraculously appear on the table beside him. He reads the menu card. Prawns pickled in lemon and ginger, chicken wings with blueberry relish, roulades of ham hock and pickle, mozzarella and roast tomatoes with a wasabi glaze. All beautifully presented on crisp slices of Italian bread. His mouth waters, fingers reaching out, he tries one after another. They taste delicious. More people arrive. He loosens up.

After a while he starts to enjoy himself, his tongue loosened by alcohol and the fact that red dots were appearing on the for-sale tickets. He takes a circuit of the room, chats to people, feigns embarrassment as they compliment his work. After a while, his mind goes to the conversation he'd had with Carlo on the phone earlier that day. Carlo had rambled on about his good friend, James. How he'd met him at a party in Chelsea, thrown by some multi-millionaire that he'd never heard of.

'James owns the gallery,' a smirk crossed his lips. 'Felicia is his daughter.'

'*Really?* How did he make his money?' he couldn't help asking.

'Pharmaceuticals – made a killing in the seventies, apparently. Doesn't like to talk about money. Quite enigmatic in that northern sort of way, a rough sophistication, new money and all that. Women fall all over him.'

'*Really?*' A vision of a six-foot lothario in a tuxedo comes to mind.

'He'll be there tonight.'

He'd felt a frisson of excitement. All at once; optimistic, flattered. His burgeoning ego pushed the fears that had been plaguing him for days out of his head. A sense of normality returned.

An hour and half has since gone by. *Doesn't look like he's turning up tonight, more's the pity.* Felicia is helping people with their coats.

'Melissa, James!' Carlo's voice raises over the goodbyes. 'Fantastic you could make it, it's been a great night! Come over here and meet Lottie, his beautiful wife—she's having a nap.'

He turns to look, sees a tall slender woman, perhaps thirty-years-old, perhaps forty, he can't tell. A sleek blonde, he thinks to himself. Her long fringe flops across one eye, her hand gently caresses the polished steel bannister as she makes her way down the stairs. There's something about her; her way of walking, of holding time in its place, her hips sway gently from side to side.

She's been a model, he thinks to himself, she must have, surely?

His heart stops as he sees the man behind her. It knocks the breath out of him; his mouth dries in an instant. The years haven't changed him much; still lithe as a boxer, his skin weathered, the cut of his Italian suit more expensive, the brown hair now completely grey. He would know him anywhere. Her nails had cut a nasty scar above his eye. Last time he'd seen him that scar had been weeping blood.

The walls close in on him. He hurries towards the entrance, grabs his coat and scarf. The door shuts silently behind him, he needs air. His pulse races. He's not seen Jimmy in over thirty-five years. This isn't the night to make their re-acquaintance. Not in public.

He steps into the doorway of an empty shop, pulls out his phone, his fingers punch a text to Carlo.

'Sorry had to go, not feeling well. Didn't want to dampen events. Look after Lottie for me, please. Get her back to the hotel.'

He presses send, switches off his phone before Carlo has the chance to ring him back. He won't be happy.

What if he saw me? Thank God that Carlo didn't plaster my face over the publicity materials.

He has always insisted on a certain amount of anonymity. His work spoke for him; those were the only images he was interested in displaying. Even in the face of adversity, he never faltered from that position.

The streets are busy. Bare shouldered, their hairy legs exposed to the weather, a stream of young men stagger out of a wine-bar. Each one dressed in a red silk basque with the words *TIMO is getting married* printed across their chest. The groom and best man teeter on red velvet platform shoes, the others wear black wellington boots. Normally this would engender a smile from him; not tonight – all he wants is to get away from the gallery as quickly as he can.

His mind clears as he walks toward the tube station; the fear in his chest subsides. Tomorrow he'll ring Lottie, make an excuse. Tonight, he'll go home, put a few things in a bag, go up North. See if the old house is still standing. Go to the old haunts, search out old friends. He's not been up there for years.

He'll erase all traces of himself from their lives.

Chapter 18

Outside the front porch of the farmhouse, her hands laden with plastic bags, Thomasine pauses for a moment. Her eyes linger on the fields, on the moorland. The midday sun stands proud in a clear blue sky; every blade of grass, every tree, every wall covered in a gleaming white crust of snow. She longs to be up there, walking with the dogs, wrapped up in a thick winter coat, her lungs filling with fresh air. Chained in their kennels, the dogs whimper and whine. Their food and water bowls licked dry – their hunger seemingly never satisfied.

She slides the key in the lock, nudges the door with her shoulder, kicks the baseboard with her foot, one final push and it opens. Dumping the bags in the hallway, she turns on her heels. *Animals first.* Her father's rule. His face comes to mind, that wide toothy smile. His clothes smelt of dried hay and lanolin. His breath of the Weetabix he ate every single morning drowned in sheep's milk. Karen's murderer took him, too.

'They can't get their own food, not the dogs. Not like sheep who graze on grass.'

Dogs fed, she gets on with the day, pulls back the kitchen curtains, thousands of dust motes shimmer in the sunlight. The other side of the room has a chill to it, summer and winter combined, a microcosm of weather, not one, not the other. She lights the fire, watches the flames lick the kindling.

Her mother's presence is everywhere. Amongst the clutter; in the silence, as the wind rushes underneath the back door. The room, the house, feels exactly as she'd left it, as though holding its breath for her return.

Thomasine checks the time. Rosie will be there in an hour, to help her out, to clean the place. Thomasine rang her earlier, they'd talked briefly. Both eager to escape the circus that the media forced upon them. Rosie offered to help her get the farmhouse ready for the funeral. Thomasine had been quick to accept. Rosie is the one person she trusts completely.

Years as a senior social worker on the Child Protection Team have toughened her up, given her a strong sense of responsibility. Two weeks ago, they offered her redundancy. Thomasine closes her eyes for a moment. It is beyond her how they can let someone of Rosie's calibre and experience go.

She unpacks the plastic bags on the kitchen table. An A4 lined notebook, a pack of Bic pens, a jar of decaffeinated coffee, semi-skimmed milk, a small sliced wholemeal loaf, a large bag of Maltesers, salt and vinegar crisps, Eccles cakes, fresh vegetables, best butter, cheese and onion pies, vegetarian lasagnes, a roll of black bags and a large bottle of bleach. All bought from the village shop – enough for a week's stay; enough to get the local gossips excited.

She fills the kettle; as it boils, she sifts mindlessly through a clutch of letters on the table. *Why hadn't I noticed these before?* A couple are stamped urgent in bright red capital letters. The thought of opening her mother's mail unsettles her.

'It's not like she's still alive, she can't do it. God knows what's inside them that might come back to bite me.' The words echo around the empty room. Or in her head. She's not sure.

It's your job now to sort this all out. The thought paralyses her. The letters lay unopened in a pile beside the milk carton. She closes her eyes for a moment. *Work—I need to get back to work. Who am I if I don't do that?*

Her work is her escape, an ironic distraction. *Distraction*, she thinks to herself… no, that sounds trite. Yet it does distract her. She was the only child left in a family devastated by the loss of a missing child. Never knowing, always suspecting. Decades of it, years blighted by anger, disappointment, bitterness – blaming.

Hope dwindling away like a trail of smoke up the chimney. The cases she dealt with gave her a sense of purpose, what she couldn't do for her own family she could do for others. From the very beginning, she had known she would never be allowed to work her sister's case. Her job eased that pain.

Images loiter at the back of her mind like unwelcome guests. Her job, in the main, is to reunite the dead with the living. To the uninitiated, it's the stuff of nightmares. She's seen so many dead people. They crowd inside her head – jostle for her attention, never resting until their cases solved. Partially decomposed, semi-naked, their bones covered in bits of flesh. Washed up by the tides after throwing themselves off a bridge or a cliff. Some caught beneath the water, beneath the rocks, hidden from sight until bad weather and fierce currents drag them out, what remains of them floating on the surface waiting to be found. Seagulls pecking at them.

God knows what all of this has done to me. What sort of person am I, truly?

What would she be without her work, alone, unable to deal with everyday life? Thomasine has seen many like that. Antidepressants thrown at them by overworked GPs. Sometimes the pills helped, sometimes they made things a whole lot worse. Weeks later they'd be discovered hanging from the back of the bedroom door, the belt from their dressing gown around their neck. Found by relatives, inconsolable, filled with guilt about the words they could have said but never did. Or had said and no one had listened to. She can never let herself slide down into that pit. Not for long at any rate.

There are five files locked away in her desk. Five human beings, all apparently homeless – their deaths unexplained. Not enough of them left to create a Photofit. The list of their meagre possessions the last thing she'd been working on. Some had so very little; a coat, a scarf, a thin pair of trousers, trainers, a lighter, four pounds sixty in change, an elastic hair band, four keys, no address, no name. DNA but no match. Some had no money at all. Their cases logged onto the database, their records uploaded to the Missing Persons Bureau, the home of the found and unclaimed.

Early on, a fellow officer spoke to her of his way of coping with the job. Some went to the pub and washed away the recollections of the day with alcohol. Or went to the gym and ran themselves to exhaustion on the treadmill. He read, immersing himself between the covers of a book. Every single night after work. So, she did the same; her front room lined with bookshelves, laden with books of all genres. A temporary respite that worked for her, too. Her eyes now search the room for something to read. Only the pile of old newspapers beckon.

She makes herself another coffee. Her head still can't process it, won't process it. There's no normality in it. *There'll be two funerals to organise. Two. That's it. That's what's screwing with my head. And Mam's death, I'll have to register it.*

It is as though Karen died along with her mother. The two of them together, in a car accident. Here one moment, then gone, snuffed out. She takes a sip of the coffee, the heat of it stings her tongue.

Thomasine recalls accompanying her mother to register her father's death. Together they sat opposite the Registrar. She almost nine-years-old, wearing a bright red coat with a black collar; her mother all in black, stoic, refusing to let either of them shed a tear. There was something else, the Registrar, the way he took the top off his fountain pen, the flourish of his hand as it skimmed across the certificate. How he pressed the ornate blotter over the registration documentation to dry the ink. His signature, small and neat. As though all these things were part of the ritual of death

Tiny, noticeable things.

She wrote it all down in the memory book, the red exercise book her father gave her to write down her memories of Karen. That's so you don't forget, that's what he said. At first, she couldn't think of what to put in it, so he helped her.

'She smiles a lot.'

She wrote that down. It became a game they played. 'Write that down for me, Thomasine,' he'd say, whenever he remembered something. Writing notes became a habit that she never gave up. One exercise book filled after another, journals of observation; the dog with three legs, the cat that turned up out of nowhere, four magpies sitting on the barn roof, the price of lollies in the village shop, Tommy Hartley's acne. The boy who averted his eyes to the right whenever he lied. Years later, in a fit of despondency, she'd thrown them on the fire one night, they'd burnt brightly. No longer able to read them without upset. Unwilling to torment herself any longer. Unwilling to remind herself that she must have been the one that let her sister escape in the night. It must have been her fault that Karen disappeared. She'd shut the window because she was cold. Karen couldn't get back in. Thomasine's face flushes... *she'd shut the window...* where had that come from?

It couldn't be true – her brain is playing tricks.

Just the same she'll check the file when she next goes back home. The one she personally compiled that documents everything to do with her sister's case.

Chapter 19

The yellow tape stretches, snaps and twists as the wind tears at it. The wail of the siren gets louder until it drowns everything out. Muted blue lights twinkle on shop windows like Christmas illuminations. Snow, thick as fog, keeps coming in wave after wave. Twenty minutes have passed since Lily's head bulls-eyed the windscreen. Since she flew over the car. Since her body lay still. As people look on, the slush around her head turns pink like a cocktail.

People get out of their cars, their necks straining to see what the problem is. As the ambulance approaches, they get back in their cars, try to move forward, pull up on the pavement, reverse. Tyres slide and skid – it's gridlock. Inch by inch the ambulance manoeuvres its way through the chaos. In the end, it stops, lights blazing, unable to get closer, three hundred yards away from the incident.

Inside the tape, a uniformed police officer kneels beside Lily, getting to her feet as the front doors of the ambulance swing open. Paramedics; one male, one female, heavy bags slung over their shoulders, drop down onto the road and hurry towards the accident. The police officer gives the Special Constable, the tape guy in charge of access, the thumbs up. Nevertheless, he asks for their names, notes them down, lifts the tape so they can get under it. He gestures towards Lily's body several metres away, her legs splayed, one arm beneath her body, the other outstretched, her head still resting against the curb.

The paramedics scramble towards her, the grippers on their shoes clinging to the icy surface beneath their feet. One of them shrugs off his backpack, pulls a torch out, drops down to his knees. He pulls on a pair of surgical gloves, uses his fingers to lift the lids on Lily's eyes, shines the bright white beam into her irises. No response. He raises his voice over the wind, 'Hello, we're here to help you, now. To take you to hospital, to sort everything out. Can you hear me? Can you talk to me?' Still nothing. He gently touches the wound on the side of her skull – a thick, viscous liquid clings to his gloves – blood.

The police officer stands a few feet away, watching.

The paramedics, heads together, speak quietly but efficiently. *Head injury, shock, possible broken neck, fractured fibulas and possibly the kneecaps.* The words flit between them, the male uses scissors to cut Lily's trousers from the heel upwards, the female sticks small electronic discs on her torso then clips in the wires. The portable ECG kicks into life. A weak pulse quivers on the screen. Seconds later, the female runs back to the ambulance, returns with a neck immobiliser and a spine board tucked under her arm.

'We're going to have to move her onto the board, got to be careful… there might be internal bleeding. And damage to the spine. We'll give her some pain relief first.'

The police officer takes a step back. The paramedic injects Tramadol into Lily's thigh. She doesn't stir. Long minutes tick by as the careful and painstaking process of cutting off the rucksack begins. They slowly lift her arm. One gentle move and the rucksack slips out from under her. She gives out a low moan, her skin is waxen, sweat pours off her face. As they move her onto the board, a loud visceral scream, so full of wretchedness, so full of pain, hurls out of her mouth. The paramedics ease the board onto a trolley, then roll it towards the ambulance as quickly as they can.

The police officer gazes at the blood-sodden patch of snow beside her feet. The snow is melting. She takes out her phone and takes a photograph; already gloved up, she dips her hand into the rucksack. There is no sign of any identification. There are several bulky items but no purse or handbag.

'We're off!' shouts the female paramedic, pushing shut the rear door of the ambulance. The siren and lights start up again, this time the road is clear. The ambulance moves off into the night.

The police officer picks up the tattered rucksack nestling beside her feet and walks over to the unmarked car parked up on the pavement. She opens the boot, inside is a cardboard box full of evidence bags. She takes a large white paper bag out of the box, lays the rucksack on top of it. The rucksack is wet and will need drying before it can be properly bagged, tagged and processed; that will have to be done when she gets back to the station. For now, she's worried that the weather will wash anyway any evidence.

Another drunk driver, no doubt, she says to herself. *Bastards! I hate them*

Chapter 20

The dogs let out a low growl, tumble out into the hallway, claw at the door howling to be let out, desperate to get to whoever is at the other side of it. Thomasine had let them in for a bit of warmth and company. *That'll be Rosie.* Her fingers tucked inside their collars, the dogs wriggle and squirm as she drags them into the front room.

'Sit. Quiet!'

They obey.

She shuts them in, opens the front door to find Rosie manhandling a large cardboard container out of the back of her Renault Koleos. Her shoulder-length red hair a flash of colour against the glare of the snow, her face bare of makeup.

'A bit of a bumpy ride up through the field, isn't it? I locked the lower gate like you asked, put the key back in the hiding place.'

'Thanks, I'm hoping it'll keep the press out a bit longer.' Thomasine gives her a weak smile. 'I'm sure they're not eager enough to walk a couple of miles in this weather.'

'I thought you might be interested in this.' The cardboard container perches precariously on her left thigh. She tries to close the boot with her elbow. 'It's been under the stairs for years, behind that old tumble dry er of Mum's, the one she made me keep for Kim. They discovered it when they cleared Gran's place. It's the last of Veronica's belongings. It was already boxed up, Mum was going to throw it out. It's her clothes, her makeup. She couldn't bear to look at them. I made her keep it for me. It was all that was left.'

'Hold on a moment, let me help you.' Thomasine takes the box out of Rosie's hands, 'Mind, it's slippy.' Both totter unsteadily across the yard and into the house.

Thomasine places it on the worktop. She offers Rosie a chair, 'Let's have a bit of something to eat before we start.' She fills the kettle, makes them both a coffee, butters the Eccles cakes. They sit facing each other at the table, the plate between them. They only meet up every couple of months, but the ritual is always the same, coffee and cake.

Rosie stirs her coffee, her eyes darken. 'I'm truly sorry, Thom.'

Thomasine takes a deep breath, 'Ironically, I think it would have been exactly what she'd have wanted. God knows how she would have coped with the investigation—' A wave of emotion catches in her throat. She changes track. 'Look, I'm not up to talking about it right now. Let's change the subject, shall we? How's Jeannie?'

Rosie nods her head, 'Not good now. She's getting more and more confused.'

'I'm sorry,' and Thomasine is. Dementia has turned Rosie's once vibrant mother into a ghost of her former self.

'Me too.' Her friend pushes her fingers through her hair, rubs her temples. 'There's an upside that I hadn't anticipated. All that sadness she carried for years, all that anger, it's all gone. She thinks Veronica visits her and I don't dissuade her of that. You know, Mum used to say that Veronica changed, in those last few months before she disappeared. It started when she went to college in September. Some girl was a bad influence on her. Pamela or Paula, something like that. She'd started getting all dressed up, loads of make-up, then she'd catch the last bus into town. Mum was worried sick about her. Then Veronica would rock up at six in the morning, banging about, waking everyone up. Mum said there was something about her that wasn't right.'

'Not right?'

'She'd be rabbiting on about things. Was too awake for someone who'd been out all night.'

A frown deepens between Thomasine's eyes, 'Drugs?'

'I don't know – drugs wouldn't have been on Mum's radar. Then Veronica stayed out all weekend, Mum went bananas with worry. Told her it wasn't a hotel. Veronica moved in with Gran after that. We didn't see her for months. Then she turned up at Christmas, thin as a rake, even I remember that. All done up in a red backless dress and platform shoes. Off later to some nightclub. When Mum asked her where she got the money from, Veronica just shrugged it off. Said that she'd got a part-time job. Wouldn't say more than that.'

'That was the last time you all saw her, wasn't it?'

Rosie nods, places her elbows on the table and cups her chin in her hands.

'Did she have any other friends?'

Rosie shakes her head. 'If she did they shrunk back into the woodwork. I guess she must have had some at school. Even then she was always one for going off on her own. She'd be gone for hours.'

'On her own? Where did she go?' Thomasine's interest is growing.

'I only know what Mum told me. Some old paper mill down in the woods, and that place called the druid circle.'

'The druid's circle? The one on tops, directly behind us, here?'

'Yes.'

'I don't remember you telling me this before.' A look of confusion crosses Thomasine's face.

Rosie shrugs her shoulders. 'You know what it's like, you get on with life. You don't forget, you just park stuff. Put it somewhere where it can't hurt you. I don't believe she just buggered off—she would never have run away. Not from us, and certainly not from Gran.

Thomasine breaks an Eccles cake in two, nudges the plate towards Rosie. A habit born out of years of friendship. They sit in silence for a moment, the sticky sweet pastry melting in their mouths.

Rosie breaks the silence first. 'I don't believe she's dead, either, I've always thought she's out there somewhere. Lost, trying to find her way home.'

Some don't care about who they hurt. They just get on with life, move on. I've met many of those. Thomasine's thoughts go unsaid. She rubs her tongue around her teeth and gums, licks away the last vestige of the pastry. A gust of wind rattles the back door.

One of the dogs lets out a loud moan, scratches the door to get out. Thomasine gets up, opens the front door, lets them out into the yard.

'They're farm dogs, farm dogs stay outside, Thomasine.' Her mother's words haunt her every time she allows them over the threshold.

'Perhaps she is alive, that does happen.' She settles back into her chair. 'I've seen it hundreds of times. People go missing, after a while they're too afraid to come back, they believe that their family won't want them anymore.'

'All we've ever wanted is to get her back. Every single anniversary we send out a message on YouTube, on Facebook and Twitter too. We just want her home.'

Thomasine reaches out for her hand, covers it with her own. 'I know. We did the same.'

'With all of this, with finding Karen, she might come back.' Rosie's face brightens for a moment. 'She might be able to tell us what happened to Karen. If she knows, that is.'

Thomasine averts her face, stares intently at the photographs on the mantelpiece. She knows only too well what that might mean. Unconsciously she edits her response. 'Yes, hopefully.'

Rosie reaches into her handbag, pulls out her phone, frowns. 'Can I ring Phil on your landline? I can't get a signal on my phone. Just to tell him where I am.'

'Of course, help yourself. You know where it is.' Thomasine wonders how Phil, Rosie's husband, is handling all of this.

Rosie leaves the door ajar, a few moments later, her voice goes up a notch. 'Why didn't you tell them to piss off? For God's sake, why can't they leave us alone.'

A few moments later, she opens the kitchen door, her cheeks are pinched red, her eyes brim with tears.

'Those bastards! On the doorstep when Phil got home. Our Kim said they'd been hammering on the door for ages, shouting through the letterbox. Scared her to death! Phil said the bloke got right into his face, camera going off and everything. He said that Veronica was the suspect for Karen's murder. *Did we want to comment?* A look of indignation crosses her face. 'They didn't even know each other.'

Thomasine takes in a deep breath, she knew this would happen.

Rosie's daughter is eighteen, the image of her mother, though the opposite in personality. Shy and reserved, always in the background, never stepping into the limelight. Kim would have been paralysed with fear.

'They're just scraping for a headline. Let it wash over you, Rosie.' She is surprised by the normality of her own voice. 'There's probably no truth in it.'

Rosie's eyes flash, the tears run down her cheeks. 'It's fine for you to say—' the colour drains from her cheeks, eyes wide she covers her mouth with her hand. 'Oh, God, I'm sorry, really sorry, I didn't mean to say that. I'm just angry.'

'Sit down.' Thomasine puts her arms around her friend, gives her a hug. 'I've seen it all before, honestly. When they find out Mam's dead, she'll be next on the list. After that they'll really scrape the barrel, it'll be me, an eight-year-old murderer with the strength of Hercules.'

'I know but... can't you—'

'No, I can't put a stop to it. They won't tell me anything. As soon as I go back to work, they'll transfer me to another team. I won't even be in Missing Persons.'

Rosie's hands start to tremble.

'What if they come for you?'

'Who?'

'The person who did it.'

Thomasine's eyes widen in surprise. 'Me? Why would they do that?'

'It's obvious, isn't it? Because, as far as everyone is concerned, you're the last person to see Karen alive. Perhaps they might think you saw them, too.'

That thought lodges itself inside Thomasine's brain; her mouth goes dry.

Hours later, when Rosie has gone home, Thomasine opens the box of Veronica's belongings. She is methodical in her approach, gloves on, she removes one item at a time.

First, a small off-white plastic container filled with nail varnishes – the liquid separated, three lipsticks, a pallet of block mascara and eyeliner. All by Rimmel. Next, a tired brown velvet clutch bag full of cheap jewellery; metal bracelets, dangling earrings, studs for pierced ears – some still on the cardboard backing, never worn. Then clothing, wrapped in plastic bags, two pairs of platform shoes with wooden soles, a pair of full-length navy-blue culottes, a pale pink dress with padded shoulders, the label still attached and carefully folded. At the bottom, curled with age and faded by time, half a dozen Jackie magazines lie flat. The most recent, November 1972 with the headline *Stories to Warm Your Heart*. She handles each magazine by the spine, lets the pages flutter then still. A solitary slip of blue paper falls to the floor. As she picks it up, her eyes strain at the faded black ink. *The Torch in Tunstall, Northern Soul Nights. All-nighters for September and October.* She turns it over in her hand, there's nothing on the back. Thomasine lies it flat on the table, takes a photograph of it with her phone. Unsure of its relevance, slips it back inside the magazine it had fallen out of.

A keepsake? There is no mention of all-night clubs in her case file. Why is that? Surely, that would have come out during the investigation? She pushes that thought to the back of her mind, then carefully returns all Veronica's things to the cardboard box.

If she can't be involved in her sister's case, there's no reason she shouldn't take a look at Veronica's. Unofficially, of course.

Chapter 21

The thin line of terraced houses has long gone; their cobbled streets and high-walled yards lie buried beneath acres of housing estates, high-rise flats and mini-markets selling newspapers, cheap bags of sweets and cans of lager in singles. He has no sense of where he grew up, where he'd escaped from, who he'd been. He's bewildered. The man he's become surely didn't come from this, he thinks to himself.

He buys himself a car out of small ads in the local newspaper, a rusting mini, destined for the crusher.

'A doer upper,' says the bulked-up bodybuilder as he gets out of the driver's seat. 'I've no time to do it – six months MOT and tax still on it.' He looks him directly in the eyes, 'No warranty, buyer beware and all that.' The man offers him a test drive, ten minutes later he buys it on the spot, five hundred pounds, twenty off for cash. 'For yer daughter, is it?'

He nods his head, eager to complete the transaction.

'The service manual got lost, okay?' A taut smile crosses the man's lips.

He nods his head again. 'Fine, yes, fine.' He doesn't ask about the logbook, won't be needing that either.

After that, he picks up the search, his eyes scour every female face for her. For any trace of the eighteen-year-old, Veronica, Ronnie. That's what everyone called her. Tears streaming down her cheeks, as Jimmy dragged her down the street. It won't be the same face. He'd done a pencil sketch of her, from the photograph in the paper, then made her look older. He keeps it in the inside pocket of his jacket for reference; he's not shown it to anyone, yet.

He feels no empathy for either girl, nor guilt. Only fear of his own plight. It's 2010, the chances of him finding anything from 1973 are zero and yet…

Why am I putting all this effort in? he asks himself. *She's dead.* But at night the doubt sinks in. He wanders around Manchester, Bolton, Bury, even up as far as Blackburn. He wonders how far she will have got if she had escaped.

Like an automaton, he cannot give up. He visits libraries, spends hours scanning electoral roles, birth, marriage and death registers, anything that might lead him to her. The muscles in his eyes ache; no amount of sleep eases them. His nights spent in cash-only B&Bs with nylon sheets where fire alarms hang by a flex from the ceiling and the switch on the shower is missing. Where continental breakfasts are made up of sliced white bread, thin slices of ham, margarine and seeded jams bought from the pound shops. All left on a tray outside his room overnight. Places that no one would think he'd want to stay, and he doesn't.

He dons dark clothes, beanie hats, no longer shaves, blends into the landscape of drug addicts, drunks and girls on the street.

His eyes catch it by chance, the headline, at the supermarket. He'd been ambling along the magazine and newspaper isle, heading for the chocolate bars. A thick banner of text – Missing Girl Found. He'd nearly shit himself. Then he realised it was Karen they were still talking about. There, slap bang underneath it was a picture of a woman with her hand obscuring most of her face, a fierce look in her eyes. He picks up the newspaper, folds it in two, pays for it at the till.

He reads the article in a café over breakfast. The media are so very helpful, he thinks to himself, quite negligent in many ways. His jaws champ on a slice of fried sausage, the smack of salty pork settles on his tongue. He puts down his cutlery, picks up his mobile phone, takes a photograph of the photograph. Then another of the article. Then he carries on with his breakfast, comfortable in the knowledge that there are more ways to skin a cat than he thought.

He hadn't intended to visit the crime scene. He had gone on impulse again, unable to keep away. He clocks a face in the crowd. White male, tanned, a camcorder on his left shoulder; his head covered by a navy bobble hat pulled low. A dark red scar runs down his right cheek. The camcorder is pointed directly at him, quickly he averts his head, turns and walks the other way. His Doc Martens slip on the sodden ground.

He's seen her at the site several times now, standing there, peering into the woods. Yesterday he decided to follow her; she went back to work. She's one of those hard on the accelerator, hard on the brake drivers. She didn't seem to notice him.

There's a dull ache in his chest, a longing. He wants to be amid the milieu, jostling amongst the media, scrambling for photographs, hailing out questions that go unanswered. He'd never seen them at work, never seen the power of the pack. They're like wild dingoes – hunting, sniffing, scavenging. He imagines what it would be like to stand in front of them, the sole focus of their attention. He feels something crystallise inside of him. A need that he had hitherto ignored.

Without Lottie to distract him life seems simpler, no one else to please but himself. He does one thing at a time, spends hours in cafés planning his next steps, putting ideas down like charcoal strokes on drawing paper. Filling in the detail later. The drama unfolding in his head, he, the leading player. A hero of sorts.

When he was younger he had a talent for getting things done, for clearing things out of the way. He was a finisher, tying off loose ends for those less capable of doing so.

He makes his way back to the car, parked a mile up the road in a layby. Lorries hammer by, throwing waves of slush and sleet up onto the pavement, stinging his face, soaking his clothes. Obscenities rise out of his mouth and into the air, only to be lost in the thunder of the traffic. It is fifteen minutes of misery before he gets into the basic comfort of the Mini. He jerks off his jacket; hangs it off the back of the passenger seat. Shivering, he takes his mobile phone from the pocket. No messages. No missed phone calls. He calls his home number, his fingers drum on the dashboard impatiently as he waits for her to answer.

Where is she? Where is she?

Last time he'd called he'd been explicit: stay in, be there for when I call. She'd told him to piss off.

He takes his wallet out of his trouser pocket, counts his money. He's running out. A couple of the twenties and a tenner, he'll need that for petrol. He's purposely avoided making cash withdrawals. Hasn't paid by card for anything. He's mindful now, wears gloves and he's got two packets of antibacterial wipes in his rucksack.

He pivots around, lifts the carrier bag nestled in the footwell of the passenger seat. He peers inside; chopped liver and kidney swish about their polythene containers. He smiles, exhales. He'd thought it all out. He can stop on the way, quick and easy; the first task on his action plan.

Then off home. Pick up more cash. Sort out Lottie.

Then the fun begins.

Chapter 22

The pain is gone, their voices fade, their bodies blur, time is running out, she knows it. She feels a separation, a butterfly casting off the pupae, a pull into the brightest light. Freedom… peace from that place that trapped her. From the cruel voice that brought the nightmares.

She looks down at the battered body on the bed. Her body. Medical staff swarm over it like ants. They cut off clothing; drop them into plastic bags, check for injuries; call out findings, insert lines into veins; pump in drugs. Gentle hands carefully wipe away the blood.

Time rushes in and pulls her out into another place, another time.

Miles of violet sky welcome her, white cotton candy clouds drift towards the horizon then melt away. The fields are a mass of blonde grass, like waves of a choppy sea, the breeze pulling them one way, then another. A warm summer sun washes over her back. The fear trapped inside her dissipates. She is young again – just seventeen. No mistakes have been made.

Her eyes fix on a golden plover, catching the thermals, the bird spreads its wings; soars above her. She tilts her head back, sees the beauty in the tip of each feather. How dark goes to light then back again.

In the distance, she sees someone walking towards her. A female form, a slow step, her head held high, arms resting by her sides.

Ahead, the narrow rocks of the druid circle jut up through the soil. She weaves her way around them, her fingers glide over their hard edges.

The ground is covered in a bed of honey-scented heather, she sinks into its comfort, looks up at the sky, drinks it in.

'It's been a long time. I'm glad you're home.' A whisper carried by the wind.

She opens her eyes wide. A hand reaches down then pulls back.

'I wish I could take you.'

It's her grandmother, Alice, a look of sadness on her face.

She feels a heavy thump on her chest—then a searing pain down her breastbone. A shard of light blinds her.

The trolley thunders along the hospital corridor towards the theatre, takes her with it.

Chapter 23

Thomasine strains to hear the noise of them, their early morning yelps for food. They didn't come, would never come. Whoever put the food down knew exactly what they were doing. Her eyes well with tears, a wave of emotion ripples up through her chest. Fists clenched, her arms ache for want of someone to punch.

Probably one of the press – no, surely, they wouldn't kill the dogs?

She'll never forget the horrible death… the thick rancid foam covering their tongues, their backs arched. The fox beside them, its snout covered in its own blood – a female. Vision clouded, she'd fallen back against the barn door, unable to believe the abject cruelty before her.

Thomasine gets dressed, the black suit and olive-green silk shirt too light for the winter weather. Nothing else seems appropriate. She didn't put the funeral in the paper, why would she? The few relatives she has left will be there, they all live in the village. They know better than to blab to the press, they'd ticked that box years ago, encountered her father's wrath.

I need to get through today. She looks in the mirror. No makeup, no dressing up. No jewellery. *Chin up, girl!* At that moment, she realises most of her life has been *chin up*. She pulls on her boots, grabs an umbrella off the coat rack, rushes out of the door. The hearse and car will be waiting for her at the bottom of the track.

The wake is at the farmhouse; the kitchen table is crammed with food. The funeral a blur that Thomasine is slowly rousing from. Rosie is making teas and coffees, Uncle Oliver handing out glasses of sherry, her cousin Paul taxiing people up and down the track in her mother's four-by-four. The field is now such a quagmire of mud that boots sink down into it and can't be pulled out. He is under strict orders from Thomasine to tell every single person about the dangers around the farm, most of the outbuildings should be demolished. She thanks God there are no children there.

People stream in and out. Time passes, the food and drink consumed. In the front room, people are standing in twos and threes, heads dipped in conversation, the sofa and chairs already taken by those less mobile.

Uncle Oliver has lit the fires and stokes the range. At least there is heat and hot water. At long last, the house feels warm, welcoming even.

For some it's the first time they've visited the place in over thirty years, their eyes soak up the dowdy walls and hand-me-down furniture.

A hand catches hold of hers, it's Karen's childhood friend, Judith. 'Are you free for a moment… to talk about Karen… about that thing I told you about, outside the church?' Her forehead is creased with worry.

'Of course, let's get a bit of privacy.' Thomasine gives her a weak smile then leads her upstairs to Karen's bedroom.

Judith's face freezes as she walks through the door. One side of the room a mausoleum, circa 1973. The other like an empty prison cell. She walks over to the window, peeks through the curtain before turning back to face her.

'It's about the diary,' she speaks quickly as though eager to be out of the room. 'I bought it for her fourteenth birthday, from M & S. Definitely her fourteenth birthday, the one when we all camped the night, in the barn; up in the hayloft. It was one of those lockable diaries. It was freezing that night; don't you remember?'

Thomasine did, she wasn't invited, wasn't allowed to go. Karen didn't want her seven-year-old sister cramping her style.

'Your mum brought loads of blankets and quilts out. Your dad made a house out of hay bales. We all brought our hot water bottles; your mum filled them up. It didn't make an inkling of difference, we were all bloody freezing and moaned like hell.' She lets out a nervous laugh. 'Karen threw a right wobbly because we wanted to come in.'

Thomasine thinks back to the night, she'd been made to stay indoors, up in their bedroom. She'd spent the night looking through the window, down at the barn. A yellow light shone out from the hayloft. Eight of Karen's friends from school had been invited. It was winter. No one truly wanted to camp out in the winter. Even if it was in the barn. Karen had told them that it would be a sign of true friendship. Apparently, none of them had been impressed. In the end, only six had turned up.

'So, what did she do with the diary? I'm sure there's no record of a diary in the investigation file.'

Judith's face clouded over. 'I don't know, I know she wrote in it, she told me that all the time. I think she hid it somewhere, not in her bedroom, I'm sure of that. She said you'd have it in no time.'

Thomasine forces a smile. 'I would have tried, junior detective even then.'

Someone shouts upstairs, it's Rosie – the vicar is leaving. Judith reaches for Thomasine's hand again, there's a sadness in her eyes. 'No one believed me last time, but I thought I'd give it one last shot.'

That was the end of their conversation, Thomasine almost files it away as nonsense, she's heard tales like that before, all had come to nothing. Yet a tiny strand of hope works its way through her psyche, by night time she's decided that she'll go looking for it.

Chapter 24

He's on his knees pulling shirts and jeans out of the washing machine when the front door slams shut. The dog wallops towards him, tail wagging, it pushes itself between him and the washer. 'Hello, boy, have you missed me.' He gives the dog's ears a hard rub. 'I've missed you, too.'

'What the—' Her heavy soled walking boots hit the base of his coccyx with such velocity he falls forward, a searing white pain roars up his spine, he knocks his head on the machine door. Tears spring to his eyes, a dark red flush floods his face. He scrambles to his feet, rounds on her.

'That *hurt*!' He towers over her, rubs his back with his hand.

'Where the hell have you been?' The words spit out of her mouth, she swings back her leg for another attack.

The dog's ears go back, it lets out a low growl, he grabs it by the collar, pulls it into him, in front of him. 'Stop! Stop—you're terrifying the dog!'

'I've had enough. What were you thinking, abandoning me at the gallery without a word.' She screeches in his face, 'Screw you!' Turns on her heels, races up the stairs, the slammed door a thunderclap that shatters his ears.

He rushes out into the hallway. Lottie's standing outside their bedroom, a suitcase in her hand. He takes the bottom step, the case hurtles towards him, he leaps back, it lands at his feet, inches away from the dog's head. Horace scrambles away, whimpering. Still in shock he steps over the case and sprints up the stairs. She moves across the landing, goes into the bathroom, slides the bolt across the door.

'I've missed you,' he whispers through the glass over and over. 'I'm home now, don't be angry with me, Lottie.' He taps on the door, 'Lottie, don't be angry with me.'

His pleas are met with the sound of running water.

'I went walking along the coast. Come out, I'll make us dinner, you'd like that, wouldn't you?'

He can see the outline of her body through the mottled glass. He shrugs his shoulders, climbs the stairs up to the studio. She'll calm down, he thinks to himself. She always does.

An image flashes across his eyes. Her and Carlo, naked, in the hotel room, on the bed. He sinks onto the wooden steps. Blinks the image away – she wouldn't. She wouldn't dare.

That first sight of her. It took his breath away. The summer holidays, the inner city, the park, the open water pool and tennis courts. The pool had been his favourite watching place. There had been so many water nymphs to watch. None, since Karen, had truly taken his fancy.

The sun glinting on the surface of the water, the yellow bikini clinging to her wet body, like an arrow she shot into the water, he could hear nothing but his own pulse beating in his neck. She burst up through the water, arms raised, the bikini top slipped to her waist. She laughed, yanked it back up, then dove beneath the water again. Her hand gripped around her friend's ponytail, pulling her under.

She'd been oblivious to his watchful eyes.

Until he'd made himself known, weeks later. A slow courtship, helped by small gifts – makeup, perfume, clothes. And, when the time came, a little something for the journey.

A new start, a new name.

Two hundred and fifty miles away, where no one came looking.

Chapter 25

It had been weeks since the exhibition, yet the memory bled into Jimmy's psyche – soured everything. He'd know that face anywhere.

The artist had turned his head, just a fraction, as he'd pulled on his coat, enough for him to see that profile. If Paula his ex-wife had been there, she would have fawned over him. Just like she had back in the day.

Shame he didn't fancy her – life would have been a lot easier. A grim smile crosses his lips. *But then I wouldn't have Fizz, Felicia, so it wouldn't.*

It was him. Still fit as a butcher's dog by the look of him, the strong nose, the full lips. He was the last person Jimmy expected to see. It seems a peculiar coincidence that they'd encountered each other. Especially after all that stuff in the newspaper. He knew then he'd have to pay him a visit, make sure he didn't go blabbing about their shared past.

He flicks down the driver's shade, squints into the distance, the long straight road disappears into the horizon, miles and miles of barren fields on either side. A woman's voice tells him he's about to arrive at his destination.

Further ahead, a couple of detached properties come into view, an ornate concrete water tower turned into a gleaming glass palace and beyond that, set back from the road with a small garden in front of it, a barn conversion, a motorbike parked in front of it. That must be it. He doesn't stop.

A quarter of a mile further along, there is a lay-by on the opposite side of the road; he does a 360 degree turn, manoeuvres the car into it. The sun hovers above the hills, giving the landscape a burnt red glow. Jimmy takes a torch out of the boot before jogging his way back down the road towards the barn.

His hand grips the large wrought iron door knocker. He tilts his head to the side, perhaps he needs to check the lay of the land first. He turns right, follows the path around the rear of the building. The path is cluttered with wheelbarrows, bags of soil and gardening tools, it opens up into a large garden, dotted with chestnut trees, with a river beyond. Jimmy feels a twinge of envy; he has no real outside space. An abstract art installation stands in the middle of the garden, a cluster of metal tubes of varying heights; floral patterns cut through the rusting metal. The setting sun soaks them in a rich ochre light.

A glaring white light burns through the French doors, hidden by the woodshed, he stands in the half-dark, peers through the glass. The kitchen looks in disarray. Pans and plates, caked with half-eaten food, are piled high by the sink. Two swollen black plastic bags lean against an overflowing rubbish bin.

They're sat at the table, alone, between them a bottle of red wine and two glasses. Jimmy gets a better look at him, has time to take it all in. He looks older than she is, still has a full head of curly hair. And has that wide-shoulder narrow waist thing going on that the girls used to love. Always the first one to get his shirt off in the club. A six-pack before six-packs were invented.

He watches as the man rubs his forehead with the palms of his hands, sinks back into a high-backed wooden chair. A look of despair spreads across his face.

The wife jumps up, Carlo introduced them that night at the gallery – she'd been drunk, said that her husband had abandoned her. Now, she paces around the room, her fingers jabbing at his chest. Her voice muffled by the double-glazed window. Her short skirt reveals slender legs, her hair bobs about in a ponytail at the back of her head. Without makeup, she looks younger – from the back, she could be late teens. Yet when she turns... but even so, she must be at least twenty years younger than him.

Silently, Jimmy steps out of the shadows, drops to his knees, works his way towards the door, takes cover behind a large wicker table and chairs. He peers through a narrow line of vision.

Her voice rings through the glass.

'What do you mean you've got to go away for a few weeks, you've just come back, for God's sake.'

His former friend jumps up from the table, grabs hold of her arm, pulls out a chair, roughly thrusts her down into it. As he squats down on his knees, her face hardens. His voice is too low for Jimmy to hear. Her lips twist into a sulk.

'What about—'

'You'll... look...wrong...' The words leak through the glass like raindrops.

Her shoulders slump, he pulls her out of the chair and into his arms, tilts her chin up to his face, kisses her full on the lips. She pulls back, thumps his chest with her fist, he runs his fingers down her spine, kisses the nape of her neck, lifts her top. She averts her face, looks out into the darkening sky, towards Jimmy, her eyes have a vacant look, her lips set in a hard line. He eases her body onto the table, a glass of wine topples over, the dark red liquid seeps into the wood, he lowers his body on top of her, his hands move up her thighs.

Jimmy blinks, he feels like a voyeur, a pervert, some sort of freak. A shudder rides up his spine, his face flushes with embarrassment. He jerks his head away, picks up the torch, silently moves away from his hiding place, around to the front of the house.

Across the fields, the sun slips behind the horizon, a row of leafless oaks stand guard like angels of wrath.

Chapter 26

'DCI Phillips? This is a surprise.' Thomasine takes a step back into the hallway.

'Hi... I thought I'd wait—until after the funeral. I tried you at home.' She sounds breathless, as though she's been running. '... you'll have to excuse... asthma...cold weather sets it off. It's—' She stamps her feet, the base of her boots clogged with snow.

'Bloody freezing up here. I know. You'd best come in.'

'Thanks. And... call me Mel... can I call you Thom? Everyone said—'

'No problem, fine.' Unbothered by her own appearance, hair unwashed for days, a tatty black sweatshirt splattered in paint, Thomasine turns her back on her, shows her through to the kitchen.

'Thanks.' Mel pulls off her jacket, warms her hands on the fire then perches on the end of the settee. She studies the room as Thomasine makes them both a hot drink. Her breathing eases.

'It's a—'

'An old place.' There is no trace of a smile on Thomasine's face. She shrugs her shoulders, 'Mam would never invest in the place.'

Mel nods her head in understanding. 'Thanks, nice and hot,' she takes the cup out of Thomasine's hands, 'just what I need. I tried your home first then it dawned on me you'd probably be here. I thought I'd take a risk, see if you were in. I had a walk through the fields first. I hope you don't mind.'

She's been snooping. A frown creases Thomasine's forehead. She sits down solidly in her seat, wonders at what point in life her smile became a stiff upper lip. She can feel the hardening in her cheeks, the clenching of her jaw. It's this place, she tells herself. She lifts the cup to her mouth; an aroma of tea and ammonia wafts up her nostrils. Her fingernails are lined with the grime of two days' work. Peeling off wallpaper; scrubbing off the mould and damp that lay beneath it for near on forty years. Then treating it with bleach.

'Oh, I nearly forgot, I brought something.' Mel leans down, rummages in her handbag, pulls out a white paper bag. 'I hope you like doughnuts.'

Thomasine shakes her head. 'Not for me, thanks.'

Without apparent disappointment, Mel slips them back in the bag. Her eyes soften. 'I hope the funeral went okay.'

Thomasine doesn't respond, it's dangerous ground that she's not ready to dig over.

'Anyway, I thought it was time you had an update, that's the least we can do.' Her hands reach out for a cushion, then another. She nestles back into the settee, appears relaxed, comfortable. Her long legs clad in skinny black jeans and wellingtons, a russet brown cable knit jumper clings at the hips.

A microscopic flash of irritation flickers across Thomasine's face. This *making yourself at home* business feels like an intrusion. She throws another log on the fire, the room is already roasting hot, a bellow of flames flies up the chimney.

'I thought I'd give you a rundown on the Coroner's report first. Would that be okay? I don't want to patronise you but—'

'Just tell me as it is,' her lips form a hard line. 'Don't dress anything up for me.'

Mel rests her mug of coffee on her thigh, takes a moment to gather her thoughts. 'I'll do the edited version if that's alright.' She carries on without waiting for an answer. 'The radiocarbon dating tests indicate the remains were in the ground between thirty and forty years. A hair sample was taken – it was dark brown, no sign of grey. The Coroner says the remains appear to be from a female, aged between five and twenty-five, although given the length of the thigh and shin bones they are likely to be over twelve years of age. One femur is intact. Approximate height was five-foot-eight inches.'

Unexpectedly, Thomasine is consumed by a sense of relief, of detachment – this is the landscape she understands, language she's heard every day of her career. 'So, she was likely to have been in the ground since the time of her disappearance?'

Mel nods her head. 'Most likely, although of course, we can't prove that at this moment. Sadly, about twenty-five percent of your sister's remains are either lost or deteriorated.' Her voice drops a tone, 'There were some animal bones caught up in the remains.' They both know what that means. Scavengers fighting— Thomasine blanks the images out as quickly as they come.

'The rear of the skull shows damage. We can't ascertain at this moment in time whether she was killed there or somewhere else.' Mel hesitates for a moment, rubs at an invisible spot on her denim jeans. 'We've found remnants of what we believe are her underwear and her shoes. So far, we've not been able to find any other clothing. There is no way of knowing—' Her face darkens, 'anyway, the Coroner said that injuries to the rear of the skull indicate that that part of the skull may have been a weak spot, the bone less dense. She could have just hit her head on something, it could have been an accident.'

The fire crackles, pops, spits out an ember. Thomasine gets to her feet and stubs it out with the heel of her boot. 'Sorry, go on.'

'There was no need for facial reconstruction as the upper jaw was intact and had already been matched against Karen's dental records. As you probably know, she had four premolar teeth removed eight weeks prior to her disappearance. Metal fillings in the lower left molar and lower right pre-molar are a full match.' Her head drops, she picks up her mug.

'Unfortunately, the tree root system did a lot of damage to her skeleton. The excavators did further damage.'

Mel is silent for a moment, Thomasine watches her facial expressions, she can tell Mel is gathering her thoughts.

'What I'm going to tell you next is confidential.' She holds up her hand, 'sorry if that sounds condescending, that's not my intent. I'm going to ask you to keep this to yourself.' Thomasine knows what is coming. 'I know how close—'

'You don't have to finish that sentence,' Thomasine's eyes lock in on hers.

'Fine, I'll leave it at that. A single gold circular hoop sleeper earring was found amongst the debris, there was no DNA on it, nothing in the records indicates that Karen had a pair of earrings like that.'

She waits for confirmation.

'Karen had her ears pierced for her birthday. We'll need to check her jewellery box. If Mam were—' A squall of wind sucks at the window, 'I'll find out somehow.'

'I'm sorry, Thom. I'm trying to find my way here. It's the first time I've dealt with a situation like this.' She puts the mug of coffee down on the floor. 'I checked Veronica Lightfoot's case file. It appears she was wearing a pair like that the weekend she disappeared.'

Thomasine sits up straight. Mel waits for her to ask her to leave.

'So, what's next then?'

'Next?' Mel feels thrown off course, she expected an argument, a heated response at least. *Did she already know?* Thomasine's face is impassive.

'I know Rosie is your friend but that shouldn't get in the way of the investigation, should it?'

A knot of irritation fills Thomasine's chest. 'I know she was wearing earrings when she disappeared. I've read Veronica Lightfoot's missing person report hundreds of times. I could probably recite it word for word. I'm not one for jumping to conclusions. What I've heard about Veronica, from her sister and mother, is that murdering my sister is the last thing she would do.'

'Okay…' Mel sits back in her chair, lets out a breath, 'let's start again then. Let's focus on Karen. I'd like to ask you about the night Karen disappeared.'

'That may be a problem.'

'Why would that be?'

The air seems to go out of her lungs, Thomasine shakes her head. 'I was eight-years-old. I've had nightmares for years, I've no idea of what the truth is and what's not.' Stone-faced, she folds her arms across her chest. 'And the second?'

'I know you'll have been expecting this. I'd like to have a look around the house, and the outbuildings. I've seen the initial investigation files, there are huge gaps that need filling.'

'Okay, when do we start?'

'This week sometime, we'll ring first.

Thomasine has the overwhelming urge to tell her to piss off, instead she says 'Okay,' unfolds her arms, rests them by her side.

Mel picks up her coat, shrugs it on. 'I'd better be off. We'll see you within the next couple of days.'

'You bet you will.' Thomasine is already in the hallway, mind racing, her hand on the lock of the front door.

Mel walks out into the yard, pivots on her heels. 'The dogs? I assumed you had dogs?' Her eyes stop on the large kennel outside the barn.

The question catches Thomasine off guard, her face fell. 'We did... she did, Mam that is. Poison... that's what I think anyway, the vet's doing tests. Probably the press, I wouldn't put anything past them.'

'Oh, God, I'm sorry. Have you any idea who—'

'No, but when I find out I wouldn't like to be them.' Thomasine tries to stop the tears from reaching her eyes. Too late, she wipes them away with the sleeve of her jumper.

'When did—'

'The funeral, the morning of the funeral.'

Mel shakes her head, lets out a sigh.

'I'm so sorry, I don't know what to say.'

Thomasine waits for a second or two, lets the silence hang between them. 'I'll be ready tomorrow, tell them to ring me beforehand. On the landline—I've had it repaired. It's hard to get a mobile signal around here.'

Thomasine watches Mel do a slippery three-point turn in the yard. It occurs to her as the car disappears down the track – the box of Veronica's things that Rosie kept under the stairs at her place; the magazines, the clothes, the jewellery, the flier for the all-nighter. She could have handed them over. She should have called her immediately, not even opened the box. But there you go, she thinks to herself, that was probably never going to happen. What the hell, she'll give them to whoever turns up to process the house and deal with whatever shit happens.

Then she changes her mind, she'll drop them off, now. It will be one small point in her favour.

She places the box in the boot of her car, shuts the front door behind her.

What if the search team turn up tomorrow?

Her heart sinks. If that's the case she's got sixteen hours to search the house before they do and she's going to need every one of them.

Chapter 27

DS Sam Ingleby's six-foot-five frame leans over the evidence table. Forensics have already done their work, DNA, fibres, fingerprints all taken and in process. He checks his watch, takes the notebook out of his inside pocket and flips it open. He writes the words *Hit and Run* and the date at the top of a new page.

His latex gloves make a snapping noise as he slips them on. 'Let's see what we have here then.' He's a man who talks to himself often, his voice has a soft Geordie lilt that gives him an advantage in interviews. People warm to him, even criminals. A smile rises to his face. There was no ID on the body, that almost always makes it more interesting for him.

Before him sits a large grey container with a yellow label, recently emptied of its contents. The victim's belongings – each item labelled, bagged, sealed and documented by the officer who'd attended the crime. Their shift now over, they are on their way home for the night. Home to their family, unlike DS Ingleby, who has another twelve-hour shift to conquer.

He works from the left, picking up each item, jotting down notes as the need takes him. Each item equidistant from the one above, to the right, to the left and below.

Rucksack, black, make Jack Wolfskin. Straps probably cut off by the on-scene medics. Before moving on to the next item, he checks the pockets and inside, everything has been removed.

Self-defence spray, small, pink, no branding. The sparkling pink metal container disguised as a tin of deodorant glistens in the glare of the overhead lighting – a self-defence spray, not illegal but the results are painful, a stinging that would last for hours.

Torch, yellow, heavy, make Varta. *That probably hurt her back when she rolled off the bonnet, poor bugger. That one thing probably did more damage than anything else.* He winces in sympathy. *Other than the car and concrete kerb.*

A pair of knitting needles. *Nasty weapons if in the wrong hands. Stabbings, gougings, rammed in places too awful to think about. The knitting pattern is a smoke screen. She must have thought that would help if she got picked up, got caught for whatever she was doing.*

A key ring with four keys attached, one of which is sharpened at the point. His eyes focus in on what looks like a copper coin. *Is that a running medal attached?*

He grits his teeth. An itch starts from his nose and rises to the crown of his head, an allergy to latex gloves that drives him crazy. Like a cat with fleas, the urge to scratch himself is overwhelming. He is completely aware that a single unconscious act like that can contaminate evidence. He learnt his lesson early on. He wriggles his nose and focuses on the task in hand. Questions pop into his head.

Why no phone? Where's her handbag? Where's her purse?

Carefully, he places each item of evidence back in the cardboard box before starting on his next task. Beneath the table, in a couple of transparent tamper evident bags, is the victim's clothing. Almost shredded to pieces by the medics, the only way of ascertaining and treating injury. Now dry, they are stained with the victim's own blood.

He checks the label. A frown creases his forehead. It's not been processed by forensics yet. He goes through each item of clothing with the same level of detail that had earned him high praise during training. After examining each one, he jots down a few words in his notebook.

One size ten, black, knee-length parka, fur hood, make Jack Wolfskin. Blood stains on hood and chest. A hard, oblong object in the outside left-hand pocket – a mobile phone. Black – make Bang. A taser. He knows this because he's seen them before, the *go-to* weapon brandished by local drug dealers.

One pair of size five, black, trail shoes, make Solomon. Laces cut (A & E?).

One pair of size six-to-eight woollen socks, make Bridgedale. They reek of damp wool and talcum powder.

One pair of waterproof trousers, black, size and make unknown – label removed. Leg length medium? Pockets empty. Cuts to the legs and groin area (A & E?). Blood stains on knee and shin areas.

One black fleece, Polar, size ten, cuts to the front and back (A & E?).

One black running bra, size ten-to-twelve, make M & S. Cuts to material (A & E?).

One pair of black panties, size ten-to-twelve, make M & S. Cuts to material (A & E?).

He lets out a long breath through his nose. Someone should have gone through the hospital bag by now, processed everything. Even a matter of hours can make a difference. The weather shouldn't be an excuse, but he knows it will be. This is one of five car accidents reported this evening. He looks at the evidence label, recognises the name, scribbles it in his notebook. There's been some mislabelling too. He'll have a severe word with the officer in question, someone who should have known better. They should be more aware of the *look-a-likey* weapons readily available on the internet. Items which, to the uninitiated, would seem harmless.

He completes the chain of custody label then pulls off his latex gloves. His conscious mind already making a mental composite. *Good quality clothes, slender, about five six, outdoor type.* He imagines her loading up the rucksack, one item after the other. Questions run through his head again. Did she do that every day? Was this a one-off? What was she afraid of? Who was she afraid of? Is she a victim or an aggressor – he's not sure yet. First things first, a name. They had put a rush on the fingerprints and DNA. With any luck, the results will be on his desk when he gets back. Although he knows the chances of that are almost zero.

Chapter 28

I cannot see.

I hear him breathing, the monster behind a mask that hides his true self, his lungs like bellows howl.

He towers above me. Above us. The earth shudders as his boot hits the shoulder of the blade, the shovel's sharp edge slicing through the soil, lifting it up, pushing deep into the dirt again. I cannot flinch, he must not know that I am awake, if he does—that spade, he'll use it on me. He used it on her. I saw it. My heart pounds so loud I am terrified he will hear it, hers so silent it makes my own beat out of time.

My mouth and throat are filled with something I cannot swallow. I must not cough it out, he will hear the wrack of my throat, he will see the rise and fall of my ribs. I must not move at all, the ground above me, around me, may shift, may give me away.

I see people moving between the roots of the trees, their fingers probing, touching. The pain in my head wants to be let out. He stops… a second later he starts again, digging, sniffing, his words come out in spurts. None of them repentant, frontal lobe, glabella, parietal, he speaks a language I don't understand.

The other girl stirs, her face pressed against mine, the curve of her lips on my lips, her skin cooling. Her fingers curl around mine; her eyes open.

'Veronica…Veronica.'

Who is Veronica?

Things crawl over me, scratch me, prick my skin like needles, slither their way in my ears and eyes, slide up my nostrils. The earth, writhing with life, wants to consume me. I want to scream out, every nerve in body trembles, every cell keeps me where I am, keeps me silent, a statue made of human blood.

He stops, there is quiet.

I hear a hissing sound then a Thump. Thump. Thump. Like some bird stamping up worms, he levels the ground above me – us. I hear the scrape of his boots on a tree root; the spade falls to the floor.

I do not breath. Must not breathe. My lungs are filled with air without my intervention.

Am I dead?

They stand around me, look down at me. They are listening. And so is he.

Chapter 29

The following morning, Mel receives two text messages. One from Thomasine Albright, informing her that Rosie Lightfoot had discovered a box of Veronica's belongings from her mother's house. She'd passed them to Thomasine, who'd dropped them off at the front desk.

Mel blows out a sigh. So, this was how it was going to be, Thomasine messing where she shouldn't. She'd thought she'd made it clear, obviously not. Why hadn't she given them to her when she visited the farm? Probably didn't want an argument or a reprimand for tampering with evidence. She shakes her head, hopes that nothing is amiss, wonders if Thomasine and Rosie had been looking for the match to the earring that had been discovered amongst the remains. She hopes there's nothing important in there. If there is she'll have a hell of a time explaining that to the CPS.

The second message is from DS Sam Ingleby asking if she can contact him immediately.

I wonder what he wants? She punches back a response.

'Hi Sam, what do you want? I'm still at work. Mel.'

The text is short, to the point and puts the matter, whatever it is, back in his court. She and Sam worked together on the Barker case. *How many years since I've seen Sam? Two, three?* She knows it's more than a year since they've spoken. No argument between them, life moves on and they'd been working on different jobs. An ugly memory long blocked out materialises in her head: four years ago, last June. Sam lying prone on the ground, the stink of old coins in her nostrils, bright red blood, a river, then a lake, eating its way through his white shirt. He'd been trying to get to his feet, he didn't even know he'd been stabbed.

A teenage girl, strung out on meth, mumbling to herself, crouched over him, a breadknife in her hand. He'd tried to talk her off the bridge above the motorway. She swearing he'd tried to rape her. Hallucinating. Screaming it was his fault. Raising the knife above her head.

Full force, Mel's foot missed the knife, the heel of her boot hit the girl full in the face, cracked her cheekbone, broke her nose. There'd been blood everywhere. His blood, the girl's blood. Mel's blood as she grabbed at the blade of the knife and wrenched it from the girl's hand.

The IPCC cleared her six months later. The girl is now serving eight years for the attempted murder of a police officer, the penalty reduced because of mitigating circumstances, her age and psychological state. It had pissed them both off.

She and Sam got on with their everyday lives, both unwilling to raise the matter, neither wanting any form of indebtedness, any form of guilt. They'd been tested for Aids, for Hep C. Both still subject to regular checks.

Mel knew that Sam would never have touched a crackhead. She'd been with him the whole time. She reaches out and takes a mouthful of the milky coffee Badger had made an hour ago.

Her lips twist. 'Ugh!' The coffee, stone cold, turns her stomach.

It's late, the outer office is deserted, lights off, the team have gone home for the night. She leans forward, rests her elbows on the desk. Her eyes ache from staring into the computer for the last forty minutes. The notes from her interview with Thomasine Albright almost finished. She'd been right in her estimation, she remembered very little of that night.

The cardboard box that Thomasine Albright dropped off earlier has been processed by a member of the team. There was nothing of real interest – half a dozen teenage magazines, clothes, makeup, nail varnish, jewellery – none of the earrings matched the one found at the crime scene. The details are written up on a second board, waiting. Waiting for what, she wonders? She isn't sure how any of it links to the Karen Albright investigation. The hooped gold sleeper earring found in the remains could have been either girl; both had pierced ears. It was the size of a pound coin, men and women wore them. It could belong to the killer. It could belong to Veronica; there was no way of proving it at this present time, any DNA long gone.

Her phone bursts into life, she grabs at it to stop the noise. Sam Ingleby clearly is in a hurry; his words rush out in a babble of excitement. He is investigating a hit and run. The victim, a woman, had no ID on her; they'd rushed fingerprint and DNA analysis. He pauses for breath then carries on.

'There's a DNA match, Mel. I think you'll be interested. The PNC flagged it up as a missing person, someone wanted in connection with an on-going investigation.' His voice gives away the smile on his face. He had always been that way with her, the joker, always wanting to reel her in. 'Guess who?'

'Come on then,' the tension eases, 'spill the beans, it's getting late, who is it?'

He's unwilling to give up. 'Who do you think it might be?'

Her heart thuds against her ribs. The left side of her brain kicks in.

'You're joking, aren't you?'

'Nope.'

'Are you taking the piss?'

'I'm a professional police officer, DCI Phillips, why would I do that?'

'Is she still alive?'

'Just. She's in the neurosurgical unit at the Royal Salford.'

'Can I meet you there in thirty minutes?'

'I can meet you in five, I'm downstairs on reception.'

'I'll come to get you.'

Thirty minutes later she was fully briefed, five minutes after that her request for him to be seconded to her team had been agreed. Two linked lines of enquiry and she would oversee both.

The hospital corridor is filled with noise – the ringing of phones, the murmur of voices, the click and ping of equipment, the sound of footsteps on the linoleum floor. People in white coats and sky-blue uniforms stream by her. Mel leans against the wall, a red foolscap file under her arm, head dipped, she flicks through the messages on her mobile phone.

Without warning the door opposite jerks open. The consultant, a lean man in a tailored black suit hurries through. Long blond dreads cluster behind his neck.

'Brandon De Costa. I'm one of the Lead Clinicians in the Neurosurgical Unit.' His dark brown eyes focus in on her. 'The patient is under my care.'

His accent throws her off centre, he reads the look on her face, a smile rises to his lips. He lets out a low laugh.

'For some reason, people are always surprised by my accent – I'm a white Barbadian.' He proffers his hand, she grasps it in her own and returns his smile.

'DCI Mel Phillips – born in Manchester, mother Italian. The victim has been listed as a missing person since 1973, we are very eager to talk with her as you can imagine.'

A look of surprise flickers across his face. 'Right, well. That might not be for some time.' He squints at her, nods his head. 'We have an office just along here on the right, we can talk there.' He takes off at a pace. 'I'm sorry, I don't have long, though.'

He holds the door open for her, lets her through first. Mel looks around the room, it's the size of a public toilet and just as welcoming. Sparsely furnished, there are three hard-backed chairs tucked around an arm's length circular table. In the bay of the window is a coffee machine, beside it a pack of bottled waters.

'Would you like a drink?'

'Thanks – just water.'

He hands her a bottle from the pack. 'No glasses, I'm afraid.'

She places the foolscap file on the table, takes a long gulp from the water bottle then wipes her mouth. 'I'd like you to describe the extent of her injuries if you would, and if possible, give me an idea of when we can expect to be able talk with her? If I can just say that at first, we thought it was a straightforward hit and run, an accident influenced by the weather. Now we have intelligence that leads us to believe there might be other factors at play.'

Brandon Da Costa puts his elbows on the table, leans forward. Mel wonders how long he has been at work, his eyelids flutter as though he's struggling to keep them open.

'Other factors?'

She looks him directly in the face. *He's not going to like this.* 'I'm truly sorry but I'm not at liberty to say at this moment in time.'

His mouth hardens, he balances his chin on his fist, lets out a sigh. 'And her name?'

Mel shakes her head, 'Not even that at this present time – I'm sorry.'

He lets out another sigh. 'In layman's terms, the head injury was severe. We've put her in a medically induced coma that should reduce the swelling on the brain and allow us to treat her injuries. It would be imprudent to comment on whether or not she'll be in a position to talk, if ever.' He looks down at his watch. His eyelids flutter again. 'My shift is due to finish in about thirty minutes, I need to do a handover before I leave. Sorry, but that's it.'

'We understand, truly we do. I won't keep you long. Could you tell me about this?' She takes the medical report out of the foolscap file she'd laid between them. She points to a paragraph near the bottom of page one.

He nods his head, reads the paragraph in question. 'There's evidence of pre-existing injuries. Probably a physical attack. We see that sort of injury all the time. Mainly in women – domestic abuse. Her nose has been broken; it looks like she's had surgery to repair it. Three of her fingers on her right hand have been broken, they don't appear to have reset properly and it's likely she didn't have full use of her hand in that regard. I've got the x-rays if you'd like to see them. All the injuries are roughly of the same age.'

Mel flicks open her notebook, jots down a few notes.

'And could you just talk me through this,' she points to a long paragraph at the end of page two. 'The one relating to the brain injury. The technical terms, just so I understand.'

He nods his head. She notices small patches of skin bare on his scalp. *Alopecia?*

Five minutes later they are finished, the consultant stands up, puts his arms above his head, stretches from side to side.

'My back doesn't like me sitting down for long,' he says with a thin smile, his humour slowly returning.

'Thanks for all your help. I realise you're pressed for time.'

'She's up having a CT scan right now; that will give us more detail, especially about the head injury.'

'Thank you for that, it was very helpful indeed. When do you think she can be brought out of the coma?'

'It's a "wait and see" process.'

'As soon as you plan to do it, could you let me know?'

'Of course. And I'd like her name as soon as possible.'

She nods her head, offers him her card. 'You can contact me on that.' The consultant hesitates for a moment, places the card in the top pocket of his coat. Moments later they both disappear down the corridor, he turns right for the Neurological Unit, and she left – for the exit.

Chapter 30

Chemicals whoosh around her body like leaves in a flood, reality and nightmare swirl in the current.

Her eyelids are swollen shut.

She pulls her knees away from her chest. She can barely breathe. Her feet catch against cold metal. A thick nylon carpet scratches the skin on her thigh. She's lying on her side. There's something behind her. She can't reach it.

Her mouth is full of blood… her blood… the sticky sweetness covers her tongue. She tries to spit it out. Her front teeth are loose against her top lip. Someone has hurt her. She can't remember who they are or why they did it. Shadows rush by her, they pull and tug at her hair.

Broken—she knows she is broken, broken bones and something else, something so terrifying she has blocked it out completely. She cannot keep in the loud wail that sears through her every nerve. Her left hand traps the noise from escaping her mouth, as if only her fingers know that she needs to be saved from herself. As though only they know that whoever did this to her is still near.

Waiting.

The tips of her fingers move over her face. The bridge of her nose loosens to her touch. A sickening pain pulses up through her forehead. She wants to cry out, beat her fists against the hard-metal roof above her. She's going to die. Whatever they plan to do with her. Whoever they are. It will be bad. She must get out of there. The only senses she has are hearing and touch. And even touch hurts. She cannot unfold the fingers of her right hand. Not without pain.

She holds her breath, hears an engine. Then music, louder and louder, by each turn of the wheel. The bass so loud that her eardrums hurt. She screams out for help, the music starts again, it jars her bones.

'Please let me out, please let me out…' she sobs the words out repeatedly. Her words are nothing to the beats of the music.

She runs her hands down over her chest and thighs. She's naked except for her knickers and bra. Her mouth goes dry – a feeling of dread saturates her; what happened to her clothes? Who took them? Why can't she remember any of this? What did they do to her? What has she done?

The car stops suddenly. She falls back against something. A sack? She tries to feel what is behind her, the fingers of her left-hand wriggle and probe through her thighs, there's something there. There's something soft, there's material, that's what it is. Her fingertips brush against the weave. Her heart bashes against her chest. She knows what it is. It's a coat. They've put someone else in here with her. It must be the girl she'd heard screaming. She's quiet now – too quiet. She touches her leg.

'Are you awake?'

The engine roars, the car leaps forward again.

'Are you okay? We've got to get out of here.' Her words clogged by blood and loose teeth. 'Come on, wake up!' She's got to rouse them, she leans back, nudges them in the stomach with her elbow. There's an urgency she cannot control. She's sure it's the girl. Perhaps they've been knocked out. Perhaps they were both knocked out. *Did he put something over my face?* Were they drugged? She can't remember.

If only she can bring her round. They can help each other escape. If there are two of them, they'll be stronger. They can do that; she knows they can. All they must do is to pretend to be dead.

She inches herself over onto her left side, her knees scrape against metal. She faces her, faces it. Tentatively she reaches out, her fingers find a pair of shoeless stone-cold feet. She pushes her knees against the girl's chest, tries to hurt her awake, she tries time and time again; her voice is hoarse from screaming. Why can't she wake her?

Wake up! Wake up! She screams until she has no breath left.

It's her fault—it must be her fault. The girl was alive earlier – she'd woken up and cried for help. Then something must have happened. What? What happened? Now the girl is dead. It must be her fault. It must be.

The monitor above her head skips a beat, then another, before falling back into rhythm.

'Just a dream, it will be just a dream,' says the nurse as she carefully smears Vaseline on Veronica's lips. 'A nice dream.'

Chapter 31

Mel picks at her teeth with the nail of her little finger, a remnant of her breakfast bagel stuck between her upper left premolars. 'Family Liaison contacted the Lightfoots yet?'

Badger nods his head. 'They spoke to the sister. The mother isn't well – she has Dementia or Alzheimer's.' Dark-haired, the flash of white hair in his widow's peak gives him the unique appearance that's earned him his nickname.

A look of sadness crosses Mel's face. After years of waiting, Jeannie Lightfoot was unlikely to comprehend that her daughter had been found alive, just. 'We'll need to interview the sister at some point, leave it a day or two – let the news settle.' She moves out of her office into the incident room, eases her bottom onto the edge of a desk. The team are already in place for the day's briefing.

'Right, team, according to the files, Veronica went missing after work on Friday the fifth of January 1973. Karen Alright disappeared from the bedroom she shared with her sister, Thomasine Albright between nine p.m. on the sixth and seven p.m. the following morning. They lived within three or four miles of each other. Records show that Veronica's work colleagues stated they thought she was going clubbing with some friends. She was eighteen at the time she went missing, lived with her grandmother in Englewick. A village six miles from the burial site. It wasn't unusual for Veronica to stay out over the weekend. Back then, her grandmother said she'd normally turn up on Sunday afternoon, just after two o'clock. She had no idea where Veronica used to go other than she thought she'd been staying over at a friend's house and that they'd been to a nightclub. There were several clubs in Bolton at that time.'

Sam pulls his face out of his cup of coffee. 'No phone calls?'

'No, no phone at home, not unusual back then,' she carries on. 'Karen Albright had not long turned fifteen, she lived on her parent's farm up on the moors. According to the families, Veronica and Karen didn't know each other. Different schools, different ages. At the time, no witnesses came forward for either case, there was the odd bit of gossip, but nothing substantiated. The officer investigating the disappearance of Veronica Lightfoot thought she was a runaway. He even made a note on file. He said she was a drug user, he found some Dexedrine tablets in her belongings at her parents' house. Her mother denied that at the time. She said Veronica didn't do drugs and nor would she run away from her grandmother. She said they were too close for that. She also said that the tablets definitely hadn't been there before the search. She complained but no one listened.

So, what else do we have?'

Badger holds up his hand. 'That's it for the moment. We're waiting on some Section 29s so we can access the medical files.'

Twenty minutes later Sam knocks on Mel's door. 'Some hairdresser has fronted up, holding onto the front page of the newspaper. Says he lives next door to her, recognised the coat. One of his girls has one just like it. They've not really spoken much; her cat is always in and out of his place though.' Arms folded, he stands half in, half out of her office, his back leaning against the frame, 'I got a Warrant signed by Dave Forbes.' He looks at the pile of interview notes on her desk. 'I know you're busy but—'

'Definitely.' Mel puts down her pen, gets to her feet, grabs her handbag. 'No time like the present.'

Veronica Lightfoot's home is like a Christmas card. Red bricked with white shutters at the windows and a topiarised olive tree either side of a shiny black door.

'A nice picture of suburbia, isn't it?' says Sam, closing the gate behind them. The front garden, drenched in snow, is littered with tiny paw prints. Fleetingly, he wonders if the chap next door has taken in the cat like he promised.

They each pull on a pair of latex gloves. Mel drops her head down to look at the locking mechanism on the door, a Yale deadlock. She recognises it. Pulls the evidence bag from her pocket. Four keys dangle from the running medal keyring. Two brass keys and two small silver ones. Both sets appear identical, but experience has taught her that they probably aren't. She tries one of the brass keys, it sticks, then tries the other, the lock releases, the door opens with a high-pitched squeak. Her right-hand reaches for the light switch. A pale-yellow glow emanates from an expensive-looking shade hanging from an ornamental ceiling rose. And bleach, she'd know it anywhere, the smell so strong it catches in her throat.

She steps inside, stands still for a moment, takes in the silence, lets it wash over her. Her eyes skim over the surfaces, the hallway is well-cared for, not a speck of dust on the skirting, no scratches on the walls. The floor is laid with original tiles, geometric shapes in blues, browns, blacks and pale cream. Against the left wall is an oak staircase; the ornate bannister running up to the first floor and along the upper hall; the candy twist spindles gleam with polish. Mel nods to herself, even the runners on the stair carpet have been restored.

She hears a cough behind her and she takes a step forward.

'Oooh, very nice, this must have cost a few bob.' Sam stamps his feet on the front doorstep, then bends over to put on a pair of overshoes, he hands a pair to Mel.

'Looks like a show home to me.' Mel drops the keyring back into the evidence bag and returns it to her jacket pocket. She leans against the doorframe as she slips on the overshoes. 'Let's have a look around then, you do upstairs, I'll do down here.'

She slides open the drawers of the hallway table, her fingers slowly move around the contents. Charger cables, safety pins, pens. In the next drawer, a Garmin running watch, an unopened packet of Power Beans.

Sam takes the stairs one at a time, careful not to put his hand on the handrail. Mel opens the first door on the right, into the living room. The décor is creams, natural fabrics – a wood burning stove sits in a contemporary fireplace. A badly folded lilac throw lies over the back of the settee, it looks out of place, out of order in a room that appears, at first glance, so very orderly. On the side table, there is a pile of magazines, on top of them a manual for an alarm system. She cocks her head, listens.

Oh shit! Probably set on silent.

She walks back into the hallway. The alarm box is set behind the door.

That's why we missed it.

There are no flashing lights, no lights at all. It's not been set. As she turns, she spots an envelope hanging from the letterbox. A charity fundraiser by the look of it. It's addressed to a Lily Probis her. She takes out her phone, takes a photograph of it, lays the envelope on the hallway table.

Lily Probisher – lodger? Previous tenant?

She goes back into the living room, casts her eyes over the walls, nothing personal, no photographs. She hears the toilet flush.

Shit! Stupid bastard, why did he do that?

She knows, he knows, that peeing on the street is more appropriate than peeing on or in anything related to a criminal investigation, or in this case, the home of a victim. She goes upstairs, sees him exiting the bathroom, his fingers doing up his flies. The colour drained from his face.

'Sorry I couldn't wait. I'm still getting…' He shuffles back into the toilet, his hand on the buckle of his belt. He shouts through the door, 'The wife's got the Norovirus, I think—'

'Spare me the details,' her voice is emphatic.

Beyond the bathroom are two rooms. Mel enters the one on the right. It's sparsely furnished: a double bed, pastel colours, no wardrobe, no cupboards, one bedside table, a dressing table. She checks the back of the door, key on the inside, four bolts above the lock.

'There's something off in this room,' she says to herself. 'You can tell there are no kids; this place is bloody spotless.'

She jumps, her heart races. 'For *God's* sake, don't creep around behind me.'

'Sorry.' A glum look spreads across Sam's face.

'Never mind. Her eyes rove around the room. 'The last time my place was as clean as this was when I bought it. I'm not even convinced we'll find any fingerprints in here.' She gestures towards the door. 'Someone is afraid of someone getting in.'

Sam raises an eyebrow, 'A lot of locks for a bedroom.'

The room next door has a wall of fitted wardrobes, all with clear glass sliding doors and no other furniture. There are vacuum marks on the oatmeal carpet.

Mel goes downstairs. The kitchen is much the same, pristine, not a crumb in sight. Three large Velux windows let in the light. A neatly laid out garden looks in through folding doors. The white quartz worktops are bare of clutter, not even a kettle. The hardwood floor gleams like a chestnut. Sleek white gloss cupboard doors run along one wall. In the centre of the room, an island unit houses a sink and a six-ring hob.

I'd kill for a kitchen like this, thinks Mel to herself, running her fingers over the worktop. Everything about this place reeks of someone with a whole host of personality problems. Someone with an unquenchable desire for control.

Sam opens cupboard after cupboard. Each one an example of organised living; cups stacked one upon another – every handle off to the right, tins of food in date order, crystal glasses sorted by shape and size, see-through plastic boxes filled with a variety of breakfast foods, cornflakes, muesli, shredded wheat, all side by side, all full, in date and labelled in neat capital letters.

Mel opens the dishwasher, there is nothing inside. It's the cleanest dishwasher she has ever seen. She sniffs inside it – bleach.

'Are the rooms you checked like this?'

Sam gives a thin smile. 'From what I saw, yes. Not a thing out of place. I get little sense of who lives here, it's weird, everything is too clean, too orderly. There's a library or study upstairs, the shelves filled with self-help books. Hundreds of them. All in plastic covers and filed in alphabetical order.'

'Self-help?' She raises an eyebrow. 'What about the other bedrooms – anything in the drawers, under the bed?'

'Not anything that tells us much about her, you don't need to be a shrink to know she has a serious case of OCD. Either that or she has a bloody good cleaner and I'd like her name. Even her knicker drawer is sorted by colour. Oh—' The blood drains from his face, he puts his hand over his stomach, goes for his belt, sprints up the stairs again.

As the door to bathroom slams shut, she hears him let out a groan. She looks under the sink for a bottle of bleach just in case.

A dark shape catches her eye. A thin black and white cat, tail erect, presses itself up against the French windows, it stands on its hind legs, cries to be let in.

She hunts around in the drawers for a key before noticing it was already in the door. As she opens it up, the cat shoots between her legs and up the stairs.

Sam's footsteps sound behind her, she turns to see him walking down the stairs, cat under one arm, a book in his free hand.

'Self-Help? I thought you might need this,' he hands her the book. *The Paradigm Shift – What if I'm Addicted to Me?* is typed in big letters on the front cover, he grins. 'It's got five-star reviews, says so on the back.'

'You *cheeky* bastard!' she lets out low laugh, shakes her head, hands the book back to him. 'I hope you've flushed and cleaned the toilet.'

Sam nods his head, strokes the cat's back, before shutting it in the kitchen. She checks her watch; they've been there nearly an hour.

'We'll get a team of CSIs to come back and process the place properly.'

'What about the cat?'

'Not me.' She can already feel the wheeze in her chest.

'I know,' he looks her in the eye, 'allergic. I suppose I'll have to take care of it then.'

She smiles. 'You can always ring the RSPCA tomorrow morning. By the way, I found this,' she shows him the photograph of the envelope. 'Someone called Lily Probisher either lives, or has lived, here.'

'Could be a lodger?'

'That's what I thought too.'

'Or,' their voices chime together, 'an assumed name.'

'Very likely. Maybe this isn't *just* a hit and run after all,' says Sam.

Mel notices a twinkle in his eye. She hopes the Sam she used to know is on his way back.

Chapter 32

The incident team hadn't turned up to the search the house. Relieved, Thomasine doesn't ring to find out why not. By four o'clock, dead on her feet, she plonks herself down on the settee in the kitchen. She wolfs down a piece of toast and marmite.

As always, she'd been fastidious, there was no sign whatsoever of the diary.

She let out a groan of frustration. Like the kitchen and front room, every nook and cranny of the house is filled with miscellanea. Staplers, pencils, rubbers, small notebooks covered in her mother's looping scrawl, appointments cards – years out of date, reminders from the vets, recipes cut from the back of Weetabix boxes, crossword puzzle books half completed and thrown aside. Then she started upstairs – her mother's bedroom cramped with yet more hand-me-downs. Three-legged bedside tables nestle against the double bed. Half-open dusky pink curtains allow a glimpse of the tops. Either side of the window, a six-drawer chest stands tall; wedding gifts – one from each side of the family. In the far corner of the room an ornate commode that had been her great-great grandmother's lies, covered in dust, thankfully empty. Opposite it a linen press crammed with woollen blankets. The stench of camphor and damp stung her eyes and cloyed in her throat as she opened it up. She'd slammed the lid shut immediately, leaving that for another day.

Other than in their own bedroom, Karen's room, there was only one place, the loft. It was the first place the police had checked, back in 1973. After the missing person's bedroom, it's always the next place Thomasine herself heads for when on a case.

Pulse racing, sweat running down her back. It's always the same, dark places set her on edge.

Thomasine wipes the crumbs of toast off her lips, washes them down with the last dregs of tea. *Best not to put it off. Best to do it now. Best to be professional.* Those nagging voices she knows so well reverberate in her head. She grabs the large black torch she'd found on the top shelf of the pantry and makes for the stairs. The loft is accessed via the upstairs landing, between the bedrooms, a narrow door with a set of wooden steps behind it. Jammed shut by a cast iron bolt with a brass handle.

She hasn't been up there since she was a child. Her mouth goes dry, her feet root to the spot. She tries to blink away the memory. Karen's high-pitched voice pierces her ears, her fingers sliding shut the bolt. 'Don't you go up in the loft, Thom… it's private. Only Mam and Dad can go in there,' her eyes widen, her lips pull into a grin, 'and me of course.' Then she'd flounced her way downstairs, leaving Thomasine alone, in front of the door, in front of temptation. She must have been about four, perhaps five-years-old at the time – always curious, into everything, easy to wind up, set running like a clockwork toy. She'd reached on her tiptoes, her chubby fingers slid back the lock. The door creaked open, she snuck inside.

Without warning, a fist slammed into her back. She pitched head first into the darkness, hitting the side of her face on the steps. The door behind her banged shut.

Thomasine brushes her forefinger over her left cheek, runs it over the blemish above her cheekbone – the scar, less than a few millimetres long yet her eyes rarely missed it when she looked in the mirror.

'I told… you… *not* to go in there,' Karen's voice muffled by a scratching noise as she stuffed the narrow gap between the floor and door with a rolled-up newspaper. The weak band of light snuffed out.

She'd pleaded to come out. Said she was sorry. Said she'd never do it again. She thought it was a joke. Karen was always playing jokes on her. Her words were greeted by silence.

Her parents oblivious to her plight, dipping the sheep in the lower field.

Eventually, Karen had let her out, open-palmed she slapped Thomasine full in the face. Told her that it was a lesson that she'd better learn from.

'Never, ever,' she gripped her by the shoulders, 'disobey my orders again.'

The memory hovers between herself and door like a ghost.

Her fingers pull back the bolt; the door swings open. She tips the beam of the torch upwards into the roof space. As she treads on the top step—the wood squeals out in pain. She freezes. Flashes the beam of the torch up to the ceiling, waits for the flurry of black wings – bats. She hates them. Nothing moves.

The noise, she'd not expected the noise. The chattering swirls around her, it's the Southerly wind hitting the roof, pulling at the tiles, letting them fall as it makes its way across the valley, towards the coast.

The size of the loft surprises her, it's huge. Six heavy oak beams strain under the weight of a sagging roof. There's a proper floor, though she can barely see a plank of it.

A dank, yeasty odour fills her nose. The bright light of the torch seeks out the source of the smell, a rack of old clothes, two floor-length fur coats, matted with spider webs and dead flies.

Chinks of light squint through broken tiles and rotting timber. On the ceiling, large patches of mould eat at the plaster – huge swathes of black fungi. A tight band of pain stretches across her forehead. The thought of replacing the roof. Even just repairing it will cost a fortune.

'What the hell!'

A pair of yellow eyes glow in the shadows. A fox, half-bald, its jaws wide open. A stuffed animal. Blood rushes in her ears; she can hear the boom of her heartbeat. In the same box, a stoat standing on its hind-legs, a dog lying curled up in sleep.

The further in she goes, the more ancient and decrepit it gets. A child's wardrobe – cornflowers, dandelions, buttercups embellish the door. A matching headboard, another commode, a school desk. All riddled with woodworm. She dips her head to avoid the hazards hanging from the rafters. Rotting lampshades – fringes tattered, a red and blue turkey rug folded over, the size of the front room, ravaged by moths and caked with dust. Five or six hessian sacks of wool.

Against the back wall, two heavy bookshelves; at least three metres high, the wood swollen with damp. She has no idea how they got up there. No recollection of them ever being in the house. In a higgledy-piggledy fashion are tens of books, their ornate jackets covered in faded gold lettering, their pages bloated and uneven.

'What a waste,' she says the words out loud as though to allocate blame to whoever put them there.

Her foot catches on something, she looks down at her feet: a book, *A Sister's Devotion*. She leaves it be – it feels like an ugly reminder of the sister she's never been. Maybe that was the problem, she thinks to herself. *Maybe I've been living the wrong life, the sister of someone painted so differently by our own mother that I could never believe it was the same person. Yet I had to pretend they were that person the whole of my life.*

She takes a step back. The bookshelves wobble a little. The boards tilt unevenly beneath her feet. She shines the torch in an arc, something is off-centre. It's the depth of the shadow. She inches herself nearer, the shelves are not proud to the wall. The gap is drenched in cobwebs, their latticework a crocheted curtain that keeps out predators and pulls in victims.

She casts the light down to the floor, it's littered with blankets, pillows, black with mould and the smell so repugnant that she covers her nose.

The initials KA are carved into the back of the bookshelf.

It's a cubbyhole. A hiding place – or it had been.

Chapter 33

He'd slept badly; violent dreams of young girls, parties, drugs – his daughter.

Jimmy fills his cup with the remainder of the coffee from the cafetiere. Through the window, in the distance, a heron drags its feet over the water.

The waitress, dressed in black skinny jeans and a burgundy sweater, appears out of nowhere. The sun catches the diamond stud in her left ear.

'More coffee, sir?' Her hand reaches for the empty cafeterie. Her voice has a warm tone, a lightness that reminds him of his daughter.

'No, thanks.' He fakes a smile. His chair scrapes against the wooden floor as he gets out of his seat. He makes for the French doors that open onto the garden, pulls a pair of sunglasses out of his breast pocket and slips them on. The morning light so fierce it hurts his eyes.

Red berries gleam on winter shrubs, woodland coppices punctuate the horizon. A fine layer of frost covers the grass. Fleetingly he wonders if he should get a place in the country. It could be the final obliteration of the man he'd once been, whose life had been fuelled by drugs, money and power. He'd been nearly forty before he truly let go of it, before it had let go of him. A bitter taste fills his mouth; an angry thought raises its ugly head. His need to be the father that his daughter would love and respect, weakened him.

A low mist hangs over the fields, above it a citrus winter sun glimmers through. Ahead of him, there's a gate with a sign above it, *The Pear Orchard*. He wanders in, kicks at the fallen leaves.

Patches of snowdrops push up through the grass. A pair of magpies chatter loudly up in the boughs of a tree. He pulls up his collar, digs his hands deeper into his pockets. The mobile phone in his breast pocket rings, it's Fizz.

'Hiya sweetheart – how's things?' He asks her about work, about what the restaurant took last night, who was in. They talk like they always do, it's relaxed, matter of fact, the occasional laugh. He weaves his way to the point he wants to make, about the gallery, about the exhibition. He laughs, says he thought the artist had the hots for her.

She giggles, 'Really?'

'Yes, I noticed how he looked at you.' The words come out in a light-hearted tone.

She chuckles. 'Since when have you been interested in my sex life?'

'Sex life? Since you were born,' he doesn't laugh.

'None of your business, Dad.'

His voice is tense. 'Has he got your number?'

'Of course, he has, I organised the exhibition.'

The air escapes from his lungs, the image of that man's hands on his daughter crucifies him. He chokes back the emotions, fakes an interruption, terminates the call. He cannot tell her not to see him because that would be a red rag to a bull – a lesson learnt years ago.

It takes him five minutes to check out of the hotel, then he's back on the road, the heel of his foot deep on the accelerator, the speed racking up as he careers down the narrow lanes towards the barn.

He drives past it, takes the first turning on the left, follows the signs for a nature reserve, the road is littered with potholes, a small gritted area serves as a carpark. He slips the car between a small red Punto and a bright yellow Ford Kia.

The air goes out of him. He puts his head in his hands. Fizz, Melissa, the restaurant. He has a different life, a good life. His eyes shine with tears. What will he do when he sees him? Threaten him? Kill him?

But now – who is he now? He's a businessman desperate for grandchildren. That's who he is. He gets out of the car, makes his way back down the main road. Within minutes he's outside the barn. The curtains are drawn, there's no sign of life. He knocks on the door loudly, moments later he hears her voice.

'Won't be a minute.' It's her, the wife, Lottie.

The door opens a crack. 'Oh—' her eyes widen in the surprise. 'You're Jimmy, aren't you?' She has the dishevelled look of someone who's just climbed out of bed, her fingers grasp at the belt of her dressing gown.

The words tumble over this tongue. 'Jimmy, James, I answer to both. Sorry it's early, Lottie. I was just passing. Fizz is in Norwich scouting for a new gallery.' He scratches the underside of his chin; a slow smile crosses his lips. 'I thought I'd check out the coast, get some fresh air. Then I remembered you telling me you lived next to a converted water tower. I saw it in the distance.' He takes a step back and holds up the palms of his hands. 'Sorry if I woke you up.'

Her cheeks pinch pink. 'No, no, I was up, just about to have a shower.' She glances down at her dressing gown, pulls it tight around her waist again. 'It's just me, I'm afraid. Rob's out.' She rolls her eyes. 'I can't believe it; you've just missed him.'

'That's not a problem.' He takes another step back up the path. 'Is there a café around here, I'll get a coffee before I head back?'

A look of concern crosses her face. 'No, no, come in. Have one here, it's the least I can do.' She opens the door. 'Come through,' she lets out a weak smile, 'the place is a bit of a mess.' Together, they go through to the kitchen, the chaos of the previous night still evident. In a flurry of activity, she loads the dishwater, the plates clamour together noisily as she lifts them out of the washing up bowl.

'Please don't make any effort for me, it's kind of you to offer me a coffee.'

Lottie pauses for a moment, runs her fingers through her hair. 'It'll only take a minute, let me just pop upstairs and get changed.'

She looks down at herself, at her dressing gown, 'I'll feel better if I do that.' She hurries out of the kitchen and up the stairs.

His eyes go to the kitchen table, to the dark red stain, to where their bodies had lain. The mask slips from his face, his jaw tightens, the knuckles on his hands go white. He takes in the room, silently he opens the drawers on the dresser, runs his fingers through the contents, he picks up a stack of letters, flicks through them. He hears her footsteps above him, panics. He picks up the house magazines strewn across the floor, wipes the worktops down with a cloth. He was about to take out the rubbish when she comes back into the room.

Lottie blushes a violent red. 'Oh… there was n—'

'Sorry, just keeping myself busy, hope you don't mind, I'm hopeless at doing nothing.' He holds up his hands, gives her a broad smile, 'I'm a bit OCD like that. And on the plus side, it'll give us a bit more time to get to know each other.'

Her eyes cloud over for a moment, she wants him to leave, he knows that he has gone too far.

'You *shouldn't* have,' there's a sharpness in her voice, 'I was about to get started when you knocked at the door.' She turns over the cuffs on her jumper, picks up a tea cloth, puts it down again. 'Take a seat, what can I make you, tea, coffee?' She puts on the kettle.

'Coffee would be great, thanks… it'll help me keep awake for the journey back home. I'm driving, Fizz will no doubt be fast asleep. That's what she usually does. Kids, eh.'

'We don't have any.' There was no sadness in her eyes, she's matter of fact. 'Just the dog, Horace. He must be out in the garden.'

'Tell me about yourself. We didn't get much of a chance to talk the other night at the gallery.'

She tucks her hair behind her ears. 'There's nothing much to tell really, we've been together for years. He paints, I look after the house.'

'How long?' he couldn't help himself, he had to know.

'Since the ark, about twenty years, maybe a bit more, I don't keep count.' She places two cups beside the kettle, scoops a teaspoon of coffee in each.

'Where did you meet?'

Her eyes falter, the clouds come back, she covers her mouth with her hand.

'Oh God, I'm sorry, it completely escaped my mind.' An apologetic look transforms her face, the kettle boils, she switches it off. 'I promised a girl from the village that I'd go to Pilates with her. I can't let her down.' She looks up at the wall clock. 'I'm going to be late.' She hurries out into the hall, grabs a padded coat from off the end of the stair rail, picks up a pea green fitness bag off the floor. She pops her head around the kitchen door. 'I'm really sorry about this but I'm going to have to—' she holds out her hand, 'I can put your coffee in a paper cup if you like, for the car.'

He's surprised, he didn't see that coming at all. 'No, it's ok, really. I probably should have phoned… I'm a bit of a spur of the moment person.'

She lifts a bunch of keys off a key holder by the door. 'Got to go now, have a safe journey.'

He leaps to his feet, she hustles him out of the front door, locks it behind her. 'Lovely to meet you, Lottie,' he says with his hand resting on the gate.

'Nice to meet you too,' she turns left, along the path towards the back of the house. Just as he had done the night before. 'I'm going to walk across the field, there's an opening at the back of the house. It's quicker.'

'I can give you a lift if you like?' He holds the gate open for her to pass through.

'No really, it's just as quick through the fields, it'll wake me up.' She casts a hurried goodbye over her shoulder.

Jimmy walks along the road, towards the nature reserve, and as he turns to wave, he realises that she's already gone. He wonders what he said that scared her, he could tell she was scared, it was the way she got flustered when he asked her when they'd met. He can feel in his gut that something isn't right, there was something about her, why would she lie to him about that? And why on earth was she with him in the first place? He'd turned into an arrogant ponce, with a plum stuck well down his mouth. He must have got rid of his accent long ago. He'd been shocked to see him at the gallery.

He's going to make sure that Fizz steers well clear of him. And he's going to have a word with Carlo, clear a few things up. He takes out his phone, checks his messages, there's an unknown number. He wonders who it is.

'Call me as soon as you can, Jimmy. I need to talk to you urgently.'

His interest is piqued, but it isn't as strong as his need to talk with his daughter and Carlo. He spots his car in the carpark and sprints towards it; the sooner he gets home the better. Then the penny drops. He stops at the next services, there's something he needs to do now. Before the damage is done.

Chapter 34

The early morning briefing that started dead on ten thirty is almost at an end. All eyes are on Mel.

'So, the police reports regarding Lily Probisher. Badger, what did you find?'

Badger stands up, pushes his wire-rimmed glasses back up his nose. 'We think it's her, same date of birth. This was in north London though. Over a twelve-month period, 1998 to 1999. Three reports, two for an affray, one attempted suicide. Tried to throw herself under a train on the underground, some bloke pulled her back. Parents refused to help. Nothing since then.'

'Sounds like she's had psychological problems.' Mel gets to her feet. 'Any record of the psychiatrist that sectioned her?'

'Not in the police files. The arresting officer found a card with a contact name and number in her belongings, someone called Ellen Williams, she arranged for a psychiatrist to do a psyche evaluation. Apparently,' Badger pauses for effect, 'there was an agreement in place that gave her power of attorney in the case of deteriorating mental capacity. Not long after, Lily was committed to a facility in West Hampstead, Harper Burgess Health. It still exists, bought out by Prima Health in 2003. I assumed the patient files were carried over. I did a Section 29 request. They weren't very happy.' He picks a large envelope up off his desk. 'Arrived last night. They look as though they've been hacked about a bit. I've noted down the name of the psychiatrist.' He passes the envelope over to Mel. 'My notes are on the inside.'

'Thank, Badge. Track down Ellen Williams for me, will you?'

He frowned. 'It might be a long job, really common name.'

'Well, give it your best shot. Try the telecoms first. Does everyone know what they should be doing?' She looks around the room. 'No dissenters? Right then, get on with it.'

The team disperses around her, eager to get on with their respective tasks. There's a buzz in the room, two interesting cold cases, unsolved for years. Everyone wants to win, to solve the crime, to give the families some form of closure. She pours herself a cup of coffee, closes the door, seats herself at her desk. The patient file overflows with paper. She places Badger's notes directly above it. His flowery handwriting and well-rounded capitals a little too much for her own taste.

She opens the file; her fingers move fluidly over each page as she speed reads line after line. This is her forte, the attentiveness to detail. Now and again she scribbles a note on the pad next to her. The records go back as far as 1983, a referral from her doctor. Anxiety attacks, severe ones. In and out of the facility for near on ten years. She runs her pen down the page, there it is – the blood type. She's sure it's Veronica Lightfoot. Her sister Rosie donated a sample years ago and the lab ran a DNA test, there's a strong familial match.

Every few minutes she turns to her computer, taps in the name of a specific treatment or drug. It's a complicated process – she realises that she needs to talk to a professional, probably a psychiatrist. Run things by them. She gets to her feet, opens the office door.

'Kinsi, have you got a minute?'

'Yes, sure.' Kinsi unwinds herself from her seat and elegantly weaves her way through the clutter of desks. She's inherited her Somalian mother's stature – tall and slight.

'Can you find out the name of the psych that's on the books?'

'Sure.' Her eyes fixed on Mel. 'Do you want me to get them in?'

'No,' Mel shakes her head. 'Not yet, I'll have to see what the budget is. Just the name right now.'

Mel returns to the medical file, there's a thought nagging her. Why had Lily Probisher given Ellen Williams power of attorney over her? She'd encountered that once, maybe twice in her career. Who was Ellen Williams? And plenty of the text had been obliterated by thick black lines – and names of her physicians blanked out. She is almost halfway through the file when she finds a name, a scribbled signature, it looks like Dr R Coleman-Wakely or Wakefield, she can't tell which. Her mood lifts a little. She does a quick Google search on the name, it's Wakely rather than Wakefield. It seems he or she is no longer practising, not legitimately at least. Then she finds an obituary from 2006.

"She leaves behind her husband, Hugh and two grown-up children, Harriet and Charlotte."

Her mood shifts again. She rids herself of the notion of interviewing Dr Wakely.

Early on there is mention of a suicide attempt. About two thirds through the file she finds what she is looking for. The skin on the back of her neck tingles. Electric Shock Therapy, drug-assisted psychotherapy sessions, surely EST was made illegal years ago, she thinks to herself. Then page after page of half-obliterated documents, she makes a note to send some of them to the lab to see what they can do with them. The thick file reveals more secrets. A further attempted suicide whilst there. More treatment. Then a disclaimer, a declaration that says that the patient is cognitive, that there may be considerable memory loss, signed by Lily Probisher.

The final document denotes that the patient was released four months later and subject to a follow-up, three months after that. Lily hadn't turned up for that appointment. There were no further entries after the year 2000.

Questions mount up in her head. Why had she been kept there for so long? Four months is a long time to recover from treatment. Then she'd not attended the follow-up, why didn't she, what stopped her? Was she okay, had her health declined? What had happened to her in those three months?

There's a signature, that woman again, Dr Coleman-Wakely. She had concluded that the patient was no longer suffering from PTSD nor Multiple Personality Disorder. That the Veronica personality was no longer manifesting itself.

The Veronica personality was no longer manifesting herself?

Her stomach flips, the words knock the breath out of her.

Chapter 35

Thomasine left everything in situ, as she should. Almost. Hidden from daylight and preying fingers, slimed by mildew, a carrier bag – a cocoon. She holds her breath, opens the bag, shines the torch in it. For one overwhelming moment, she is glad that she gloved up.

There it was – the diary.

She gulps in a mouthful of dust filled air, coughs; the floorboards beneath her creak.

Don't you dare read it! Karen's voice shrieks in Thomasine's head as she hurries out of the loft and down the stairs to the kitchen.

Once read, it cannot be unread. Cannot be unlearnt. Cannot be unsaid.

She knows that, yet her body quakes – the desire to turn its pages one by one, such a rush of emotion—who would blame her? Who do they belong to anyway? Karen's dead so she can't claim them. And who else has paid so much for the right to read it first? Certainly, not Mel Phillips.

She takes a small china plate out of the cupboard, lays the diary on it. Places the carrier bag on the side of the sink.

The painted roses have parted company from the cardboard; the pages ripple and pucker in response. She turns it over in her hand – it's light, two pages to a week, a reminder for birthdays – so it says on the back. She closes her eyes, imagines what's inside this Pandora's box. The secrets it might hold, the scathing comments, the hurts.

The killer's name?

What if it's someone I know? Someone I like, never suspected? Hiding amongst us, crushing us under their feet as each day went by. What if they're dead?

She clicks the lock. The diary falls open in her hand, a dimpled picture of a grey kitten looks back at her. Carefully, she turns back the pages, turns back time. The first entry is Saturday the eighth of January 1972.

'It stopped raining, went down the park, Wayne Harris tried to kiss me. I slapped him. He's fow.'

Thomasine lets out a laugh, she can hear her voice, that high pitch, that giggle, that broad Lancashire accent that never had a chance to leave her. The slyness of the last word.

Her eyes drink it in, page after page of scribbled notes, sometimes only a single line, other times so much to say, the writing so small it's barely legible. Red, blue, black inks, crossing outs, thick lines cut through long words misspelt. Capitals for confrontations and retribution.

Is the rest of it up in the loft, she thinks to herself? School books, pictures, cards, anything like that, they all disappeared.

'Where did you put them, Mam?' She cocks her head to the side as though waiting for an answer.

Fow – she's not heard that in years. Ugly, that's what it means. A flash of memory ignites it back to life.

Fow cow, fow cow!

She blinks, the world changes. She's up on the moor, running along the tops – Karen in front, hair bouncing in a ponytail, her arms wide open, gusts of wind against her back, scooping her forward. Thomasine behind her, hands stretched out, her chubby legs unable to keep up, she stumbles, her ankle turns out on a rut of soil. She cries out in pain. Karen doesn't stop, her face raised up to the sky, twirling around, caught by the airstream, oblivious to her sister's cries.

She'd been found by the dogs two hours later. Her eyes and nose blood red from sobbing, huddled inside the gnarled trunk of a tree. Shivering. Her ankle swollen to twice its size.

Thomasine closes her eyes, lets it play out in the recesses of her memory.

'She's only three-years-old, Karen.' Dad was shaking. 'Leaving her here, up on the tops.' His shoulders slump, his voice cracks to a whisper. 'For God's sake – she's your baby sister. Why can't we trust you with her?'

Karen, dry-eyed and white-faced, straightens her shoulders, pulls herself up. 'You never asked me if I wanted a sister, did you?'

'You—' unsaid words hang between them. He rubs his fingers through his hair, heat rushes across his face, he grabs her by the shoulders, shoves her in front of him. 'I'll let your mother deal with you.' She never did. Her mother always had a softness for Karen that went beyond love.

Thomasine flicks through the pages. Like plaited hair, Karen's memories weave together with her own. Not quite the truth, not quite a lie. The disdain, the disapproval when she didn't do exactly as her sister asked. It comes back in fits and bursts. Make her bed, get her a drink from the kitchen, make her a snack, clean her shoes, become invisible when her friends were around. How she borrowed Thomasine's dark green kilt because on her it became a mini-skirt. How Thomasine wasn't allowed to tell Mam and Dad. The Chinese Burn that she'd get if she refused. The pinching. Her neck, her inner arms, her inner thighs. All the places that would hurt the most.

These are things she told no one, not even Rosie.

'She's stolen my Mary Quant lipsticks, the bitch won't tell me where they are, I hate her.'

Thomasine has no recollection of stealing her lipsticks. In that last year of her life, her sister had been particularly nasty. Accusing her of wearing her clothes, using her make-up. Lying to their parents, even to Mam. Saying that she'd been with her when she wasn't. Sneaking out on a Sunday afternoon, making her go with her, only to abandon her out in the fields with the strict instructions of where and when to meet her. If she followed her she'd get a slap. Often, Karen would be gone for hours.

How have I forgotten all of this? Is my mind playing tricks with me? Her own questions are met with a stony silence. She takes in a shallow breath – the air in the room is stale with sadness. Thomasine places the diary back on the china plate, she pulls off her latex gloves, backs away from it, goes out into the hallway. She yanks open the front door, a cold blast of air hits her face. A murder of crows squawks off over the barn roof. Across the valley, clumps of slate-grey cloud cling to the horizon, the woodland where her sister's remains were found is drenched in mist.

Hardacre was right – I can't deal with this. My objectivity is completely screwed. I hated her at times. I must be honest about that. Even if only to myself.

She walks across the yard, turns right behind the barn, climbs up onto the wall just as she had as a child. The sheep huddle around the water trough, their tongues lick the ice, their backsides caked in thick grey mud. Their coats will be sheared in spring, the wool sold for next to nothing. The stench of rotten eggs blows into her face – the slurry pit, a few yards in front of her, sunk into the ground, the crust so thick it looks like a compost heap. She remembers her grandfather telling her that it had taken himself and his brother, four days to dig it out, back-breaking work; he could barely stand upright for days afterwards.

The cold cuts into her, she clambers down the wall, makes her way back to the farmhouse, closes the door behind her. Her mother's voice tells her to turn off the hallway light, she's not got money to burn. Her sister's voice drops in, tells her to leave her things exactly where they lay.

God, I need a drink. To drown them out if nothing else. She tries to recall a kinder memory, one where there was happiness.

And hormones, says the voice of logic in her head, *puberty, don't forget that, that would explain it, it wasn't her fault; it was nature's chemicals flooding through her. Would she have become kinder as she grew into an adult? When puberty was over?* So many of her contemporaries say that happens. Before she knows it, her fingers hover over the half bottle of red left over from last night's dinner.

'What the—' A thunderous banging noise startles her. Her heart leaps into her mouth, she rushes towards the front door, wrenches it open, still attached to the door knocker, her cousin Paul falls into the hallway.

'Who—' At the sight of his face, she apologises profusely. 'Sorry, sorry. I hadn't meant to drag you in. Are you okay?'

Paul trips over the mat, stumbles against her. 'Yes, I forgot... yer mam. You had to knock hard for her to hear yer.'

'Right, well ease things off a bit, my hearing is pretty good.'

He raises an eyebrow, nods at the open bottle wine on the worktop.

'Started already, have you.'

She knuckles him on the shoulder, a childhood banter that they never grew out of.

'Come in, would you like a brew?' She put on the kettle without waiting for an answer.

'I thought I'd come over. See how yer was. See if yer needed a hand with anything. And I brought yer these.' He places a large bag of Maltesers on the table. A treat they shared as kids.

'That's really kind of you, Paul.' She jerks open the packet, offers them back to him. He takes a handful.

'You've looked a bit rough of late, to be honest, I thought I'd cheer you up.'

'Thanks, always good to know when you look rough.' Their eyes met, she laughs and so does he.

Paul takes a seat at the table, she talks as she makes the tea, her voice rises in volume as she describes the clutter, the roof in the barn and the loft full of woodworm.

While taking another handful of Maltesers, he lets out a groan. 'I bet it's not as bad as ours, Dad never throws anything out. I'm surprised the bedroom ceilings are holding up.' He waves his hand around the room, 'This is alright – a bit of decorating and it'll be fine.' He picks up the mug of tea, blows on it. His free hand reaches out, he spreads his fingers, ready to pick up—

'*Don't!*' Thomasine pulls the plate away. He always was curious and into everything. It was a family trait.

'What is it?'

'It's a diary I found up in the loft, there's some other stuff up there too, Karen's, I think.'

'Once a copper, always a copper,' he smiles, pulls the plate towards him.

'Best not to touch it. I'm planning to hand it in.'

He shrugs his shoulders. 'I was just trying to get a better look, that's all.' He picks up the mug of tea instead. His eyes narrow. 'Why are you handing it in?'

'It was just stuff that I found that I thought might help the investigation.' She watches the expression change on his face.

'A diary?' His eyes narrow, he rubs his nose with his thumb as he covers his mouth. His cheeks redden as the words tumble out of his mouth. 'D-d-does she mention me?'

'Not so far, I'm in there. Nothing good.' She wipes her hands on her jeans. 'You know what she was like,' she shakes her head, smiles. 'always a bit scathing.'

He picks up the mug of tea again, puckers his lips, blows on the liquid before taking a sip.

'She c-c-certainly was.' He looks up at her for affirmation.

The memory of Karen affects him, she can tell. The stutter that so blighted his youth returns only when he is anxious. It rarely rears its head when they are alone together.

His gaze returns to the diary. 'Have you t-t-thought of what you're going to do n-n-next?'

'Next?'

He looks around the room again. 'This is all yours now, I g-g-guess?'

'Oh, God. It'll take a long time to sort this place out. And a bucket full of money that I don't have.'

He stands up, moves towards the mantelpiece. 'Where's she g-g-gone?'

'Karen? The picture…it was freaking me out. I put it away in one of the drawers. Her eyes kept following me around the room.'

His eyes widen, his jaw drops. 'R-r-really?'

'Yes, really. Does that surprise you?'

He closes his eyes for a moment.

'No, I s-s-suppose not. Occasionally your mam would say she saw Karen about the p-p-place.'

'God, I hope that doesn't happen to me, I'll be out of here like a shot.'

'Old age, p-p-probably.' He puts his mug in the sink. 'Anyway, I'd b-b-best be off. I'll see myself out. If you need any help just give me a ring.'

'I will.' She watches his back as he leaves the room, his shoulders slumped, his feet scuff the floor as he makes his way down the hallway, the front door scrapes shut.

She decides to go home, to her place, to have a bath, to clean up. She locks the back door, checks the windows. She's interrupted by the loud clatter of the landline.

It's Rosie, she can barely hear her voice.

'Thom, Thom.' Rosie is crying, she can barely make out what she is saying. 'You won't believe this.' She takes in a gulp of air. 'It's probably not true. They say they've found her, Thom, they've found Veronica—'

'Up in the woods?'

'No, no, here. We're at the hospital. She's alive—'

'Where?' There's a trace of disbelief in her voice.

'In Salford, sorry, but it's the first time I've had a chance to contact you. I've just texted you the details. They found her, she had an accident. She's been there for days. She had no ID on her, they did a blood test, did DNA.' The words rush out of her, 'She's in a coma. I'm at the hospital. I'm sorry I didn't ring you but...' Her voice trails off.

Thomasine is out of the door within minutes, at long last, there may be a chance of finding out the truth.

Chapter 36

I need caffeine.

He limps into Sophie's Café, rubbing the base of his spine. The café is newly renovated, or so it says in the window. Unplastered walls painted white, heavy oak tables on iron legs, chairs right out of a schoolroom, flooring torn up from a long-abandoned factory, stripped and cleaned. He orders a double shot cappuccino from the counter. Fakes an apologetic face, as he hands the teenage girl a fifty-pound note. She gives him a withering look, runs some sort of pen over it before putting it in the till. Without a flicker of a smile, she counts his change into the palm of his hand.

The place is half full, morning commuters on flexitime. He spots a vacant table by the window, ambles toward it, slips off his backpack, pulls out the seat. Winces as the base of the seat nudges at his bruised coccyx.

He checks his watch; it's just gone quarter to ten. He'd gone into Norwich to get money from the bank. The thousand pounds he's withdrawn from his account lays thick in the inside pocket of his coat. All in fifties. All new. He'd not been brave enough to ask for used notes. Then he'd dropped into the local computer supplies shop, a Chinese boy with a large waist and splayed feet wandered out from the back, the sides of his head shaved, a long black lock of hair hanging over his right eye. Another unsmiling teenager, the high street seemed to be full of them. He'd proved surprisingly helpful, recommended something called a dongle, preloaded. Told him he'd be able to use it wherever there was an internet signal.

He pulls his MacBook out of his backpack, places it on the table, slips the dongle into the USB port, logs on. Without comment, the girl places his cappuccino on the table beside it. He waits for the northwest news service to load.

Missing Woman Found. Woman? He almost skims over it.

A reliable source stated that a woman, missing since 1973 had been discovered in a local hospital. The victim of a hit and run accident, she was now recovering in intensive care. Could it be her? No, it couldn't be her, how could it be? He searches for a name, there isn't one.

Surely there should be one? Why hadn't they given a name?

His stomach cramps. The chair legs make a high-pitched scraping noise as he shoves himself back from the table. His eyes scan the room in a panic. The teenage girl points to the door behind the counter, the engaged sign on red. He hunches over in his seat, counts the seconds down one by one. His sore back now the least of his worries. Jimmy Fairfax is now top of the list, if he talks, they'll both be screwed. Through the door, he hears the loud hum of the hand dryer, a teenage girl with braided hair slinks out. He manages to place his backside on the toilet just as his bowels loosen.

Chapter 37

Rosie stands rigidly at the end of the bed while the work of the Neurological High Dependency Unit goes on around her. Her fingers wrap tight around the cold metal frame. High-pitched electronic beeps, the trill of phones, the scurry of feet, the doors swishing to and fro, all skim over her consciousness like blades on an ice rink. Her whole attention consumed by the woman lying in the bed before her – a tube down her throat, lines coming out of her arms, her fingers cramped into a fist. Three monitors above her head glow with jagged lines that move with the beat of her heart, a thin grey stubble covers the right side of her head, a thick line of black stitches curves over her scalp from her left ear to the crown of her skull. Her face is covered in bruises that have gone from a swollen deep purple to an olive green. Beneath the blanket, both shins are wrapped in a thick white plaster.

She could be anyone. Anyone.

A ventilator helps her to breathe, a catheter measures how much liquid is taken in, how much urine passes out. There's a tube inserted into her scalp that measures the pressures in her brain. Then a feeding tube into stomach.

The statistics aren't good. She'd looked them up. Of the ten patients on the Unit, probably only two will make a good recovery. Two might die, six will likely be disabled for the rest of their lives. This isn't the homecoming she'd imagined for her sister. If this woman is her sister at all. She seats herself by the bed, looks at every curve of the woman's face. A hand taps her on the shoulder, she jumps.

'Sorry to scare you. There's someone outside to see you.' The nurse frowns, 'Only family allowed in, I'm afraid.'

Thomasine waves at her through the glass window in the door, Rosie goes out into the corridor.

'Are you okay?' Thomasine puts her arm around her. 'Shall I get us a coffee?'

Rosie nods, wordlessly they walk down the corridor, both caught in their own thoughts.

'You get a seat, I'll get them in.' She returns a few minutes later, a plastic cup of coffee in each hand. 'How is she?' She takes a seat beside her.

Rosie shrugs her shoulders, the lines on her forehead deepen. 'A bit difficult to know really – alive, asleep. No idea of how it will all turn out.' She takes a coffee off Thomasine, her hands tremble, the coffee ripples in the cup. 'It's been a shock.' Her eyes glaze with tears, she goes to get to her feet. 'Sorry I need to get back in there.'

'Give yourself a little break,' Thomasine rests her hand gently on Rosie's knee. 'A few minutes won't hurt. Drink your coffee. Besides, I've found out a bit more, if that helps.

Rosie's eyes widen, 'Go ahead, tell me.'

'I've been talking with DCI Phillips, the woman heading both investigations, she's on her way now. Veronica's been living the other side of Manchester for years, under the name of Lily Probisher. She was some form of psychotherapist. No one's been caught yet for the hit and run. It could have been an accident; it was snowing heavily that night.'

'A psychotherapist?' Rosie frowns, 'I'd never have—' Her chest heaves with a sob, 'I'm sorry, really sorry, that I've not been able to be there for—'

Thomasine puts her arm around her friend's shoulder. '*Honestly*, I'm fine, I can cope. It's you I'm worried about.' She gives her a hug. The wail of an alarm interrupts them, she disentangles herself. 'Go on, go back in, I'll be fine, I'll get in touch in a couple of days. I promise.'

As Rosie makes her way along the corridor, a woman catches her eye. There's something familiar about her. The dark curly hair, the narrow waist, the way she moved. Her upper body seemingly static, the legs taking long strides. The woman reminded her of Thomasine, that was it.

She presses the buzzer with her thumb, gives her name. The door clicks. Barely a few steps in a male nurse yanks the curtain around Veronica's bed. She rushes over, grabs the edge of the curtain, a woman in blue scrubs appears in front of her, blocks her way.

'I'm sorry you can't come in here right now.'

'What's happening?' Her mouth is dry; her fingers squeeze the plastic cup in her hand.

The nurse's dark brown eyes soften. 'I'm sorry,' With a gentle force, she guides Rosie away from the bed. 'She's not very well, we need you to stay calm. I need you to go out into the corridor while we deal with it.'

Rosie backs her way out of the room, her heart slamming against her breastbone.

Behind the curtain, a voice pulses out with urgency. 'One, two, three…'

The door opens just as Rosie's legs give way, the coffee showers the floor, Thomasine and DCI Philips just manage to break her fall.

Chapter 38

Someone is sitting on my chest. It's her.
You killed me.
It's not her fault, I tell her that. She doesn't believe me. She hits me in the chest with her fist.

I couldn't breathe. I was weak. She was heavy. I tried to save her. I tell her that.

She shakes her head. *You killed me. You killed me. You crushed the life out of me.*

I must have.

I tried to wake her up. I tell her that. It didn't work. Nothing worked. Her eyes turned into pools of thick white jelly.

She hits me again. My ribs crack. I beg her to stop. I didn't mean for her to die. I tell her that. I'd pulled her out. Held her hand in mine. Wiped the soil off her face. Ran my fingers through her hair. Kissed her on the cheek.

He buried us both, I try to tell her that.

She doesn't believe me, she scratches at my clothes with dirty fingernails.

I tell her again, 'I tried to save you.'

She looks away. *You didn't try hard enough.* Her head swivels. Her eyes slice into me. *Then you put me back where no one could find me.*

Her fingers wrap around my wrist.

My heart stutters. A high-pitched noise bursts my ears.

'STAND BACK! HANDS OFF! STAND CLEAR!'

The pain wracks through her. Her back arches, her eyes flip back in her head.

Then silence. She counts the beats of her own heart. One, two, three. Someone coughs. She tries to prise open her eyelids, move her hands, speak. Nothing responds. She's caught in a river of pain. It drags her under. Takes her with it.

Chapter 39

Mel walks through the office in a daze, her mind still not made up. It had been the last thing she'd expected from Thomasine Albright. Offering up what she'd found without a murmur of discontent. From the look of her, the case was clearly taking its toll. Greasy hair, dirty blue jeans, an old grey cardigan frayed at the elbows. The manicured fingernails now bitten down to the quick. Hollow circles under her eyes – the crust of a cold sore at the edge of her lips. Her life a concertina of events collapsing in on her. And living up at that place wasn't helping, up there without a soul around her.

Or was she manipulating them all, going behind their back?

The second cardiac arrest had caught them all by surprise. Thomasine had stayed with Rosie, she was in shock. If they'd not been so near she would have hit the floor like a brick. At least Veronica was stable at present.

A day later, Thomasine had given her the key to the farmhouse, told her where the diary was. She'd gone up there at first light, met Sam there and right now he was going over the loft along with a forensic team.

The diary lies open on her desk. She turns the pages, one by one. In the first six months, there is nothing of great interest but the humdrum life of a fourteen-year-old in 1972. Going to school, swimming, the youth club, the dilemma of choosing subjects for GCE. Coming sixth in the school cross-country race. The fallings out. The makings up. How the father refused her pleas to go on a school trip to the Lakes. How everyone else was going, how she was the only one who'd miss out. How she hated him because of it. How he wouldn't give in. How Thomasine had been using her pale pink nail varnish and matching lipstick. How she'd put on her clothes, tramped around the bedroom pretending to be her.

That had made Mel smile, brought back memories of her own childhood in Manchester, her mother's clothes, her high-heeled shoes.

Karen's writing flickers between easy to read to almost indecipherable. She talks about asking her father for money, about her mother picking her clothes, about Thomasine not behaving, about her being a pain. *Still no change there.*

Badger shoves open the door. In one hand a coffee and in the other a bacon sarnie from the canteen.

'Thanks, you're a life-saver.'

He smiles then disappears back into the office.

Things change in July, Karen writes about walks through the fields to the village, about how boring the boys in the village are, about how they kept trying to touch her, their fumbling hands trying to flick her bra strap.

Mel remembers being fourteen – the spouting breasts, the periods that brought her pain and foul moods. The acne blemish on her cheeks that disappeared six months later.

August brings gossip about school friends, how Judith had a boyfriend, how Judith was boring, how Judith never had time for her anymore. How she was lonely and couldn't wait to get out of the village, away from the moor. Karen complains about the sun and the rain and everything in between as though the weather was purposefully trying to thwart her.

The bacon sarnie disappears, as does the coffee. Mel's eyes ache from trying to decipher Karen's scrawls.

Then the tone changes, she writes about a boy she meets. The hair behind her neck bristles, she picks up her pen in readiness.

'I could see him looking at me, so I slowed down, looked the other way. I pretended I was shy. He's *sooo* good looking, long brown hair, grown up. He took me in his car up over to Belmont, he took me over to Rivington. I told him I'm sixteen, everyone says I look sixteen anyway.'

She has an uneasy feeling in her gut that tells her this is the beginning. From that date, there are no missed entries, no negative talk. No name either. One mention of long brown curly hair. But that's it.

Twice a week she meets him on the moor road or up in one of the abandoned cattle barns on someone else's land. He starts buying her gifts, perfume, make-up; lipsticks, mascara. Then he moves onto buying her clothes; maxi-skirts, loons, T-shirts. He asks her to put them on. He asks her to change in front of him, she refuses. Mel's pen scratches across the lines in the notebook, more questions.

Surely, her parents should have noticed something going on.

It's balling up in her stomach, the anger. A teenager being groomed by an older boy. She knows that back then, with that sort of money, he would have been older than eighteen.

Something big happens in November, on the twelfth. It had to be big, it was written in code. Time for a team task. Mel gets to her feet, goes into the Incident Room.

'Game time, whoever gets this right wins a bottle of prosecco.'

'I don't really like prosecco, boss.' Badger's voice complains over the rattle of the photocopier as it churns out copies of the medical report.

A voice pipes up, 'I wouldn't worry about winning if I were you.' There's a smattering of laughter amongst the team.

Mel holds up the diary. 'Here it is, twelfth of November 1972. She's had a boyfriend for a few months, older, probably in his early twenties. She writes the code up on the whiteboard.

Gd'r oqnlhrdc sn szjd ld sn z mhfgsbkta.

Badger raises an eyebrow. 'I hate stuff like this.'

Kinsi leans forward, 'It's basic teenage stuff.' She picks up her pen and notepad, goes silent for a few moments as she scribbles a few notes. 'This one is easy, it's the alphabet, just moved on one.'

'And?' Badger's voice has an edge of frustration to it, everyone in the team knows he's dyslexic and finds any type of word puzzle infuriating.

She walks over to the board, crosses out each letter, puts one above it.

'Da Da! "He's promised to take me to a nightclub."'

'No name?' Mel's voice cuts through the air.

'No name.' Kinsi answers back with a shake of her head.

Mel lets out a sigh, 'Thanks, Kinsi. Right, everyone – noses to the grindstone, eyes peeled for any mention of a boyfriend.' She goes back into the office, carries on reading the diary. She scribbles down a note of the code.

Karen Albright's life reveals itself to her, how she'd run through the fields and meet him down on the road. He borrowed his brother's car, that's what he'd told her. It was – a Capri of some sort, white. He's going to take her to a nightclub.

Then she mentions someone called Paul, that he's spying on her. Who's he? Another note, this time to ring Thomasine.

The final entry is on New Year's Eve. Her father had banned her from going out. He'd said he didn't want to go down into the village to get her. She writes that she hates him. Then a sentence in code again.

'*Gd vzr fnhmf sn szjd ld sn zlzkkmhfsdq*'

"He was going to take me to an all-nighter."

Mel rests her elbows on the desk.

Perhaps that's where she was going the night she disappeared.

A young girl trying to grow up fast.

The passenger door swings open. Sam dips his head in, his thick black hair gelled back like a blackbird's wing. His skin looks even paler than usual.

'Morning, boss!'

Mel senses a hint of sarcasm. She hitches herself upright in her seat, rotates the stiffness out of her shoulders.

'So, what did you find up at the farm, up in the loft?'

He eases himself into the passenger seat. His six foot five bulk seems to squash the air out of the car. 'Not much, a right manky place, that. Wouldn't want to spend much time up there.' He hands her the plastic-wrapped sandwich he bought ten minutes ago from the canteen. 'I got you the last one, sorry it's only cheese and tomato.'

She takes it, gives him a weak smile. 'Thanks, how much do I owe you?'

His smile twists into grin. 'Ah, it's alright, you bought me that curry last week, call it quits.'

She laughs out loud. 'That curry cost me twenty quid!'

He sniggers, his dark blue eyes light up. 'Yeah, well, you earn more money than me.'

She rips the wrapping off the sandwich and takes a mouthful of cheese and tomato. 'So, what did you find?'

'Not much, like I said.' He takes his notebook out of his inside pocket, skims through the pages. 'A bunch of comics, teenage girl stuff, stuck together in a clump, a hand torch and a small biscuit tin, both half eaten by rust. A pair of horn-rimmed NHS glasses so filthy they could be sunglasses. I can't remember seeing anything about her wearing glasses, did you?'

Mel shakes her head.

'Anyway, it must have been her hiding place, or someone hid her there. Who knows? And there was something else, a tin of crayons, completely covered in rust. I opened them up, showed Kinsi, they're lip pencils apparently. I brought it all back, it's with forensics now.'

'And what did Badger find then?' She takes another bite from the sandwich.

'Well, he worked his wonders on the internet. He found a birth record for a Lily Probisher, same date of birth, born in Norwich in 1957. He checked the records for that person, in 1972 she seems to go off grid and resurfaces in 1975. He managed to trace her parents, both still together. I rang them – the mother picked up. At first, she said that she didn't have a daughter.' He raises an eyebrow. 'No love lost there. She had one of those upper-class accents and I clearly was too Geordie for her. After I said I had a copy of the birth certificate in my hand, she fessed up that her daughter had run away from home when she was fourteen. Apparently, she'd had a drug habit, heroin, and was a bad influence on their son. She'd thrown her out. Told her to go live with her "druggie" friends. Clearly, she hadn't run away after all.

Badger forgot to mention she wasn't the girl's mother. Lily's mother died when she was three-years-old. Her father remarried when she was seven, it appears she and the new Mrs Probisher didn't get on. I'm surprised no one from the girl's school flagged this up. She said she couldn't be of more help then put the phone down.' Sam looked across at her. 'So, it looks like our first question for Veronica when she wakes up is where is the real Lily Probisher? Here's hoping there's not another dead body hidden somewhere.'

Mel nods her head as she chews the last bite of the sandwich. 'It's hard to believe the father never tried to find her. *Surely…*' She shakes her head. 'I sometimes wonder why some people have kids. What about the brother? She might have kept in touch with him. Where's he?

'Apparently, he lives in New York. I got his number off her though she complained like hell. I wonder if he wanted to get away from *mummy* and *daddy,* too.'

'I'd like you to get yourself down south to see the Probishers. Afterwards, give the brother a ring and see what he can tell us about his sister.'

'Do I have any choice?' He'd arranged to take his wife out for dinner.

She smiles, shakes her head. 'Not really, take this one, it's faster,' she hands him the keys. 'Make sure you talk to Mr Probisher. Don't come back without his side of the story.'

'Yes, *Boss*. There is one thing, I can't see him disowning his daughter, surely, she's the one thing he's got that reminds him of his wife. It's not like they divorced, she died.'

'I'm wondering whether the new Mrs Probisher actually told her husband what was happening. Maybe the girl was a bit of a shit, caused too much trouble, maybe they thought they were better off without her in their lives. Addicts can make life very difficult.'

'Well, I thought I'd check it out, nevertheless. Thought I'd see if I could find any friends of Lily's whilst I am down there.'

'Good thinking, Batman,' a wide grin spreads across Mel's face. 'Don't forget to liaise with the local team while you're there. Just in case.'

She gets out of the car, runs across the car park, disappears into the building just as Sam catches the crotch of his trousers on the handbrake as he slides over into her seat.

Chapter 40

My head hurts, at the back. It's sore. I try to move it, just a little. I can't.

They've changed the stinky stuff. What's the name for it? Disinfectant, that's the word for it. It smells of oranges.

I can hear voices. This near one sounds foreign. I wonder what my voice sounds like? There's someone singing. *This little piggy…* am I small?

The phone jangles. I hear that voice again. The foreign one, she's mumbling. *They're going to bring her out of the coma, soon.* That's what she's saying.

Is it me? Have I been in a coma? No, I haven't, I've been awake. It can't be me.

I can't move, I'm strapped down. Just like before. I wanted everything to be over. Why isn't it? She promised me it would be. That nasty bitch who fried me. My eyes won't open. They always open without me thinking. Why won't they do that?

Maybe I'm dead and this is hell.

'Still asleep then ma girl,'

That voice again. A northern accent. Lancashire, Yorkshire, maybe some Caribbean.

'Yer poor girl, that bang on yer head must have hurt, don't yer worry though, they'll catch that man that did it.'

What man? The memories tangle, untangle, then tangle again. *Are you talking to me?*

'And that policewoman, she'll be back to talk to you.'

The woman is touching me, I try to pull away. My brain's not working, nothing moves, the woman strokes my hand.

'She'll find that bad man that ran yer down, she will. She's that sort. I like her.'

I don't remember being knocked down, I don't remember any man. The woman runs her fingers across my cheeks, I smell patchouli oil on her skin. I don't like it. Grab her hand, push it away, grab it! Why the hell won't my body do what I want it to? Everything hurts, I can't move my legs. Why did he run me down? What did I do to him? I've done something wrong. I can feel it inside of me. I'm sorry! I'm sorry!

Whatever it is, I'm sorry!

'Anyway, ma darling, that nice physio is going to come and see you later, she'll get yer muscles moving.' She shuffles away, her shoes flip-flop.

'Hello, ma love, it's Carmela. How are yer my sleeping beauty? I've just come on duty and thought I'd come and say hello to ma girls first.'

His footsteps, I can hear his footsteps.
He's found me again.

Chapter 41

Thomasine jabs at the buttons; the burglar alarm makes a *dah duh* sound then goes silent. Her back against the front door, she rubs her forehead with her fingers. A rabble of press had been outside; she'd pushed her way through.

She'd left Rosie at the hospital, eyes half closed, slumped in a chair.

'I'll be alright,' she'd stretched her neck. 'Honestly. Go home, get some sleep.'

The letterbox rattles against her hips, a card drops down onto the pile of mail by her feet.

'Thomasine, Amanda Palmer,' the rasping voice peppered with the stink of cigarettes. 'Sunday Record… I just want to give you my condolences.'

Thomasine raises her foot, kicks back at the door, someone lets out a cry, she hears the scuff of heels on the doorstep. A hard smile crosses her face. She looks down at the floor. Sympathy cards, utility bills, a reminder that her car tax is due, business cards with notes scribbled on them. She kicks them away from the door, leaves them where they landed.

The hallway is airless, cold, the other downstairs rooms aren't much better. She switches on the gas fire in the living room, overrides the central heating system so it comes on. She does all the things she normally does when she gets home. Except for the curtains, she leaves them drawn. She fills the kettle, goes through the routine of making a drink, opens the fridge door, pulls out a carton of milk, checks the date. It's okay. Every now and then a voice shouts through the letterbox. Her phone pings with messages and voicemails. She ignores them all.

She has the feeling that she's forgotten something, it niggles away at her – just out of sight. The last weeks have been a miasma of emotions, wanting to remember the best of her sister, yet only the worst bubbling up. There were good times, they did get on, it's as though those memories have been washed out by a flood of negativity. The diary threw her into a tailspin, and then Veronica. Alive. She hadn't expected that, none of them had expected that. Especially in the state that she's in. An accident— that feels all too convenient. Had she tried to kill herself? Her sister's case had been on the news, so that was possible. They've not caught the driver yet. The questions won't leave her alone. Was it Karen's killer? Was Veronica a witness? Had the killer managed to trace her? Was it a gang of them? Was Veronica in the gang? Was it a prank that went wrong? It wouldn't be the first time something like that had happened. Adrenalin pumps around her heart, the muscles in her chest tensed. She needs to relax, to get rid of the stress.

She takes her mug upstairs, runs a bath, throws in some salts. She sits on the toilet seat drinking her coffee, waits for the bath to fill, that bothersome forgotten thing still worrying her.

She shrugs off her mother's cardigan, casts off her clothes. The hot water steams the air, she sinks down into the bath, lies back, closes her eyes and falls asleep. Dreams.

Her head breaks the water, *an all-nighter*! She grabs a towel, wraps it around her, forgets to drain the bath. She scrambles downstairs, grabs hold of her phone. A rush of energy pulses through her as she flicks through the photographs. She lets out a hoarse laugh, bingo! *There you are*, she emails herself the photograph.

I should have remembered this days ago, I'm going crazy. Thomasine takes the stairs up to her office. She unlocks the door, this room is her enclave, her place of secrets. There's a hint of apples – air freshener. Everywhere is covered in a fine layer of dust, the result of weeks of inactivity. She switches on her PC. It makes a chundering noise as it loads up.

There's a whiteboard to the right of the door, covered in newspaper articles, pictures, post-it notes, anything and everything to do with her sister's case. Three rows of large white storage cubes line the wall to the left of her, laden with sky blue storage boxes, all bought from Ikea and assembled by herself.

Hidden from sight behind the locked doors of a large metal filing cabinet are four files. One for each missing girl. Karen Albright (aged 15) disappeared 7/1/1973, Veronica Lightfoot (aged 18) – disappeared 7/1/1973, Candy Wharton (aged 15) – disappeared 30/5/1980 and the final box was Charlie Arnold (aged 14) – disappeared 23/8/1987. Except for Veronica, each girl shared physical characteristics – long auburn hair, brown or hazel eyes, slender and around 5'7" in height, Charlie had been a few inches shorter, all had outgoing confident personalities. All of them disappeared into thin air. Thomasine shakes her head; they never *simply* disappear. It's far more complex than that. All classed as runaways by their initial investigating officers.

Each box contains a complete copy of the set of the documentation currently held by her team. No one but her knows that these files exist. One of the joys of being on the Missing Persons Unit – an almost unbridled access to information. She can't remember the exact point when she decided to set up her own incident room. Not on a whim, she's sure of that. Probably when she kept getting the runaway story from the people who should have cared. Usually men, old coppers long retired but who still hung out in the local pub, downing whisky and regaling the good old days when political correctness didn't apply.

She'd borrow documents, photocopy them at home, then take them back the following day. No one noticed the drip feed out of the door, certainly not the upper echelons, the higher-ups, the ones that had the big offices up on the top floor. It had taken her years to compile all that information, but for what? She'd never turned anything up in the intervening years. She cast her gaze around the room. *All of this was for now.*

She sits down at the desk, tries to clear her head. *I'll be right up shit creek if they decide to search this place.* If they do she'll have to call in some favours. A wry smile crosses her face. Mel Phillips owes her a few.

A sudden sense of urgency spurs her on. She logs on to her computer, accesses her private email account. Prints off a copy of the photograph she took of the nightclub flier – the one she found in Veronica's teenage magazines, lays it down to the right of the keyboard. She flips her notepad open at a clean page. At least now she has a new place to start. Mindfully, she types in the words *Golden Torch 1970s,* then presses enter.

Her heart sinks. There are over hundred and forty thousand hits. She limits herself to the first twenty pages, screen-dumps page after page of website addresses. Ticks them off as she works her way through them. There are specific websites that advertise reunions, all-nighters in Manchester, Leeds, all over the northwest and as far down as Bristol. There are chat rooms, Facebook pages, Twitter accounts. Her stomach growls; she checks her watch. Three and half hours have gone by. She goes down to the kitchen, pings herself a readymade macaroni and cheese in the microwave. Washes it down with strong black coffee.

Then she's back on the job again. The muscles of her back tight from hunching over the computer for hours, sifting through pages and pages of information, much of it completely useless. Back then it would have just been *good old police work.* No internet then, no national police database, no DNA, no HOLMES, no social media, no Missing People page on Facebook. She sits in envy for a moment, considers the resources that Mel Philips will have at her disposal. The resources she'd have if only they'd let her back in the office.

The muscles in her eyes ache from staring at the screen, from analysing each photograph, crowd scenes mainly. The Golden Torch, The Wheel, Wigan Casino, Blackpool Mecca.

Arms stretched out, heads flung back, spines flexing as they flung themselves up into the air. People looking on. Teenagers, most of them. Thomasine scrutinises every single human being, side on, in the shade, half hidden by someone's hand, an eye peering out between two heads, a half-averted smile, the curve of a back.

Her mobile bursts into life just as she clicks the cursor to move onto the next image. It takes her completely by surprise. The photograph. She's wearing false eyelashes, looks older, at least eighteen. He's wavy-haired, the man behind her. his hands on her shoulders; an intimate gesture. Neither of them are smiling.

It's Karen. She'd know her anywhere, even with all the makeup.

There in the centre of the dance floor, looking up at the photographer or at the DJ or whoever it was.

Her hand goes to switch off her mobile. She clicks on the website, it's a chatroom. Her hands tremble with excitement. The photograph was posted six months earlier. The Golden Torch, October 1972. Jacky2422. Email me at jackymail2422.

Chapter 42

Mr and Mrs Probisher sit together on the settee. She, in particular, hadn't been pleased when Sam turned up on their doorstep unannounced.

The couple live in a leafy suburb, a double-fronted 1980s detached house – a soft top, silver Saab convertible on the drive. The colour had drained from her wan-coloured olive skin as he'd held up his badge in front of her. A short woman, she almost fell off her six-inch stiletto heels. Her eyes blinked in the harsh glare of the morning sun.

'I'd like to have a word about your daughter, Lily Probisher.'

'I've not—'

Her husband joins her on the step, Sam speaks over the woman's shoulder. 'Your daughter, Mr Probisher.'

'What about my daughter?' A flash of anxiety crosses his face.

'My name's DS Sam Ingleby. I spoke to your wife yesterday.'

A pinched look freezes on the woman's face, she crosses her arms across her chest. The man's voice hardens. 'Move out of the way, Ingrid. DS Ingleby has travelled a long way, let him in.' He steps back from the doorway and offers his hand as Sam noisily wipes his feet on the doormat. 'Ralph Probisher. Did you say you were here to talk about Lily?'

Sam nods. 'I did, your wife tells me that you've not seen or heard from her for many years.' Sam found, in general, unexpected visits created unexpected results. And this was proving the case. His intuition tells him that Ingrid Probisher would have sent him on his way with a denial if her husband had not been stood directly behind her.

Ralph Probisher offers a weak smile, clearly shaken by Sam's presence. 'Tea?'

'Thanks, long journey, that would be great.'

'You'd best come through here.' There is no warmth in Ingrid Probisher's tone.

Sam follows her through to a large, heavily decorated room, dominated by an L-shaped white leather settee and marble fireplace. 'Take a seat.' She gestures towards the only single chair in the room. It matches the settee and, like the settee, is laden with black scatter cushions covered in silver sequined hearts. He takes the cushions off the chair and places them on the floor in an untidy pile. Ingrid Probisher gives him a look of disdain.

'Bad back,' he explains, easing his large bulk down into the chair. This isn't true. He just wants to wind her up, unsettle her a bit. Sam glances around the room before taking out his notepad.

Ingrid Probisher seats herself in the corner of the settee, her dark red lips, painted in a cupid's bow, purse like a prune, she crosses her legs one over the other, one high-heel pointing towards him like a weapon. She has deep lines running down either side of her cheeks. She keeps sniffing, as though there is something off in the room. Sam feels ill at ease; he's met her type before, the aspirational middle class. Either that or she's got a serious coke habit. Part of him wishes it were the latter, perhaps then he could arrest her. Now that would be fun, he thinks to himself.

Ralph Probisher reappears moments later, a wooden tray between his hands, three cups of tea along with a plate of Jaffa cakes.

'Thanks,' says Sam as he takes a cup and saucer. He declines the Jaffa cakes, a small nod towards keeping diabetes at bay.

Ralph Probisher takes a seat next to his wife, the cup and saucer waver in his hand. He remains silent, a grey man, thinks Sam. A dark grey cardigan covers a pale grey shirt, open at the neck. Thick, grey, wavy hair is brushed back off his face, a shallowness of skin gives him the look of a man with the life sucked out of him. Dark grey eyes nestle under thick eyebrows. He is colourless, in contrast to his wife, dressed like a peacock in a bright turquoise knee-length dress. Something more suited to a cocktail party than knocking around the house. Sam balances the cup and saucer on his knee, a look of horror crosses Ingrid Probisher's face. She rises to her feet, briskly crosses the room, picks up a small black lacquered side table and places it next to the chair in which Sam is sitting.

'Oh, thanks,' says Sam, placing the cup and saucer on top of it. He's tempted to let his hand tremble a little just for the hell of it.

'Lily was a bad influence, the drugs.' She returns to her seat, her eyes focus in on him, she clears her throat. 'Heroin—she hid it here in the house. Our son found it, he was only five-years-old at the time. God knows what could have happened if he'd swallowed it.'

'Where is your son now?' he said, knowing full well he had been living in New York for the last four years. 'Edmund, did you say his name was Edmund?'

'Did I? Yes, he's our son. Ralph's and mine. He's in New York. He works for a bank.'

Ralph Probisher interjects. 'He's not been home for a while, he's busy with work and all that. And Ingrid doesn't like to fly.' There was a sadness in his voice.

'How long is it since you've last seen him?'

'Four years, perhaps more. He has an important job, high up,' Ralph Probisher looks down at the palms of his hands, 'he doesn't get much time off. We speak on the phone about once a month.'

Irritation crosses Ingrid Probisher's eyes, she opens her mouth to speak. Sam interjects.

'And how about your daughter?'

'We don't talk.' The woman glares at her husband, as though daring him to contradict her. 'We haven't for over thirty years, not since the early seventies. We thought it best to close the door on that relationship.' She looks out of the window and into the distance. 'Given her problem with drugs.' She returns her attention to Sam. 'Serious drugs. Class A.'

He raises an eyebrow. 'You seem to be well acquainted with drugs, Mrs Probisher.'

'No, no.' She flashes a look at him, her lips twist. 'Just what I hear on TV.'

Sam tilts his head to the side, transfers all his attention onto Ralph Probisher. 'And how about you Mr Probisher, when did you last hear from your daughter?'

A look of confusion settles on the man's face. He shrinks back into his seat, lets out a sharp cough, his head drops, he scratches the back of his neck. There is no eye contact.

'Last week.' The words are barely audible.

'Could you repeat that Mr Probisher, I didn't quite hear it.' A warm feeling fills Sam's chest.

'Last week, on Friday.'

'What—' Ingrid Probisher, in the process of swallowing a mouthful of tea, almost chokes. She rounds on her husband. The words splutter out of her mouth. 'You... you... didn't tell me.' Her cup and saucer clatter back onto the coffee table. 'You've not been—'

'Giving her money? No, I haven't.' Ralph Probisher's mouth hardens as he stares into this wife's face. 'She's my daughter, mine and Penny's daughter and there is no reason at all why I shouldn't talk to my daughter. And if I want to give her money I bloody well will do. I've worked hard enough for it.' His hands curl into fists.

Sam represses his urge to smile, he knew he was right. Given the wife's reaction, this was clearly a revelation she didn't want to hear. Sam doesn't know whether the man wants to let it all out or slap his wife around the face. It was hard to tell. He'd certainly not been expecting the man to be so open so quickly. Normally, in situations like this, they walk to the car with him, leak out their secret when their partner is out of earshot. Ralph Probisher was clearly a man who didn't want to lie to the police.

'I think it would be better if Mr Probisher and I spoke alone about this matter.' Sam focuses his eyes on the woman in front of him, her cheeks burn with anger. 'Don't you, Mr Probisher?'

She wipes a spittle of tea off her chin and lips, it smears her lipstick. 'I—'

'Yes,' he interjects. 'Ingrid, leave me and DS Ingleby alone for five minutes.'

'What?' she folds her arms across her chest, sinks back the pile of cushions behind her back.

'Leave us alone, please.' He rubs his hand over his mouth.

She gets to her feet, throws him a look fit to kill. '*This* isn't finished, Ralph,' her voice drips with indignation. She slams the door behind her.

Ralph Probisher takes his head in his hands, inhales a slow breath. 'I'd divorce her if I could, that woman drains the life out of me.' He looks up at Sam, pleads with him, 'Please, don't tell her that.'

'Why don't you?'

'She'd take every single penny I have.'

Sam decides not to explore that subject. 'Your daughter, Mr Probisher, you said you spoke to her last week.'

He nods, a small smile crosses his lips. 'Yes, we've been in touch for years. I speak to her every week.' He rolls his eyes towards the door. '*She* doesn't know. Lily turned up one day after I'd finished work. Back in the 1980s. Said that she was getting married, that she wanted me to give her away. Apparently, she and Edmund had been in touch for a while.'

'You didn't tell your wife, then?'

'What do you think?' bitterness floods into his voice. 'She'd have made the whole thing an absolute misery.' He rubs his eyes. 'I told her I'd been invited on a golf trip up in Scotland, that's where the wedding was, that's where she still lives. Ingrid hates golf, she took herself off to a spa for the weekend.'

'When did Lily first contact you?'

'1984, summer I think. She got married in 1985. She'd straightened herself out, managed to get into one of those government-funded rehab clinics. The ones we paid for never worked. Then she went to Canada for a bit. That's where she met Tom, the man she married. He doesn't know, you know, about the heroin. She's a completely different person now.' His face suddenly glows with pride. 'She's lovely, a bright smart girl. She went back to university. I have grandchildren too – Bella and Will.'

'Does your son know all of this?'

He nods his head in accent. 'Yes, it's because of him she got in touch with me. He hired someone over here to find her. He's sworn to secrecy. When he lived here we used to visit her. Father and son weekends away – fishing.' He gets to his feet, goes to stand by the window, looks out into the garden. 'He's not overly fond of his mother either, Lily had doted on him, before the—' There's a tremor in his voice. 'I–I've got two great kids and have to lie to my wife whenever I want to see them.'

Sam rests his notepad on his knees. He lowers his voice. 'So, what was your daughter like, before she left?'

Ralph Probisher gazed off into the distance. 'She was a handful. I'll admit that – she would never be the girl that Ingrid wanted her to be.'

'And what was that?'

'Quiet, she wasn't quiet. Ingrid wasn't used to little girls, not boisterous and full of energy ones. She's not the maternal type. Penny and Lily, they spent all their time together, they adored each other. Lily was broken-hearted when her mother died, as was I. And of course, Lily took after my wife,' his eyes light up, 'she had beautiful red hair and a beaming smile.'

'How did she get into heroin?'

'At school, one of her friends, I think that was it, anyway. I never asked. I was a different man after Penny died.' He looks down into his hands. 'Weaker, I was weaker. That's why I married Ingrid, everything was falling apart. I was about to lose my job. I thought Lily needed a mother.' He lets out a sigh, hangs his head. 'Worse mistake I ever made.'

'I'm sorry to have to ask you this, but were you aware that the police rang you after your daughter tried to commit suicide?

The man is taken aback, he looks aghast. 'Suicide? No.'

'They spoke to your wife.'

'Suicide? Lily?' His eyes widen in disbelief. 'No, she's never tried to commit suicide. What the hell are you talking about?'

Sam flicks the pages back in his notebook. 'Our records show that she tried to commit suicide on the fourth of December 1999. The booking sergeant rang your wife. She refused to help, said that she didn't have a daughter anymore.'

The colour rushes to Ralph Probisher's face. 'That can't be true—Lily would never do that.' He strides across the room, away from the window, stands directly in front of Sam. 'But Ingrid, that's bloody typical.' His hand balls into a fist. 'No, she didn't tell me that there'd been a call.' His spits the words out. 'I know it was years ago, but I would have remembered if she had. Lily moved out of Edinburgh after she got married, to the north of Scotland. She would have been pregnant with Will. He was born that year, on Christmas Eve. It must have been a mistake, someone with the same name.' He looks down on Sam, a sheen of sweat covers forehead and cheeks, his agitation clear to see.

'I'm sorry this is difficult, especially after all this time.' Sam makes some quick notes and stands up. 'I know it's been uncomfortable for you, but you've really helped. I've just got a couple more things to ask of you. I need to take a DNA sample, is that okay with you?'

Ralph Probisher, steps back, pulls himself up, takes in a deep breath. 'Of course, no problem at all.'

Sam removes a testing kit from his shoulder bag and takes a sample from Ralph Probisher's mouth. He labels it up before placing it in an evidence bag. 'So why did you come to see us. It seems a long way from Manchester?'

'Didn't your wife tell you I'd rung?'

'No.' Ralph Probisher shakes his head, the edges of his lips turn down. 'God knows how many calls I've missed over the years. You must think I'm really foolish – weak.' He looks expectantly at Sam, as though seeking some form of denial.

'You're not the first, shall we leave it at that?' Sam smiles, 'and at least it's out in the open now. Could I have your daughter's phone number?'

'Yes, of course. It's in my office upstairs.' He hurries off to get it.

Sam hears raised voices out in the hallway. Moments later, Ralph Probisher comes back into the room, red-faced, a sheet of paper in his hand. He shuts the door behind him.

'Here it is. Lily Jamieson, she's probably at work right now.'

'Thanks,' Sam takes it from him, pockets it. 'You've been very helpful, Mr Probisher, I'll be speaking to your son later. He'll confirm your version of events?'

The man stares into his face for a moment. 'Right, yes, I'm sure he will.' He turns his head, looks towards the door. 'I'm glad it's out in the open now. Edmund has asked me to go and spend some time with him and his partner in New York. I'm going to go.'

Sam smiles, offers out his hand, the man takes it in both hands, shakes it vigorously.

'I'm sure he'll be delighted to see you.'

For a second, Ralph Probisher's eyes light up, then they dim. 'You never said why you needed to know all this. Has someone else been pretending to be my daughter?'

'I'm sorry, I'm not at liberty to tell you that right now. All I can say is that it's linked to another case. But when it's all over I'll let you know more, I promise. I won't leave you in the dark.'

Ralph Probisher's shoulders slump down, he stands immobile for a moment, then rubs his thumb along his lower lip. He seems lost in his thoughts. 'It seems that I've been in the dark for a long time anyway. A couple of months won't make much of difference. I've always worried that Lily's past would catch up with her. I've put my private mobile number on there too. Just in case you need to get in touch with me. Clearly, I can't depend on Ingrid.' He shows Sam to the door, his wife nowhere to be seen.

'I'll be in touch,' says Sam, shaking the man's hand again. Then another question pops into his mind.

'Mr Probisher, did Lily have many friends?'

He touches Sam lightly on the sleeve, 'Ralph, call me Ralph,'
'Ralph, then. Did Lily have many friends?'

He shakes his head in response. 'You'll have to ask her that one
yourself. There were some, but heaven knows where they are now.'

'Right, thanks, bye again then.' Sam strides off in the direction
of his car. When he's settled in the seat, he calls the number on
the piece of paper. Lily Jamieson answers, he briefly explains the
purpose of his call. He hears her voice break, clearly unsettled by
his call. She asks if she can ring him back, she's at work, can't talk.
They agree that he'll ring her tomorrow, her day off.

He starts up the car, switches on the satnav, makes his way
back to the M1. His mind wanders as he drives, he imagines
Ingrid screaming at her husband, he sees the tall grey figure of
Ralph Probisher leaving with a paltry suitcase, just like he had
when he'd broken up with his wife. She'd thrust it into his arms as
he'd walked through the door, her face blazing with anger.

'You can go and live with that tart you work with.'

As usual, his wife had got the wrong end of the stick. He wasn't
Mel's type. And, of course, he couldn't explain; some things are
best left unsaid.

Thankfully, they'd made up. He checks the time on the
dashboard if he's lucky he'll be back by dinner.

Chapter 43

Mel's jaw tightens as she reads over her notes. The list of queries seemed endless. Back in 1973, the investigating copper's interest must have dissipated within weeks. In the case of Karen, at least one witness had come forward and said that they'd seen her with an older boy. There was no sign of it being followed up – probably brushed aside as tittle-tattle. The witness, probably long dead.

Veronica, on the other hand, was portrayed as a druggie, yet there was no investigation into who supplied the drugs. The fact that both the mother and grandmother stated that Veronica would not have run away went unacknowledged. No wonder they had felt abandoned, let down by the very people who should have been helping them. Mel lets out a sigh of frustration. At the least, both cases have been reopened – fresh eyes, better science and even better policing hopefully will find them closure.

The office is a buzz of noise, Kinsi and Jenny are on the phone. The HOLMES team are entering data into the system. She loves days like this, when everyone is on board, on purpose, and all those other terms she'd learnt on the management development course she attended last year. Veronica Lightfoot is proving an interesting case – for everyone on the team, she can see it in their eyes. Concentration, determination. They want to be let off the leash, they want to get on with it.

There was still one big unanswered question – when did Veronica become Lily Probisher? Those early police files, did they relate to the real Lily or to Veronica using her name. They hadn't been able to find anything to guide them in that direction. She'd hoped Sam would bring light to that.

Badger pops his head around her office door, fresh from fighting his way through Lily Probisher's financial files. 'Can I see you for a few minutes, boss?'

He places a plastic storage box on the floor by the door, parks himself in the chair opposite her desk. He pulls the metal rimmed glasses on the top of his head down to his eyes.

'Her financials gave up some surprises; she owns a couple of properties.' He raises an eyebrow. 'Although, as far as we know she's not legally Lily Probisher, so I'm not sure who actually owns them.'

Mel gives a wry smile. 'Let's hope the Probishers don't find out.'

'That's a point, I'd not given much thought.' A pained look crosses his face. 'Some interesting legal issues will definitely raise their ugly head whichever way this case goes. Anyway, she owns the place she runs her business out of, the one on Bennetts Road. It's split into two flats. Downstairs is her practice. I assumed that she would have rented the top flat out, especially as she has that place on St. Georges Road, the one you visited.'

Mel listens with only half her attention; the other half wants to get back to checking out the medical records.

'Well, I was wrong.' He smiles, taps his knuckles lightly on her desk as though to bring her back to the conversation. 'It's not rented out. She's had work done on it. There was a desk, a couple of chairs, a single bed, no sign of an occupant. That was about it. The desk drawer was full of receipts, the woman never seemed to throw any of them away,' he sniffed, took a tissue out of his pocket, blew his nose noisily, 'going back years. Among them, there was bill for a garage door repair. Clearly, it wasn't attached to the house. I thought it might be worthwhile having a look to see what she's been using it for. I contacted the repair company; they gave me the address of the garage.'

'Right, when Sam gets back, you and he have a look. I want to finish these.' She places her hand on the pile of medical records.

He coughs, raises his voice an octave. 'Been there already, boss. Thought I might try out the remainder of those keys that we couldn't find anything to fit.'

'Oh, right.' Mel's attention is fully focused now, she pushes the pile of documents off to the left, leans back in her seat. 'Tell me what you found?'

'These.' He places the plastic box on the table. 'Locked away in a filing cabinet. Very old school technology, I had to use one of the tape machines in the interview room to play them back on.'

She lifts the lid, peers inside in the box.

'Lots of cassettes, I played a few. Recordings of some sort of therapy sessions.' He peers through his glasses, 'A bit weird, if you ask me. Unusual name too – Mnimi – it's Greek for memory.'

Each cassette has been bagged for evidence. Mel picks one up after another, they look as though they've been played repeatedly. The thin brown tape is creased in parts. The labels are stained with age. No dates, just five words, handwritten in the same hand on every cassette.

The Mnimi Project – Patient Number Eight.

'Did they come in individualised cases?'

He shakes his head. 'I wondered about that, too. I think someone must have thrown those out. They certainly weren't in there,' he points to the box.

She leans forward. 'Fingerprints?'

'Some... but they're badly deteriorated. Nothing identifiable.'

She frowns, sinks back into her seat. 'What's on them? Her clients?'

'No. I had another look in her office, I found her client records locked in a wall safe. She recorded everything, video, a camera hidden in the room sensor. All on DVD, everything labelled, name, date, time, organised in alphabetical order and then by date. Very OCD. I doubt that her clients knew she was doing that.'

'Anyone contacted any of them yet?'

'Hmm, not yet.' He scratches his chin.' I've put together a list of her clients, it's a long list.'

'Give Kinsi the list, tell her to give them a call, she's good at stuff like that. No mention of the recordings though, don't want them demanding access or threatening to sue us. Tell her to inform them that we've just found an appointment book with their telephone numbers in.' She leans forward, rests her elbows on her desk, rotates her neck. 'She'll get them to open up, hopefully. At least they'll be able to tell us more about her.' She moves her seat, dips towards the box. 'Tell me more about these?' She picks up another bagged cassette.

'I wasn't sure at first, after checking a few I realised that they were the same two people on them, patient number eight and someone who I think might be a psychiatrist. I compared one of the DVDs with one of the cassette recordings. The voices sound very similar. However, on the cassettes, the person is patient eight, on the DVD she's the therapist. There's a little difference in the accents, she's got a bit posher over time.' He smiles. 'Whatever problems she had, she'd clearly got over them.'

'Any dates on the cassettes?'

'The couple that I listened to were recorded in 1999. Nothing noted on the actual tapes themselves though.'

'Well, whilst we're at it, we'd best get on with that, too. Get Jenny to transcribe them. The cassettes that is, make them a priority. Then ask her to put them on a timeline. See what turns up.'

He gets to his feet, picks up the plastic box, tucks it under his arm. 'This case seems to be getting weirder and weirder.'

She nods her head; stifles a yawn, the lack of sleep is catching up on her. 'Still, we're making progress. You've done a good job there, Badger.' She feels a sense of relief, the relief that her team is nothing like the one back in 1973.

A thought spins through her head, Thomasine Albright must have read every single document in the missing person's file.

I'd be filled with anger and bitterness if it was me.

Her mobile phone vibrates across the desk.

'Thanks, Badge, I've got to take this, it's Sam — let's see what he's found out from Ralph and Ingrid Probisher.

Chapter 44

Thomasine drags herself out of bed, her bare feet sink into the bedroom carpet, her eyes feel like they're filled with sand. She slips on the furry pink dressing gown her mother bought her last Christmas, draws back the bedroom curtains. She'd worked well into the night, forced herself to bed at three o'clock, with a glass of whisky and two paracetamol for the pain across her shoulders. A common complaint in her line of work. Soon her dreams soured into nightmares. All the cases she'd investigated concertinaed in her head, the bagged hands, the bloated faces, the burnt bodies.

I bet I look like shit.

Late yesterday she'd rung the boss, asked to come back. After the niceties, he'd been direct.

'Not yet, take another week,' He wasn't one for messing around. 'I want you back fresh. Your head clear.' He knew what he was talking about, his own daughter wreaked havoc on the family, drugs, stealing money. She disappeared at least once a month. Thomasine knew that if he'd thought she was up to it, he'd have her back at work in a heartbeat.

She goes through to the office, looks down at the black and white photographs strewn across her desk. The computer hums in the background. She has a name to follow up on, a new lead to follow – Jacky2422, the woman who posted the pictures, the woman who probably was there that night. Someone who might be an important witness.

Those other missing girls—what happened to them? Perhaps there could be links there too.

Thomasine picks up the photograph of Karen, and of him. Her eyes wander across the page; they settle on his face again. What did he have that attracted Karen to him? He looks older than the eighteen she said he was. He must be at least twenty. He has a beard and moustache, dark eyes, long dark eyelashes. She tries to imagine what he'd look like now. Grey hair instead of brown, a receding hairline, the skin on his face slack, his shoulders rounded; the muscle wasted from his arms and chest. That's if he's alive even.

The doorbell goes, she reminds herself to take out the batteries. Someone shouts through the letterbox. She tells herself she must tape it over, ring the post office to keep her mail there. Instead, she closes the office door, blocks them out.

Her eyes return to the photograph. Dozens of people surrounded them on the dance floor. It's hard to tell how old they were, some look very young, the girls in particular. She clicks back on the website, reads through the blog postings, to see if anyone has tagged themselves in the photograph. No one has.

Boys in sleeveless T-shirts, thin waistcoats, some bare-chested. Girls in short-sleeved blouses and culottes. Thomasine can't tell whether it's summer or winter by the clothes they're wearing. Wherever they are it must be hot, everyone is sweating. Other than Karen, she doesn't recognise anyone in the photograph, or in any of the photographs.

There's one thing she does know, most of the people in them will look very different now. She wonders which one is Jacky2422. She emailed her last night, asked if she could see her tomorrow, now today. Jacky emailed her back, she was away for a few days. Would she mind waiting until she got back? She had no choice.

For a moment, she wonders why Judith had told her about the diary. She'd had plenty of time over the years. She saw no mention of the diary on file. She scribbles a reminder to ask her who interviewed her. If she can remember that is. Then she texts Paul. Lets him know that she'll be staying at her own place for a few days.

Her eyes catch the name on the wall – Charlie Arnold, the most recent case, 1987. It had been over a year since she'd contacted Belinda Davies, her sister. She was due a visit – to show that they were still looking, still cared. Keeping the connection alive even though the case might be cold. Faces changed, parents and grandparents died, brothers and sisters grew older, sometimes moved away.

Then there were the families where the missing child was their only child. That was perhaps the hardest. The fear that when they were gone, no one would be there to keep looking. To look after them if they turned up alive or to organise the funeral if it was the other. Sudden tears prick Thomasine's eyes.

Pull yourself together girl. Those words had been her mantra for over thirty years.

She knew Belinda Davies' number by heart. Charlie could be in those woods, too. It rang for nearly a minute before she picked up.

'Hi Belinda, it's Thomasine.'

It's clear from the moment she hears her voice; Belinda is not in a mood for a chat.

'I thought you might ring, Thom. I don't know why but I did.' Her tone is clipped, brisk, her reluctance obvious. 'I'm happy for you, truly. I want you to know that. At least you know now. At least you can bury her.'

Then she put down the phone, she didn't slam it. She's never been one for long conversations, she didn't even let Thomasine get a word in. But the call was brief, even by her standards. Thomasine lets out a sigh of disappointment, pulls herself out of the chair, goes downstairs, throws some cereal in a bowl, splashes on some milk. She eats two spoonful's and throws the rest in the bin.

She sees no point in getting upset, nevertheless she does. Belinda's voice was like a paper cut, sharp and unexpected. She goes out into the garden, down the bottom, to sit on the bench that she had built herself. She has a cry, allows herself five minutes of wallowing, then she pulls herself back together. She stands up tall, pulls her shoulders back.

Like Mam used to say, no point in crying over spilt milk. No, I'm not giving up, I'm going to talk with her, I just need to adjust my strategy. Her sister disappeared the same way as Karen, out of the blue, that's why I'd copied the file. There were other parallels too, same age, dark hair, hazel eyes, the same precocious personality, fourteen going on twenty-two. And yet no one made a connection. Just another runaway.

She goes upstairs, showers, puts on some makeup. Pulls on a pair of fitted black trousers, they're loose at the waist. The milk-chocolate coloured jumper looks off against her skin, she's sleep deprived, washed out. She seizes her bag and coat and sneaks out the back way. Her car is parked down the street, out of the sight of the journos.

Belinda lives in Wickenshaw, rents a house there. It's about thirty minutes away. As she drives through the streets she sees hundreds of young girls, layered in make-up, heads stuck in their mobile phones, in complete denial that it could happen to them. A shiver goes down her back, what if the woodland has more bodies to give up? Back then, girls were a lot more naive.

The street is run down; it's all back to back housing, abandoned cars on the scrub ground where they knocked houses down, ready for the regeneration grants that never came. Drugs, high crime, high unemployment, too many people thrown out of decent housing that they can't afford or don't take care of, with no place to go but this... five rows of Victorian terraces, surrounded by a field of squalor. Two-up-two-downs, downstairs bathrooms, low rents and even lower standards.

Within seconds of being out of the car, her body is covered in a freezing cold drizzle that turns her hair into springy black curls that stick to her head and soaks through the heavy black coat that she'd slung on earlier. Hidden in her bag lies a bottle of prosecco. Picked up from the Tesco's around the corner. Belinda's favourite tipple. As she gets nearer, she sees that the curtains are half-drawn, there's a light on. Someone must be home. Outside the front door is a large green recycling bin overflowing with bottles and tins.

She knocks, she hears a dog bark. *Why is it they always have dogs?*

Belinda shouts through the half-glazed door. 'What do you want? Didn't you get my message?'

It must be a bad day. Thomasine wonders how she knows it is her. Belinda unlocks the door. Her leg holds back the brown and white Jack Russell that's trying to escape. She points towards her watch.

'I've not got long.' Her mouth twists in a sour expression. 'I've got to go out.'

Her face is puffy through God knows what. Lack of sleep, too much alcohol. Thomasine tries not to hazard a guess. The skin on her neck is losing its tightness, her eyes are lined with kohl, her lips covered in a thick layer of lip-gloss. Her long brown curly hair pulled into a top-knot on the crown of her head.

'I brought a gift.' Thomasine holds out the prosecco.

'You'd best come in.' She takes the bottle from her hand without even a thank you.

Thomasine follows Belinda through to the back room, her dark grey slippers flip-flop on the laminate floor, there's a sickly-sweet aroma of Chinese food, the kitchen table is covered in half-empty takeaway cartons.

'You'll have to take me as you find me.' There is no warmth in her voice, the dog rushes around her feet, she picks it up, nestles it under her arm. It bares its teeth. Thomasine smiles back at it.

Belinda lets out a sigh, 'What do you want anyway?'

'I'll be honest. I reviewed your sister's file recently. I remember looking at Charlie's picture and thinking how alike she and Karen were. Now we know that Karen didn't run away, I thought perhaps that Charlie didn't either.'

The silence hangs between them. That same cold smile spreads across Belinda's face again. When they'd first met, Belinda had been pretty in that clean, wholesome way that hadn't fitted with the current fashion. There was a softness to her. Now, her clothes are too small, the bright red blouse she's wearing looks like the buttons are about to burst off. Her skirt creased – it's not been ironed, and there's what looks like a long smear of sweet and sour sauce across the hem. All in all, there's been quite a change in Belinda.

Her eyes zoom in on Thomasine, her words to the point. 'I bet no one is looking for Charlie's body up in those woods, are they?'

Thomasine coughs, clears her throat. 'They're still excavating, but sorry, I don't know for sure, I'm off work at the moment.' She feels a sudden flush of embarrassment, of helplessness that she doesn't want to explain.

Belinda walks out of the room without a word. Thomasine's stomach plummets.

I've probably said the wrong thing. She hears her feet tread on the stairs, then a door open and shut, the dog barks voraciously, she must have shut it in. Moments later Belinda saunters into the room, her slippers making the same slow flip-flop sound.

'Do you want one?' She picks up the bottle of wine, takes off the top.

Thomasine nods. 'Why not?'

Belinda takes two glasses off the side of the sink and washes them thoroughly, dries them off. At least she understands the need for some basic hygiene. Thomasine looks around the room, it's tidy and clean. She'd not noticed that at first. The overflowing bin outside and the food cartons on the table had switched her other senses off. Belinda appears to have read her mind.

'Patricia, my sister, it was her twenty-first yesterday, last night… just family. I was just finishing clearing up.'

'How is everyone?'

Her eyes soften momentarily. 'We still feel guilty whenever we allow ourselves to have a celebration. But then you know all about that, don't you? Dad, he tries to be strong, Mum… she's not well, hasn't been for years. I don't see her much these days.'

Thomasine nods her head; she knows only too well how families fair in that direction.

'Take a seat.' With intense concentration, Belinda fills one glass, then the other. There's an irony about the occasion. The bubbles give a sense of celebration where there is none. She hands Thomasine a glass. Takes a quick sip of her own. 'I still worry to death about her.' Her eyes settle on a photograph hung on the wall, a school photograph. 'Our Pat's like Charlie. Out all hours, real party girl, hard to keep a track of. Thank God for mobile phones.'

Thomasine lifts her glass. 'To Charlie… wherever she may be.'

'To our Charlie.'

'Tell me more about her?'

Her eyes widen. 'Who? Our Charlie? Haven't you heard everything there is to hear?'

Thomasine hesitates for a moment, then throws caution to the wind. It'll get out eventually anyway. 'What I'm going to tell you I want you to keep to yourself. You can't tell anyone else. Are we clear about that?'

Belinda takes in a quick breath, goes to speak but closes her mouth.

Thomasine holds gaze, leans forward. 'I need you to promise me you won't share what I'm going to tell you with anyone else.'

The woman lets out a sigh, gives Thomasine a look that says *you must be joking.*

Thomasine puts an edge on her voice. 'I'm being completely serious.'

'Alright, I won't blab. I promise.' She offers her hand to shake on it, Thomasine takes it in her own, Belinda's skin is dry and soft.

Thomasine leans back into her seat. 'Okay, I've found something out. About Karen. A boyfriend, one we didn't know existed. Someone older, he bought her things, clothes, makeup and the like. I wondered if the same was happening to Charlie before she disappeared. There's no mention of it in the notes.'

'The same man?' Confusion crosses Belinda's face. 'There's twelve years' difference. Surely there can't be a connection between the two of them?'

'Men like that don't change their preferences. They have a type, they invest a lot of time and effort into getting to know the girls, spend a lot of money.'

'I find it hard to believe our Charlie would have gone for an older bloke.'

'She might not have seen him as a boyfriend, could've been a friend. Men like that worm their way into teenage girls' lives in all sorts of ways.' The word grooming looms large at the front of Thomasine's mind, she doesn't say it. 'He was very generous; girls can be swayed by that. Karen certainly was. It had been going on for months. We had no idea at all. I think he might have been about twenty at the time Karen went missing.'

Thomasine can see Belinda mulling things over in her head, she takes in a breath, a look of distaste flashes in her eyes.

'Let me clear this away first.' She takes a black plastic bag out of a drawer. 'I can't think with this mess.' She throws the half-eaten cartoons of food in it, takes it outside. She opens a window to let out the smell, wipes the table top down with a cloth, then drops it in the sink.

'That's better.' She sits back down opposite Thomasine, takes another mouthful of prosecco, holds it in her mouth a moment before swallowing it. 'I can't remember much. I was just tiny back then, only three.' Absentmindedly, she rubs her forefinger around the rim of the glass. 'She was always out at some club or another, that's what Dad says. She was just thirteen when it first started, she'd be gone for hours, not tell Mum and Dad where she'd been. They had huge arguments about it. She started wearing makeup, making herself look older. Mum and Dad couldn't stop her, they tried but she wouldn't listen, she kept sneaking out. Then she went missing. Mum said that the police looked all over the place for her, couldn't find her. Her friends said they'd only seen her at school, that they thought she was hanging out with someone new, they didn't know who it was. No one had seen her with a stranger. Whoever she was spending time with they must have taken her somewhere private.'

'Did she have any boyfriends?'

'Probably, we never met any of them, though. She was really pretty, dark hair, brown eyes, skinny as a rake.' Her eyes go to another photo on the wall, Charlie in her school uniform, next to pictures of Pat and Belinda. The similarities between the three girls less obvious, their heads tilted to the right, broad smiles, full lips. Hair colour, skin tone, facial features, in that there is no apparent resemblance.

She carries on. 'She used to buy her own clothes, she got a paper round when she was about eleven. Dad said she was very enterprising, always wanting stuff that they couldn't afford. Always trying to look older than she was.' A look of sadness crosses her face. 'Mam and Dad argued like cat and dog when she didn't come back. Mum blamed Dad for not being harder on her, she said he was too soft. That was the end of their marriage really, they've not divorced but…'

'I know how that feels, it was the end for my dad. He didn't even make forty-one.

Belinda's eyes widen in surprise.

'We're not meant to talk about personal lives, unprofessional. And besides, it's my job to help find other peoples' loved ones.' A wry smile crosses Thomasine's lips.

Belinda's eyes suddenly streak with tears.

'I never knew, I just thought—'

'I know,' Thomasine shrugs her shoulders, 'you and everyone else.' She places her glass down on the table. 'I was wondering if you still had any of Charlie's things?'

She shakes her head. 'Not much. Like you know, the coppers take most things, they're probably in a box somewhere deep in the bowels of the police station.' She raises an eyebrow. 'There is one thing though, I'd taken it before she left, I thought they were crayons, I'd been drawing with them.' Her eyes soften. 'I kept them as a keep-sake, stupid I know.'

'Have you still got them?' Thomasine tries not to sound too eager.

Belinda hurries out of the room, her previous reticence evaporated. The dog starts barking again. Minutes later she is downstairs. She offers out her hand, opens her fingers. In the centre of her palm is a yellow tin with a white daisy on it.

Thomasine feels the air inside her lungs contract. It reminds her of something, she wracks her brain trying to think of it as she takes the tin out of her hand.

'Is it important?' Belinda leans forward, waits for an answer.

'I don't know yet.' Thomasine's turns the tin over in her hand. Her fingers tremble. 'Look, I'm really sorry but I need to get back home, to check something, I'll be in touch, I promise.' She lurches to her feet. 'Can I take this?'

'As long as you let me have it back, it's the only thing I've got of hers.'

She promises that she will. After a quick thank you, she's out of the door. Once in the car, she drops the tin into a clear plastic bag. She doesn't know why. The chances of any prints other than her own and Belinda's are remote. Not after all these years.

All the way back she keeps repeating the words in her head, *please, please, please let me be right.*

She's almost home when she remembers that Sam Ingleby took everything for processing. She carries on back to the farm regardless. She can check that the press hasn't been all over the place.

It still feels strange not to be greeted by the dogs. It seems so silent at the farm, just the birds cawing on the roof, the wind whistling through the barn. For once the hairs on the back of Thomasine's neck start to rise. What if someone is waiting for her? What if someone has broken into the cottage. The person who took Karen. Murdered her? Perhaps they've come back. She lets out a nervous laugh.

But what for? There's only you here now, stupid cow.

The darkness of the hallway pales as she opens the front door. She stands totally still for a moment, listens for movement. A blackbird squawks as it lands on the chimney.

She keeps her coat and gloves on. First things first, she thinks to herself. She turns on the lights, plugs in the radiators she brought up last week. Tries to take the edge off the cold. Then she freezes.

Upstairs, a door opens and shut. Her legs go weak; she's positive she'd shut all the doors before she left.

She creeps up the stairs, a shiver goes down her back, rats, bats, what if they'd managed to force their way through the roof and into the house. She lets out a gasp, footsteps, she can hear them overhead. She almost jumps out of her skin. Her mouth goes utterly dry. Her mother's rifle is in the pantry, she hid it there, she could use it. The footsteps get nearer.

Someone must have broken in, not through the front door, she'd just unlocked that. They must have come in the back way; she wants to kick herself for being so unobservant. Have they heard her? Did they hear her come into the house?

Thomasine continues up the stairs, the loft door swings open and shut. The floorboards squeal and moan above her. Perhaps they've not heard her, the wind makes a lot of noise up there, the rattling of the roof tiles drowns everything out.

She takes the first step, closes the door behind her, at least they won't be able to see her silhouette. Places her feet carefully, trying not to make a sound. Seconds later she eases her head above the attic floor, just enough to see what's going on, see who's in there. A pale-yellow light moves around the room; he, she is down at the opposite end of the nook. She ducks her head down, holds her breath. She has no idea how big they are, she'll need an advantage, will need to take them by surprise. It takes her seconds to come up with a plan.

Tentatively, Thomasine makes her way down stairs, checks for signs of a break-in. There are none. Whoever they are, they have a key, or they've picked the lock. She picks up her bag, slings it over her shoulder, makes her way silently back upstairs. The ceiling above her groans beneath their weight. She slides open her mother's underwear drawer, takes out a pair of her thick nylon tights. Tucks them in the band of her jeans. She draws the curtains; the room sinks into a dark grey gloom. Her fingers wrap around the small cylindrical tube in the outside pocket of her handbag. She takes it out, presses the cap, drops it at the bottom of the stairs. The piercing noise screeches in the silence.

Heavy footsteps clatter across the floor – then a thud – the sound of a body falling to the floor. It's a man, it must be a man, the weight, the ungainly movements. Then the scrambling of feet, the footsteps hammer down the stairs, his hands scrape along the wall, the door explodes open. She's waiting on the other side, she swings her torch into the middle of his face, hits him hard on the bridge of his nose. The wail of a wounded animal bounces off the wall, he drops to his knees. She swings the torch again, to the back of the head. The blow knocks him forward. The toe of her boot hits him centre spine. His hands flay about as he hits the floor, her heel digs deep into his shoulder blades as she wrenches his arms back, binds her mother's tights around his wrists. She jerks the nylon like catgut, binds his ankles then – in one quick sweep – ties his hands and feet together. His body immobilised. She grabs his hair, pulls back his head, glares at him.

'Who–*Paul?* A look of incredulity springs to her face. 'What the—'

'I can't b-b-breath, g-g-get off me.' Tears mix with blood as they stream down his face, over his sweatshirt onto the floor; sobs rattle out of his chest.

Her heart pounding in her ears, she fumbles with the knots she wound tight only a few minutes earlier. He slumps forward, his body juddering in shock.

'Shit – I'm sorry! I thought you were—'

She grabs him a towel out of the linen chest. He holds it to his nose.

'Why did you hit me?'

'Why do you think, Paul?' Her voice clipped, she helps him to his feet.

He doesn't answer.

'I come home and hear someone in our loft, an intruder. Surely, you're not that naive to think I'd just say hello, tell them to just get on with it, help themselves. I'd no idea who it was, I just heard footsteps in the loft. This beggars belief...'

'I didn't think—'

'You certainly didn't *think*, Paul. I'm a police officer, I'm trained to respond. You're bloody lucky I didn't have my taser on me. I could have done you some serious harm. I could have…' She looks at his face, the penny drops.

Of course, I should have guessed, I should have anticipated this, he wanted to know what I'd found up in the loft, wanted to see if there was anything else. He'd even asked if there was anything about him in the diary.

'Let's go downstairs, have a proper talk, I still can't believe you've done this.' She shakes her head in exasperation. 'Anyway, how did you get in?'

He coughs blood into the towel, his voice is muffled. 'Yer mam left a spare front door key in the barn.'

'Great,' Thomasine shakes her head in disbelief, 'she never told me that.'

He follows her downstairs, she soaks the towel under the cold water, bright pink blood seeps out. She gestures towards the kitchen table.

'Sit there.'

He sits down without a fuss, face streaked with dust and blood, his skin the colour of beetroot. Tentatively, she feels the bridge of his nose between her fingers. He lets out a whimper. Her patience frays. 'Don't be a wally. You're okay, it's not broken.'

She makes them both a drink, they sit in silence, their hands wrapped around pint pots of tea. Thomasine breaks the ice first.

'It's about the diary, isn't it? What did you think it would say about you?'

A sullen look transforms his face. 'I d-d-don't know.'

'Don't mess me about, did you see Karen with someone? It might be important.'

Purple shadows are forming around his eyes; he'll have two black eyes before the evening's out. She wonders how he'll explain that to his father.

'Not at first, it was November time when I saw them together, I can't exactly remember when. It was when the weather had changed.

It was r-r-raining. I spotted them out in the fields. I was out hunting for r-r-rabbits with the dogs.'

'And what?'

'It must have been a weekend. I saw them walking up through the back field. Her and him, he had a beard, I remember that. I remember thinking she was with an old bloke. Why would she be with an old bloke?' He looks out through the kitchen window. 'They went in the old bomb shelter – y-y-you know, that one she locked yer in. I was just curious. It was the once, that's all.'

The memory of the bomb shelter flashes into her conscious – a rat invested hovel – a shudder runs down her spine.

'So, what did you see?'

He averts his eyes, picks up his tea, his hands are shaking. 'I didn't see anything, they went inside and shut the door.'

'What happened next?'

'I can't remember.' He snivels; wipes his nose on his sleeve. Right in front of her he transforms into his fourteen-year-old self.

'Yes, you can, Paul. I can tell that from the tone of your voice.'

'Well, I heard things, laughing, things like that?'

'Did he rape her?'

'No, no.' He has a look of horror on his face. 'I don't think so.'

'Then what happened next?'

'I heard her cry out. She told him to stop.' He averts his gaze again. 'One of the dogs barked, I couldn't shut it up. I heard her calling me like she used to. "Spaz, Spaz – go away, Spaz." She sounded afraid.' His eyes glint with unshed tears. He hated that name and she knew it. He looks down at the floor, the sadness that this particular memory brings him written all over his face. 'Yer could never tell with her. Anyway, I ran off.'

'So why didn't you tell anyone about it?'

'I saw her at school a couple of days later, she p-p-pulled me aside, told me not to tell anyone. I know yer p-p-probably think I'm a coward, but I didn't know what to do, I were t-t-trapped.' His words rush out. 'I couldn't tell anybody; she would have known. My life would have been sheer bloody misery.'

'Okay,' she breathes out. Takes the black and white photograph out of her bag. She slides it towards him. Points to the man in the centre of the dance floor. 'Is this him?'

He stares at it for a few moments.

'Yeah, th-th-that's him.' He clears his throat. 'I've had that face in me head ever since.'

She let out a low groan, all these years wasted.

'Where did yer get that picture from?' His voice cuts through her thoughts.

'What?'

'The picture, where did yer find it?'

'On the internet.' She leaves it at that. The trust she'd always had in him dissipates into thin air. 'Did you take anything out of the loft?'

He shakes his head, stands up, clears his pockets. Two keys clatter onto the table, his own and the one from the barn.

Her fingers wrap around the latter. 'I think I'd best have this one back.'

His face flushes. 'I'm sorry, Thom, r-r-really. I should have talked to yer about it. I just—'

'It's done now, let's move on. Come on, I'll take you home. I've got some more work to do.'

'Can I help?'

She shakes head. 'No, I'm on top of it. I'll take you home. We can face your dad together.' At least that was like when they were kids.

He gives a weak smile. 'It's alright, I'll tell him meself.'

Chapter 45

The welcome aroma of fresh coffee washes over Mel as she enters the meeting room. The team are already there. 'Sam's on a call to Lily Probisher, the *real* one. I'll bring him up to speed when he gets back.' Her eyes rove around the room. Scattered on the table are coffee cups on placemats, a large plate of blueberry muffins and a tape recorder on temporary loan from one of the interview rooms. 'Best get a start on this, we've got a lot to cover.' She eases herself down in the vacant seat at the head of the table.

Jenny Welbeck's eyelids flutter shut as she downs a couple of tablets with a glass of water.

Mel leans over towards her, touches her lightly on the arm. 'You alright?'

'Just a bit tired, this job was a bit unsettling, stays in your mind, if I'm honest.' She sinks back into her seat, inclines her head towards the tape recorder. 'Long job, we might need to bring a few more transcribers on board.'

Mel nods in agreement. 'I'll have a word.'

Kinsi switches off her mobile phone and stuffs it deep into the bowels of the large black and gold Gucci handbag hanging on the back of her chair. Badger places a cup of coffee in front of Mel. She looks up at him, gives him a quick nod and a smile.

'Let's start then. Jenny kindly transcribed the first ten tapes out of the box. No small task given the age of them. Those transcripts will be handed out at the end.' Mel looks around the room, 'I thought it would be useful for the whole team to listen to them together. So, notebooks out and pens ready, folks.' She gives a quick nod to Badger, who presses the play button.

An uncomfortable burst of static fills the room. Jenny swiftly interjects. 'The tape has probably been damaged at some point.' Then a clicking noise, as though the record button was being switched off and on. The room fills with the sound of rustling paper, a cap being pulled off the top of a pen.

'How are you today, Lily?' a woman, the voice is accented, nasal, American.

'I'm not Lily.' Another voice, a woman, disinterested, irritated, Mel can't quite decide which, there's a trace of a northern accent, middle class.

'Who are you right now?' There is no sarcasm in the American's voice.

'I'm me, Veronica.' Agitation rises in her voice. 'Who are you?'

'You can call me Rosalee,' There's a smile in her voice. 'We aren't very formal here. I'm a psychiatrist… your psychiatrist. My role is to help you get better.'

There's a bubbling sound from a water cooler in the background.

'Get better?'

'Yes, you've been very sick.'

'I have?' Veronica sounds disbelieving.

'Don't you remember?'

'No,' there's a sadness in Veronica's voice that tugs at Mel, and that's rare.

'We help you make sense of those voices in your head. The one that you say is called Veronica.'

'There are no other voices in my head. Veronica is me, I've already told you that.'

'Who is Lily?'

'Lily is who I had to become, I had to hide. If he finds me…' she stops speaking, there's a sound of water being poured into a glass.

'In case who finds you?'

'Him, he's looking for me,' she takes in a breath. 'I got away, he won't like that if he ever finds out. He thinks I'm dead.'

'Dead?'

Veronica ignores her question. 'He won't let me get away. I know what he did.'

'Who is he?'

'I can't tell you.'

'Tell me about Lily then, who is she?'

'She's the fake one.'

'How do you know that, Veronica.'

'Because I took her name, she didn't need it anymore, I did.' There's a sharp intake of breath. 'I don't want to talk, I've had enough.'

'What's his name, Veronica – this man who'll hurt you?'

There's a pause, the tape makes a crackling noise. 'I can't remember.'

'What can you remember?'

There's a choking noise, a sob rising out of her throat. 'His hands, I remember his hands,' she swallows, takes a breath, 'he had long fingers, I could feel them as he put his hands around my neck.'

'Tell me about his face, what does he look like?'

'He's—' There's a tremor in her voice. 'I want to go back to my room,' she sounds flat – weary.

'We have a drug that will help relax you, it won't hurt, just a prick.'

Someone sniggers, there's a muffled laugh. Mel looks towards it – Kev's face straightens immediately.

'A drug?'

'Yes, a sedative.' the smoothness of the American's voice cuts the ice.

'What *kind* of sedative?' the sense of fear in her question is palpable.

'No need for you to know that right now. It will help you remember; you'll be safe – I promise you that.'

'Drugs do bad stuff to me.' Her voice drops to a whisper. It's impossible to hear what she then said.

'Your friend, the one who brought you here, Ellen. She tells us that your name is Lily, that she's known you for nearly twenty years.'

'Ellen?' Veronica is incredulous. 'Who's Ellen?' Her voice is on edge.

'I have—' a loud crackling noise mangles whatever is being said. '—emory is like this tape recorder. We can erase those memories.'

The room is utterly silent.

The American carries on, 'We have a drug. Propranolol. We use it alongside other treatments. It is completely safe. Almost a hundred per cent.' There was a dishonesty in that statement that boomed in Mel's ears.

Veronica hesitates before responding. 'What other treatments?'

'Talk therapies such as cognitive behavioural therapy.'

'And what else?' There's an intensity in Veronica's voice.

'More traditional methods, well-proven to be effective.' A moment's pause, 'Electro Shock Therapy. People think it hurts – it doesn't.'

A chair scrapes across the floor, the words come out cold. 'Like I believe you.' Muffled footsteps shuffle across the floor; a door opens then swishes shut. The tape clicks, more crackling sounds, then it clicks again.

Jenny leans forward and turns off the tape. 'That was it, there's nothing else on this recording.'

Mel looks around at the team. 'So, any ideas, any comments?'

Silence, before Badger pipes up. 'Well, as obvious as this may seem, it sounds like the psychiatrist didn't believe she was Veronica.'

'Definitely.' Mel nods her head. 'Jenny, what did you gather from listening to the other tapes?'

'There's a disjointedness about the whole thing, sometimes she remembers things, other times she doesn't.' Jenny taps the pile of transcripts in front of her. 'It's all in there, I've done copies for everyone.' She tilts her head to one side, 'One of the tapes I listened to was dated ten weeks later, there is no mention of Veronica at all. The psychiatrist refers to her as Lily throughout the session and Veronica doesn't correct her. They talk about what she wants to do with her life. I thought that was strange.' A smile of embarrassment spreads across her face. 'I wondered if that mind wipe stuff had really worked.'

Mel mulls Jenny's comments over in her head. 'Mindwipe eh, let's listen to a few more tapes, ones you've not transcribed. See where that takes us. Best get some more coffee in, it might be a long session.'

Kinsi leans forward, elbows on the table, head in her hands. 'What if what this psychiatrist says is true, Lily Probisher may have no memory of Veronica at all.'

Mel blinks, she turns the comment over in her head, 'What did you say the name of the programme was?'

Both Jenny and Badger answer at the same time. 'The Mnimi Project.'

'Greek for 'memory', Jenny interjects, noticing the frown on Mel's face.

'Thanks for that. Kinsi, nip out and do a quick search on that, then come back and tell us what you find.'

Ten minutes later, and notepad in hand, Kinsi returns. 'Well, there are lots of differing opinions. The Mnimi Project was a controversial psychotherapy programme back in the 1980s and 90s. Run by the same woman.' She grimaces, 'By the sounds of it, it was a testbed for psychotropic drugs – of course, funded by the drug companies. They claimed it was the solution for all sorts of psychological conditions, including post-traumatic stress syndrome. It was shut down in 2001 after two of the participants committed suicide. I've not read the reports yet but from what I can gather it was pretty gruelling. There's a couple of videos on YouTube, participants talking about the abuse. I'll go through them properly when we finish – I thought I'd best get back and let you know what I'd found.'

Badger suddenly stands up. 'It sounds like a bloody plot from a Stephen King film.'

Mel shudders at the thought, 'It certainly does.' She scratches her head. *It'll be a hell of a job explaining that to the Superintendent.*

Chapter 46

'Have something to eat and then go for a relax in the family room.' The nurse smiles at them both. 'I'll come and get you if anything changes.'

Rosie and Thomasine walk down the corridor towards the café, both lost in their own thoughts. Neither of them had breakfast that morning. Rosie knows they must eat something, but she feels sick, she's felt like that for days. The police won't tell her anything.

Her mind is crowded with questions. Why did her sister abandon her? Had she done something wrong? She'd been three-years-old when Veronica left to go live with their grandmother. That had been bad enough. A few months later – after she disappeared completely – Rosie became inconsolable, raging at her father for driving her away and blaming her mother for not stopping him.

She can't sleep, can't rest, she needs answers. Why has Veronica been calling herself Lily Probisher all these years? Is it just a name she decided she wanted? If it wasn't, did she hurt the real Lily?

Where is the real Lily, is she dead?

Is it Veronica's fault that Karen died?

Rosie's own memories of Veronica are faded by time, but the sister she knew was kind and thoughtful, would never harm anyone. Did something or someone change that?

A rush of sanity washes over her, her life prior to Veronica's reappearance was a lot more comfortable. She had hope then; reality is completely different.

Thomasine pushes open the swing doors into the restaurant. The sweet sugary fragrance of newly-baked cakes fills the air. Two young men are serving food, their voices rise and fall, Jeremy Vine is on the radio, a teenage girl sits in the corner, her head stuck in a magazine. A Victoria sandwich dusted with icing sugar is on special offer, two pieces for the price of one. Teacakes, colourful macaroons, flapjacks and millionaire's shortbread lay behind the glass counter. The menu on the wall lists all-day breakfasts, nutty porridges, vegetarian soups, mozzarella and sundried tomato paninis.

They make their way over towards two empty seats in the corner, Rosie picks up the menu and passes it over to Thomasine.

'What do you fancy, Rosie?' Thomasine looks over the menu with limited interest.

'Shall we share something?'

Rosie reads down the menu, chooses something sweet, 'Teacake?'

'Okay, I'll have the same – butter, jam?'

'Both. I'll get them.' Rosie has no appetite at all. She wanders over to the counter and places their order.

A few minutes later a pot of tea and two large tea-cakes are placed on the small round table between them by a boy with blond highlights in his hair; several gold earrings pierce his left ear. He nips back to the counter for two mugs and a jug of milk. 'Sorry about that. How are you today?' There's a softness in his voice.

'Fine, Ryan, and you?'

Thomasine looks on, Rosie has always had a way with young people, the ability to strike up a conversation.

'I'm good, got exams next week.'

'All the best of luck for them,' she gestures towards the far corner of the restaurant, 'I've seen you over there, surrounded by books. I'm sure you'll pass.'

'I hope so,' he lets out a giggle, 'Dad has said he'll give me a right bollocking if I don't.'

'Thom's a copper. If he does, let her know, she'll sort him.'

'Oi! I'm not sure I'm allowed to do that,' Thomasine interjects playfully. Fully cognitive that a little light relief is exactly what they need.

Ryan gives them a broad smile. Then hurries back to the counter with a spring in his step.

A serious look settles on Thomasine's face as she pours milk into the mugs.

'Have you thought about what happens when Veronica gets discharged?'

Rosie's eyes widen, tears prick at her eyes. 'I think I need to focus on the now, we don't even know what she'll be like when she comes to. I've been reading about it; she may be very disabled. They won't know until she wakes from the coma.'

A shadow crosses Thomasine's face. 'Is there anything I can do to help you?'

Rosie shakes her head. For nearly ten minutes they sit in silence, eating, drinking tea. Unable to voice their fears.

When they return to the ward, a nurse is dry-washing what is left of Veronica's hair. Then she cleans her teeth, wipes her face with a flannel, rolls deodorant under her arms. Every task is done with a light touch. *Such gentleness,* thinks Rosie, *I'd never be able to do that.*

Her sister looks peaceful, there's not a line on her face. The hair on her head is already starting to grow back into a thick grey down. If Rosie hadn't known better she would have thought they were in conversation together, the nurse's voice twitters like birdsong, she laughs, strokes her sister's arm, gently unfurls the fingers on her left hand, rubs lotion into them. Within seconds the fingers go back into a claw.

Rosie feels that heaviness, the one she has always carried in her heart, it floods every part of her body. A DNA match is not evidence enough for her. Her sister is like a cuckoo in the nest. She hates herself for even having that thought.

Chapter 47

'I'm really sorry, I couldn't talk there.' Lily Jamieson's voice has a soft, slow Scottish lilt to it. 'I didn't want to talk when Tom or the kids were around either.' She swallows. 'I'm not that person anymore. I thought—'

'You thought it was over.' Sam Ingleby senses the reticence in her voice; her unwillingness to say the one word that she was terrified would define her. Heroin. He'd heard it all before.

'I understand that.' He cuts to the quick. 'I've got some questions that I need to ask you though – we believe someone has been living under your name. It's regarding a case we're investigating.'

'My name—' She clears her throat. 'Who would do that?'

He hears the fear in her voice. 'I'm not at liberty to tell you right now… but your help could be invaluable.' He carries on. 'Are you aware that someone has been using your identity?'

'No,' she blurts the word out.

'Your father told us about your previous drug habit.' He imagines her sitting down, the phone to her ear, wondering how all this has caught up with her.

'Tom doesn't know about this.' She sounds horrified. 'I'd stopped months before I met him, I'd sorted myself out.'

'When did you meet him?'

'In the eighties, we were both living in Canada. I was clean by then.'

'In Canada?' His pen scratches noisily on his notebook.

'I went over there when I came out of rehab.' She hesitates for a second, 'I wanted a new start.' Her tone of voice changes. 'Needed a new start. I moved to Vancouver. After a few years, I married my ex – it didn't work out, but it gave me residency. A couple of years later I met Tom.'

'Where is your husband from?'

'Where we live now, Skye.'

He already knows the answers, but he asks the questions anyway. 'When did you get married?'

'Back in 1985, in Edinburgh.'

'Our records show that you tried to commit suicide in 1999.'

Silence, then only the sound of her breath.

He repeats the statement and waits for her response.

'That can't be right... Dad told you, I was pregnant then.'

'I'd like you to think back. Take your time. Have you ever lost your passport, birth certificate, bank cards? Anything like that?'

He can hear the ticking of his watch against his ear; the shallow beat of her breath against the phone.

'Just one time that I can remember, back when I was an addict – most of that time I was out of it, so who knows. I was very angry back then. I hated her, Ingrid... she's a cow. I hated Dad for marrying her. Hated Mum for dying. For leaving me. Heroin was the only thing that took it away.' He can hear a choke in her voice. 'I... I just slipped into this dark pit and couldn't get out of it.'

'So, what happened?'

'I needed a fix. That was it. That was always it. I got the stuff off someone at the squat. It had been cut with something else, I don't know what. I OD'd. When I came to some of my stuff had been taken. All I was left with was my passport.'

'Your passport?'

'I guess they thought they couldn't do anything with it. It had expired.'

'What did they take?'

'Nothing much; no money, a P45, my NI card and a couple of references. I'd had a job for a while the year before I'd...'

'Who do you think took it?'

'I didn't know at first, too out of it to care. There was this girl though, she disappeared afterwards. It could have been her. People came and went. One minute there, the next gone.'

'Can you remember her name?'

'I can't remember. I think it was a boys' name. Probably a nickname. I'm sorry.' She takes a deep breath. 'I remember she was in a bad state though, worse than me. She had terrible nightmares. You'd hear her screaming in the night. Someone told me that she'd been beaten up by some guy, left for dead, her and this other girl. It sounded a bit farfetched to me.'

'Do you know his name?'

'I can't remember it. I'm not sure she told us – she didn't talk much, kept herself to herself.' He hears her fidget with the phone. 'It was such a long time ago. I've spent a lifetime trying to block it all out.'

'So, what did she look like?'

'Long red hair, quiet, didn't speak much like I said. Her face was a bit of a mess. I think her nose had been broken, sort of crooked in the middle. A couple of times, people had got us mixed up, we had the same colouring – pale skin, freckles. She always wore the same coat, herringbone. Never had it off her back.'

'And when was this?'

'I don't know, probably 1974. Mid-seventies. I'm not sure...' she hesitates for a moment.

Sam interjects. 'Where were you living?'

'On the outskirts of Manchester, I can't remember the place. Probably knocked down by now. One of the guys there said it was his grandfather's. He said he'd inherited the place. No one believed him though.'

'Why was that?'

'It just seemed unlikely.' She falters, swallows. 'He was a lowlife, he had us out begging, stealing, I hated it.

'Right. How about the rest of them, have you kept in touch?'

Silence.

'No, they weren't the sort to keep in touch with.' There's a hardening in her voice, 'When I came out of rehab I couldn't go back there, not with that lot. The place was full of drugs. I would never have survived.'

'Was she an addict – the girl who might have stolen your belongings?'

'I don't think so, but I wasn't around all the time. You'd have to ask someone else.'

She hesitates for a second, then the words rush out. 'What did she do with my name?'

He could tell she was afraid. 'Like I said, I'm not at liberty to give you any information right now.' He knew she would have many sleepless nights until all this was cleared up. 'What happened after that?'

'As I already said, I got into a rehab programme, when I got out I went to Canada.'

'On your own?'

'No, with a girl, I met her in rehab. She lent me the money for the ticket.'

Sam moves quickly on. 'Can I have her name?'

'Sure, but we've not kept in touch. It's Wendy Harris.'

'Will she still be in Vancouver?'

'Honestly,' Her voice holds a sad tone. 'I'd really like to be more helpful, but I've no idea.'

'Will you talk with your husband about this?' Sam knows only too well the chaos that hits when someone has built their lives on a lie.

'I don't know, perhaps. We're a little off the beaten track up here in Skye. I'd hoped to forget that time in my life.'

'I think it might be a good idea if you did. No more surprises after that, eh?'

She doesn't respond.

'Well, thanks, then. Thanks for your help, I might need to get back to you, okay?'

'On my mobile, not my home line—I don't want the kids or Tom to know.'

'I understand. On your mobile, then.'

She puts down the phone. Sam shakes his head, grateful for the misspent youth he never had. He sinks back into his seat for a moment, reflects on what life might be like for Lily Jamieson. As soon as the press get hold of this they'll have a field day, he thinks to himself, at least it won't be coming from me. Everyone deserves a second chance.

In reality, he knew that many didn't. He makes a record of the interview, hands it to the HOLMES team, grabs a coffee. Just as the rim of the cup touches his mouth, his mobile buzzes.

He lets out a loud sigh.

A text from Mel.

'They're bringing her out of the coma.'

Chapter 48

Mel presses the play button.

'Well done for finding this, Badger. Will I be handing out a gold star?'

A hesitant smile crosses his face. 'You've not watched it yet, boss. Got it copied from VHS to DVD,' he said, the edges of his mouth turn down. 'Second time back at the garage isn't necessarily a good retrieval rate. Should have found it first time. I found it stuck down with masking tape behind the filing cabinet, easy to miss.'

'True. But, if this is any good, we'll wipe that particular slate.'

The whole team gathers around the screen. The quality isn't great. A woman with short blonde hair lies on the bed, she looks peaceful, drowsy, her eyes are shut. The psychiatrist's voice drifts in. She's not in shot.

'Tell me about that night, Veronica, tell me what you see.'

'Do you mean what he did to me,' her voice trembles.

'From the start, you were in the club, near the dance floor, like you told me before.'

The girl shifts on the bed. 'I can see myself there, on my own, in the club. The lights on the glitter ball shine like confetti on the dance floor.' Her voice is slower, on the verge of sleep, she sounds younger. 'They look so pretty.' She lets out a sigh, opens her eyes, they take in the room.

'The walls are red, a velveteen red. I'd forgotten that, the colour of the walls.' She raises her wrist, looks at an imaginary watch. 'I'm waiting for Paula. It's gone midnight, she said she'd meet me here at half-eleven. She's always late – I never am.

The club is a rabbit warren of rooms, dance floors surrounded by little alcoves where people sit and talk, where couples kiss and grope.' Her face transforms, brightens. 'The big dance floor is my favourite place. I say big, it isn't as big as The Palais on George Street – that's huge. This one, the one at the Connaught, is barely big enough to hold a hundred people, but, if you get there early, you can have the floor to yourself for a while. There's masses of people, all milling about. It's like they're all waiting for something to happen. Something always does. A fight, a tussle, broken hearts, wounded egos.'

An adult voice creeps in. 'The lights are dimmed. It's a shit hole, really.' Her nose wrinkles. 'Filthy. The air is thick with smoke. It gets worse as the night goes on. Those little rooms are like ovens. The condensation rises up to the ceiling and then drips back on to the dance floor. It's like a skating rink.'

The smile again. 'I love it – finally I found a place where I can be me. Where I fit. When I'm alone, at least.' She moves her head side to side. *Give Me Just A Little More Time* blares out from speakers hung above the dance floor.' She starts to hum the tune, then laughs. 'I'm under orders, from him, to wear the dress, the red one.' Her voice drops to a whisper. 'You never ignore his orders, no one does. Beautiful eyes,' the teenager again, 'that's what people told me I had – beautiful eyes. An illusion, but there you are.'

Is that Lily or Veronica speaking, Mel wonders?

'That's always been the nature of the female form. We colour ourselves in. False eyelashes, olive green irises like the rings on Saturn, large dark pupils, glitter sparkles on my eyelids. Long silver earrings that dangle from my ears. A present from Mum and Gran for my eighteenth birthday. I never take them out. Hundreds of teeny weeny freckles cover my face. The disco lights pick them up, too. I'm high. Another present from him. It's my weekend ritual, all-night clubs, sometimes all-dayers in Blackpool.' She frowns, 'Paula still hasn't turned up.'

She breathes out, there's a weird tone to her voice. 'I'm not the girl she met in September, she's made sure of that. She's given me a complete make-over. Before, I was just freckles, blonde eyelashes and an inferiority complex. Now I'm part of the crowd that everyone wants to be in.'

Then sadness. 'Until that is they find out what it's really like to be in it; to be subject to his moods.'

Her eyes glance around the room, Mel is confident that Veronica is there, in the nightclub, at that very moment.

'I walk onto the dance floor, drop my bag in the centre by a group of girls that I vaguely know. It was all vague back then, shallow conversations about drugs and where you'd been the night before. They see me, the girls. They smile at me. I want you to know that they see *me,* and I know they have because they smile back at me. Thin smiles forced out. Every single one of those girls sees me. They will deny it later.'

She points into the distance, 'That one, Jacky, with the auburn hair tied back into a ponytail, she always says hello, she's always taking pictures with that little Kodak camera of hers. He has his eye on her, too. I've seen it. She has the thickest Liverpool accent I've ever heard and dances like she's got bolts through her knees.' A sly look crosses her face, 'I smile back. They move away a little, give me space to dance. I spin around on one heel. It's like I'm hovering above the floor. The hem of my red polka dot dress splays out around me. I lean backwards, bend my knees, fling my right arm out behind me, momentarily my fingers drag along the floor before I spring back up again. I look at no one, not even the boys, although they often try to catch my eye. It is all about the music, about moving, about becoming. I stare at someplace in my head. Somewhere where I am alone on the dance floor.' Veronica shifts on the bed, 'My head nods, my shoulders sway from side to side in time with the beat. I slip and slide across the floor, spin – my arms outstretched. I catch my reflection in the eyes of the girls that line the edge of the dance floor. I'm the queen of Northern Soul. '

Her voice trembles, she blinks.

'He's there. His fingertips run along my spine. I don't turn to look. It's him, right now I can't remember his name. It's a blur, even the sound of it. I think it was Jimmy. Maybe it wasn't. Maybe he was called Derek or Stephen. There were a lot of Dereks and Stephens back then. Jimmy, that's what I'll call him, it's either that or snake face.'

Mel writes those words down.

Veronica's mouth twists into a smile.

'*Snake face* doesn't make me sound very nice, does it? He's not very nice. I carry on dancing. Those girls I mentioned earlier, they blend into the walls, they disappear. Even the auburn-haired girl. He has that effect. Jimmy and I circle each other, shoulders moving, feet shuffling over the floor. *Papa was a Rolling Stone* fills the room. We kick, dip and spin. The beat gets faster. More people cram onto the dance floor. The room gets hotter and damper. Two of the other boys join us. One slides onto the floor, his arms outstretched. The other drops into a push-up. The competition is on. Sweat rolls down my back. I kick, they spin, I dip, Smithy does a backflip.

Jimmy shakes his head and moves off towards the bar. Towards Jacky. She's minding his drink. Paula turns up two hours later, strutting across the floor. The bruising on her cheek has faded, her face is covered in makeup. I don't ask her where she's been. She's wearing that chocolate brown hot pants all-in-one she bought last week from Vamps. It cost a bomb. You should see the heads turn as she makes her way through the crowd. It's always the same – and I can't really understand why. It isn't as though she's good looking. It's just something she exudes, something that catches their attention.'

Veronica's eyes narrow, her voice changes, there's a bitter edge to it, 'Boys, that is. And men, there are plenty of them in here. They can't take their eyes off her. Paula has this *availability* gene that's always switched on. She wants to know where Jimmy is. I nod towards the bar. I have no real idea of where he is. He's always in corners doing business. She said she'd see me later.'

Veronica's mouth twists again, the northern tones leak out, 'What she really means is goodbye. Gone very unreliable she has. Ever since I had that problem with the LSD she gave me. And since that other thing with Jimmy. Away to her new best friend, Jacky she is. The girl with auburn hair and bolts through her legs. Paula always has to have a new friend in the pipeline. A protégé.

It's then that I notice him, on the dance floor.' She lets out a long slow breath.

'Notice who?' a disembodied voice in the background – the American.

'The boy with the beautiful dark skin.' A small smile comes to her lips, her body moves. 'His arm brushes against mine. He's not wearing a shirt; his skin glistens with sweat. His face is covered in tiny grains of salt. I feel my heart go thump, thump; something tingles at the base of my stomach. His scalp is covered in ringlets of jet black corkscrew hair. He has eyelashes like my baby sister, long and thick.

I look away, but it's too late. He knows I've been taking him in. He leaps up in the air, drops and spins. As he puts his arms out I notice that the palms of his hands are white. I want to ask him why that is, but I don't. I pull myself away, turn my back, move away, look over my shoulder, his eyes are off their stalks, he looks straight at me, drops down into a half split.'

The tremor in her voice comes back, she blinks. 'Wrong, wrong, wrong. Stupid, stupid, stupid. You never know who's watching. Jimmy hates black people, he says he likes Jamaicans, but that's it. But that boy in Blackburn, he was Jamaican, so that can't be true. Jimmy carries. A knife, that's what I mean. He's nasty with it. I don't know where this boy is from. I've never seen him before.' She closes her eyes, gives a sleepy smile, 'I only know that he is the most beautiful boy I've ever seen.' She touches her face. 'I wonder what he looks like now?' She swings around, sits upright on the edge of the bed, it freaks Mel out. 'He might not even be alive. Jimmy was very strict about the rules. His rules. He was like a magician, made people disappear. One minute they'd be there, the next gone, erased from our memories by fear. I never found out where they went.'

Hastily, Mel scribbles a note on the pad in front of her, a name in large letters. JIMMY.

On the screen, Veronica's eyes flick around the room, at ghosts the viewers cannot see. 'A slow record comes on, so I disappear, up to the ladies' toilets on the next floor. For safety's sake. I don't want anyone to ask me to dance. Definitely not the dark-skinned boy—that would be too big a risk.'

Her face darkens. 'Paula's up there with a group of girls. She's leaning back against the wall, pulling a lipstick out of her handbag, a cigarette hanging off her lower lip, the ash dropping down onto her chocolate brown hot pants.' Her eyes flash. 'God, at that moment I hate her. Jacky stands next to her, laughing, a small bottle of sherry from Yates's Wine Lodge in her hand. Australian – real cheap it is. She's offering Paula a swig. I'm flabbergasted. Paula never drinks. Her predilections are of the chemical kind.' She whispers the words out. 'I walk back out. Don't talk to them or anything. I hate Paula even more. It wasn't my fault she couldn't… I don't want to say it, so I don't. Anyway, it wasn't my fault he hit her. I know what she's like now.'

Seconds tick by before she starts again.

'The dark-skinned boy is waiting for me at the bottom of the stairs. He must have seen me go up there. He has his shirt on now, a brown Ben Sherman with a white collar. Two drinks in his hands. He parts his lips in a smile, his teeth almost perfect. The front two cross each other, just a little. It is as though someone so beautiful needs a flaw. And that is his. Something happens inside of me, not in my head, in my body. It starts in the soles of my feet. Not a tingle, that sounds stupid, electricity, that's what it is. Up through my legs and right into my solar plexus. I smile back. Stuff them, who cares about Jimmy and Paula. He offers me a glass. It's lemon and lime. He's bought it for his mate, but he's buggered off somewhere. He sounds just like me. I don't know what to do. Then I think about Paula and the girls, and Jacky, her new best friend. I take one of the glasses out of his hand. He asks me if I've ever been to an all-nighter.

I tell him yes and that I've been to the Torch, too. And Blackpool, for the all-dayers. Suddenly I feel superior – special.

Veronica blinks. 'He looks around, I keep my head down, not wanting to call attention to myself. He might be Jamaican. If he is that will be alright.

He asks me if I fancy a sit-down, and gestures towards one of the booths on the other side of the dance floor. The place is still heaving with bodies, Bobby Womack's *What Is This?* is blaring out of the speakers. I can see Del leaping about – he's off his head. Sweat streaming down his face, his chest is bare, KEEP THE FAITH

tattooed in big letters between his nipples. The leatherette seat sucks against my bare back.

The dark-skinned boy leans forward, puts his mouth against my left ear. I feel the warmth of his breath. He tells me his name is Benjy and asks me what mine is. I pull back a little, just enough.

Veronica, I say my name is Veronica. That my mam likes Veronica Lake, that I was named after her. He looks back at me blankly. I explain that she's an American film star – my mam's favourite film star. But that everyone calls me Ronnie, though.

He smiles politely at me. I ask him if Benjy stands for Benjamin. He tilts his head, tells me it's a nick name. It's because his dad is from Bengal. He said, my real name is Krishna.'

Veronica lifts her hand to her mouth, her face flushes. Mel hears the panic in her voice.

'I inch away from him. I can feel their eyes on me. Everyone knows but me. I put the drink down on the table. Hang my head, I want to hide my face. I feel a flush of shame; my dad hates racists. In that moment, I hate myself more than I ever have.

He leans forward, the tips of his fingers glide slowly over mine. I jerk my hand away. Across the table, I feel the heat from his body. I can hardly breathe. I want to get up, get away. I don't know what to say to him. He tells me that I'm really pretty. He slides along the seat towards me. I move away. If I don't move quick one of the boys will have him.'

Veronica's eyes are wide open. She seems to look at Mel through the screen.

'They'll be on him like dogs. They hate Pakis and Hindus. No one is allowed to touch a white girl. Not one of *their girls*. The polka dots on my dress feel like huge big targets. For one stupid, *stupid* moment I wonder what it would be like to kiss him. I've never kissed a boy like him. I go to stand up, he looks up at me. He knows.'

There's emotion in her voice, a terrible sadness, her eyes pool with tears. 'He knows I can't sit and talk to him. Then he smiles, a big smile, as though it's a joke. As though he's played a joke on me. As though it's a big joke between him and Jimmy. A test. Yes, he knows about Jimmy. At that very moment I'm sure of it.

Then I change my mind. No, it's Paula. It's definitely Paula. It's the sort of thing she'd do.' There's a wail of anxiety in Veronica's voice, 'It's payback time. The bitch has set me up. The walls shrink in on me; my heart beats like a hammer in my chest. I have to get out.'

The words rush out of her, her eyes are wide open staring into the distance. 'I get up, push my way through the crowd. A voice roars up in my face, Jimmy, red raw with hate. *No, No, it's a mistake!* I want to scream that out, but the words freeze in my throat.'

Veronica becomes more agitated; she tugs at the sheet beneath her. 'I try to push him off. He grabs me by the hair, drags me off the dance floor. He twists my arm up my back, properly, not a little bit, all the way up. I cry out, tell him that we only talked.

'He doesn't hear, I feel the muscle tear in my shoulder.

I beg him to let me go.

He slaps me across the mouth. Tells me to shut up.'

Tears glide down her cheeks.

'I plead for someone to help me. No one does, I'm suddenly invisible. I can see her, Paula. She sees me, her eyes glaze over; a smile crosses her face. She's wrapped around some second-rate football player. His hands stuffed down her blouse. She gives me the finger. Benjy, he's disappeared, too. Those mates of his, they'll have dragged him off somewhere.

Jimmy shoves me through the crowd, forces me up the staircase, out towards the exit. The bouncers disappear into the cloakroom, big lads with black Crombie coats on, their backs turned, their hands stuffed down deep into their pockets. Cowards, that's what they are, and he pays them money, Jimmy pays them money to look the other way. And the drug squad too. I've seen him do it. He paid that copper.'

A sob shudders through Veronica's chest, she rubs the tears away with the back of her hand, pushes herself back against the wall. Her words choke out. 'He drags me out onto the street by my hair, I try to fight back. I do. It's raining. Freezing. I don't even have a coat. My whole body is trembling. It's really cold.'

Her face is drenched in sweat, she blinks, shivers repeatedly. 'I… I'm sorry, I've got a pain in my chest. I can't talk anymore. It really hurts. It really hurts just remembering all of this.'

'Can you see his face, Lily?' The psychiatrist's voice is calm.

'You know I can't see his face; I've told you that before. Just bits of it, like a mirror, like a mirror that's been smashed.'

The camera lens draws back, the woman sitting in the seat by the bed comes into view. She's leaning forward, her long legs are curled beneath the chair, her thick brown hair is tied back with a satin bow. 'Are you sure?' her voice is calm, distant.

Veronica's face pales; tears glisten on her cheeks. 'Yes.'

'His name, before, you said his name was Jimmy, is that true?'

'I think so, I can't remember, I don't want to remember.' Veronica lies down on the bed. Her back to the psychiatrist; her knees curled into her chest. 'All you do is pump me full of drugs and hurt me. Have you ever had that thing done to you? *You're* no better than he is.'

The woman doesn't react, seems unperturbed. 'We need to know everything, those memories are like viruses, Lily. If we don't root them out, they spread.'

Veronica sits up, looks the woman directly in the face. The words rush out of her mouth. 'His name is Jimmy.' She hesitates for a moment. 'I don't know his last name. I don't care whatever else I forget,' Her hands ball into fists, 'I can't forget him, his name, his smell. He's going to stand there in front of me one day—' She frowns, a look of confusion flits across her eyes. 'Why do you keep doing that, calling me Lily? I'm not Lily. I keep telling you I'm not Lily.'

'Would you like something to calm you down?' the voice is saccharine. Mel wants to hit her.

'No, I don't want anything to calm me down.'

She goes to stand up, two pairs of hands push her down by the shoulders. The picture freezes, her face void of colour.

'That's the end of the mind wipe session.' The spell is broken. Badger's voice brings everyone back to the present. 'I don't know about you lot,' Badger grimaces, 'but it bloody well freaked me right out.'

'I know what you mean,' says Mel, her knuckles prodding the base of her spine. 'God, it feels like months since I've had a good sleep. This case is keeping me awake at night.' She knows snatching an hour or two isn't doing her any good. 'Were there any notes that went with it?'

Jenny shakes her head.

'No date?'

'No,' Jenny points at the TV, 'I played through the whole session just to make sure.'

'Does anyone think she'll be able to tell us more about him when she wakes?' she voices the question that is on everyone else's lips.

'I don't see it happening,' says Badger, a look of disappointment on his face. 'This is running like an episode of the Twilight Zone.'

Kinsi pulls her hair back into the elastic band that had been wound around her wedding finger. 'It might be months before she can speak.'

'We can't rely on her, then,' says Badger, brushing some imaginary dust off the table with the palm of his hand. 'Back to the legwork and my old pal the PNC.'

'How do we know it's a hypnosis session?' The scepticism in Kin si's voice rings loud. 'There's nothing to indicate that. It could be one big act.'

No one answers, Mel can see a whirr of internal thoughts on the facial expressions of everyone in the room.

Kinsi continues, 'I'm wondering what drugs they used. We all know there's a lot of stuff out there that could generate that kind of response. That can make people open to suggestion. And make them very confused.'

'Oh God, you're not telling us she just made all that up.' Jenny's voice cuts in.

'Hopefully, not,' interjects Mel. 'Let's go with what we've just seen and heard.'

Every single one of them had written down the names of those mentioned. The name of the nightclub, and anything else that they thought was useful. On Mel's notepad, there was one word written in large black letters. JIMMY. Everything in her gut tells her it's him.

Chapter 49

It takes Thomasine a while to find Jacky2422's house; an old converted railway cottage about ten miles from Chester. There's a small garden at the front, an arched trellis over the gate. All very twee. She walks towards the house – a knot of discomfort sitting in her chest. She has been in two minds all the way over. Should she call Mel and tell her what's she'd found online? If she does, Mel will refuse to involve her in the interview. She mulls it over for a moment – the door opens before she gets the chance to ring the bell. The decision is made for her.

There's a hesitant smile on Jacky's face. 'Did you get lost?' Her accent has a trace of someone trying to move away from their Liverpudlian youth 'People always do.' She's slender, petite, her pale grey eyes look back at Thomasine through thick, mascara-covered lashes. She tries to guess her age, late fifty's or early sixties. It's hard to tell.

Thomasine offers out her hand, 'Thomasine Albright.'

'Jacky, Jacky Wainwright. You can't keep calling me Jacky2422.' Her hand is clammy, uncomfortable to touch.

Jacky welcomes her in. The small sitting room is shabby chic, bright and airy. A gas fire blazes away in the fireplace. Motivational quotes, stencilled in italics on thin panels of whitewashed driftwood, are dotted around the room. If Thomasine were a betting woman, which she isn't, she'd say Jacky Wainwright was in the interiors business, but she doesn't ask. Jacky gestures for her to take a seat and disappears into the kitchen for a few minutes then returns with a tray in her hands.

'I've made some refreshments.' She places the tray on the large footstool between them, pours thick black coffee into white cappuccino bowls, asks whether Thomasine would like cream and sugar.

'Milk, no sugar, please.'

Jacky disappears into the kitchen again and brings out a small jug of milk. 'I have cream myself,' she looks Thomasine in the eyes, 'you know like the Americans do?' Then edges a plate of biscuits towards her. 'Help yourself, they're from Waitrose. Organic, chocolate chip.' Her eyes widen as though expecting a comment.

'Thanks, I'll just let the coffee cool.' Thomasine resists a smile.

'So how can I help you? Are you interested in Northern Soul?'

'Not particularly.'

A confused look crosses her face, 'Oh, I thought you were.'

Polite protocol would dictate that – right at that moment – Thomasine pick up a biscuit, bite into it, tell her how organic is 'worth paying the extra for', but she does neither of those things, she wants to get to the point.

'It's about the picture, one of the ones you posted on the internet,' she takes an A4 folder out of her bag, flips it open, takes out a photograph. 'This one.' She holds it out for her to see.

Jacky places her coffee cup on a coaster. She smiles again, 'Yeah, that one at the Golden Torch, those were the days, I loved that place.' Then her gaze shifts to the fireplace, to the flames. 'Young and free, eh.'

'This man here,' Thomasine point to his face. 'Do you know who he is?'

Her eyes narrow in on her for a moment, then flick down to the photograph. 'Why do you need to know?' her voice is light, conversational. She picks up her cup again.

Thomasine's voice tightens, 'I'm Karen Albright's sister, that girl's sister.' Her finger points to the girl directly in front of him.

There is no trace of recognition on Jacky's face.

'The girl in front of him, the one whose shoulder he's resting his hand on. She went missing back in 1973. That girl.' She lays the photograph on the tray. Waits for Jacky to pick it up; she doesn't. 'She is, was, my sister.'

'Oh God, I don't know what to say.' Jacky blinks, puts down her coffee.

Thomasine hesitates before speaking. Jacky Wainwright is the first stranger she's sharing this information with. 'They found her remains two weeks ago.'

The colour drains from the woman's cheeks. Her hand goes to her mouth; the words mumble between her fingers. 'Oh, I'm so sorry.'

Thomasine presses on. 'Are you sure you don't remember her?'

Jacky shakes her head. 'Yes, I'm sure of it.'

'How about him?'

The woman picks up the photograph; stares at it for a few moments. Swallows before she speaks. 'Yeah, I do.' She has that piqued look on her face that people get when they suddenly realise their past may have come back to bite them. Her jaw clenched, her teeth a barrier to the words she fears letting out.

'I don't want you to worry, I'm just trying to chase up people who might have known her, for the funeral.'

The woman's face clears, the tension dissipates. 'Oh, right.'

'Didn't I put that in the email?' She knows she hadn't.

Jacky opens her mouth to speak, pauses, Thomasine can sense her formulating the words in her head. 'His name was Billy.' She traces a brightly painted fingernail over his face. 'I can't remember his last name. He had a car – white. A Capri. His pride and joy. Lots of the girls fancied him. He never seemed interested in them, though. He was one of...'

'One of what?' Thomasine copies Jacky's light conversational style. She makes a mental note of the car. Karen had written about a white car in her diary.

Her face clouds over. 'Nothing, I was just thinking, remembering. He liked to dance, was a good dancer.'

'There was another girl who went missing that night. Maybe you remember her, Veronica Lightfoot? Is she in any of your photographs?' She lays out the black and white photographs one by one in a row.

The hum of the gas fire fills the silence. The woman's heavily mascaraed eyes scan the photographs. Her hands begin to tremble; she clings more ardently to the white cappuccino mug. 'No. I don't think so.' She nibbles at her lower lip.

'Look again, take your time.' Their eyes meet, the woman turns her head away.

'No, I'm sure.' She glances down at her hands, then returns Thomasine's gaze. 'Look, I didn't load them all though, I have others. I was always taking photographs. I copied them all onto my computer about six months ago. That's why I put them on the website, I'd forgotten I had them. Shall we have a look? Perhaps there are more of your sister and Billy?'

Thomasine almost kisses her.

Jacky disappears up the stairs and returns with a laptop. An hour and fifteen minutes later Thomasine has six photographs, sadly none have her sister in them. There was one of Jacky herself. Standing at the edge of the dance floor. Her body thin as a paper knife. Next to her is a tall girl with short frizzy hair and long thin legs. Beside her a wiry looking boy with a shaved head.

'Who's that?' Thomasine asks pointing to the girl.

'Just someone who we used to hang around with now and again.' She tilts her head to the side, frowns. 'I can't remember her name for the life of me.'

'And him?' Thomasine points to someone else.

Jacky shakes her head, 'John – Jim, not sure.'

'Who took the photographs?' Thomasine gathers the prints up.

'Smithy, Del, I think Smithy might have taken that one.' She leans back against the cushions. 'I'm not being much help, am I?'

Thomasine's disappointment sinks into the pit of her stomach. Smith, one of the worst names to trace. 'Can you remember full names?'

Jacky shakes her head, 'We only met them now and again.'

Thomasine wonders if Jacky's selective memory is real or an act. 'Do you ever keep in touch with any of them?' Thomasine leans forward, rests her elbows on her thighs, a dull ache starts up behind her right eye.

'Not really, I saw a couple of them at the reunions, I've not been to those for years though.' She gazes over Thomasine's shoulder and out through the window. 'Billy turned up once or twice, back in the eighties. I've no idea where any of them are now. Life moves on, doesn't it?'

Thomasine nods and gestures towards the laptop. 'Are there any photographs of the reunion?'

Jacky shakes her head again. 'Only the ones on the website.' She hangs her head momentarily, 'I'd like to pay my respects at the funeral if you don't mind. I know we never met but…'

For a moment, Thomasine's mind goes blank. *Funeral? What funeral?* Then it flashes back in, her lie, Karen's funeral.

'As soon as the Coroner's Office release her remains I'll let you know. It might be months.' An idea slips into her consciousness. 'I'm thinking of having a memorial. Perhaps we could put the date on the website. See who turns up.'

'Thank you, I'll do that for you if you like. Just send me the information.' She gets to her feet. Takes a scrap of paper off the mantelpiece, 'Here's my mobile number, I'll post the date of the memorial on the website for you. I'm so sorry that…'

'It's okay. At least it's over.' Thomasine knows this is untrue. It's just the start. She stands up, 'I'd best be going.' She makes for the door; Jacky follows her.

Halfway out, Thomasine turns to say goodbye. The woman wraps her arms around her. 'Let me give you a hug,. It must be such a difficult time for you.'

'Thanks… thanks… it is,' Thomasine disentangles herself from the embrace, 'thanks for all your help. You've been really kind. I'll text you my mobile number later.'

As she navigates the car out of the street, it dawns on her that Jacky Wainwright hadn't asked how Karen died, nor where she was found. She didn't talk about Veronica either. Why was that? People are curious. People like her, anyway. Her intuition tells her that Jacky Wainwright is holding something back. Something important. The names she gave her Smithy, Billy, Del… surely, she would remember the last name of one of them? She wishes she'd been able to impound her laptop as evidence.

She pulls over to the side of the road and takes out her phone. Mel can do what Thomasine can't – interview Jacky Wainwright under caution. And she can get the tech guys on the laptop, too.

Chapter 50

The incident room is under pressure, evidence boxes piled high, voices raised, fingers punching at keyboards. Jenny's brain hurts, a tight band of pain rages mercilessly beneath her temples. Even her ears are sore. She pops two maximum strength paracetamols onto her tongue. Washes them down with a cup of strong black coffee. Only a couple more hours and then she can head off home for the night.

The last few days have been frenetic. Transcribing the cassette tapes required her full attention and concentration. The sound quality is poor. At times, she struggles to hear not only what is said but who is saying it. The result: eye-watering headaches that kick in after a few hours. She's dog tired and living on painkillers.

She's had to block out distractions. Remove herself from the organised chaos of the incident room, as well as ignoring the constant stream of texts from her daughter, Amy. It's exam time and her teenage stress hormones are raging. Every couple of hours, Jenny takes herself off to the toilets and knocks out a reply. None of which seem to pacify her daughter.

The task has been laborious; days of start-stop-start-replay, type it up. This final stage is perhaps the most taxing element. Checking each tape off against its transcription. Just two more tapes and that's it.

Mel owes me for this one.

The therapist, psychiatrist, whoever she was, proved the most arduous to make out. She spoke quietly. Often didn't respond verbally, or Jenny assumed that was the case. And there were gaps, seconds lost, sometimes minutes. As though the tape had been tampered with.

Each session followed the same format. Typically, drugs administered by injection at the beginning. By the psychiatrist herself; allegedly to help Veronica recall memories she had repressed. Her reaction to the medication varied. Her mood swung up and down. She flitted between the two personalities and often it had been difficult to know who was talking – Veronica or Lily. At times it was only her tone of voice that gave her a clue, and that was subjective.

Coffee drunk, and another one in hand, Jenny gathers up the cassettes and typewritten notes. She's sequestered herself a room in the Interview Suite again. Whilst not comfortable, the small windowless rooms allow the benefit of isolation. Through the walls, she hears the occasional scrape of plastic chairs on lino and the odd rumble of conversation when voices are raised.

Just two to go, just two to go, Jenny keeps reminding herself of that. She sits down, slips on her headphones. Each cassette is numbered and in sequence. She inserts the penultimate one into the player. Pen in hand, she places the transcript in front of her then sets a ruler underneath the first line of the text. Everything must be one hundred per cent accurate before distributing it to Mel and the team. Her work will, very likely, form part of the evidence. It could be challenged by the defence. She doesn't want anything coming back at her.

The psychiatrist's voice flows into her ears as soon as she presses the play button.

'Tell me about that night, when you first met Jimmy?' She sounds calm, distant. Jenny ticks off word after word on the transcript.

'Me and Paula were at the bus station, the main one, the one at Bar Lane. Before Christmas, a Saturday night I think. It was late. Huddling together to keep warm. The wind roared through that place, even the bus shelters were open to the elements. I was blocked, we were blocked.'

'Blocked?'

'High... high on amphetamines. Both of us. Everyone we knew took them. They kept you awake. I'd lost a lot of weight.

Everyone had. Paula sold drugs. I didn't know that at first. That's why she always had money. That's why people were friends with the bitch. Did I tell you she was a bitch?'

There's no response.

Jenny presses the stop button on the machine. Tries to clear her head. She would have asked her for Paula's second name. There's so much she wants to know; wants to ask her. Everyone in the team will feel the same. Listening to the tapes has given her a sense of Veronica. Who she was and who she became. Piecing her story together has been interesting. Jenny has been diligent. Never making a note of anything that wasn't on tape. Never adding or taking away. At times Veronica's accent changes. It thickens. As though the young Veronica, the teenage northerner, is narrating her own past. As though Lily is merely a vehicle for her voice. At other times the accent disappears; it matures. Her language morphs into something more educated, cultured.

Jenny brings herself back to the present. To the task. She doesn't want to have to redo it again. Her forefinger presses down on the play button; the words flow again.

'I need a drink; can I have a drink of water?'

There is a sound of a chair being pushed back, footsteps, the pouring of water into a plastic cup.

'Here.'

Moments later Veronica carries on, her voice laboured.

'There was a crowd of us, dozens, all around the same age, eighteen. Maybe some as old as twenty-one, but not many. Everyone dressed the same, like a code, like a tribe, the boys in short leather jackets, sleeveless T-shirts, Oxford bags, hands cupped around their cigarettes. Stamping their feet to keep warm. The girls all in long thick winter coats and boots, talking, huddled.

We were waiting for the midnight coach… to an all-nighter… I can't remember where.' Her speech slows, the medication must have started to kick in. 'There was music. Paula had brought a cassette player along. One of those battery-operated ones. Everybody started moving side to side, shuffling their feet.' She started to hum. Jenny recognises it straightaway, 'Marvin Gaye, "Ain't That Peculiar". 'I love Marvin Gaye,' says Veronica. 'Sometimes I play that song in my head. Those four beats going again and again. I shut her out, Lily that is, that *other* me. I imagine my body spinning, my arms outstretched. Lily hates Northern Soul. She's more of an *Abba* and *Queen* sort of girl.' A sly tinge leaks into her voice. 'She has shit taste in music.'

Another pause, she coughs.

'The lights at the bus station went off at half-eleven. I didn't feel nervous. It didn't feel dangerous; not to me. I was one of them.' She pauses, waits, as though the information has to be downloaded into her head. 'A big cheer rose up. It always did when the coach turned up. It was passing the Odeon. Lights on full beam. Smog pumping out of the back – freezing in the air. I wonder if the Odeon's still there? It used to be filled with hundreds of teenagers on a Saturday morning. I can remember it. I can remember being a kid and screaming my head off at some Beatles sound-alike band.' She let out a sigh.

'As the coach pulled up, Paula pulled me towards her, linked her arm through mine. Told me she had some acid, Jimmy had given it to her. I'd never taken acid before, didn't want to. I didn't tell her that. I asked her who Jimmy was.

He's over there, she hissed. Told me not to look. Said he was he was the one with the black bag over his shoulder, the one with *Keep the Faith* on it.

It's weird, isn't it? Weird how some memories are so clear, even though I've spent years trying to forget the night I met him. Years covering it up, pushing it deep into the back of my mind. Blocking it out. Now, now, it's like I'm there, right in that moment.'

She breathes out noisily, wearily. Jenny hears the creak of a chair, Veronica must have sunk back into her seat.

'I tried not to look at him, I really did. I sneaked a look out of the corner of my eye. He saw me. He must have been waiting for that one glance. He came towards us, the wind pulling at his Oxford Bags, hands tucked deep into his pockets. He draped his arm around Paula's shoulder, smiled at me, a hard tight smile, like he knew he was smart and wanted to make sure I knew it too.

Then I noticed something that made my skin crawl. The nail on the middle finger of his left hand was long; like a girl's. The rest of his nails were bitten down to the skin.' She scratches at something, clothing perhaps, there's a rustling noise in the background.

'He fancied himself, I could tell. He bounced on the balls of his feet, like a boxer. He kept pushing his hands through his hair just like Paula did. He was full of nervous tics. Even back then I noticed stuff like that.

He raised his eyebrows, tilted his head in my direction; said he assumed I was the lovely Ronnie. He didn't have a Bolton accent. Not like me, not like Paula. Not like everyone else I knew.

Paula laughed, that throaty laugh of hers. She said that he was a grammar school boy, through and through. That he was *posh*.

Posh – that was her nickname for him. He didn't like it. I could tell. The smile dropped from his face for a moment. Paula was busy laughing at her own joke. Casting her eyes around to see if anyone was listening.

He turned his attention to me. Looked me up and down. From my platform-soled shoes right up to the brass buttons on my navy-blue coat. He took a step forward, I took a step back. Something about him made the hair on the back of my neck stand up. He tugged at my sleeve. Ran that long nail along the back of my hand. I froze, felt my face redden. I stared at the ground.

He said that I was a quiet one. Not like her, not like Paula.

She told me to ignore him. I couldn't. He was right in my face.

Then something else caught his attention. A couple of Indian lads. Stood by the newspaper kiosk, in the dark. As bad as it sounds… I was relieved.

He reminded me of a copperhead snake. The one I saw at Chester Zoo. When I was a kid. The slow blink of his eyelids. His pale thin lips. He sprinted off in the direction of the kiosk, one of the lads followed him. Only then, I realised I'd been holding my breath. I didn't want to breathe him in.

I don't know where they went after that. All I know is that they didn't get on the coach with the rest of us.

Months later I heard someone say that two Hindu boys, twin brothers, had been found badly beaten that night. Left for dead. I knew it was him. It had to have been him, and that other one that followed him about, that—'

There's an intake of breath.

'I've had enough.'

A chair scrapes back, footsteps slap on the wooden floor, the door slams shut.

Chapter 51

It's noisy here. Too noisy. Beeps, whooshes, footsteps. Gurgling drains. Or at least that's what I think that sound is. Singing. Crying out. Laughing. Coughing. I shout at them. *Shut up! Shut up!* They ignore me. That's the worst.

I play a game to distract myself. I call it *Command*. Move fingers. Nothing. Move thumb. Nothing. Move toes. Nothing. Blink. Nothing. My brain isn't making my body do stuff. That can't be right. Then I fall asleep, I'm always falling asleep.

I can't give up. I'm going to do it ten times more. I shout louder – BLINK! My eyelids open a little. I can't focus my eyes. There's a blur of people moving around me. Fast then slow. It's a dream. I'm on a roundabout. I must be. My brain plays tricks. I don't know what's real and what's not.

Am I real? Is this a dream?

I wonder where I am. Is it a hospital? I don't like hospitals. The light is too bright. I want them to turn it down. What if it's a prison? I'm tied down. It could be a prison hospital. I want to turn over, my back hurts. I shout for help. No one answers.

I hear snatches of conversations – coma. I hear them say that a lot. And the other word, clean. Then people touch me. I hate being touched. I shout at them to stop. It's dirty.

They never listened to me last time either. Last time I was in hospital. No matter what I said. I pleaded with them to stop. They didn't. I pleaded with her to make them stop. She didn't. I remember the pain in my head. I remember her dark hair tied back into a ponytail. I told her she was Miss Taken. She laughed. I didn't. She was the biggest bitch I've ever met.

I think I stole something. I can't remember what it was. I can't move my hands and feet. I must be dangerous. I keep screaming at them. Asking them what I've done. No one tells me.

She's here again, that woman. She always says her name, Camila. She's the nurse. My nurse. That's what she says. I don't believe her. Miss Dirty Bitch that's what I call her. She's the one that touches me in places she shouldn't. I don't like it. She lifts my breast, wipes a cloth underneath it. Then does the other. I hate it. She says she's taking care of me, keeping me clean.

Grab her hand! Grab her hand! I scream at my brain. *Concentrate! Concentrate!*

'Get your fucking hands off me!'

'Oh, my Lord, you're coming around, girl.' She squeezes my hand.

I must be real.

Chapter 52

The final tape, the last check for accuracy and, after this, she'll endeavour to put them into a timeline. She's transcribed every single one. As usual, there was not enough money in the budget to get anyone to help. At least there'll be consistency, she thinks to herself.

Jenny slips on her headset, presses the play button.

'This won't hurt,' the lie the psychiatrist tells at every session as she administers the injection. The small cry Veronica lets out gives that lie away.

'I need a drink.'

'Water? Will that be okay?'

'Thanks,' Veronica sounds despondent, lost.

Jenny hears the psychiatrist get to her feet, walk towards the water cooler, just as she had on every single tape. Briefly, she wonders why the woman never offered Veronica a glass of water at the start of every session. Was it a control thing?

There's a sudden sense of urgency in Veronica's tone 'You said you'd help me get rid of the nightmares, the flashbacks. This talking, this talking isn't working... not for me... the flashbacks. They've not stopped. I can't sleep—'

'It only works if you're telling me the truth.' The psychiatrist's nasally whine seems more pronounced.

'I am telling the truth.' Veronica's reply is flat, unemotional.

'I'm not sure you are,' then a pause, 'not all of it, not Jimmy, I want to understand why you needed to escape, to disappear, to become someone else, to become Lily.'

'Are you taking the piss?' She's indignant. 'Haven't you been listening at all? He was violent. He really hurt people. I saw him...'

Jenny hears the tapping of feet, of agitation.

There is no verbal response from the psychiatrist, not that she can hear on the tape.

'He was an evil bastard, probably still is.' Jenny senses Veronica getting more anxious. 'He knew where I lived, he knew where my sister went to school. He said he'd give her to his mates if I ever—'

She stops mid-sentence.

'Do you think I'm making this all up?'

'I believe, that you believe what you remember is real.'

Jenny's back goes up, *the patronising bitch.* She hates psychobabble.

'Of course, he's *real.* Would I be this scared, this damaged, if he wasn't real. Haven't you seen the x-rays of my face and hands, I said you could, don't *you* remember that. Did you even bother to look!'

'I…' there is hesitation in the woman's voice. 'Tell me about it then, tell me how you got those injuries.'

Even though she had listened to the tape several times, Jenny wishes this was on video, there was so much more that could be added, the interplay of emotion, facial expressions, non-verbal reactions that would be invaluable. A videotape would give them more leverage with the CPS.

'He called me a paki-whore, a slag. In front of everyone. I hadn't done anything. I tried to tell him. I told him that Paula set me up, that she set him up. He didn't believe me, so I made a run for it. I didn't—'

There's a loud noise in the background, an alarm going off. A few seconds later it stops, someone must have silenced it.

'I thought I got away from him,' her words are filled with sadness. 'I thought I'd be safe, that I could hide. I ran into a side street. I'd forgotten about the cobbled stones. They were slippy. It had been raining. I went down like a ton of bricks. Smacked my knees and sprained my wrist.

I heard the slap of his boots coming towards me.' Her words quicken, 'He grabbed my hair, nearly tore it off my scalp—dragged me into the dark, through the mess, broken bottles, rotting food… abandoned cars. The houses were all boarded up. I tried to kick him off me… I couldn't see anything. His knuckles hit the side of my head. I nearly passed out. I'd never had to fight anyone—' The pitch of her voice rises higher and higher. 'He was going to kill me, he wanted to kill me—'

The psychiatrist mumbles something out. Jenny hadn't been able to transcribe it.

'What sort of stupid question is that? I was terrified! He pushed me on top of a car bonnet, started to lift up my dress. Put his hand over my mouth. I thought… I thought—'

A mangle of words tumble out, some hers, some the psychiatrist. Jenny still struggles to make sense of them.

'Do you want to take a break?' The psychiatrist's voice suddenly clear.

Veronica carries on. 'What's the point?' She takes in a deep breath. 'My arms were loose. He must have thought I'd just give in. Just let him. As if I'd do that. Something went off in my head.

I went for his face, tore at his cheeks with my nails. Dug them in as deep as I could. He fell back, screaming. I scrambled away, hid behind a car. Everything went quiet. I couldn't stop crying; I tried to cover my mouth. He must have heard me.' Her speech becomes more intense. 'He came out of nowhere. Grabbed me by the hair. Headbutted me…the pain.' The tremor in her voice worsens, 'There was blood everywhere. My legs gave way. I wrapped myself around his thighs,' she gulps for air, 'tried to stop him kicking me… he smacked me around the head. Stamped on my hand. He was going to kill me—' Sobs wrack up through her body.

'He shouted at me, said I'd made a mess of his new shirt. That's all he said. Like he'd not hurt me at all. I thought he'd finished, I thought he'd let me go.' Veronica cries out, 'He threw me onto my back, put his knees on my chest, put all his weight on me.' Her breathing becomes erratic, 'He put his hands around my neck. He pressed—'

There's a loud thump, the sound of a metal chair clattering to the floor.

Jenny, heart pounding, full of adrenalin, reaches out and presses stop. She knows there is nothing more to listen to. Whatever happened next wiped away long ago.

She takes a break. The walk back to the Incident Room gives her time for reflection. If Veronica was acting, was faking it, she deserved an Oscar.

Chapter 53

She's back at her own house. Eyes trained on the computer screen in front of her. Much to Thomasine's disappointment, the call hadn't gone well. She'd hoped to get professional courtesy, at least. Mel had been unwilling to talk, said she was on the way to another meeting. Jacky Wainwright would go on the list of people to be interviewed. She thanked her for getting in touch. Said she'd get back to her.

Instead of letting her frustration get the better of her, Thomasine calls in a favour, a long shot, a contact at the Department of Transport. A small lie of omission, no mention of the name of the case, she's trying to trace someone called Billy or William, probable owner of a white Capri in 1972, likely to be within a twenty-five-mile radius of Bolton. It takes him a while to get back to her. A list of four people.

Only one fits the profile – Robert William Bennett, born in 1953.

Thomasine enters his name and date of birth into 192.com – searches for his address. The basics turn up, the town. She needs more information – it's pay per view. She hurries downstairs to grab her credit card. Minutes later his current address is written on her notepad – Owl Barn, Wassington, Norfolk. Then she does a full search on the Land Registry Database. There are details of another property, in London – Bow. She finds it on Google maps, it's a garage, and a large one at that.

Why wait? she thinks to herself. The feeling in her gut tells her that this man is connected to her sister's death. Which address should she go to first? Her intuition tells her that Mel will have already dispatched a team to Norfolk. They might have missed the garage.

London, it is.

Chapter 54

'So, this is what we've found out so far.' Mel straightens her back and casts her eye over the whiteboard. She counts on her fingers: 'One – the psychiatrist diagnosed Lily as having Post-Traumatic Stress Disorder. Two – her medical team found evidence of numerous physical injuries. Three – she was experiencing flashbacks. Although there isn't a police record of those events as far as we know. Four – in the therapy sessions she describes being attacked by someone called Jimmy, a drug dealer. Five – it sounds like she became hyper-alert, tried to keep herself awake all the time to avoid the nightmares. This ultimately led to exhaustion and a mental health crisis which resulted in her attempting to take her own life.

'Finally, and perhaps most salient, the psychiatrist concluded that Lily had Multiple Personality Disorder and Veronica was an alternate personality generated by PTSD. She then told Lily she could rid her of the flashbacks that were the source of her problems.'

Sam Ingleby steps forward, hands stuffed deep in his trouser pockets. 'From what we can see, the main thrust of the treatment was to block the memories that triggered the manifestation of the alternate personality. Electro Shock Therapy was used extensively over a four-week period. Sometimes up to four times a day. Plus, they were pumping her full of something called Propranolol, God knows how the poor lass coped with it.'

'The next thing we need to confirm,' interjects Badger, 'is how she got hold of the tapes. She could have made an application under the Data Protection and Access to Medical Records Acts. If that is the case, we might assume that Lily Probisher was fully cognitive and aware of her true identity.'

Mel eases herself onto the edge of a desk and folds her arms across her chest.

'Badger, we can't assume anything.'

The procedure for waking Veronica up was going to start the following morning. Of one thing Mel is completely clear. There was no way any other member of her team was going to hear whatever Veronica had to say when she woke up. She wanted to be the one that did that. Veronica could be the killer and, if she is, a brain injury wouldn't make her any less guilty.

The hospital carpark is almost deserted. She pulls the collar of her coat around her neck. She hears someone clear their throat. The hair on her neck bristles. She stops dead and glances over her shoulder. A man in a thick black coat lumbers off towards the pay and display machine. His hands jangling the coins in his pockets.

Pull yourself together. It's probably some poor bugger whose wife's been taken in. She carries on, her boots slapping on the wet tarmac.

It's gone nine p.m. She's standing at the end of Veronica's bed waiting for Brandon Da Costa to finish his checks.

The consultant's eyes scan the numerous monitors that cluster around behind the head of the bed. Unconsciously, he makes a clicking noise with his tongue, then gently digs his fingernail into the skin on the back of Veronica's hand. She doesn't flinch, eyes closed, breathing steadily, she appears asleep.

He writes a few lines on her notes, then slips his pen into his pocket. He returns his attention to Mel. 'I need to speak with you for a moment.'

She follows him through the double doors. He leans back against the wall, arms across his chest, hands tucked into his armpits. 'We don't know how long it will take for her to fully wake. In layman's terms, we're reducing the medication that's been keeping her in the coma and it will take time for the medication to work its way out of the system. She may be in a lot of pain. We have to be very careful indeed. That earlier episode when she woke could be a one off.

It may be hours or even days before she wakes. We don't know how she'll respond when she comes to. It can be very distressing for everyone.' He winces, rubs the back of his neck with his hand, 'I've agreed with the family that we'll contact them as soon as there are signs of recovery. I'd prefer it if you waited with them.'

'I'm fine where I am, I'll wait.' Her jaw clenches. 'It's important that I'm here when she comes to.' Her eyes widen. 'She may say something important to the investigation. Not only about the accident, but also the murder of Karen Albright.'

He looks her directly in the face. 'DCI Phillips, you're being very naive.' He lets out a sigh, his irritation obvious, 'Look, she might not even be able to speak and if she can it might not make any sense.' A porter walks by, pushing an elderly lady along in a wheelchair. The woman looks up gives them both a gentle smile. Da Costa carries on regardless, 'Let me make it clear, my priority is to make sure that she can recover the best she can from the brain injury. I don't want the family suing me because we allowed you to be at the bedside when she woke up. She's already had two cardiac arrests, another might kill her.' He takes the ballpoint pen out of his top pocket. Clicks it on and off with his thumb. 'I've advised the family not to allow you to be by the bedside. We have no idea how Veronica may react to your presence. You seem like a very nice person, but in all honesty, I think you might do more harm than good. Until she wakes and stabilises, I'm afraid you won't be allowed on the ward.'

Mel meets his eyes, holds his gaze, says nothing.

'Do I have to repeat myself?'

'No,' the word is tinged with frustration, she feels like a ten-year-old being told off by a parent.

'She may wake very confused and upset, even terrified, and that may have a fundamental impact on her well-being. I can't risk that.'

Mel nods her head, she must be careful, she's no fool. It may be weeks before Veronica is cognitive. He gives her a final deep stare before striding off down the corridor.

God knows who'll she'll wake up as, thinks Mel to herself. Will she be Lily Probisher or Veronica Lightfoot? It could be either or both, if the historical medical records are anything to go by. She peers through the glazed window in the door. Head lopsided, Veronica lies prone on the bed; a ventilation tube down her throat. The craniotomy carried out to alleviate the pressure within her brain has left a shallow depression in her skull the size of the palm of her hand. Somewhere in the hospital, the section of bone removed is being stored in a freezer, ready to be re-inserted when the conditions are right. Mel is filled with sadness—what if they can't? The reality of Veronica's situation sinks in. Her broken legs will be fine, but the brain doesn't heal in the same way. She may have to learn to walk and talk all over again. Her mental capacity may be severely affected. Days ago, she'd heard someone from another family telling Rosie that she must have hope. Hope was what got them through it. Mel wonders how useful it will be as Rosie endeavours to navigate her way through the carnage of a murder trial.

She hurries towards the exit, struggles on with her coat. Her phone falls from her hand to the floor. A text message from Thomasine flashes up as she picks it up. She leaves it be, pushes open the doors, a blast of air hits her face.

It's bloody freezing!

As she runs across the carpark, it's almost empty except for a couple of cars, two beams of light shine across her path. She plonks herself in the driver's seat, calls up the message from Thomasine.

'Have you been to see Jacky Wainwright yet?'

And that was it.

She hasn't. The muscles in between her shoulders knot. Perhaps it's time to remind Thomasine Albright that she's not the one in charge of her sister's case. She shrugs it off, Thomasine is unlikely to send them on a wild goose chase. She's too smart for that. She'll go see her tomorrow. Right now, Jacky Wainwright might be the best lead they have.

Chapter 55

Jacky Wainwright looks alarmed as Mel thrusts her badge in her face. She sways a little, steadies herself on the doorframe. 'DCI Mel Phillips, can I come in?' Her tone is firm but polite.

The woman nods her head, her attention elsewhere. Mel looks over her shoulder; someone is doing a three-point turn in the road. The rear of the car inches away from a silver-grey Audi. Jacky lets Mel pass by her into the hallway, she herself continues to stare out the door. Mel hears the sound of an engine going off into the distance. Jacky shuts the door, tells her to go straight ahead into the living room. Whoever it was disappeared swiftly. The room is as Thomasine had described – a cacophony of wooden plaques and motivational sayings. Mel silently chuckles to herself and wonders if Mrs Wainwright had one for this occasion. She doubted it.

'I'm not sure if you're aware but there's now an active investigation into the murder of Karen Albright.'

'Karen Albright?' The woman's face blanches – there's a sharp intake of breath.

'I'm here on a different matter, although we believe it is linked to that case. I'm also investigating the disappearance of Veronica Lightfoot. I'm sure you've seen it in the media. She's been found alive.'

The woman nods, gestures for her to take a seat.

'Thank you. I believe you may have known Veronica.' It was a statement, not a question. The woman's mouth opens. Mel can see her struggling to form an answer – nothing comes out. 'We have evidence that strongly indicates that you and she knew each other and that you were there on the night of her disappearance.'

'Evidence?' the word is barely a whisper. Her face crumples, thick tears slide down her face taking her eyeliner and mascara with it.

'What sort of evidence?' Her lower lip trembles.

'I'm not at liberty to say more than that. You, amongst other people, are in a line of enquiry that we're exploring.' Mel dips into her handbag, takes a tissue out of a packet and offers it to her. The woman takes it out of her hand. 'No need to get upset, Jacky – may I call you Jacky?'

She blows her nose, nods back in assent, sniffs.

'Thanks, Jacky, I'm sure we can sort this out. I just want to check a few things with you. I could kill a cup of tea, though.' She stands up, gives Jacky Wainwright a wide smile. 'Shall I make it?' She knows that it will throw the woman off-guard. It does.

'No, no, I'll do it.' Together they go into the kitchen. Her hands shake as she fills the kettle.

'Shall I get the cups out?' Mel opens a cupboard at random. Purposefully makes her words light-hearted, casual, 'In here, are they?'

A few minutes later they seat themselves back in the living room. A light sheen of sweat covers Jacky Wainwright's face. She cradles her cup of coffee tightly between her hands.

'Are you okay?' Mel feigns a look of concern.

The woman nods her head. 'Just nervous. I've not been interviewed by a police officer before.'

'Well, always good to get the first one out of the way, then.' Fear consumes the woman's face.

'The *first* one?' Her eyes widen.

Inside Mel feels slightly guilty, after all, the woman had supplied Thomasine with the photographs. Without her help they might not be as further forward. She takes a tape recorder out of her bag. 'I'll need to use this, is that okay?'

Jacky swallows, her lips go into a solid line. 'That's fine.'

Mel gets the feeling that it isn't fine at all.

'We believe you met Veronica in a nightclub, is that right?'

She nods, looks down at the tape recorder, blinks.

'Is that a yes?'

'Yes.'

'Thank you, could you tell me who you were with, the night Veronica disappeared?'

Jacky's eyes widen, her fingers play with her wedding ring.

'I wasn't—'

Mel raises an eyebrow and tilts her head slightly to the side.

'I… I mean, I'm not sure, there were hundreds of people in the Connaught. I only knew a few of them.'

'That's the Connaught nightclub? So, who did you know?'

'Billy, Smithy, Del, Paula, I didn't really know Veronica other than to say hello to.' Other names tumble out, 'Then there was Carol, Christine and Linda – my friends from Liverpool.'

'What's Billy's surname?'

'I don't—'

'I think you do.' Mel purposely drops her gaze to the digital recorder.

'Billy… Bennett, I think it was Billy Bennett.'

'And Jimmy, where was he from?' The name off the cassette tapes, Mel is sure Jacky knows him.

Her voice breaks, 'I'm not—'

'I believe there was someone called Jimmy?'

Two pink circles prick Jacky Wainwright's cheeks. 'Gosh, I've not heard that name in years.'

Mel leans back into her seat. Her smile fades. There's a burst of vibration in her pocket, a text message, she ignores it. Her mouth twitches. 'You do realise that this is a police investigation, that you may be interviewed under caution, I'm giving you the chance to tell me the truth. After all,' she pauses for a moment, 'you didn't come forward in 1973, we're going to want to know why not.'

The woman looks like a rabbit frozen in the headlights.

'I'm sorry but—'

'I know it was a long time ago.' Impatience flashes across Mel's face.

'Back in the seventies it was different times. The police were, well…' Thick black tears run down Jacky Wainwright's face. 'On the take, not all of them.' She snuffles. 'The ones in the clubs. You couldn't trust them.'

'Who was paying them?'

'I don't know.'

'I want you to take a few moments to think about it.'

The woman tugs at the tissue between her fingers and takes in a deep breath. 'He's a good man now, turned his life around. I don't want to harm him.'

'Nevertheless?'

She closes her eyes, swallows. 'Jimmy – it was Jimmy Fairfax.'

'Are you still in contact?'

Jacky shakes her head.

'Is that a no?'

'No, we've not spoken for a long while.'

'Who was on the take?' Mel imagines the cogs whirring in Jacky Wainwright's brain.

She shakes her head. 'I can't remember. I'm sorry.'

It is almost twelve thirty when Mel leaves. Jimmy Fairfax and Billy Bennett had been very bad boys indeed. Her gut feeling tells her it's Jimmy Fairfax. He'd argued with Veronica that night. But this was circumstantial, and she doubts the CPS will accept the tapes as evidence. Especially as Veronica had been heavily medicated at the time.

Jacky Wainwright said that she'd not seen them argue. Perhaps other members of the group had. At least she had more names now for the team to investigate.

What if Karen saw him attack Veronica? She'd been to a nightclub with Billy, it said so in the diary and they had photographic evidence of that. Billy could have introduced her to Jimmy. Billy was his lap dog and, according to Jacky, he used to clean up Jimmy's messes. What if Jimmy thought Veronica was dead and didn't want any witnesses? Her pulse races, she's on to something and knows it.

She takes out her mobile phone, texts Jenny. Gives her a list of names to get the ball rolling. No point in waiting until she gets back.

Chapter 56

It's been three nights since Rosie last slept in her own home. Curled up, she sleeps in a chair by Veronica's bed.

There will be no miracle recovery.

Now weaned off most of the drugs that kept her in a coma, Veronica is constantly agitated. The thin cotton sheets wrap around her body, catch on her nightie. She turns over every few seconds, trying to get comfortable, forgetting she has already turned moments before. She tugs the bedsheet over her head. Tries to block out the light. Never settling; never sleeping. Always exhausted.

Her short-term memory has been severely affected, whatever she hears slides into her head and right out again. Her speech is slurred, her tongue swollen. Words come out randomly, regardless of the conversations she has with herself or someone else.

Occasionally, she points at the wall, eyes wide with terror. Her mouth gapes open in an empty silence. A nightmare brought into the broad daylight.

'What do you think it is?' asks Rosie, her hand unfurling her sister's clawed fingers as she turns again.

A look of concern crosses the nurse's face. 'A nightmare, probably. Maybe something to do with the accident. It could be the drugs. That sometimes happens. It's hard to guess.'

Rosie sits back in her seat, picks up her journal. She keeps a diary of Veronica's progress; she jots down a few words.

She's afraid of something and I have absolutely no idea what it is.

Chapter 57

S am lets out a growl of frustration, there are no criminal records on the PNC for a Billy Bennett or a William Bennett born in Lancashire between 1950 and 1954. He tries births and deaths – kicks the heel of his shoes against the legs of his chair. There are hundreds of William Bennetts that fit that criterion. 'This is going to take me bloody ages.'

Jenny's voice rises above the milieu of voices. 'Have you refined the search, put the car in?' The whole team are working down the list of names supplied by Jacky Wainwright.

'No, but I will.' Two-finger typing, he punches in the information. *Why the hell didn't I think of that myself?*

The Department of Transport records bear fruit. His eyes quickly run down the results.

Robert William Bennett, born 1953. Registered owner of a white Capri between June 1972 and January 1974.

'Thank you, *Jenny,*' he whispers under his breath. He inputs the data into the PNC, and this time he gets a hit, Robert William Bennett reported the car stolen in 1974.

'*Found him!*' he exclaims. He leaps to his feet, punches the air, relieved at last to be making progress. Their heads dipped in concentration no one seems to notice. His next stop is the electoral roll. An address in Norfolk comes up. Robert William Bennett had been the sole occupant of the property since 1979. Sam wonders what he did between 1974 and 1979. 'Jenny, will you do a general search on the internet for Robert William Bennett, that's Billy Bennett's full name.' He scribbles the address down on a piece of paper and hands it to her. 'Best to try the Land Registry, too.'

He sits in silence for a moment, tilts back his chair. His eyelids flutter then close. That morning he'd woke early, way too early. Exhausted and drenched in sweat. His sleep plagued by dreams of a young girl with wires attached to her head, convulsing, screaming at him to help her.

He pushes those thoughts away and concentrates on Karen Albright. *We could have so easily missed her.* The photographs could have been on the internet for years, waiting to be found. *Thom Albright must be pretty pissed off, too. Those magazines had been at her friend's place for years.*

The press will have a field day when they find out. If they find out. Hopefully, they won't. The team had been working hard to find Karen's killer. It galls him that the CPS will probably reject anything that's had Thom Albright's involvement. All the work they've undertaken on the back of it will follow it down the toilet.

Kinsi shouts across the room. 'Sam, what's the name of the woman Mel saw earlier?'

'Jacky Wainwright? Why?'

'I thought it was. We've just had a call. Husband found her unconscious – at home. She's with the paramedics now.'

Chapter 58

It doesn't take him long to pack; a few crumpled shirts, thick hiking socks crusted with mud, two pairs of jeans – unwashed clothes that he'll dump on his way to the airport. He's already got rid of most of his stuff, thrown in the local clothing bank in a rare moment of charity.

A double-decker bus thunders past the window; the glass vibrates in its tarnished metal frame.

Naked, he pulls on the merino thermal underwear Lottie bought him for Christmas. He layers on top two long-sleeved T-shirts and the fair isle jumper he bought from Oxfam. Over his long johns he slides on a pair of waterproof trousers, commando green, two sizes too big. He secures them with a black leather belt. He's lost weight – the curve of his hip bones, the broadness of his chest – a new body is emerging.

He shaves his head, just as he had for the passport photograph, takes the clippers to his skull, short clean strokes just as he'd done before. Clumps of fine grey hair fall to the floor – he finishes off with a razor, careful not to nick his scalp, careful not to cut. Two minutes later he is done; a dab of shaving oil rubbed into his newly domed head the final finishing touch. He gazes at himself in the mirror. Fleetingly, a confused look crosses his face; a lack of recognition, a hint of doubt. Finally, he puts on a pair of horn-rimmed spectacles, to match the passport photograph. A total transformation, he thinks to himself. *Even Lottie wouldn't know me.* He feels a tinge of sadness – how will she cope without him? He never prepared her for the single life. His eyes glisten as he blanks those thoughts out.

He wanders around the room – black and white geometric shapes glare back from the walls. The owner's futile attempt at modernity. Against the wall, a copper monstrosity – a double bed whose mattress sinks in the middle. The lurid black and pink silk duvet slips off with every movement. It had driven him mad. The place was one of those *walk in off the street* places; cheap, cheerless and strictly cash. *Probably used by prostitutes.* He studies the bed for a moment. *Perhaps I should have availed myself of the local delights?*

With a shake of his head, he finishes off packing the rucksack, stuffs in a pair of trainers, two pairs of waterproof gloves, wraps the chisel and hammer in his sleeping bag and positions it on top of everything else. A bag of latex gloves lies open on the dressing table. He tucks them in one of the outside pockets, for convenience. Lastly, he packs the toiletries, his razor, clippers, tooth whitening kit, toothbrush. Along with his phone charger he distributes them amongst the outside pockets. He pulls the tie tight, snaps the clasp shut.

'Done.' He takes a final look around the room. *Should I clean it, wipe all traces of myself from it? It would take too long and, anyway, the people here are unlikely to report me. I can't imagine they'd want the police streaming all over the place.* He'd only been there a couple of nights, the woman behind reception barely looked at him. *Nah.*

Then he chastises himself, he's getting sloppy, the old language coming back.

He eases his padded jacket over his clothes, slips the rucksack over his shoulders.

Leaves the room without a backward glance.

Chapter 59

At least the rain has stopped.

Thomasine hates London, hates the crush of people; lemmings rushing to some unknown destination, roadworks everywhere.

'Turn right,' the electronic voice of the satnav pipes up. 'You have reached your destination.'

On one side of the road is a row of garages, the other a run of viaduct with units built into the arches. The slip of white paper in her hand notes the address, 4B. There's a door next to a roller-shutter garage, both painted a dull grey. Thomasine sits in the car for a while, watches for any sign of life. After a while, she eases herself out of the car, strolls towards 4B, in her pocket a picking hook. She knocks on the door, knocks again. No answer.

She looks up and down the street before sliding the hook into the lock, a few twists, a click and it's open. With tens of unlabelled keys at the farm, she's had plenty of practise lately. Her mother didn't believe in labels, not for keys anyway.

'I know what goes with what.'

It's like a prank she planned for after her death, something to chortle over. Thomasine feels a knot in her stomach. Her mother's voice now a constant companion, getting louder and louder.

There's a flash of light as she walks through the door. She jumps back—blinded by a row of enormous halogen lights that hang from the ceiling. It takes her seconds to get rid of the green patches of light that blur her vision. Whitewashed brick walls rise high above her. The place is cavernous. She turns her head, looks over her shoulder. Quickly glances through the door before locking it behind her.

She takes the place in. It looks like a crime scene – the rugs, the walls, the concrete floors, all splattered in dark red paint. She slips on a pair of latex gloves. Turns off her sense of smell – she'd learnt to do that years ago. It went with the job – half-consumed corpses have an odour that not everyone can bear. She walks around the room, stopping now and again to explore whatever is within hand's reach. There's a pungent odour of methylated spirit and rotting food that cloys in her throat. It stinks like a pub that's not been cleaned in weeks. A mound of empty wine bottles lie in a plastic box just right of the sink; red, white, cheap, expensive. *Billy Bennett clearly has a drink problem.*

Next to it, a black bag filled with empty pizza boxes, half-eaten chunks of food, chips, bananas, burgers, gangrenous bread that's a putrid olive green. If it hadn't been winter, there would be maggots and flies everywhere. At the back there's a small oblong room with a white door; a cheap metal plate marks it as the toilet. She opens the door, shuts it just as quickly. One look at the toilet was enough to turn her stomach. In the other corner, a metal sink caked in paint; the bowl filled with unwashed cutlery and crockery. Above it, several shelves laden with painting supplies. There's a pile of rags—they stink of methylated spirit. No, something else, she lifts one to her nose, her head spins a little. The smell is familiar, she can't quite name it.

Thomasine hadn't expected him to be an artist. *Dug deeper, I should have dug deeper.* She'd been impulsive, set off without thinking it through. *That's not like me. Not like me at all.*

She casts her eyes over the paintings. They're not to her taste; too depressing, too dark. Rather weird. Dark red swirls, mouldy greens, gloomy browns. Unsettling images of mould, mushrooms and decay.

Exhibition posters litter the walls; their yellowed paper curling at the edges. All advertising his own work. His name in bold letters in the foreground. Some go back over twenty years. She wonders when Billy Bennett became Robert William Bennett.

In the centre of the room is an Ikea daybed – the duvet is covered in stains and reeks of stale air and sweat.

There's a large antique oak easel with wheels on it. On the floor beside it, there is what appears to be a matching box, both riddled with woodworm. She opens the lid, inside there's a jumble of business cards and photographs. She takes them out. Most mean nothing to her – names she doesn't recognise. Melancholy landscapes of God knows where. She gives each one a quick glance before moving on to the next.

Halfway through, a photograph stops her in her tracks – a black and white. Her stomach flips—time stops. Karen dressed in summer shorts, legs tanned, her hair tangled by the wind. Stood amidst the long grass. Seemingly unaware that she was the centre of someone's attention.

It's him. It must be him.

Then another—Candy Wharton, she recognises her immediately. In a nightclub, standing just off to the left of him. Then several photographs of what might be a reunion. A group of middle-aged people stand in the midst of a dance floor. Smiling, posing – dressed in Northern Soul garb.

She takes a copy of each one, then places them back in the box.

Her feet create an echo as she moves around the room, even her breathing sounds loud. Shrouded in cotton bedsheets, four enormous canvases hang high on the wall. As she stands in front of the first one, she takes a small torch out of her pocket. Reaching up, she lifts the sheet, shines the light on the canvas.

'What the—'

Her legs crumple beneath her.

Chapter 60

On the way to the car, he'd taken a detour, drawn into a corner shop by the potent aroma of turmeric and coriander. The girl behind the counter scrutinised his face as he passed her—she wrinkled her nose. Did he smell? Her long, jet-black plaited hair swung across her back as she focused her attention on the closed-circuit TV fixed on the wall above her head.

He felt an uncomfortable shift, he saw her watch him as he walked up and down the aisles. She had taken too much interest in him. Her eyes lingered on his face. Had the police released a photograph of him?

That foolish bitch from Liverpool said there was a photograph of him and Karen. That the sister, the one with the funny name that Karen had taken the piss out of relentlessly, had a copy of it. He hoped his little gift has distracted them for a while, he knew the card would come in handy. It was as though he was applying the fine detail to a painting, a tiny touch of white in the lens of the eye to reflect the light.

He'd wondered for a moment whether it would be better to disappear, right then and there, into thin air. Just as Veronica had. His fingers curl at the thought of her, if it wasn't for her, none of this would have happened. And that photograph, if only he'd known about it. *It's years out of date, what good will that be?* He can easily say that they just had one dance and that was it. He'd chided himself for the bout of negativity, bought a sliced white loaf and some ham. Smiled at the girl as he handed over the money. She didn't smile back.

Chapter 61

They play *The Name Game*. Veronica, propped up against the pillows, smiles. Barely lined, her face has a translucent quality to it, blonde eyelashes, almost non-existent eyebrows, pale pink lips. She bears no resemblance to the eighteen-year-old girl that disappeared from their lives so long ago. Her pale green nightie and floral cardigan hang loose on thin shoulders. Only her eyes give a clue to who she really is, dark green irises, an exact match of her sister's.

'Who am I?' asks Rosie, pointing to her own chest.

'Mum, Mum.' A cheeky grin crosses Veronica's lips.

For a moment, Rosie wonders if it's better to say *yes*. To play along. Or is Veronica having fun with her, is it joshing? Hard to tell.

'I am Rosie. I am your sister.'

'Sis, Nosie, sis.' Veronica laughs, eyes open wide, her body shakes. As yet unable to get her tongue around the *r* in Rosie.

Rosie holds her breath, won't let out the hurt. Her sister may never be reunited with their mother; dementia was eating at her brain. Her memories of Veronica's disappearance, and the years that followed, have themselves disappeared. At first, it had been a gift – but now?

They play the game again. This time it is, *where are we?* Veronica's laughter turns into hiccupy giggles that she can't stop.

'Nosie's stupid, Nosie's silly.'

Rosie chides her. 'Now, Veronica, don't be naughty.' It has no effect.

Anything can prompt it, someone walking by, someone crying. As yet, she is unable to differentiate between what is an appropriate response and what's not.

Suddenly, Veronica's attention is caught by one of the nurses, the giggles stop. She shrinks back at the sound of the woman's voice, turns her head away.

Rosie's stomach churns, so many questions still go unanswered. For now, her place is by her sister's side helping her recover. Easing out her clawed fingers, massaging her feet, talking about the life they had until she went missing.

And she'll have enough time now. The redundancy offer— she'd accepted it.

Under her breath, Rosie whispers a silent prayer.

Please God, don't let my sister end up in prison.

The sister she knew wouldn't harm a soul.

Veronica's eyes close, she lets out a low whimper, tries to cover her face with the bedsheet. As though she'd heard every word that Rosie said.

Chapter 62

'Has Jacky Wainwright recovered yet?' Mel rubs the tiredness out of her eyes.

'Aye, just about. Nasty attack. We're waiting for the full forensics report to come back.' Sam fixes the satnav on the windscreen, it starts up automatically. He'd put the destination in earlier – Wassingham, Norfolk. Securing the seatbelt over his stomach, he glances over at Mel then switches on the ignition. 'She'd thought it was you coming back to ask more questions. Apparently, the attacker put his foot in the door, grabbed her by the neck then pushed her back into the hallway.' He shakes his head, switches on the heater. 'Unfortunately for us, he kept his mouth shut, didn't say a word, or so she says. He threw her up against the wall, wrapped his fingers around her throat, tried to throttle her. Fortunately for us and her, she passed out, he must have thought she was dead.'

He eases off the handbrake, manoeuvres the car out of the carpark.

'She didn't recognise him?'

'Nope.' His fingers tap on the steering wheel. 'All she can remember is that he was wearing a black coat buttoned up to his chin. And black leather gloves.'

Mel frowns, 'Any take on who it might be?'

'Jimmy Fairfax? Billy Bennett?' He narrows his eyes on the road. 'Badger's checking the phone records, to see if she spoke to either of them recently. Kinsi is over there with her now, it'll be a few hours before Mrs Wainwright will be ready for a formal interview. She's still in shock.'

'It must have scared her to death.' Mel looks out of the window; a homeless man shivers in a doorway. She caught his eye, he averted his gaze. 'Have Forensics picked anything up?'

'Just bits of stuff off his boots, we're not sure if he had transport. Unfortunately, all the tyre tracks were obliterated by this last lot of snow.'

There are a lot of unfortunates in this case, thinks Mel. They continue in silence for the next fifteen miles. Sam lost in his own thoughts, she ponders the information they'd garnered from the medical files. It had made uncomfortable reading.

Suddenly Sam jabs his fingers on the steering wheel. 'I can't believe she's getting there before us. It's like she's taking the piss.' He swivels his head to look at her. 'I thought you'd warned her off.'

'Who?' The tone of her voice is sharp. 'Eyes on the road, please.'

'Thomasine Albright—I thought you'd had a word with her.'

Irritation flashes in her eyes. 'I did—we did. She's on compassionate leave. We can't be babysitting her; checking whatever she's doing.' A little admiration leaks through, 'And let's be honest here, we'd both be doing the same, wouldn't we?'

He snorts out an uncomfortable laugh. 'Probably.' The tension dissipates, he puts his foot down on the accelerator as they slip onto the motorway. The speedometer inches up to 90 mph. 'Still, let's hope she's not made a dash down the M1 with a shotgun on the back seat, those farmers always have one stowed away somewhere.'

Her stomach plummets, a bright red BMW swings out in front of them, Sam flashes them to get out of the way. The driver ignores it, he follows it up with a blare from the sirens, the BMW swiftly manoeuvres into the second lane. Then it hits her like a slap on the face. They'd been so consumed by the Lightfoot case that they'd not considered alternative scenarios.

'What if Karen hadn't been the only one to disappear?' A lorry changing gears nearly drowns her out.

'Veronica Lightfoot did.' There's a lilt of sarcasm in his voice.

'No, what I mean is what if other girls have disappeared?' Her pulse races. She messages Jenny, 'Do a long-term missing persons for girls aged between fourteen and eighteen. Specifically, anyone with the same physical profile and within sixty miles of the crime scene.'

There was something else she wanted her to check but she can't remember what it is. She puts her phone on charge, leans back in the seat, lets her eyelids shut.

Sam kills the engine; parks outside the barn conversion, the curtains are drawn. 'The place looks deserted. 'Shite—driving all this way and he's not in.'

Mel shakes her head in frustration. 'Let's not make assumptions.' They get out of the car, open the gate.

Sam knocks loudly on the front door. They hear a dog barking inside, within seconds it's directly behind the door, growling, its nails clawing at the wood.

'Let's give it another ten minutes.' She checks her watch, 'He could be out in the fields for all we know.'

'Without the dog? I doubt it.' Sam kicks at the stone chippings beneath his feet. 'This place is in the middle of bloody nowhere, boss. There's no guarantee he's even here.'

'Don't sulk,' her mouth twists in irritation, 'Go check the neighbours' place, who knows, he could have gone over for a coffee.'

'Aye, like that's conveniently going to happen.' He opens the gate and walks up the road towards the converted water tower.

Her mobile vibrates in her pocket. It's Badger; his Lancashire accent booms in her ear. He only has one volume on the phone – loud.

'We've traced Jimmy Fairfax.' His voice is full of excitement. 'He's got a place a couple of miles away.'

Mel feels a burst of elation. 'Great! Check where he was when Jacky Wainwright was attacked and get him to give us a DNA sample. And check his mobile, see if there are any calls between them.'

'Will do. I'll let you know how it goes.' He hangs up.

Moments later Sam jogs back down the road, a look of disapproval hangs on his lips.

'The woman's in, she says he's gone away for a few days, doesn't know where.'

Mel holds out her phone, Sam stops, in front of her, a look of confusion on his face. 'Badger's located Jimmy Fairfax.'

He thumps his fist into the palm of his hand, '*Get em in*—all we need now is him to turn up and we're quids in.'

She slips the phone back into her pocket, raises an eyebrow. 'If only we were so lucky.'

'Let's go have a chat with the woman next door, then,' Sam looks over his shoulder at the sparkling glass-covered tower, 'my gut tells me we should. She's seems rattled about something.'

As they make their way over, Mel's phone vibrates again. An email from Jenny – a list of names with photographs attached. She gives the message a quick once-over, pockets the phone.

The woman welcomes them in, offers her hand. Mel shakes it, she senses a trembling, a discomfort. She doesn't close the door after them.

'I'm Kerry Marchant,' a weak smile comes to her lips, 'nice to meet you. Would you like a coffee?'

'DCI Mel Phillips, no doubt you already know that this is DS Sam Ingleby. Tea would be good, if that's okay.' Mel takes in the room. The glass panels and concrete finishes, not her thing. 'Milk, no sugar, same for both of us.'

The woman opens the cupboards, roots around, her face flushes. 'Sorry, we've had someone looking after the house for us, they've moved things around a bit.' Eventually, she finds three cups, opens the fridge. It's empty.

Kerry—' the woman doesn't answer. Mel taps her on the shoulder. 'Kerry, that's okay.'

'What? They've not left me any milk, I asked them to. I'll pop next door—'

Mel gestures toward a seat. 'Let's not bother about that, shall we?'

'I'd rather stand, if that's okay.' The frown lines on the woman's forehead deepen.

Mel folds her arms across her chest, she seems deep in thought for a moment then lifts her head, her eyes drill down on the woman in front of her. 'You don't live here, do you?'

'What—what do you mean? Of course, I do.' A look of fear freezes on her face.

'Who are you?'

'I'm Kerry Marchant, like I said.'

'You've not asked us why we're here. Aren't you curious?'

'No, I assumed it was something to do with Rob next door. It's none of my business.'

Sam interjects, 'I'm afraid I don't believe you, either.' He sits down at the kitchen table, takes in the view across the fields. He raises his voice. 'Sit down.'

The woman seats herself opposite him, her eyes go to the open door. Is she expecting someone else, Sam thinks to himself. Or is she planning to make a run for it. He gets up, strides over to the door, slams it shuts.

Mel takes out her phone, calls up the email she'd received a few minutes earlier. She clicks on the photographs until she finds the one she wants; her fingers stretch out the picture. 'Who are you really? I don't want to have to arrest you, but I will.'

Tears form in the woman's eyes, stream down her cheeks. 'Lottie Bennett, I'm Lottie Bennett. I'm Rob's wife.'

Mel's lips twist in a smile. 'I don't think so, he's never married.' There's a sarcastic edge to her words. 'We've checked.' She leans forward, puts her phone on the table, swivels it around to face the woman. 'Do you recognise this girl?'

The woman blanches, her lower lip trembles, she steadies her hands on the base of her seat. 'No.'

Sam looks on in surprise.

Mel taps her fingers on the table. 'I think I do. You're Charlotte Arnold, aren't you?'

Sam's jaw drops.

'Do you realise your family has been searching for you for over twenty years?'

The woman looks up, her eyes shine with anger. 'I don't know who you're talking about. I've already told you who I am. I'm Lottie Bennett.'

'To be absolutely accurate, you lied.' Mel inclines her head towards Sam. 'You told us your name was Kerry Marchant. Now you're saying your name is Lottie Bennett. It seems you have a problem with the truth. We've been looking for you for a long time, Charlie. It will be quite easy to establish who you really are. A quick DNA test will prove that beyond doubt.' Mel looks over at Sam. His face is impassive. She realises he has no idea who Charlie Arnold is. She should have told him but there hadn't been time. The email arrived just as the woman invited them in.

Mel retrieves her phone, hands it over to Sam, he peers at the photograph.

'Your sister, Belinda has been looking for you all these years.'

The woman stares out of the window. 'I have no idea what you're talking about, I don't have a sister. I want you to go.'

'I'm sure you do, but I want you to think of the three-year-old girl whose whole life has been a misery because he stole you away. That's how old Belinda was, that's if you can be bothered to remember. She was heart-broken.' Mel has no idea if this is truly the case, but it usually is.

The woman refuses to look at the photograph. 'He didn't steal me away.'

Mel gets out of her seat, sits next to the woman, decides to take another track.

'Do you know why we're here?' She sees the woman swallow, run her tongue over her lips.

'No.'

'Sam, ring the RSPCA, see if they can pick up the dog.'

'Why?' it was barely a whisper.

Mel decides to take a chance. 'We're investigating the murder of Karen Albright, aged fifteen when she disappeared back in 1973.

Robert William Bennett, the man you say is your husband, is a person of interest.' She couldn't resist it. 'We believe he is her killer. I believe you are Charlie Arnold, that he abducted you in 1985.'

'But… I'm not her,' she points to Mel's phone. 'I… I don't have a sister.'

Mel lets out a sigh, two words flash into her consciousness, Stockholm Syndrome. She decides to change track again. 'Lottie, Mrs Bennett, where is your husband?'

The colour drains from the woman's face. 'I have no idea.'

'I think he's left you,' Mel spreads out her hands, 'left you to deal with all of this.'

'You're lying!' The woman spits the words out, stands up, lashes out at Mel with her fists, knocks her to the floor. She swings back her right leg, the full force of her foot heads towards Mel's chest.

Sam launches himself towards her, grabs her in a neck hold, hauls her to her feet.

Mel scrambles to her feet, her cheeks flaming red. 'I don't think attacking a police officer is going to help your case at all.' She brushes herself down as Sam pulls the woman's arms behind her back and snaps on a pair of restraints.

'So, who are you, then?' This time Sam asks the question.

The woman looks over her shoulder. 'Go screw yourself!'

'I am arresting you,' Sam's voice is clear and firm, 'on the grounds that you have assaulted a police officer. You do not have to say anything, but it may harm your defence if you do not mention when questioned something which you later rely on in court…'

Mel, arms folded across her chest, stands by, observes. The expression on the woman's face transforms. Eyes dry, she lifts up her chin, speaks without tremor, says what they all say when cornered.

'I want a lawyer.'

'I believe you've been covering up for him for years. You have, haven't you?' Sam tugs at the restraints, the hardness in his voice cuts through the silence. 'You're his accomplice. You're going to need that lawyer.'

Lottie's eyes unfocus, she hesitates for a moment, frowns. 'You're wrong, he's crazy, he's dangerous. He said he'd take Belinda if I didn't go with him—she was just a kid. What choice did I have?'

'Why didn't you leave?' Mel's voice cuts in.

Charlotte Arnold hangs her head, and doesn't utter another word.

Chapter 63

The hood of his coat blows back, the freezing cold wind stings his scalp. He yanks the black beanie hat down over his ears – it keeps slipping off his newly shorn head. He'd already taken the glasses off, condensation clung to the inside of their lenses rendering him almost blind. Hands grasping the straps of his rucksack, he presses on, stumbling over the rutted ground, never sure where his feet will land next. The snow, up to his knees, blusters around him, clings to his lips and eyelashes.

The bitterness of it all gags at the back of his throat. All these years, those girls – people forgot them, he forgot them. Then he'd been torn, that's how it felt, literally ripped back into the past. All because some rich arsehole wanted to build luxury houses for even bigger arseholes. They wanted a view of the moorland. That's what the developer had named it, Moorland View. The press renamed it Murder View, he'd been disappointed, the perspective had been completely inaccurate.

He stops abruptly, squints into the distance, tries orientating himself. He'd left the road a while ago, decided to take an alternative route, the one he'd trodden along back in 1973. His tracks will be less visible, less likely to catch the notice of prying eyes. The true landscape eludes him, hidden beneath a fakery of white and black. It doesn't bother him, not much. Long ago he painted this place, in summer not winter, an orchestration of colour and space, the rocky landscape folding in on itself; the hard, siliceous sandstone juxtaposed against the life that clung to it. Miles of swirling, purple cotton-grass, sapling trees that hugged the rock, drystone walls that gave the land shape and form. The lucent sky, puffs of cumulous cloud tinted pink by the afternoon sun. Three matchstick people punctuate the landscape. It hung on the wall of his studio for years. On impulse, one Christmas, he'd presented it to Carlo, whose face denoted no pleasure; he was not a fan of sunsets, he'd said, handing it back. He'd choked back the hurt, never forgot it. *He'll probably sell his story when it comes out.* He never painted over the canvas, didn't have the heart, it was a reminder of his time with Karen, although she herself isn't in it. Now it lies under the bed in the spare room. Loved only by himself.

A thin line of oaks appear out of the mist, half a mile away, the Albrights' farm beyond it in the distance. He presses on, snow clinging to his calves and feet, his waterproof trousers no longer waterproof. Overhead, a flash of shimmering coal-black wings, a pair of ravens bicker and screech as they swoop down to hit the ground. The victor rises – the head of a dead mouse in its beak.

Shivering, he veers off to the right, to the old barn in the high field, he'll camp there for the night.

Chapter 64

The band of pain from his back to his sternum is crucifying, the seat of his trousers soaked with sweat. His buttocks stick to the black plastic chair he's been sat on since they *invited* him in for an interview three hours ago. All this time he's been left waiting.

All he can think of is Felicia, what will she think of him? She'll be afraid for him—terrified. They've taken his phone off him, he can't contact her. He'd been allowed one call, to his solicitor. What use was that? His was a commercial conveyancer, with absolutely no experience of criminal law. He rang him nevertheless, asked him to find him a *proper lawyer*. The tone of the man's voice told him that he was offended. Whoever he found has yet to turn up.

The interview room is cold and airless. There's a shadow of footprints on the wall, toe marks, heel scrapes. Four chairs tuck under what looks like a breakfast bar. He's seated in one, waiting. A tape recorder is screwed to the table.

He hears a scramble of a fight through the wall, raised voices, someone kicking in the door, there's a rush of feet down the corridor, more shouting. His pulse races—he wants to be away from this, away from the future he'd been avoiding for years.

Over the years, Jimmy wanted to tell his daughter, he'd planned to tell her at the right time. He truly had. But he didn't have the guts. Yesterday he'd worked himself up to it. When he was young he was foolish, reckless, he'd done things he'd regretted, he'd start with that. He'd made her lunch at his place, bought her a bouquet of flowers, Baby's Breath and twelve deep, red roses. Her face lit up as she'd cradled them in her arms.

'Dad, you are such a sweetie.'

Now, tell her now, *he'd said to himself.*

Across the table, an empty bottle of red between them, he'd opened his mouth, 'I—' The doorbell startled them both. The words froze in his throat. Their faces filled the security screen. Two of them. Police. She'd wanted to stay. He couldn't let her. She didn't understand. How could she understand? And when she did, she'd hate him. She hated bullies and always had.

The door opens, he jumps up from his seat. DS Parker and MacLeod walk in, seat themselves down in front of him. Neither are smiling. 'Take a seat, Mr Fairfax. Your solicitor still hasn't turned up,' the tone of her voice lacks empathy of any sort. 'We'll get you put in the cells until he does. We need this room for another interview.'

He slumps back in his seat, he feels sick, the unease that consumes him turns into vertigo, everything around him spins.

'No—let's get on with it.'

DS Parker flips open an A4 notebook, then reaches forward, presses the button on the recorder.

'DS Kevin Parker and DS Kinsi MacLeod interviewing Mr James Fairfax. Mr Fairfax has decided to continue without representation. Is that correct, Mr Fairfax?'

Jimmy nods his head.

'Mr Fairfax has nodded his head. Could I ask you to confirm your decision verbally?'

'Yes, yes.' Anything would be better than waiting, he wants it over. 'I've decided to continue without representation.'

'We'd like to take you back to the night of the sixth of January 1973 – a Saturday. Tell us what you were doing that night.'

He doesn't hesitate to answer, it's all he has been thinking about for the last three hours. 'The Connaught, I was at the Connaught, always was, back then.' His words tumble out. 'I have witnesses, you can ask them?'

'Witnesses, after all these years?' DS Parker leans forward, his mouth sets in a hard line. 'That's rather convenient. Won't they find it hard to remember, after all these years?' He leans back, taps the base of his pen on the desk.

Jimmy blurts the answer out, 'We're still friends—mates, have been for years, still meet up.' He shifts in the chair; his left buttock numb. 'They come in the restaurant. We were at the Connaught, we went there every Saturday night.'

DS MacLeod scratches a note in the notebook in front of her. 'And Karen Albright – was she a friend?'

He turns his head, stares into her face. 'I've told you I didn't know her. All I know is what I've read in the papers.' His fingers cling to the edge of the table. 'If I knew her I'd tell you, what's the point in holding anything back.'

'Tell us about your relationship with Veronica Lightfoot?' She smiles.

'Veronica? The other girl?' An image flashes in the corner of his mind, long red hair, green eyes. 'She was a friend of a friend. That's all. Look, like I've said. I've got witnesses, they'll tell you I was in the club all that night.'

DS MacLeod raises an eyebrow, 'Shame they didn't come forward back in 1973, isn't it? Neither did you, did you? I'd say that was perverting the course of justice?'

'Definitely.' DS Parker interjects. 'Without a doubt.'

Jimmy pulls himself up, 'Look, I've not seen Veronica since the night she went missing. I didn't even know she was called Veronica, we all called her Ronnie.' The pressure builds up behind his temples. Felicia's face rushes up inside his head.

'A friend of a friend? What's that friend's name?'

'Paula, my wife, Paula. Ex-wife, we're divorced. She knew her better than me.'

'Ronnie?' She jots down the word. 'We have evidence that you knew Veronica well. That something happened between you the night she disappeared.'

'Evidence?' The air goes out of his lungs. 'What sort of evidence?'

'We aren't at liberty to say at this moment. However, we have a witness who is willing to testify that you and Veronica had an argument that night.'

The words echo in his head, he watches the police officer unconsciously play with the gold bangle around her wrist. Veronica's voice echoes in his ears. *Please, please, don't.* Splinters of memory rise to the surface. The broken nose, blood splattered over his new Ben Sherman shirt. He imagines the look in his daughter's eyes when she finds out what he used to be. 'We didn't argue, it was me.' He sucks in air through his nose, 'I'm not proud of who I was.'

'Who were you?'

Head between his hands, he tells them who he used to be. The violent racist who controlled people with drugs. 'The last time I saw Veronica was the night she disappeared. Paula, my ex, it was her fault, she set her up, set me off. I dragged Ronnie out of the club,' he rubs the back of his knuckles, 'taught her a lesson, told her that I never wanted to see her face again.'

'And what did teaching her a lesson involve, Mr Fairfax?' There was a loud thumping noise. A raised voice carries through the wall, 'Sit down.'

DS MacLeod, impervious to the interruption, carries on. 'What did that lesson involve?'

'I beat her up, pinned her up against the wall, held her by the neck.' The shame of it appals him, 'I headbutted her. She was in a state when I left her, unconscious.'

'Did you rape her?'

He is back there, in the alley, his eyes bore into Ronnie's face, his fist smeared with her blood. He stood over her, spat in her face.

DS MacLeod taps the table with her pen, 'Did you rape her, Mr Fairfax?'

The words explode out of him. 'God, NO!' Panic sets in his chest, he can see it in their eyes, they don't believe him. It's written all over their faces. 'I was violent, yes. But I never would have done that.' The thought that they might tell Felicia he was a rapist petrifies him. 'I have *never* raped a woman.'

'But you left her to die in the alley?'

'No... no... I was angry,' his shoulders slump, 'I didn't even think about it.' He hangs his head again. 'There are witnesses, I wasn't long, I went back into the club.' He feels the heat rush to his cheeks.

DS Parker leans forward, the is room deadly quiet. 'And Jacky Wainwright, when did you last get in touch with her?'

The wind goes out of Jimmy's chest yet again. His forehead creases. 'Jacky Wainwright, what's she got to do with this?'

The police officer smiles. 'There's a message from her on your mobile phone. When did you see her last?'

Jimmy shakes his head, he blinks. 'I can't remember—it must be years, twenty years, maybe more. She called me, a couple of days ago, I forgot to get back to her. Why?'

DS Parker places a small clear plastic bag on the table, there's a yellow label on it. 'Because Mrs Wainwright has been attacked.' He turns it over, slides it towards him, gives a half-smile. 'Because we found this sticking out from under the settee.'

Jimmy stares at the card, his heart batters against his ribs, the room swims. It's his business card. 'How the hell did that get there?' He is incredulous.

'That's what we'd like to know too, Mr Fairfax.' DS Parker shifts in his seat, the plastic chair creaks as relaxes into it.

'Is she alright?' The colour drains from Jimmy's cheeks.

Kinsi watches every tiny movement on his face.

No, it's not him—he hasn't got the balls.

Chapter 65

I slept for two hours today, in one go. The nurse says that's good.
'What day is it?'

I stare at her, watch the smile form on her face. I look in my brain for the answer, nothing comes to mind. She waits for a minute then repeats the question.

I still don't know.

We are creating memories. New memories that I can hang on to. That's what she told me. It's all about creating new short-term memories. Why is it that I can have these thoughts in my head, orderly thoughts but can't make them come out of my mouth?

'Today is Tuesday. What day is it, Lily?'

'Tuesday… today is Tuesday. My name is Veronica.'

I don't remember being Lily. I remember being Veronica.

'Where are we?' Yet another question.

I'm tired. 'No.'

The nurse sticks her hands in her pockets, she's unhappy. I can never remember her name. She doesn't like that, either. The lower lid on her right eye tics.

Rosie speaks, she's my sister. 'Maybe we can give it a rest for today?'

I have two sisters, Rosie and Thomasine. Thomasine isn't a real sister. Rosie says I've got fifty-two *Get Well* cards. I must have a lot of friends. She tells me I was a therapist. When I was Lily. I can't remember any of it.

Every day is the same. I keep clean, I like clean things. Rosie says I'm very tidy in my house, I didn't know I had a house. She says I've got two. What's the point in that? I live here now.

Get your limbs moving, someone told me that. They lift my leg, ask me to resist. Sometimes my leg moves. Sometimes it doesn't. I want my limbs to move. I want to do it on my own. I don't like being touched. I don't mind Rosie doing it. She's gentle. She loves me. She told me that. She's Miss Delicious.

My voice is broken, it croaks—that tube broke it. Rosie understands me when I speak. They've moved me to a different place, I think. I'm not sure. The room looks different.

There's a woman to help me talk, to form words. We repeat words over and over again. I want to talk properly. I want to be understood. The words in my head don't come out of my mouth. Sometimes they do, sometimes they don't. They aren't always in the right sequence. I know what I want to say, mostly.

I can focus my eyes now, look around. They tell me I broke my legs. That I was in a car accident. I have a brain injury. It's on a poster on the wall. So I can remind myself. I can read words. Rosie said that they found who did it. A young girl, drunk, or was it a boy, I can't remember. She didn't do it on purpose.

Am I young, too? I still don't know.

They shaved one side of my head and made a hole in it. They've not let me look at myself yet. There are no mirrors in this room. I touch the soft place with my fingers. I don't like what I feel. Mushy. I don't know what I look like. I want to know what colour my hair is. I think it's red. The nurse said grey. Why would someone dye my hair grey? I certainly didn't do it. Perhaps Lily did.

I can move my legs a bit, they've taken off the clamps, the bindings. The doctor says my legs are healing nicely. They took me down for a scan. I didn't like it. Something isn't right, I don't know what it is.

I don't want games today. I don't want to move my little toes. *Piss off, Piss off.* Rosie says I'm naughty. I slap her hand. I pull her hair. She cries. Tells me to stop.

I'm tired. He came in the night again. Put his fingers around my neck. He laughed. His fist smashed into my nose. I scratched his face. He slides in through the window when it's dark. It's their fault. I keep telling them to lock it.

They forget.

Chapter 66

He's in the room.

Heart thundering against her ribs, drenched in sweat, Thomasine jolts awake. A smell gags in her throat—turpentine. Hand over her own mouth, she smothers the cry for help before it leaves her lips. Blinded by darkness, her ears seek him out. Nothing but silence. Then she tunes into a low hum, a heater perhaps.

Where am I? At the edge of her sight there is a flicker of light. *A curtain, window?*

A draft of ice cold air touches her bare shoulder. The luminous digital display on her watch shows just gone four o'clock. *Too early for daylight.* Her eyes adjust to the dark, a flat-screen TV hangs on the wall in front of her. Silently, she slides off the bed, her hand reaching for her car keys on the bedside table. She slips a key between her fingers, her body tense and ready to strike.

Come on you bastard, where are you?

A toilet flushes; she flinches. It comes to her. Exhausted, she'd booked into a Holiday Inn Express, outside of Nottingham. The only room available recently renovated, the receptionist informed her, the smell of paint still lingered, would that be a problem? It hadn't, not until now.

Thomasine sinks back onto the bed. A three-quarters drunk bottle of red stands on the vanity unit opposite her. Self-medication to dull the gut-wrenching numbness that's had her in its grip from that moment in the lockup.

It's scored into her memory, the large canvas. She lifted the cover, peered beneath it in the half-light. At first, thought it was some form of fantastical landscape, and was about to let the cover

292

drop when she changed her mind. The word *tardiness* came to her, not the painting, but her work if she lost that methodicalness that was central to it.

The painting was of a woodland, a slice of the world above and below. The top third of the large canvas a Prussian blue sky littered with stars. Beneath that a copse of trees, layers of dark brown leaves litter the ground, dead man's fingers – mushrooms – protrude up through the soil. A large rat twists its tail around the base of the tree, its nose rooting in the earth.

Her eyes continued to flick over it. Below was the underworld. There's a sprite, or a woodland goddess, a girl at any rate, naked, lying prone, her legs slightly apart. One leg raised above the other. Her face turned outwards. The girl's skin had been painted an ivory grey, her long brown lashes fringed milky white eyes. Chestnut coloured hair hung about her shoulders, stained a deep velvet red at the tips. A trail of woodlice wove its way up her neck towards her ear. The long yeasty coloured roots of an oak tree held her in an embrace. There was something sick about it.

Her eyes settled on the girl's face for a moment, took it in. Immediately, she felt the icy gaze of the girl tear right into her.

Pale brown freckles littered the nose and cheeks, even white teeth lay beneath blue lips, the girl's lower lashes rested on her cheekbones.

Karen—her sister, Karen.

Her legs gave way without warning—the side of her head hit the concrete floor with a crack. Stomach acid burnt her throat as her breakfast shot up her throat and splattered onto the floor. She'd lain there, in her own sick, unable to move. A white-hot pain wrapped around her forehead, the stench of vomit soaking into her clothes.

It took her a while to pull herself together. To clean up after herself, to push her anger somewhere to the back of her mind where it wouldn't overwhelm her. She changed her gloves, tucked the contaminated pair in her handbag. The best she could, made sure that all traces of her were obliterated.

It was only then she removed the covers off the remaining canvases.

He'd objectified them all, backs arched, legs open, lips parted in slow smiles that made them appear complicit.

Karen, Andrea Wharton's sister – Candy. Belinda Arnold's sister – Charlotte.

He must have killed all three. Are the girls buried up on Anglezarke, are they in the woodland, too?

Every bone in her body had wanted to rip the canvases from the walls, burn them.

It took all her effort to collect herself; she splashed cold water on her face. Got on with searching the rest of the lockup. Against the wall stood a wooden cabinet of sorts with long narrow drawers – the sort used to store maps in. She slid open the top drawer, picked through its contents – pencil drawings, nature, landscapes, mushrooms, trees – then moved on to the next. Charcoal sketches – tens of them. Teenage girls in swimming costumes, lying by a pool, on sunbeds, limbs splayed, spines flexed. Their wet hair dangling on their shoulders. Her stomach clenches—he must have been watching the girls for weeks.

A stack of photographs had been carelessly stuffed into the next drawer down. Mostly torn and tattered at the edges, the colours faded and washed out. Skinny girls in hot pants, long coats, maxi dresses – the seventies and early eighties. None looking directly at the photographer. Bennett was obsessed with teenage girls, she's convinced of it. She had chided herself, what use was a gut feeling. She needed proof—actual evidence. He could probably talk his way out of the paintings. Put herself and the other families through sheer misery.

She had pushed on, given the task all her full attention. The rest were landscapes, the moorlands, Anglezarke, the mast at Winter Hill, Rivington Pike, lower Rivington reservoir. A brown envelope is tucked against the rear of the drawer. Again, more photographs, faded colour prints that must have been taken years ago. Her breath faltered… there was a familiarity about them.

She lays them out, then picks them up one by one.

In the distance a drystone wall circles the house, the roof of the barn shimmers in the sunlight. Then in another a tractor stands idle in the field, a man kneels beside it, nearby two dogs out of focus as though taking flight. There are two of a dark-haired woman, arms lifted, pegging a pair of dark grey overalls on the line. The long sleeves of a white shirt are caught by the breeze. In the foreground a young girl, long grass swirling around her legs, clothed in blue cotton shorts and a white gipsy top embroidered at the edge. Her dark curly hair caught up in pigtails. A frown on her face, she looks directly ahead. Hand raised in a wave.

It can't be—it can't be.

It was.

Chapter 67

His gloved fingers wrap around the heavy iron padlock that secures the gate. It's locked. His lips twist. *This is bloody laughable. Does she really think it will keep anyone out?*

The farmhouse is deserted, no car, no tracks, the cobbles buried beneath virgin snow. He wonders if she's living there, in a matter of hours the snow changed the landscape. It could have wiped away all trace of her.

The place is a mess, a decaying cacophony of rubble. He is wary of tackling the barn, he'll need a ladder. He'll do the house first, from around the back. There's a gap in the wall circumventing the farm about ten metres away, an easier entrance. The ground beneath his feet is a health hazard, hidden by the snow, tumbled down lumps of stone lie abandoned. As he climbs through the gap, he spots that the curtains are drawn. *She might have closed the house up.* An unease settles in his stomach. *I'm not stupid, the police will have been all over the place*, any new finger prints will flash up.

He shrugs off his backpack, props it on the doorstep. Tugs his gloves off with his teeth, the wool stinks of wet dog and urine, he drops them by his feet. He retrieves a pair of blue gloves from his bag; the latex digits tear as he struggles to get them on. His hands are freezing cold and wet, he can't feel his fingers. In a fit of frustration, he wrenches his hands back into the sodden woollen gloves. Stuffs the latex ones into his pocket.

He endeavours to calm himself, other than what he finds inside the house, every element of his plan has been worked out fastidiously. Even the clothes he's wearing will be despatched into the clothing bank at Sainsbury's. Miles away from this place.

The silence is deafening. He takes the hammer and chisel from beneath the folds of his sleeping bag. Lodges the chisel between the door and the frame. One swipe with the hammer and the lock breaks. He throws his shoulder against the door; it gives way beneath his weight.

His stomach somersaults; his memory of that night awakes. It's thirty-seven years since he's been in this room.

It looks exactly the same.

Chapter 68

Sam is here, I like Sam. He likes me. I can tell. It's the way he smiles at me. I'm his *Bonny Lass.* He strokes the back of my hand. He's got a sing-song voice. He's going to catch who hurt me. He keeps telling me that.

I reach out my hand, the words won't come out. I want to say thank you.

'Hello, Veronica, how are you today?'

'Go-o-d.'

'Me too.'

I laugh. Rosie likes it when I laugh. I do it again.

He looks at Rosie. She looks at me. Is something wrong?

'Are you sure this is okay?' His eyes crinkle at the edges.

I wonder how old he is. Am I as old as Sam?

Rosie nods her head. 'Sam wants you to look at some pictures, is that okay, Veronica?' She leans towards me. Her breath smells of apples.

I nod my head. It only hurts a little bit. I like pictures.

'They're old pictures, Veronica. From when you were young.'

Am I not young anymore?

'Is that alright?'

I nod my head. This time it hurts, I let out a little cry. Rosie strokes my face.

Sam takes a picture out of a brown envelope. 'All I want you to do is squeeze my hand, Veronica. I'm going to tell you who someone is and I'm going to ask you if you know them. Is that okay? Like I said, just squeeze my hand. One for no, two for yes.' He puts his hand in mine. 'Is that ok.'

I squeeze his hand twice. I like this game already.

Rosie takes hold of my other hand. 'Are you sure, Veronica?' I squeeze her hand two times, then two times more.

'Is this Jimmy?'

Jimmy. I remember Jimmy. Jimmy slides through the window. He crushes the bones in my neck. He kills me in the night. Every night.

The bed shakes. I am shaking. I want to say no. No isn't right. It is him. I hate him.

Rosie slips her hand into mine. 'Don't be afraid, Sam won't let him hurt you.' Her eyes are shining and wet. 'Just squeeze my hand if it's him.'

I scream at my hand, move hand, move hand!

'Aye bonny lass, you're doing alright. It's him, is it?'

I squeeze his hand twice.

'Good girl,' he's not smiling.

I can see something in my head. It's him. He's thin. He's kicking out his leg. Dancing. He kicked me. Kicked me in the back. Move hand twice. Squeeze. Squeeze.

I look at Sam, open my eyes wide.

'Did Jimmy hurt you?'

My fingers claw at Sam's hand. Two squeezes. Two squeezes. My throat tightens, the air won't come in. I can't swallow. My heart is bumping against my chest.

'Is that a yes, Veronica? Squeeze my hand again if it is.'

Yes. I squeeze his hand. Did I do it twice, I can't remember? I gasp for breath.

'*That's* enough,' Rosie's voice sounds angry. We need a break. She needs a break.'

My eyes open. The wind is loud. It lashes on the roof. I like that word – lashes Is this a new day? No, it's not. Rosie is wearing the same clothes. So is Sam. He has soft hands. So has Rosie. Rosie loves me. I wonder if Sam loves me. I'm his *Bonny Lass*, he tells me that.

'We need to check whether she knows Billy.'

Is Sam talking to me? He's not looking at me. Billy? I know that name. My heart hurts. Something bad inside me is happening.

'Just the one more photograph, that's it. No pressure either. Am I clear?' Rosie sounds angry again. She looks at Sam. Sam makes Rosie angry.

I nod my head. I think I'm going to be sick.

'Remember, Veronica. Two squeezes for yes, is that alright?'

I squash his hand twice. His hand feels nice. Soft.

'She's alright, Rosie. See.' He points at me.

I smile. He holds up the photograph. My heart hurts. Like someone is stamping on it.

'Him!' I slap my hand against my ribs. 'Him!'

'Is she saying Jim?' Sam asks Rosie.

I shake my head. It hurts. I squeeze his hand. Once!

'Bi…b—'

'Billy?'

Speak words. I need words. I'm crying, I can't stop crying.

'He… he—'

'Did he kill the girl?' His eyes stare into mine.

'Ye–s!' Squeeze twice, squeeze twice.

'Did you help him?' His words hurt me, how could he think that?

Squeeze once, 'No!'

I must not let go of his hand.

Chapter 69

His eyes adjust to the gloom, the same gloom. It is as though he's walked through time; so little in the kitchen has changed. He wants to smile but the muscles in his face tighten, his teeth clench.

Perhaps it will be easier than I thought...

His frozen fingers switch on the standard lamp, the dull yellow light flickers on, the same fringe hangs down from the silk shade, once olive green now a washy grey. He drinks it all in. The sagging settee, flock cushions, the long wooden table covered in ring marks. A pile of cards lies unopened on top of it. Pale blue, melamine kitchen units; the worktop bare of space. Littered with cups, bags of food, empty bottles of wine, used plates.

Thomasine Albright is as sloppy as Lottie.

The tin breadbin lies open-mouthed, battered metal cooking utensils hang from hooks on the wall. The pantry door cracked open a touch. A microwave and a large boxy shredder the only nods to 2010.

He remembers sitting on the settee as quiet as a mouse, waiting. The whole time knowing her mother and father slept upstairs, along with her younger sister. Outside, the dogs lay sleeping – drugged. He'd crushed up two of his grandfather's sleeping tablets, mashed them in with their meat.

A damp rag lay hiding in his pocket. Karen stood in front of him, flushed of face, modelling his latest gift – a long brown, herringbone Biba coat. An expensive belated birthday gift that cost him four week's wages. He told her she could keep it, all he wanted in exchange was a kiss. The effect was immediate. Eyes shut and arms resting by her sides, she'd puckered up.

Without hesitation, he snatched the cloth from his pocket, covered her nose and mouth with it. She'd not struggled, not really. As his homemade concoction filled her throat and lungs, her body collapsed into his.

Who knows what life we could have had if that stupid bitch hadn't stopped me.

It occurs to him that his life has come full circle. The last thirty-seven years gone, not wasted but not lived to their full potential. Always on the edge of critical acclaim. Surely hiding his past for so long deserved some sort of credit. Four cases lay unsolved for over twenty years, he the answer to all of them – the police incompetent, not every girl can be a runaway. Yet he knew that each one had been classed so.

Thomasine Albright the Family Liaison for two of them, how ironic. How inconvenient.' His foot hovers mid-step, he turns, closes the door behind him. Shuts out the wind and the snow.

He's ready to escape from the boredom of his rural life, Lottie's nagging, Carlo's arrogance, painting wall-fillers. No doubt they'll be surprised when they discover his real talent, that is if they ever do. It will appear obvious to all that look, that Lottie is complicit, she could have returned home at any time in the last twenty years. That's what they'll all think.

His face transforms, his eyes light up. This is another chance, he can be reborn, the phoenix rising from the flames, a new beginning. His lips contort in a smile, he already has a new name. He feels no anxiety, he'd been surprised at how easy it was to get a fake passport, the Lithuanians, marvellous forgers, eager to take his money. His wanderings around the north, and the internet, have brought many benefits. Drugs, girls, people sympathetic to his leanings, he could have anything he wanted. Just like the old days. And of course, his smile broadening, since he'd cleared out his bank account, he has much more money.

The only evidence against me is hidden here somewhere, the dresser catches his attention, *I just have to find it.* He heaves it away from the wall, the feet scrape against the flagstones, the crockery rattles against the glass. There's nothing behind it, he checks inside, nothing there. He quickly moves around the room, picking up this and that, scraps of paper loose on the worktop, old receipts. The larder door creaks open, it spooks him a little. A shudder runs down his back, someone has just walked over his grave. Although he's no believer in that sort of drivel. *Don't be a pillock!* He jerks open the door, tugs at the light pull that swings in front of his face. His mouth gapes open. The pantry is full of produce: glass jars filled with ruby coloured winberry jam, tomato preserves, plums with rum, apple and onion chutney, pickled onions... all the things that Lottie had planned to do but never did.

His fingers run along the top shelf; they catch against something. The long metal snout brings a smile to his face, what a wonderful coincidence, a fortuitous gift, he thinks to himself. The walnut stock cold to his touch. Carefully, he slides the gun off the shelf, takes it down. He nestles the butt into his armpit, uncocks it, just one shot of ammunition, no chance of practise.

The floor creaks the other side of the door, he recocks the gun, slips his forefinger onto the trigger, eases open the door with his shoulder. Nothing. The room is empty. He lays it on the table and continues his search of the kitchen. Poking out from beneath the unopened cards, a document catches his attention. His finger and thumb ease it out.

His eyes read the letters that flow across the page. A receipt for evidence, found in the loft. Mary Quant makeup, magazines—a diary. His nostrils flare, his hands curl into fists, the creature inside of him unleashed.

'Stupid bitch—stupid bitch!' His right-hand grabs the hammer, the left the chisel. He lunges at his first target, the dresser, wielding both weapons with an uncontrollable rage, the glass panels explode into thousands of tiny shards that hover in the air before him. The chisel gouges deep rifts in the wood. He carries on, teeth bared, the carotid artery bulging in his neck, one blow followed by another. Nothing safe. The kitchen table covered in potholes, the roll top desk in the front room, both shattered beyond recognition. The china dogs no longer stand guard at the window. The glass in every photograph broken. He works his way through each room, never stopping to think. Never stopping to see the havoc he's unleashed.

The clanging of the landline stops him dead.

Chapter 70

She'd thrown on her clothes, set off immediately from the motel, drove through the night. There was only one way she was going to find out. Halfway up the track, Thomasine puts her foot down on the accelerator, the four-by-four lurches side to side as it rumbles in and around the potholes that clutter the lane.

It can't be true—it can't. I never saw him. I never met him. Dad's photograph albums, Mum kept them in her bedroom. Bennett must have got hold of them. Or did Karen give them to him? Why the hell would she do that?

Every muscle, every nerve, aches. Fear clings to her like a wet sack. Her eyes sting, almost blinded by the glare of the snow. One thought plagued her, raged at her for the last hundred miles. Had she all along known who the killer was? Only too afraid to admit it as a child. Had she repressed the memory?

No, I'm sure I haven't. That photograph of Bennett, his hands on Karen's shoulders, in the middle of the dance floor, I didn't recognise him. It was definitely the first time I'd set eyes on him.

The farm buildings rise out of the mist – long thin shards of ice hang from the guttering. Angry with herself, she gets out of the car, goes to open the gate. Her fingers wrap around the padlock, she inserts the key. The clang of the phone drowns out the rush of wind. She throws her weight against the gate, it doesn't budge, a thick swathe of snow and ice holds it in place. The bell hurts her ears, she shrugs her shoulders, whoever is at the end of the line must wait. She leaves the four-by-four on the track and climbs over the gate. The cobbles are covered in a deep layer of virgin snow. The clanging stops, unconsciously, she looks to the right.

To the kennels, waits for the riotous greeting. She feels a rush of emotion, of hate, for the bastard who poisoned them.

As she crosses the yard, she stops dead. Something unnerves her, the curtains hang loose in the windows. She'd left them shut. The china dogs are gone from their places. Warily, she treads towards the window, her boots pierce the crisp snow with a crunch. She squints through the break in the curtains, unsure of what to expect. Large chunks of painted porcelain lay on the window sill. The room has been trashed, it's in chaos. Her stomach summersaults, the house has been burgled. *The press, the bastards!* That's the first thought in her head. *No, they're not that stupid, they'd never do anything like this.* She checks the front door; undisturbed snow climbs up against the porch. *Whoever they are must have got in through the back.*

The only person who would trash the house would be Bennett, looking for evidence. For one awful moment, she's grateful for Rosie's warning, that the killer might come back. Then the fear weaves it way into her psyche, she pacifies herself with the thought that he's probably already come and gone.

Thomasine leans forward, puts her ear to the door. She hears the sound of glass breaking, then the thud of something heavy hitting the floor. Key in hand, her fingers hover over the lock. *He must be still inside.* Her mouth goes completely dry.

She makes her way around the back of the barn. Tentatively, clambers up onto the drystone wall – the only place to get a signal on her mobile phone. The wind whips up the snow swirling it around her. The phone almost directly in front of her face, she taps the number at the top of her Recent's list.

Mel Philip's voice competes with the wind, 'DCI Philips, please leave a message.' In a heartbeat it goes to answerphone.

Her hands tremble, the words croak out. 'I'm up at the farm, I think Bennett, the guy from the diary, has been here, is inside the house. He's trashing the place.' She pauses, takes a breath, 'I need your help.'

Silently, she makes her way back to the car, eases the boot open. Large flakes of ice cold snow cling to her hair and eyelashes.

She is on high alert, every nerve in her body attuned to the sounds and sights around her. Her kitbag lies open, she pulls out her body-armour, takes off her coat, slips on the vest. Her hand grabs the taser she'd bought from the internet only days before. She transfers it to her coat pocket, then shrugs the coat back on, zips it up. Fully kitted up, Thomasine retraces her steps, makes her way back around the barn, huddles behind the drystone wall and waits for Mel to call her back. Confident that, when he sees the four-by-four, he'll come looking for her. Her clothes already covered in a down of crystal white snow, she waits.

'Hello, Thomasine.' The words are caught with the wind, the hair on the back of her neck bristles. The voice speaks again, it's coming from the other side of the wall. 'Hello, Thomasine… or shall I call you, Thom?' There is no trace of an accent, no hint of where he's from.

She lifts her head up, just enough to see over the barrier between them, peers into the mist, can't see a thing. Thomasine dips down, pulls the hood of her coat over her head, tries to block out the howling wind.

'No point in hiding from me, Thom.' He laughs loudly, pretentiously, 'I know *exactly* where you are.'

A cold shiver slaloms down her back. She raises her head again – the world about her is shrouded in a thick smog of snow.

He's bullshitting. He's a fool, if I can't see him, he can't see me.

Thomasine climbs over the wall, eases herself down in front of it. 'Careful, careful,' she tells herself softly, her gloved hands clinging to the rocks. She stands tall, cleaves the back of her heels to the base of the wall.

'The police have all the evidence.' She shouts loudly into the wind, gestures towards the farmhouse, 'There's nothing in there for you.'

'I know,' there's a slyness in his assertion, 'that made me a little angry. I'm afraid I've made a bit of a mess.' He giggles like a child, 'Not much left of the family heirlooms, not that you'll be needing them.' The owner of the voice materialises out of the mist. A tall, thin, bald man with two rows of startlingly white teeth. He bears no resemblance to his younger self, the fingers of his left-hand wrap around the stock of the shotgun. 'Which is a shame because I quite liked some of them, especially that secretaire.' With the back of his sleeve, he wipes the snow from his face.

Her heart beat pulses erratically against her breastbone; a sudden panic about what she might find in there. The taser nestles in the palm of her hand. He takes a step towards her, swings the gun in front of him, steadies the stock into his elbow. He's playing with her. 'Why did you kill my sister?' Her chest constricts, 'What did she ever do to you?'

'Quite a bit really,' He rubs his hand over his bald head, 'Karen and I—'

'*Yeah*, like she'd be interested in *you*.' She loads her words with sarcasm, 'You're just a paedo who couldn't keep his hands to himself.'

He throws back his head, laughs, 'You're wrong, completely wrong. Karen and I,' he lets out a sigh, 'it was *special*.'

His conceit rankles her. She wants to tear the gun from his hands, point the barrel in his groin. Listen to him beg.

Get a grip girl, slow down.

She knows she needs to take control, it's not the first time someone has threatened her with a gun. 'Why don't you put that down before you do some harm with it.'

The smile disappears, he takes another step forward, wobbles slightly as if unsure on his feet. For a second, a microscopic look of confusion flickers across his eyes. 'That's the whole point of a gun, to do harm, isn't it?' The barrel drops slightly. 'I fully intend to do you harm. I think I'll start with the face.' He raises an eyebrow, winks.

'Start where you like, you'll probably miss,' *play the game, Thomasine, play the game.* She takes a shallow breath, tries to push back the angst that's hammering in her chest. Behind her in the barn, a pair of crows squawk and fight. She pushes back into the wall, brushes the snow from her eyelashes. 'I've seen your paintings, your private collection, down in London. You're very sick in the head.'

Bennett grimaces, lets the stock of the gun slip into his elbow. He's still twenty-five feet or so away from her, the snow churns up around them.

He looks like he's handled a gun before. It's definitely Dad's. She wonders if he's checked it, whether it's cocked ready to fire.

Her response is emotionless. 'Yes—they've been taken for evidence, and what a load of shite they are.' She watches his face twitch. 'They'll be used in court then chucked in the incinerator.'

He flinches, his mouth contorts—she's hit her target.

'I doubt if a jury would convict me based on four paintings,' he snorts, laughs, 'that's stretching it a bit, isn't it? Besides, I think you'll find that all the fingers are pointing towards Jimmy Fairfax.' He pulls himself up, presses on. 'No time for talking now. Time to terminate this particular ending.' There's an eagerness in his tone. 'I'm thinking suicide, after all, you're the only one left, and it would make sense, wouldn't it?'

'Aren't you interested in the diary?' Thomasine pulls her shoulders back, ignores the fear knotted in her stomach, her smile fades. 'It makes such interesting reading. She mentions you by name, and that Capri you had. That's how I found you.'

'I think *I* found you, is more accurate.'

'I think not,' She shakes her head. 'Is that Dad's gun?'

He lifts it up, smerks, points the barrel towards her. 'Sorry, you can't have it back. I'm going to need it in a minute.' That slyness again.

'So, aren't you interested in what Karen said about you?'

'She loved me.' He places his hand on his heart, 'I was her first.'

Keep it in, don't react, keep him talking. Thomasine fakes a laugh, wags her finger at him. 'Is that what she told you? Well, we've got it in black and white, in the diary. Apparently, you were an impotent twat who couldn't get it up.'

The pretence drops. His face flushes, 'Time to say *bye bye*.' He looks straight down the sight.

'So how did you kill her?'

He eases the butt of the gun into his shoulder, closes one eye, aims. 'You don't need to know that.' He lifts his feet, wades through the snow, it's up to his knees. He must need to get nearer, to get a good shot.

Automatically, her hand grips the taser, her heart batters against her ribs. 'Go on, tell me. It's not like I'm going to be telling anyone else, not with my head blown off.'

He doesn't respond, continues on, step by step. There's a breaking sound, a crack, his face clouds. He looks down. His legs have completely disappeared into the snow beneath him, he is knee deep in shit and urine. The colour drains from his face.

'Wha—' The sour smell of the slurry pit fills the air.

She lets out a breath, 'Why did you kill—'

He presses the trigger.

Chapter 71

Thomasine blinks. Her blood courses through her ears in a thunderous rush. She stands transfixed, the toes of her boots centimetres from the rim of the slurry pit. Its snow-covered surface splattered in bright red blood.

His blood.

The shotgun nestles in the snow about a metre ahead of him. Whimpering sobs rise out of his chest. His hands cover his face, his legs struggle to keep him upright. He lifts his head, lets his arms fall to his side. The kickback shattered his cheekbone, his left eyeball hangs loose in the socket. Blood streaks across his forehead and cheeks. He tries to move, the slurry thickened by the cold weather, clings to him like a brace. The wind carries the stench of ammonia towards her, she covers her nose and mouth.

An icicle drops from the guttering on the farmhouse, slices through the snow like a knife.

He cups his eyeball in his left hand, winces, tries to put it back in its socket. He clearly has no idea of how much damage the gun has done to his face. *Drugs*, she wonders if he's taken drugs.

'Who's a silly boy then?' Her mouth hardens, 'Who didn't check the gun first?' She inches along the wall; moves away from the stink. Away to safety, the only clue to the size of the pit, a pile of granite rocks that protrude through the snowfall.

His mouth slackens, the scream that follows turns her cold. He tries to wade out of the slurry, apparently still unaware of the futility of his plight. Torn muscle and tendon ravage his face.

'Welcome to the slurry pit.' She gives out a hard laugh, 'I would have thought you would have recognised the smell.' When the milking parlour had been demolished, the circular slurry pit sunk beneath had been left untouched. The job of cleaning it out too much for her mother. And no money to pay for it to be professionally cleared. Her cousin, Paul used it for silage, as a compliment to their own. Until her mother's death, the gelatinous mass was covered by planks of wood and a tarpaulin, open at the edges to allow the gases to escape and tightened weekly so the rain didn't pool on it.

It had taken Thomasine hours of back-breaking work to get the cover off, literally inch by inch, a dangerous job that required her full concentration and strength.

Heavy snowfalls had finished the job. Within days, the pit and warning sign were completely hidden from view. Exactly as she'd hoped.

Bennett doesn't respond to Thomasine's taunt. His whole being now focused on lifting his body out of the thick grey noxious liquid. The world around him blurs, exhaustion creeps into his bones.

She shouts over the roar of the wind. 'Tell me why you killed her? If you tell me that, I'll get you out.'

Bennett scowls at her, 'I can get out myself,' Suddenly energised, he twists and turns, the viscous liquid sucks at his waist, pockets of ammonia bubble out.

'There's a rope in the barn it'll just take me a moment to get it, you've only got minutes before you—'

'Piss off!' There's venom in his voice. 'You won't let me die—it's not in your DNA. You're a copper.'

She whispers the words out, 'My mother's blood is in my DNA.' The cloying stink of the pit wafts up towards her, she ambles her way across the yard, then turns to look at him. 'The gas will get you soon.'

'What *gas?* He sniffs the air, 'I can't smell anything. You're lying!' The nasal infection that took his sense of smell now corrupting his senses. He tries to move. His body feels like a dead weight. With terrifying clarity, he watches her head towards the barn. He realises he has no chance of escape without her help. She disappears from his view.

'For God's sake,' his shrieks become more intense, 'For God's sake—please don't leave me here.'

Inside the barn, Thomasine coils the rope over her shoulder. She pauses for a moment, takes in some clean air before returning to the pit. A gust of wind carries her voice. 'You're in a tank of shit and piss, ten feet deep.' She stops by the pile of rocks, squats to her knees. 'Here's the deal, Robert. If you tell me why you killed her, I'll throw you the rope, pull you out.'

The world around them is an eye-watering white, she waits for the information to sink in.

Bennett panics, he's not tall enough to stand up in it. His lungs strain for oxygen; his words come out in a slur, 'She let me in, through the back.' For some bizarre reason he laughs, 'I brought her a gift.'

'You're lying,' a bitter taste fills her mouth. 'We would have heard you, I would have heard you. The dogs would have barked.' She drops the rope to the ground, it coils like a snake at her feet, 'Tell me the truth.'

'It's the truth—' his breathing is laboured, 'sleeping pills in the dog's food.'

The wind catches the drone of a siren, she wonders if her mind is playing tricks. Has she too been affected by the gas. Her lips form a hard line, 'Don't worry, *Billy*, you'll soon be asleep, death is only moments away; you're going to hell. I'm going to send you there.' Her voice raises, 'Hydrogen sulphate, ammonia, methane, carbon dioxide – they're killing you right at this minute.'

Frantically, he struggles to move, the pit holds him fast. Panicking, he gulps in the toxic mix of air, *'Please—please,'* his face ashen, the words wheezed out.

Thomasine turns away, gazes into the distance, seeing nothing. An overwhelming flood of sadness consumes her. She had loved this place, he stole it from her along with everything else. She won't be able to live here after this.

'Tell me.' Her eyes narrow in on him.

'Throw me the r-r-rope,' his teeth chatter, his body shudders. The eyeball hanging loosely on his cheek stares at her.

She drops to her knees, picks up the rope, takes hold of the end. Casts the rest of it out across the slurry. He tries to grab it. The end of the rope falls centimetres from his grasp. She throws it again, it hits his face, he whimpers, arms flaying about as he tries to catch the end of it before it slips away.

'Be quick!' he sniffles, spits.

She drags it back, throws it again, it hits him in the chest. This time, he snatches it up, wraps it around his fist. A look of relief floods his face. Fingers numb with cold, he uses his wrists to grab the rope, pushes it underneath his armpits, manages to tie it in a knot across his chest, 'Pull me in—' a coughing fit consumes him momentarily. 'You… you promised to get me out!'

'Tell me.' Thomasine stands rigid. Unmoved by his demands, 'Tell me—tell me what you did.'

His eyes widen, the pressure on his chest takes his breath. He looks towards the farmhouse. 'It was her fault. We were in the kitchen, she let me in, I wanted…' There is no repentance in his voice, only self-pity. 'Chloroform… she collapsed—' another coughing fit breaks his words. The slurry sticks to him like glue, drags him deeper into its depths. 'Got to help me—*please.*'

'And, Veronica?' Her voice pierces the howl of the wind. He is only interested in his self-preservation. 'What did Veronica do?'

'She saw me… the car.' His chest heaves, he starts to hyperventilate, 'She was walking up the road… out of town,' he gulps in air, with each gasp poisoning himself. 'She flagged me down… walked in front of the car, she,' his lungs are about to give out, 'heard Karen screaming… I had—'

'*No choice?* That's what they all say, Billy.' She tilts her head, 'I'd keep still if I were you,' a smile freezes on her face, 'and you can stop calling for God, heaven is not *your* destination.' She picks up the length of rope, slides it between her fingers tantalisingly. 'And Veronica?'

The energy has gone out of him, 'I… buried them.' He stops kicking, thick streaks of slurry cover his face and chest. ' Karen came to… I don't know how Veronica…'

'The photograph, the one of me, how did you get it?'

He doesn't answer, his body sinks deeper.

Her pulse quickens, 'Did I ever meet you?'

The movement is almost imperceptible, he shakes his head, '*No, Please—*'

'Okay,' that is all she says.

Teeth gritted, she pulls the rope tight, reals him in. With every beat, the knot of rage in her chest burns, fuelling her strength. She could let him die, leave him there, it wouldn't be enough. Digging in her feet, arm over arm, she pulls him towards her.

When she is within arm's length, he lets out a groan. She tucks the rope under her arm, drops to the ground, reaches out with her hand. He grabs it, she sucks in a deep breath, the final struggle saps her strength. He's a dead weight, his upper body lies prone on the crust, blood streams down his cheeks. She grabs hold of his elbows, tugs.

Suddenly revived, teeth-bared he grabs her head, jerks her towards him, pushes her face down into the pit, tries to clamber over her.

In a blind panic, mouth shut tight, she pulls the taser out of her pocket, rams it into his ribs—fires. His body spasms, his fingernails claw her scalp. She fires again, his body fits; his grip loosens.

Lungs screaming, she wrenches herself from beneath him, scrambles back, safe from his clawing fingers. Her body convulses as she vomits up the slurry, rams snow into her mouth, spits it out.

If he'd pushed her under, she would have never got out. Her body armour, the weight of it—it would have killed her.

She turns her head to look, his body sinks beneath the quagmire of snow and slurry, limb by limb.

Chapter 72

They appear out of the blizzard, see her crouching in front of the wall, arms curled over her head, shivering uncontrollably, her upper body caked in thick grey slime and snowflakes.

Sam shouts out to her, 'Thom, Thom, are you alright?' He makes his way towards the shotgun.

Her eyes spring open, terrified she lets out a scream. 'Don't move—not one more step. I won't be able to get you out.'

Confused, Sam and Mel look down, the ground is already covered in white virgin snow, there is no sign of where Bennett's feet had tread.

'Don't move an inch.' Thomasine struggles to her feet, waves them back. 'I'll come to get you.'

They look on, perplexed, as she makes her way towards them, mindful of the lumps of granite that seem to show the way, each step carefully taken.

Mel peers into Thomasine's face. 'Are you alright? Where is he?'

'Dead—he's in there.' she points in front of them, to the expanse of snow, 'the slurry pit. He fell,' her hands shake. 'When I tried to get him out, he…' Teeth chattering, her knees go weak. Sam steadies her.

Mel steps back, horrified. 'What it's under *there*?'

'Bloody hell—where's the warning sign?' Sam's eyes open wide.

'The snow covered it up.' Thomasine wants to lay down, to sleep. Her eyelids droop, she's been outside in the freezing cold for over an hour, her clothes soaked through.

'We followed footsteps round the back of the house. The back doors been broken in.' He looks at Mel, 'Come on, let's get you inside lass.' Sam slips an arm under her shoulder.

'It's bloody freezing out here, you'll do your death.' His nose wrinkles, 'Aye, you'll want to get those clothes off too, you smell like a dog's arse.'

Thomasine's legs give way, his arm tightens around her. Mel hurries to take her other elbow. 'We got your message,' Her forehead creases. 'I'm sorry I didn't answer. We found out he had a lock-up down in London, we were on a conference call with the Met, I had my phone off.' Thomasine doesn't interject. Without missing a beat Mel carries on. 'Then we couldn't get our vehicle up the field, the lower gate was locked. We heard the gun go off, did he shoot you?'

'He tried.' Through weary eyes, Thomasine takes in their appearance, both look soaked to the skin and dishevelled. Sam had a suit on and Mel wore jeans and a jumper, her hair is plastered to her scalp; neither are kitted out for the blizzard that consumes them.

Sam's eyes narrow in on her, 'Have you got your body armour on under your coat?' A look of concern crosses his face, 'What happened?'

Thomasine can see his mind ticking over, she shudders, untangles herself from them both. Without another word, she points towards the slurry pit, now completely hidden from view by the snow. Her chest heaves as she speaks, 'He broke in when I was out. As soon as I got back, I knew he was in the house. The curtains were open, I'd left them shut. He had Dad's gun—I had no idea until I saw him with it,' she wraps her arms around herself to stop the trembling. 'He just came out of nowhere. I was out by the barn waiting for you to call back… it's the only place to get a signal.' The words stumble out, 'The gun misfired, it knocked him off his feet, the kickback shattered his eye socket. I tried to get him out but…' her voice trails off, then flashes in anger. 'The bastard tried to pull me in with him.' She starts to shiver uncontrollably. 'It's sunk into the ground, over three-metres deep. It's a death trap.' Despair washes over her, 'There were so many things I needed to know.' Fat tears carve through the grey slime that covers her cheeks, she wipes them away with the cuff of her sleeve.

'Did he tell you anything?' Mel's voice interrupts her thoughts.

Thomasine closes her eyes, 'He killed Karen—tried to kill Veronica, he must have thought he had.'

Both?' Mel looks surprised, 'Not Jimmy Fairfax? On the tapes, Veronica implied it was Jimmy.'

Thomasine shrugs her shoulders, a grim smile spreads across her lips 'I can't explain that. I told him I'd get him out if he told the truth. He said he'd done it. Said that Karen let him in the house. He'd clearly planned to abduct her.' She goes to sit down on the ground, they lift her up. She carries on, 'He knocked her out, chloroform. It's relatively easy to make – bleach, acetone, ice. He'd have most of that to hand, he—' She stops mid-sentence, suddenly remembering the rags at the lockup. 'I guess he used it on Veronica too, he didn't say.' Her voice drops, more tears come. 'He buried them together, Karen came to as he was digging the grave. He—' She stops dead. 'Look, I just need to get inside. Can we do this later?'

Sam looks across at Mel, 'Boss, do you want me to wait here to see if he gets out?' Sam's face is completely straight, 'Bastards like that always seem to come back to life.'

'He's dead, believe me,' Thomasine is emphatic.

A look of relief spreads across Sam's face. He takes the key out of Thomasine's hand, opens the front door.

He looks over his shoulder, directly into her face, 'We have to be careful, it's a crime scene now.' He helps her on with a pair of protective cover shoes and gloves.

The hope goes out of her as they walk along the hallway and into the kitchen. 'He said he'd wrecked the place.' Bennett had spoken the truth. Bar a single kitchen chair, not another piece of furniture nor ornament had gone unharmed. The hammer and chisel casually thrown down by the back door to taunt her. She sits on the chair, waits for them to process her.

It takes the CSI Team a while to get there. Whilst waiting, she gives a full account to Sam and Mel, well, almost full. She doesn't tell them about the gun, that she knew it would misfire. Nor, that she'd fully intended to lure him outside. That she'd stood back against the wall so that she wouldn't fall in it. She told them about the taser, that it was for her own protection. She doesn't ask them what was discovered in the lockup. She knows exactly what was found.

When the CSI's arrive, they are meticulous, one processes her body and clothes, the other takes photographs. Unembarrassed, she stands there compliantly, grateful that it is over, grateful that she doesn't know either of the CSI's in front of her.

The snow abates, the wind drops, Robert Bennett's body is recovered hours later. White-clad CSI's with breathing apparatus carefully bring it to the surface. Thomasine stares into his face, his mouth gaping wide open as though mid-howl. All her emotion spent, she says just two words.

'That's him.'

Two weeks later, with Thomasine's help, Candice Wharton will be found in the same woodland. Her bones entangled in the roots of a tree – just as her sister's had.

Jimmy's past finally catches up with him. He will be charged with perverting the course of justice and bribing a police officer; a European arrest warrant will be issued for Frank Tanner.

Charlotte Arnold will be back with her family. For years, Bennett had been feeding her ADHD drugs to restrict her growth. She was the last girl he abducted and couldn't have been involved in any of his crimes. Months of psychotherapy lay ahead of her.

For now, a sense of calm descends upon Thomasine. He's dead. He died a terrifying death. Just as she promised her mother he would.

She takes in a breath, the heavyweight she's been carrying for thirty-seven years evaporates into thin air. She walks around the house, tries to feel her mother's presence, a waft of her perfume, the sound of her voice.

She's no longer there.

Nor is Karen.

Epilogue

Tuesday, 26 July 2011

It's been a long slow recovery. My name is Veronica Lightfoot. I have a sister called Rosie. I no longer need to clean clean things. I allow the dust to settle on the skirting. I have a cat called Boston. He sleeps on my bed.

No one is ever going to steal my life again.

Thomasine killed him, I'm glad.

I'm not completely healed, I know that. Bones mend, but memories, well, brain damage can mean those memories are lost forever. But, bit by bit, I am piecing my life as Lily together.

The doctors say the ones before Lily are probably gone. They're not. They come back in my dreams – the touch of my mother's hand, Rosie's childhood tears, eating tea at Gran's, walking through the fields. Wimberry bushes covered in bright red ladybirds.

My hand gripping Karen's wrist as I claw my way out of the ground. Banging on her chest. Breathing through her lips. Begging her forgiveness as I put on her coat. Burying her again because I couldn't carry her. Because I didn't want the animals to take her. Because if Billy came back, he'd see I'd escaped. Every night I wake, my heart thundering against my ribs.

The doctors, they want me to see a psychiatrist. Why on earth would I do that? She probably did more damage than anything else. She left her voice in my head. I should never have said yes. But I did, and that is that. The police traced Ellen Williams, the one who got me sectioned. I know it's cruel, but I never want to see her again. I've told Rosie that.

One of these days I will go on holiday, maybe even find somebody to love, someone who'll love me back. I've discovered lots of new things, like eBay and Amazon. I've even bought an iPad. I have a life to live and goals to achieve. The list is on the fridge.

Read it if you like.

Life goals list 2011/12

- Learn to swim – still want to do a triathlon.
- Re-learn to drive.
- Run three times a week.
- Get back to work.
- Sort out the legal issues.
- Sell both my houses.
- Find myself a place back home.
- Spend time with Mum and Rosie.
- Get to know Thomasine.
- Find Paula.
- Pay the bitch back.
- Make her forget.

Acknowledgements

My most heartfelt thanks to all those involved in the journey of this debut novel.

In particular, my fantastic agent, Jenny Savill, who took me on when the manuscript was in its early stages and whose insights and suggestions made an immeasurable difference.

For their unending support, my Writers' Group – Tanya, Penny and Rica. For encouraging me to do the BathSpa MA in Creative Writing, my friend Pat. To Dr Colin Edwards, my wonderful manuscript tutor, and tutors Nathan Filer, Lucy English and Samantha Harvey who drew out the potential in me. For their insightful feedback and positivity, my fellow students Morag, Linda, Rachel, Eleanor and Tracy. For answering my endless questions into police work and medical procedure, Rachael, Caroline, Jon, Debra and Bev. Any mistakes are purely my own. And to Tanya, Debbie and Pat whose proof reading and observations of early drafts were much appreciated. To writers such as Val McDermid, Clare Mackintosh and Mo Hayder who inspired me.

My publishers, Bloodhound Books, have been wonderful. In particular Betsy Reavley and her team, and my editor, Ben Adams. Without all of whom this book would not have been published.

A huge thanks to my family whose belief in me is unfailing.

To my friends, whose ongoing encouragement has been incredibly important.

And, most of all, the biggest thank you is to my husband, Mark. He's supported me all the way and without him I probably wouldn't be writing at all.

Printed in Poland
by Amazon Fulfillment
Poland Sp. z o.o., Wrocław